BOOK FIVE OF THE DEAD HUNGER SERIES

Dead Hunger V
The Road To California

By Eric A. Shelman

Dead Hunger V: The Road To California

is a work of fiction by

Eric A. Shelman

All characters contained herein are fictional, and all similarities to actual persons, living or dead, are purely coincidental, except of course, where characters are based on real people, but the personalities and relationships are mostly fiction.

No portion of this text may be copied or duplicated without author or publisher written permission, except for use in professional reviews.

Cover Art By Gary McCluskey

FROM THE AUTHOR

When writing a series, an author relies on his readers to want to follow his characters. That makes it extraordinarily risky to do what this book has done.

While Dave Gammon has been with the story since Dead Hunger II: The Gem Cardoza Chronicle, he has not developed into what people might see as a leader. Dave, with his awkward moment jokes, could be seen as reliable and caring – but a hero? Not necessarily.

So to let Dave take the reins in a book series where Flex, Gem, Hemp and Charlie – four very strong personalities – have dominated, is obviously a risk. And while I wasn't sure when I began, I have decided that Dave is up to the task, in my opinion.

When I first began this book, even I had to fully investigate who Dave Gammon was. I had to know his motivations for leaving his established life with Serena to take a risky journey across the country to find an uncle he could not be sure was even alive. I had to create Serena's back story, which you will  we fully learn in this book, *and* I had to figure out who his Uncle Bug had become and why Dave would risk so much to seek him out. I also had to come up with some people to join Dave and Serena, the first of whom is an old friend of ours, Nelson Moore. He comes quite a long way in this book, too – which is the longest of the series. That surprised me, because in concept, I wasn't sure if I could come up with enough "moments" to carry this book over 400 pages.

Well, I think I achieved that. As the reader and the most important piece of this puzzle, I hope you agree. It's been quite a ride so far, and we have one more to go: Dead Hunger VI: Homecoming. I hope you're in for the whole ride, and it is also my great hope that I haven't let you down along the way. A book series is only as good as each entry, and I've always wanted to make sure you wanted to grab that next book. If you're reading this, I succeeded. Thanks.

All that said, I hope you enjoy Dead Hunger V: The Road To California.

It's that awkward moment when you realize nobody's listening, so you kind of just drift off and fade out …

*****

SPECIAL THANKS TO:

Thanks to my brother Don Shelman and his wife, Marion Shelman. Both brought up some great points, and Don helped tremendously with the wrap-up of the book. I'd also like to thank Sharon Berget, who is a Facebook friend and Dead Hunger fan. She found a ton of typos and some continuity issues. Thank YOU! I always have to thank Megan Sweetness (not sure if that is her REAL name) who is also a Facebook friend, a DH fan and a good beta reader – she came up with an important character inconsistency that needed addressing. Thank YOU, Megan! You guys rock.

4

PROLOGUE

My name is Dave Gammon. I'm a relative late-comer to Flex and Gem's family, but they welcomed me with open arms, and that's all that's important. I think I've been an asset to them, and I plan to get back to where they are as soon as I can.

That really depends on what happens in California and it also depends on what happens with my Uncle Brett.

Since I've never done this before – written a chronicle, that is – I suppose I should remind you that in June of 2012, the world went to crap. I mean *really* went to crap. According to Hemphill Chatsworth, a super smart scientist who is now a part of my family, a gas emitting from the earth's core is responsible for transforming most of the people on this planet into the walking dead.

This is where I'd normally say "Seriously." It's not necessary. You know very well *what* happened, but depending on where this all goes from here, I'm not certain you know *how* it happened.

Hemp's theory is that as the planet formed and fireballs and gasses of unimaginable kinds were being injected into the nucleus of the planet and outward, they were trapped there. For as long as this planet has existed, there they were.

What released them is unclear. Hemp figures a very deep earthquake or a secret, deep underground nuclear test caused a fissure in the planet's core. This, he hypothesizes, allowed one gas, or a combination of them, to escape and seep through the layers of the earth, up through the water and soil, eventually reaching our oxygen-enriched atmosphere.

The stuff we breathe became contaminated with it. It literally emits from every surface in every part of the world. It has changed 90% of the human population into dead things that walk around and try to eat the rest of us.

That's the long and short of it.

Then there is the problem of the Ratz, but they seem to be dying off, though some still exist.

Getting back to the purpose of our run to California. My uncle's name is Brett Ulrich Gammon, and he's always been very cool to me. He's my dad's brother. His friends have always called him Bug, and I've only known him as Uncle Bug as long as I can remember. I haven't thrown that out before, because it just sounds weird, and everyone can relate to Uncle Brett.

We've always connected, even though I've thought he was a total trip since I was old enough to notice that he *was* different. And while he's not like anyone else I've ever known, the guy's pretty damned special to have predicted the apocalypse that bitchslapped the world.

Yeah, he did. He really did. I don't know if it really counts, though. I mean, Uncle Brett's been predicting it for at least thirty years. It had to come to pass eventually. Even a blind squirrel finds a nut now and then, if a zombie doesn't eat it first.

Not the nut. *The squirrel.*

If I'm going to get really specific, I'd say how soon Serena, Nelson and I get back to our family – our other family, that is – depends mostly on who my uncle is these days – or if he *is* at all.

You may have determined that Bug is a survivalist. He's been stockpiling food and weapons – and I mean not just dabbling at it; *really* stocking up – for double digit years. The last time I saw Bug was around 1995. Nineteen or so years ago, which blows my mind. We've communicated via internet since then, but when I was at his place, I was just blown away at his stashes. An underground poly tank with literally thousands of gallons of potable water, sealed and treated to remain drinkable indefinitely. Guns and ammunition to put together his own small army, and vacuum-packed food stock that filled several rooms. Generators, solar equipment (Nelson will be in Heaven) and even an entire room where he grows insane vegetables and marijuana hydroponically; without soil.

Yeah, you heard me right. Nelson Moore, our resident, misguided environmentalist, is here. I'll get into that later, but first let me say that he's not a bad asset. The bastard can throw a Ninja star like no tomorrow, and to be honest, it's fun to watch. I have no interest in learning how to do it. I've gotten comfortable with my traditional weapons, but I did consider and discard the idea of grabbing a crossbow in honor of Charlie. In the end, it would've just been too much equipment for the bike, and more of a novelty for me.

So, we're on the road, but we haven't gotten very far yet. We thought we were all set, for reasons I'll explain later, but when Nelson showed up, all that changed.

We now plan to hit another Harley store, and when we get there, Nelson is dumping his damned scooter. We aren't going to be putt-putting around the country waiting for his ass.

Serena. Wow. After what happened to me in Florida, I guess I didn't think I'd be able to be with another woman for a long time. But Serena isn't just another woman. She saw me through one of the hardest times of my life; when my sis Lisa died. I was powerless to stop it, and I honestly could have seen myself taking my own life when I was trapped in that little, cinderblock building with Serena,

7

under attack by a huge horde of abnormals … and a couple of red-eyes besides.

Serena had been my rock then. She'd been the one to tell me to go ahead and grieve, but for God's sake, don't throw everything away.

I know now what she meant, I think. She didn't want me throwing *her* away. She wasn't done with me yet. In fact, I now know that she hadn't really even begun with me yet.

I'm glad I listened to her and let her help me through that time when I was right on the edge. She did it with a gentle touch and the love she offered me at that desperate moment. She's reminded me in the months since that we never really had the opportunity to say a quiet good bye to Lisa. That time will come. Probably when we get back home to our family – and hopefully with my uncle beside me.

Beauty still exists. You just have to be fully prepared to wipe out any ugly that shows up to muck it all up.

And we are.

Let me tell you how I see Serena Casteneda. She's around 5'11" tall. Her eyes are brown, her hair is almost jet black, and I'm not dumb enough to put her weight down in this chronicle. But it's kind of the point. When I met her, she was living in the Zombie-Free-Zone house in Shelburne, Vermont with Tony Mallette, Nick and Jason DeSante, and others. They didn't eat well, and the girl was wasting away, but still fiery and determined.

During the brief period of relative peace and beauty in Concord, she began eating well, and I saw Serena settle back into what I assume was her natural weight.

My woman has curves, and I like them. When I put my arms around her waist, it's like I have a woman in my arms, and she's as solid as a rock, too.

And gorgeous. Did I mention that? Sometimes when I tell a story, it's almost like I expect you to just know what I know. Imagine Penelope Cruz, plus twenty or so pounds. Then you'll have some idea of the beauty of Serena Casteneda.

We were stoked to see little Flexy born before we left our friends. Cute kid, and big! I swear that little guy could already bench press a large can of tomato sauce by the time we hit the road. I wonder if he'll be walking when we get back.

I wonder more if it will take us that long. I hope not. If my uncle is alive, and you're probably wondering why I would even give him the benefit of the doubt, there's no guarantee he'll want to come back with us. And if he does, it will depend on who he has become since this all happened. A little more than a year in this crazy ass world can really tweak you.

And he was already tweaked, a bit. In a good way.

So here's why I think he might be okay. I need to let you know I'm not just nuts, because if I didn't know this, then I really wouldn't be going at all.

By now, if you've read everyone else's chronicles – and I hope you have – you know that Hemp discovered if you have an immunity to something called urushiol, then you are also immune to the zombie gas that is jetting from every pore of the earth. This oil is the stuff in poison ivy, poison oak, poison sumac, cashew shells and mango skins. It gives those who aren't immune to it anything from a severe, red rash, to angry huge blisters – at least that used to be the worst of it. Now, without ever having seen or touched it, the lack of an immunity can give you stuff like no heartbeat, blackish-red blood and a taste for human flesh.

I don't get any of those things, and neither do Serena or Nelson. I also know from many camping trips with my

Uncle Brett that he does not get it, either. The bastard used to show off by eating the stuff.

He never let me touch it, but as it turns out, he could have. I was as immune as he was.

So if Uncle Brett was as ready as he professed to be, and he was on top of this crazy, zombie apocalypse, then it's my bet that he's fine.

We shall see what we shall see. He's near the Oregon border in northern California. A place on the outskirts of Dunsmuir. It's all I remember from my last trip, but I'm hoping when we get there, more will come back to me. If not, with Uncle Bug's big personality, I'm fairly certain that some survivors there will know who he is and will be willing and able to direct us to his place.

So that's where we're headed. Sure glad it's spring.

But before I go on with this chronicle, I want to lead you through my beginning and tell you what happened before I found Lisa again and had to kill her dad. There are lots of other things that were no less horrible than that, because before I beat that dead son-of-a-bitch with that chair, he had killed our mother.

And all of this all leads up to how we both got stuck in that little church in Knoxville, Tennessee, surrounded by zombies. That wasn't too long before Flex, Gem, Charlie, Hemp, Trina and those huge, crazy dogs saved our lives and my sanity.

Before all of that, I was doing what everyone else was; I was hanging out with people I loved. And while this chronicle is about our journey to California to find Uncle Bug, it's going to seem like *The Road To Knoxville* at first.

It's okay. It allows me to remember the time with Lisa – not the best of times, but a time when we grew closer, even if neither of us knew it then. A time of terror, perhaps, but a time that made me realize how much I loved her. Not that I'd forgotten. Now I never will.

10

So on with Dave Gammon's story.

It's that awkward moment when you realize the chronicle is in your hands now, and you're trying to fill some big ass shoes.

*****

Chapter One

Just like for everyone else, it was June, 2012. It's hard for me to write this, because Lisa is such a prominent driving force in what got me to where Flex, Gem and the others found us. Oh, well.

Here goes nothing.

Just before I realized that my life had taken a twist for the worse, I was sitting in my house in Panama City, Florida waiting for my girlfriend to get out of the shower. That sounds perfectly normal, right? Well, it was, except for the reason she got in the shower in the first place.

In the middle of sex, while I was down south and doing what I do so well, I felt her body rippling with what I thought were shivers. That would not have been out of the ordinary.

Then she screamed. That might have been normal, aside from the intensity and shrillness of her scream. It was spine chilling and eardrum piercing. I actually jumped.

"Jesus, babe, what did I do? Are you okay?"

"No!" she shouted, her hands down by her sides, clenched into fists, her body responding to what seemed to be rippling shivers, though I was no longer the cause. Not by a long shot from the looks of it.

"What's wrong, L?" I pleaded. "Your ... skin looks kinda strange, baby."

"Head's pounding," she said. "All of a sudden."

"Jeez. I'm sorry. Want me to get you some aspirin or something?" My hard on was a distant memory now, but it wasn't at the top of my priority list anymore.

"It's not ... your fault, and yeah ... maybe in a minute," said Leona, her voice pained. "I ... I ... fuck!" Tears streamed from the corners of both her eyes.

I slid off her and sat on the bed beside her. "I'm calling 911."

"No," she said. "I ... I think maybe if I get in a cold shower or something. Might make me feel better."

I grabbed the phone anyway. She didn't open her eyes, so didn't tell me to stop. I used the house phone so they'd have the address right away. It rang. And rang. On the tenth ring I almost hung up, but decided to give it five more.

I slammed the phone down and felt her head with my hand. It was blazing hot, her face flushed bright red. "Shit, babe. Feels like you're on fire."

That was no lie. I could feel the heat rising from her body, and as I looked at her, I saw her skin changing before my eyes. I vaguely wondered if she had been bitten by a spider or something that was working its way through her bloodstream.

Leona Skye had been my woman for five years. She was older than my 36 years, but not by much. She was close to average height for a woman, maybe a bit on the shorter side, with dark hair and eyes that could tell a thousand stories with just a glance, depending on the look she chose. Leona's facial features were soft, her smile subdued, but her love for me was more than I had ever imagined I would find.

She possessed shoulder-length, dark hair that made her brown eyes seem full of light, yet somehow even darker, and a smile that could tell someone that everything was as it should be ... if it was. If everything was not right – and *you*

13

were the problem — her eyes would express that in no uncertain terms. And her voice would follow to fill in the specifics. Leona was not inhibited.

Her heritage was native Canadian, Ojibiwa/Mohawk, and if the Indian in her affected her in any way, it allowed her age-old wisdom to see into my soul and read it like a spiritualist reads tea leaves. If you knew me, you would know this ability was necessary. I'm not the most outgoing guy, and when I wasn't working, I didn't go out very much. I pretty much lived for Leona, and almost never went anywhere without her.

She validated me. When I was with her in public, I was suddenly not as shy or self-conscious. In my mind, I know it was like, *Look at this beautiful, interesting woman. If she thinks I'm a good guy, then I'm good enough for any of you.*

It's true. As haphazard as it might appear, I think even my look is carefully crafted to make me seem more approachable to strangers. The strangers I'd care to meet, anyway.

Hey, that guy with the blue eyes, long, wavy hair, mustache and kinky beard looks cool — probably even has weed on him. And look at that chick he's with ... those are the kind of folks I'd like to hang out with.

I'm not muscular like Flex or Hemp. I'm Flex's height, around six feet, but I'm kind of skinny, actually. Not as thin as Nelson Moore, because that guy's a beanpole, despite the fact that on the day we met, he knocked me on my ass using his self-styled martial arts method, Subdudo.

Still makes me shake my head and smile.

So anyway, hefting and firing all the damned automatic weapons has beefed me up a bit, as has all the running back and forth between danger and safety, so while I'm more toned, I'm not all that much thicker. You tend to work off a lot of calories fighting zombies. You just do.

I have a few tattoos, but nothing that really told any major stories in my life, just ones I thought were pretty cool. So that was Leona, and that was me. The odd couple and a perfect match. We communicated without words, we loved one another. Had this day never happened, I would have been with her until I took my last breath.

I hate speaking about her in the past tense. Even as I look up and see Serena here with me now, realizing how I feel about her, I cry inside for my Leona.

But I digress. Back to the story that worked out better for me than it did for her, at least from my current perspective.

She lay on the bed with the palms of her hands pressed hard against her eyes.

"Leona, tell me what you need and I'll do it. Does this have anything to do with how you slept last night? That was insane. I couldn't even wake you up."

"Terrible dreams," she managed. Then: "Help me up."

I did. I put her arm over my shoulder walked her to the shower. She stepped in, steadying herself on the tiled wall. I reached in and turned on the water, adjusting the mixer valve to warm.

"No, not fucking warm! Cold!"

"Okay, sorry," I said. I turned the knob all the way to cold.

"Close the curtain please," she said. "I'll be out in a little bit."

I nodded, still naked, and closed the shower curtain. Plodding into the bedroom, I threw on my underwear and jeans, leaving my shirt off. It was summer, and it was hot in north Florida. Not many people realize it, but even being in north Florida it's hot. In fact, if you look on a map and take notice, the entire state of Florida is south of the entire state of California. That means it's hot here.

Fifteen minutes passed. The water ran. I sat on the sofa and turned on the TV. There was a news alert about some guy who walked into a 7-Eleven and attacked some shoppers.

Not with a gun or anything; he bit and clawed at them. Then another story about an attack at a bank. Same MO. As I watched, the weird stories kept coming. Then they had video. This was from the bank. Out by the ATM. A woman had been standing there, a lineup of people behind her. In the video, you see her turn, and her face is strange. Even in the poor quality video, you can see that her eyes are flat.

Her purse drops from her arm and she staggers toward the old woman in the line directly behind her. At first, it appears she knows the woman and is hugging her. But seconds later the old woman is beating at the bank patron whose mouth is now buried in the thin flesh of her cheek.

She knocks the woman to the ground as others watch in stunned horror. The old woman's legs are kicking outward as she lies on her back, the younger woman on top of her now clawing at her flesh.

The video is cut, and the newsroom comes into view. As the camera focuses on the pretty blonde reporter, her pleasant face becomes confused. Then Summer Storm, the weather girl who is in between segments, runs through the camera shot, screaming.

The camera that was steady, rocks, and now the entire picture goes sideways as it apparently falls over. Screaming fills the newsroom, and as the camera continues to capture the image of the shocked reporter, Allyson Terry, she raises her arms and a huge man with his cap on backward charges her, falling atop her and growling.

They disappear behind the news desk, and I've never been happier to stop watching something in my life.

And that includes the Twilight movies.

Screw this, I thought. I jumped up and ran into the bathroom. I heard the water still running, so I opened the door and went in.

The bathroom was L-shaped. As you walked in, the shower was on the left, and down at the end, it hung a left and that is where the vanity and toilet area were.

The shower curtain was closed, and I thought I heard her moaning over the sound of cascading water. I spoke without pulling back the curtain.

"Leona, hurry," I said. "Something weird is going on. You have to come see this."

She didn't answer. I pulled open the curtain. The shower was empty. I looked at the falling water, and it didn't register. Why would she be out of the shower and leave it on?

I felt her, rather than saw her, as I reached in to turn off the water. She was emerging from the corner, and came fully into view. Her face had … well, changed. It was so distorted, I hardly recognized her. Leona's eyes, once windows not only to her soul, but to mine, were rolled back and blank.

As she stood there nude, blue-black veins, so tiny, streaked visibly across her face, down to her neck and all the way down to her toes. I registered all of this in a split-second because she was staggering toward me and I caught her by the shoulders, holding her away so that I could look at her.

"L! What's wrong with you?" I asked, horrified. Her arms both flailed out toward me, her long ago bitten off nails unable to scratch, which in retrospect is just lucky – I was the one with the long nails.

She growled and pushed forward.

"Leona!" I screamed, terrified. She struggled to get close to me, but her mouth was open, her eyes dead, and her growls were completely unintelligible.

I felt myself crying, and I suddenly felt completely alone. Leona, my best friend and lover, stood before me like a wild animal. She was, I could see at that moment, essentially insane, so I had nobody else to call. If I had let her go she would've attacked me and I knew it.

Though she had just gotten out of a cold shower and was still wet, I could not shake the feeling that the coldness I felt as I held her away from me was from more than just the water temperature. She had no body heat emanating from her as she had when I put her in the shower.

I moved backward through the door, my arms still holding Leona away from me. She grew more frantic, and her mouth began to gnash and chew.

When she bit her tongue in half, I screamed. She growled on, the blood pouring down her chin and onto her neck and chest, and I tripped on the woven rug on the floor of the kitchen and fell backward.

Leona came down on top of me.

It was official. She was scaring the holy hell out of me, and I could no longer pretend that her intentions were anything else but to sink her teeth into me. As much as I loved her and as devastated and sad as I was then, I wasn't going to let that happen. Incomprehensible thoughts slammed around inside my head, none of them gaining any traction but these:

It was like the woman on the news at the ATM.

The cameraman at the news station.

"Leona!" I tried again. She growled and snapped her jaws and bloody, destroyed tongue at me, and her breath now stank like decay. That fast. Her body was slick and wet with blood and water, and the floor beneath me was slippery as I pushed her hard off me and scrambled out from under her, charging into the living room.

I glanced at the television, and the cameraman had dragged the anchor from behind the desk. He was beside the lens now, and he was eating her with satisfied snarls. The image on the TV was now in a crimson hue and I guessed it was from blood that had splashed the camera lens. Nobody had yet cut the feed, which at first surprised me. I quickly reached the conclusion that there was nobody focusing on broadcasting excellence right about then.

Leona was on her feet and rounding the corner. I felt a thousand chills streak down my body and I ran to the front door, yanked it open and charged outside, slamming it behind me.

I heard her slam into the closed door, but she did not open it and come out. I stood on the porch and stared at the knob. It didn't turn. There was scratching on the door and as I backed away, I heard something from the front yard.

It was Denny Steele. My neighbor. His arms hung down by his sides and he moved toward the porch.

"Denny, go home!" I yelled. "There's something going on, and you need to stay in your house!"

Denny kept coming. I watched him as he bee-lined straight toward me, his movements clumsy. "Stop!" I yelled.

Denny didn't. He was a big guy, pitch black hair and eyebrows like Brezhnev. His arms were like tree stumps, and I was no match for him, even if he had just been the level of pissed off that he had once been when Leona and I were doing tequila shots and blasted classic Foreigner at the top of our stereo's capabilities.

Now he was either crazy drunk or attack-level angry. He was moaning, and as he drew closer, I could see red shit all over his mouth and hands. As I ran off the porch he jerkily changed direction. The house to my left was owned by Mrs. Dunaway, who was a retired school teacher. She was 73 years old, and now I saw her in her front lawn.

She was wearing a flowered robe, but the front was wide open and she was barefoot. I waved my arms at her and yelled, "Mrs. Dunaway! Get back inside! Go in! It's dangerous out here!"

And like a parade of fucking crazies, she, too, began to head my way, her old tits swinging to and fro, almost as disconcerting as her lack of modesty. She had the same jerky motion as Denny and the same lack of response.

"Fuck!" I said. "Fuck!" That's not me, you see. I don't scream that word much unless something is really, really bothering me. Well, let me tell you. This shit was *really, really* bothering me. And scaring me. They were getting closer and I didn't know where to go.

I looked back at the front of my house and the blinds were being clawed at from the inside. As I watched, they came down, and Leona was there, buck naked and pressing against the glass, pounding on it, falling against it.

Finally, as I watched in horror, the front window shattered and my love fell through, the glass slicing deep into her in several places.

Instinct took over and I ran to her, glancing back now and then at Denny and Mrs. Dunaway, who continued their slow but steady trek in my direction.

"Leona!" I shouted again, like I was broken and it was all I could say. She lay there with an enormous, triangular-shaped piece of glass jutting from her neck. Leona gnashed and clawed at the ground and as I watched in heartbreaking agony, she chewed on the half of her tongue that remained, eyes locked on me as she tried to get back on her feet.

There was blackish-red blood oozing from her wounds, but not fast. Just coming out as if no heart muscle pumped it.

I staggered away from her again as she finally pushed herself to her feet, and she moved toward me once more, her eyes dead, her intention obvious.

Get to me.

I didn't know then exactly what the end game was, or why everyone was heading toward me. I knew that others were being attacked, but while biting is an age old method of fighting without a weapon, there was more behind the bites. It was not just to inflict injury – otherwise, why chew long term like the news cameraman?

It was then that I first realized the true horror. These things – yes, even Leona Skye, the love of my life – wanted to *feed* on me.

I turned and ran toward the porch railing, for Denny was now coming up the three steps. Mrs. Dunaway was just outside the low rail on the north side of my house, so I put one hand on top of the railing and jumped over it and the hedge on the other side, into the yard. I ran into the middle of the lawn and as one, they all turned toward me.

Not toward one another. It was as if they didn't notice each other – only me. But if we had been on Sesame Street and this was a *One of these things doesn't belong here* question, the answer would have been Dave Gammon.

I wasn't the same as them. I didn't belong there.

Looking back on it now, I think of what I might have done differently. Even as I was realizing that Leona was very sick, as were many others, intellectually, I think I knew she and everybody else were way too far gone to help.

Think of the questions you asked yourself in the world before zombies. Did I put my dog down too soon? Was she really in that much pain? Or did I do it for my own convenience?

Guilt.

Was my dad really so difficult for me to take care of that I had to put him in that nursing home? Or was it just because I wasn't a good enough son and didn't want the hassle.

Guilt.

Was Leona really a creature, beyond my help? Or was I too frightened to risk myself to help her?

Guilt. Late at night, even now, I ask this question of myself. I know the answer because Flex, Gem, Hemp and even Charlie have shared their stories with me, and they all either killed or abandoned those they loved.

Still, it nags. What would she have done? Would she have allowed herself to become like me, just so we wouldn't have to part? It would be *so* Leona.

Either way, I ran. I ran away from the three on my porch and I went to Denny's house. The man had guns and I didn't. Since he was a showoff, I knew where he kept them and I knew where he kept the key to his gun safe.

I didn't count on almost falling over his dead wife in the den.

*****

Beth Steele lay on her back just inside the open front door where I charged in without looking. Her neck was torn open, and there were clumps of her hair on the tile floor on either side of her. To be more precise, the hair was adhered to the now sticky pool of blood that had initially flowed from her damaged skull, but that no longer possessed a viscosity that would allow it to course further.

I leapt in the air as I came upon her, like a cat surprised by a jack-in-the-box. I wasn't shocked I had that much energy; I felt like a coiled spring, having seen in just ten minutes, more horror than I had seen in all of my thirty-six years.

Anyway, I flew clean over her, missing the sticky muck of blood, and when I stopped and looked back, I saw her head had been bashed open. It had probably been smashed against the tile because I didn't see any other weapon around.

The skull was pretty destroyed, and there were chunks of something I did not stay and get a better look at before charging though the living room, down a short hallway and into the den.

I saw the safe in the corner – nice and big. The key was in the nightstand from what I remembered, and I opened it.

An assortment of vibrators and oils greeted me, but there was also a gun in there. It was a revolver of some kind with quite a long barrel, but I didn't know what kind, because while I liked and respected guns and wasn't afraid of them, I'd never really been that guy. Denny had invited me to the range a few times, and I'd taken him up twice. It was fun, and he paid for the ammo.

If I had unlimited funds I would likely have owned a few guns, but that had never been the case. I worked my ass off in construction, but I was still always hand-to-mouth.

I flipped on the light and looked the gun over. It was a Smith & Wesson, which was good, I guess. At least it wasn't made by ACME. I found what I thought was the safety and held the pistol out, squeezing the trigger.

It was locked. Not even a click.

I was intent on avoiding that awkward moment when a demented person whose objective is attacking you is one second away and you first require a 2-second gun training course.

I looked the Smith & Wesson over again and flipped the switch back, then held it out and pulled the trigger again.

The explosion threw my unprepared arm back, and I almost dropped the gun. A small hole appeared in the far wall of the room, and I immediately worried about police showing up.

Then I thought again. If the news I had been watching was any indication, I would be low priority about now. I put the gun in my other hand, careful to keep my finger off the trigger, and shook my right hand, trying to get the feeling back.

I flipped the safety back on and shoved the gun in the pocket of my jeans. It did not go in far enough and fell directly to the floor. I bent down to retrieve it, and when I stood up, Denny was barreling through the goddamned door at me.

I staggered away and fell on the bed, where I spider-crawled, the gun in one hand with the safety on, and my other hand feeling for the opposite corner of the bed.

I reached it and swung my legs off and stood just as he fell onto the mattress, his eyes glowing pink and putting out some kind of strange vapor. I ducked down, as the vapor seemed to be floating in front of his face. Flipping the switch back off, I held up the gun and said, "Denny, man, I don't want to hurt you! What happened to Beth?"

He growled, snarled and ground his teeth and his hand reached to within four inches of me. He didn't look right. His skin was like Leona's had been, only worse. More roadmap-type black veins and lines crisscrossing his face and arms, his movements unnatural and not in any way fluid. His eyes were blistered with dark, bloody veins through a pinkish haze.

I squeezed my eyes shut and fired into him. When I opened them again, there was a simple hole where his heart would be – almost center chest, slightly to my right – but nothing had changed. His mouth opened in a grotesque display of hungry desire, and I staggered backward at the unexpected lack of reaction, slamming the wall.

I pressed myself into the corner, but Denny kept coming, tumbling off the bed and onto the floor. He was no more than a foot and a half from my feet now and his hand reached out and snatched my ankle.

I had no shoes on, and this touchy-feely shit was freaking me out good. My adrenaline returned full force and I jerked my leg free of his grasp, springing over him as he scrambled to his hands and knees. I jumped up onto the bed, and stood, the gun held down on him. Though I realized the new danger I had put myself in by taking my current stance on the bed, it was too late to reverse the decision.

My head immediately got wacked good with at least two blades of the ceiling fan. Because it was probably running on high speed, combined with the fact that I just wasn't prepared for it, I practically flew into the back wall, and fell off the other side of the bed, my shoulder smacking into the steel gun safe.

I was a fucking comedy of errors. I never thought I would write about it later, but after seeing what Flex, Gem, Hemp and Charlie included in their chronicles, I did not think that being embarrassing qualified anything for omission.

As I got back to my feet, I saw my strange adversary did the same, but now he was crawling back over the bed again. I held the gun out. Right at his head. Again, I did not wish to see the bullet go into his body, so I closed my eyes and fired, point-blank range, into his skull.

The boom reverberated. I opened my eyes. Denny was face down and still.

Mrs. Dunaway staggered into the room, robe still wide open, her dead old tits wagging, and she was moving toward me as fast as her vein-riddled, old lady legs would carry her.

As I raised the weapon, wondering how many bullets it held, I saw Leona stagger up behind her and my heart caught in my throat.

I couldn't shoot her. I felt my eyes tear up, and it felt like I was about to break down and bawl.

Now, as I skirted back around the bed away from Mrs. Dunaway, I saw Leona was worse. Her skin had gone darker, her eyes had their own pink glow, but no mist. I jumped back onto the bed, avoiding the dead man there as I got to the other side of the room by the window. I stood there, the gun held out, saying nothing.

Leona stared at me and came around the bed while Dunaway crawled right over the dead body of Denny Steele without even a glance down. My head, my brain, every part of me was screaming inside. Nothing intelligible. Just screaming.

I reacted out of fear and sorrow, but I wanted out of there so bad, and I couldn't look at the woman who had caressed my heart with her unique brand of love for the past years; so much so that I knew she was my soul mate – even as stupid as that sounds to my own ears.

She was. I shook my head, met her eyes and tried one last time to see any sign of recognition there, and saw none. When Dunaway reached the edge of the bed and Leona was three feet from me, I threw myself through the closed window back first, tucking in my arms and lowering my head. The framework broke away and I dropped to the bushes and grass below, feeling as though I escaped any serious injury.

I only just thought that I was as lucky as hell that Denny didn't have hurricane windows. I'd have been just dazed enough to feel myself getting bitten. I didn't know at that time that it involved any more than biting and chewing – the fact that they actually *consumed* human flesh was still a little nugget that I would have the horror of learning later.

I hauled ass around and ran back to the front door, checking myself for cuts along the way. I got back to Denny's front entrance and ran inside again, this time yanking it closed behind me. Then I charged to the bedroom where I had just been. I stopped, breathing hard, watching Leona standing there staring at the broken window, as if she hadn't a clue as to what to do.

Mrs. Dunaway had already dropped out the window through which I had retreated. I saw the top of her head as she moved aimlessly around in the yard beyond.

Leona slowly turned, her mouth moving as though she were chewing, and her eyes met mine again. Gone. Dead. My Leona was dead. I pulled the gun from my pants and held it toward her, my hand trembling.

She seemed to hesitate. Leona stopped completely and stared at my hand holding the gun. I lowered it. She resumed her trek toward me instantly, dragging her left leg and reaching out to me with both black-grey arms.

I raised the gun and pulled the trigger. Yes, my eyes were closed. I loved her with everything in me, which is why I pulled the trigger in the first place.

When I opened my eyes I expected to see her mid-fall, but she was now a foot from my arm, her teeth bared as she prepared to bite my gun hand.

I fired again, this time the bullet passing through her nose. I hadn't had time to close my eyes. This time Leona fell and lay motionless.

I ran out of the room and slammed the door.

I turned my back to it and slid down to the floor, where I sat for an amount of time that I can't calculate or comprehend. In my mind, I had just shot the woman I loved. A little while ago we had been making love together.

Or had *I* just been making love to *her*? She hadn't slept well that night. I knew that from her tossing and turning in her covers. I had barely slept because of her thrashing. Leona was a sound sleeper, so it was unusual. She'd moaned and cried out, but didn't wake up.

I struggled to my feet and turned to face the closed door. I leaned forward, my forehead resting against the cold wood. My tears began to come again and I welcomed them. Leona deserved all of them, for all of eternity – all I had left to cry.

"I love you, Leona," I whispered. "I'll miss you. I'm so sorry this happened and I'm sorry I couldn't just give myself to you." I was quiet for a moment and added, "Sorry I didn't have the balls to do that for you."

My tears came on too heavy for me to finish what I felt had to be said, tough I knew she was beyond my words now. If her spirit was as powerful as I had always believed it to be, she was listening.

"Leona, you're an eagle now, or a hawk, or some kind of goddamned bird of prey. Whenever I see you soaring overhead, I'll whisper your name, I promise. That way you'll know you still give me strength to go forward no matter what happens from here."

I stood up straight again, my breath beginning to settle a bit, but my mind ramping up; planning my next moves.

Chapter Two

I rushed to the living room and found the remote for Denny's huge 70" Sony television. I hit the power button and flipped to Fox News.

The picture was sideways, and I could hear the voice of a remote anchor, but I could not see him. The camera was moving, but it was pointed at the ground, and occasionally, a hand would swing into the picture.

This shit was happening in New York. I was in Florida. It was all over.

The skin of the hand that I kept catching brief glimpses of looked strange. I hit rewind until the hand swung back into view.

Thank God for DVR technology. The hand paused on the screen when I hit the button, and I walked toward the TV. It was riddled with veins, the nails dark.

Like Leona. Like Mrs. Dunaway. Like Denny Steele. I hit play again and watched intently.

"What are you doin', Frank? What the fuck's wrong with you? Same as these guys? Stay back, Frank! Stay back!"

But I could tell by watching that Frank the cameraman was going toward the anchor, not staying back. The voice of the anchor was still loud, as though he either still held a hand-held microphone, or he had a lapel mic on.

Now he was crying. "Frank, it's me, Shep! If you'll just sit down, I can try to find a – Frank!"

The camera fell to the ground and for a moment, nothing appeared in its line of sight. Seconds later, I saw legs running through the shot, and a second pair – not running.

Shambling.

It's that awkward moment when suddenly we're all the same, and it's way more fucked up than the diversity some of us opposed in life.

But *I* wasn't like *them*. Not yet.

The guys had run out of the picture so I turned the channel. Fucking Wheel of Fortune was on, and because it was pre-taped, everyone looked stupid, happy and normal.

I'd take that. I'd take that if I could have my Leona back, because I was used to that shit already. I'd be as brain dead as those contestants if it could be with my Leona the way she was before her headache kicked in.

Only thing is, Leona would never have accepted me that way. She liked smart, crazy and strange, which is why I was her man. Stupid, happy and normal and she'd have flushed me like an inverted goldfish.

Too late for that. I'd already shot her in the face, hadn't I? I hadn't even known then exactly what she had become, or any of the others. I just instinctively knew that they were very dangerous. None of them had taken a chunk out of me, but when a dog chases you with its teeth bared, you run, assuming the worst.

When it's people doing the same thing, and when a gunshot to the heart doesn't do shit to stop them, you'd better assume that what's coming is far worse than a dog bite.

I flipped again. This time there was a reporter on who seemed to know something, and who seemed to be filming himself. I came on in the middle, so missed what he said to start out.

" ... run and find a secure place. From what I've found, just a closed door is enough, but lock it anyway. If you hear someone asking to be let in, ask them if they were bitten or scratched, but if they can talk, they are not affected."

I almost called out a question before realizing this man, who looked anything but the part of a reporter, was not available for questions.

"... reported odd dreams last night and many called in themselves or were called in by someone else. I'm locked in here now, and there are a lot of noises outside. I've heard some screaming, and I initially heard someone you all know begging for their life, but that ended ... I don't even want to say how."

He was standing in front of a floor camera, and as he spoke, he kept jerking his head from side to side, as though watching for something. His eyes were wild and his voice was not broadcast quality. He answered why when he spoke next.

"I'm normally the operator of the camera here. I came under attack when Janelle Jameson ... changed. She came in this morning saying that some man bit her on the subway, and we all chalked it up to typical New York crazies. Then ..."

He stopped talking and turned his back to the camera. He ran straight away from the lens, and you could see him off to the right grabbing something from the floor. When he stood again, it looked like a broken boom microphone arm.

He hefted it and swung it in a wide arc as another man, very thin, his shirt torn open, took the boom to the head and went down. The man who had been talking to me pulled back his arms and swung that piece of metal downward as hard as he could.

31

And again. And again.

Then he held the boom in his hands as he stared down at the body on the floor, breathing hard. He swallowed hard and threw the boom onto the floor, then rushed back to the camera.

"Shit, you see what's going on. They attack you. No talking, no nothing. They jerk, they don't move. They move like they're stiff, and when you hit them, they feel that way. Their skin is mushy feeling, but they're strong. Their eyes glow, and some of them pump some shit out, but I haven't been close enough to any of them to find out that's about."

His voice was rising in both pitch and speed. I stood there, mesmerized, watching and listening to him, wishing I knew how to use all this information.

"I'm getting out of here if I can, and I'd recommend that anyone who can hear me now get moving and find your family. Try their cell phones first. If they answer, tell them to isolate and keep away from anyone else who either has a major headache or was bitten or scratched. If they had horrible dreams last night, write them off. It's the only way to stay … the same. Not like them. Good luck. I don't even know why I stayed this long."

I stood and stared as he walked away, feeling extraordinarily lonely for the first time since I realized that Leona wasn't just a little sick. I'd seen what Denny did to his wife and I'd seen how determined he was to get to me – likely to do the same thing.

And then I hadn't shut the damned door to his house and they all came in. Now Leona was dead in the room with all the guns, and I just wanted to get as far away from there as I could. I could not go back in there where she was. Stupid, but I couldn't.

Denny was a lot bigger than me, but I could fit into his clothes at least. I wasn't going back to my house; not with the broken front plate window where anybody – or anything – could get in with no resistance. I needed speed, and I knew Denny had just the thing.

Let me tell you that Leona and I lived in a nice neighborhood. Not because we could afford it, but because she knew the landlord and he intended to sell the house in a year. In the meantime, he wanted to offset the mortgage, but didn't want to rent it to people who would trash the place.

So we got it. I'm telling this to explain to you that just because *we* struggled paycheck to paycheck, Denny Steele did not. I jogged into his bedroom and went to the dresser. I didn't know which drawers were his, so I yanked them open until I saw underwear and socks. I pulled a handful of each out and threw them on the bed.

Then I went through more drawers, but there were no jeans. Then I remembered. This dude would hang his jeans. No way would he fold them.

I ran to the closet and hit the light switch. There, against the wall, in the California Closet Organizer, was a straight row of jeans.

Now Denny had gained weight over the last year or so, and I knew as well as I knew my own name that overweight people never toss their clothes when they get too big, because they're sure they'll be able to fit into them again.

I went to the most inconvenient jeans hanging there, and sure enough, they were three sizes smaller in the waist. Since we were about the same height, it was all good. I took five pairs.

I pulled a bunch of shirts down. There were both long and short-sleeved pullovers. The wick-away-the-sweat kind, Under Armor or something. I carried my wad into the bedroom and dumped it on the bed. Then I ran back to the closet and looked up.

There were some duffels on the top, but I couldn't reach them. Then it hit me again. Rich people. Convenience.

I looked and found extension poles with convenient hooks on the ends. I used one to lift the perfect, black backpack down and threw the pole on the ground.

It was called a *Porter Heat*. Didn't have any clue, but I was sure it was expensive as hell. My shoes would have to do. For a guy his size, Denny had tiny ass feet. I would not be shoving my size twelves into his ten and a halfs.

A sense of extreme urgency struck me, and even though I knew where I intended to go, I needed to slow my ass down and make some kind of plan. My mother and eighteen-year-old sister would need my help, and now that Leona was dead, they were all I had left. I had no idea what had happened to Lisa's dad because he wasn't my blood, but if I was okay, I supposed there was a chance my mom and Lisa weren't sick with this shit, either. I guess I was subconsciously counting on any immunity being hereditary somehow.

It hit me. My cell phone was at my house, but Mrs. Steele had one. I ran into the kitchen with my packed duffle and dropped it on the floor. I saw her purse on the counter and pulled the Gucci bag toward me. I saw the bejeweled phone tucked inside and pulled it out. The only numbers I had memorized were my mom's cell and Lisa's.

Lisa was never without her phone, while my mom would often let her battery die and leave it places. I dialed Lisa's number and waited. She answered.

"Hello?" she said, her voice tired.

"Lisa?" I said, frantic. "Lisa, are you okay?"

"Davey?" she asked. "Where are you? Did you get a new phone?"

"No, Lisa," I said. "Now be quiet - and I mean really be quiet – and listen to me. Do you have a television in your room?"

"How did you know I'm in my room?"

"Because you're alive, Lisa … turn it on."

"What?"

"Lisa, turn on the television, but lock your bedroom door first. Hurry!"

"David, what's wrong? You're freaking me out."

"I'm freaked out, Lisa. Please, just do what I'm saying. I'm coming for you and mom."

"Why?"

"Just turn on the TV. Where's mom?"

"In her room I guess, Davey. Hold on," she said. "Okay. Got it. TV's coming on."

"Go to a news station or something. Maybe local. I can't imagine every channel's not either off the air or looping their broadcast."

She was quiet, but I could hear the television. "Lisa?"

"Dave, what's going on? What is this? Some hoax?"

"Hoax?" I was confused for a minute. "Lisa, this isn't a hoax. This is an insane disease or something, and everyone is going crazy. Leona … she's … I don't know how to say this. She's dead." I began to cry and knew I had to keep my shit together.

"David! Leona's dead?" asked Lisa, her voice incredulous.

"It's big, Lisa. Bigger than anything I've ever seen. What's on the news right now? What do you see?"

"They're showing people staggering in the street. It's a view from a traffic camera."

"Where's the broadcast from?"

"Downtown Knoxville, I think."

"Shit!" I said. "Lisa, stay there. Have you heard your dad? Or mom?"

I mentioned it earlier, but Lisa had a different father than me. I was from my mom's first husband, who passed away. Her dad was cool, but he wasn't mine. I knew she loved him a lot, and from what I knew, he was good to her.

Not that such former good behavior meant much right then. Precedent had died. Now it seemed to be a whole lot of *chase and terrorize your ass*, no matter what used to be the norm.

"I slept in this morning and my door's been closed and locked. You know I sleep with my iPod on, so I don't hear anything."

"When I hang up I want you to try mom's cell phone, okay?"

"I can do it now," she said. "From the house phone."

I hadn't thought of that. Leona and I had dumped our land line long ago. "Do that, Lisa. Call now."

There was a pause on the line. Then: "I hear it ringing out there, but she's not answering."

"Just leave it ringing," I said. "Maybe she's just asleep or something."

"I'm going out there," said Lisa.

"No!" I shouted. "Stay in there, Lisa."

"I'm starving, Davey. Are you sure this is everywhere? I don't hear anything strange."

"I think they are, too, Lisa. Starving. The ones outside."

"What?"

"I haven't seen any others like *me*, Lisa. Only like them. Watch the news more if you have to convince yourself, but you're safer in that room. Keep an eye out through your window if you have to. Do that now, okay?"

"Okay," she said. Then: "Oh, my God!"

"What?" I asked.

"The street!" she said. "There's ... people out there. Some of them are naked!"

"What?"

"I think that's Bill Pace from down the street. Dave, he's running around naked!"

"He's not in his head, Lisa. And he's dangerous as fuck. Stay there. You know it's going to take me a while to get there, but whatever you do, you have to stay safe. Don't move. You've got an attached bath, so you have water. Just wait."

"Dave, he's attacking a woman! Bill Pace! What the hell's going on?"

"It's bad. Don't trust anyone, and don't leave your room."

"I won't. When will you be here?"

"I don't know, but I'm leaving now," I said. "I'll take this cell with me."

"Okay, I have the number showing on my phone."

"Charge it up."

"I will," she said.

"Bye."

"Dave," she said, her voice worried.

"Yeah?"

"Be careful, okay?"

"From your lips to God's ears," I whispered, and hung up.

I grabbed the bag from the floor and jammed into the garage. I searched for the light, but as I fell into the room, it went on automatically.

Motion sensor.

The 2012 BMW S1000RR gleamed in the florescent lights. My eye caught the key in the ignition and I fed my arms through the straps of the stuffed, ritzy backpack, situating it on my back. I jumped on the bike and turned the key. Full tank. Using the electric start, I fired the engine, leaving the stand down. I jumped back off and ran to the door, hitting the garage door opener. There was a helmet hanging on a peg by the door. I grabbed it and stuffed it on my head, snapping the strap as I returned to the bike.

I sat down, pulled the clutch and put it in first gear.

I was very aware, as the garage door rose, that I didn't have the guns I needed, but I would have to deal with that later. I never said I was the brightest fucking bulb in the box.

I was in panic mode, but some of my decisions weren't bad. The BMW would handle beautifully and get me outta Dodge.

Right now I wanted the protection of speed; something these things did not seem to be in possession of.

When I saw enough light to jet, I let out the clutch, cranked the gas and rode for daylight, the rear tire squealing on the painted garage floor. Poor Mrs. Dunaway had severed part of her right arm as she followed me through the window, and I tried not to think about Leona, dead in the spare bedroom.

I would try to always picture the beautiful woman I had known and loved for those years, and work to convince myself once and for all that what I had seen her turn into was not something that anyone could come back from.

For Christ's sake, Mrs. Dunaway didn't even seem to notice that her arm was dangling from a few straggly tendons, never mind that her tits were still out.

I loved Leona, and it killed me to know she wouldn't be there to listen to all my bullshit, support me when I was struggling, and to hold onto when I needed someone to keep me from going insane.

But I wasn't Flex then, just as I'm not him now. I was scared, Leona was gone and I had my mom and Lisa to think about.

My little sister, whom I now knew was okay, was my only real hope for sanity at that moment. In my heart, I think I had begun to fear the worst about my mom. The house wasn't that big that she wouldn't hear her phone from her bedroom, even if it were in her purse in the kitchen.

I was in the clear as I hit the street, and I was glad to feel the wind whipping my long hair against my back as I realized I still had no shirt on.

I rode. I'd deal with that later, too. There were shirts in the backpack.

*****

Cars were driving crazy, and it didn't take me long to figure out why. Some people had clearly been on their way to hospitals when the person in their car with them made their terrifying conversion into something that wanted only to attack. I couldn't imagine the horror that ensued at that point then, and I don't like to think about it now.

But I will, if only for those reading about this later.

If you were driving when it happened, you'd be helpless to do anything with one arm on the steering wheel and the other fending them off. As it turned out, the BMW motorcycle was the perfect escape vehicle. I dodged around several crashes and was able to avoid more than my share of vehicles driving even crazier than is typical in Florida. Season was already over and most visitors from up north had already gone home to suffer their transformations there. That was good, but for six months out of the year, Floridians saw a ton of visitors from Indiana, New York, Minnesota, Ontario, Canada, New Jersey, and everywhere else, so we were used to people driving like they owned the road.

This was different. It wasn't just *possible* that a car was going to careen toward you at any given moment; it was likely.

The Beemer had a GPS that I figured out how to use while I guided the bike down more open stretches of road, but I didn't need a bitch in a box to tell me how to get to my sister's place, just to guide me around blocked roads should I come across any.

The helmet had an intercom system with Bluetooth, and luckily, it had automatically paired with the system on the bike. This meant I could mess with the radio and try to get signals, but also could hear the GPS lady when she had the urge to tell me things I mostly knew. I had ridden maybe thirty minutes and had only gotten just over two miles. It was almost immediately after turning onto East Avenue when I first saw these new creatures in greater numbers. I was struggling with the process of accepting the truth about the once-humans, but they were doing their share to convince me what I and the rest of the uninfected world faced. I can tell you that at that time I kind of looked at it like a horrible fire or a riot or something; the blind faith that ultimately, our government would find a quick cure and put everything back to normal. After all, I wasn't catching it yet, so there had to be a lot of people like me working on this.

But as I rode on, I realized I wasn't seeing a lot of people like me. As I worked my way north up East Avenue, I took the horror in that surrounded me. I could see the colorless, vein-riddled skin of the afflicted from a distance; the way they moved as though stiff – somehow unpracticed in the art of walking.

I slowed the bike initially, a morbid curiosity or maybe just spacing out a bit as I observed them – I'm not sure which – but soon snapped to reality and remembered that to allow any of them to reach me was to die at their hands.

I'd seen my share of them feeding and tears ran from my eyes beneath the helmet's shield as I watched what was happening. I never saw an uninfected person actually get taken down, but I did see them fleeing for their lives. I saw uninfected people locked in cars, obviously without keys, looking out at me in desperation as I rode past; me avoiding their faces like they were dirty, homeless people on the corner looking for a buck.

The truth was, I gave *those* guys a buck. I could *not* risk my life for these doomed souls. Not at the risk of letting my sister die. No way. I put on my heartless fucking mental blinders and stopped looking, and I used my high-aim steering to chart my path through the more congested parts of East Avenue, anticipating my arrival at US 231 that would roll me onto the 431 into Dothan, Alabama.

The whole trip was around 500 miles, so I'd need gas sometime, and that I'd play by ear. If I came across somewhere that seemed safe enough, I'd swing in and do a quick fill-up.

*****

Mrs. Steele's phone was a Droid Razor Maxx, and the son-of-a-bitch really did have all-day battery life, according to everyone I knew that had one. I was happy to see a solid battery icon on it when I'd pulled it out of my neighbor's purse, but I also thought it wise to grab the car charger that was tucked in beside it. I couldn't afford it to run empty, because as I approached the house, I wanted Lisa to know I was there. I also wanted to call her and let her know I was safe, like right now.

Thank God I was safe.

After getting off East Avenue, I'd gone about sixty miles in just over an hour. I saw a Racetrack gas station and pulled in.

To my surprise, a cop car was parked in the lot with its lights on. The siren was silent, and I rode toward the car with caution, easing my bike to a stop about ten feet back and off to the passenger side. If the cop was jumpy – and who the hell could blame him if he or she was – I'd feel better if I sat in their blind spot.

With my left foot I kicked the kickstand down and eased myself off the bike. I still had the gun stuffed into the front of my pants, and hadn't even realized it. I instinctively turned away from the police car in case the officer was aware and watching, and carefully pulled it out of my pants. I rubbed the painful, dark purple impression the bulky weapon had pressed into my skin at my belt line, forgot it and opened the cylinder.

Four of the brass cartridges looked different, which corresponded to the number of shots I had fired. There were five left. I was okay for now, so I closed the cylinder again and hoped I was on a live round. I held the revolver in my right hand.

I looked again at the police car. The engine was turned off, yet I could hear the tick-tick-tick-tick-tick of the almost silent lights as they flashed. I moved to the passenger side of the car and approached the back seat, where I pressed my face to the heavily tinted glass and tried to see inside. The cage separating the criminal element from the good guys eventually came into view as my eyes adjusted.

I was squinting, trying to see if anyone was in the front seat, when a face slammed into the glass, directly against mine. An involuntary scream left my throat as I tripped away from the car, falling flat on my ass. The face slammed into the glass again and again, its teeth shattering with each impact until only cracked, jagged shards remained. Alternately, it pounded the window with gnarled hands, mad eyes demanding that I come closer, closer, open that door and let it get at me.

I looked in all directions as I scrambled back to my feet and picked up the dropped revolver. I was freaked out then, I won't lie. I shook like someone who had no right to hold a gun of any kind, but I gripped that thing like it was a lifeline.

I moved around the back of the police car to the other side. As I did so, the creature in the back seat, which wore a tank top and tattoos beneath its black, roadmap veins, pounded on the glass, desperate to reach me. From this side it was more illuminated, and I could that half its chest was ripped away; the musculature – stringy tendons and raw, rotting meat – exposed, making me want to vomit.

I swallowed my fear and steeled my nerves, moving to the front of the car to see inside the front seat area. As I did my best to ignore the frantic display of desire coming from the back of the car, I saw the cop.

It was a woman, and she was lying on her back on the bench seat, her hand hanging down with a pistol still in it. Her brown hair was cropped short, and her eyes were wide open, staring upward. She did not look like the thing in the back seat. She looked uninfected like me, only female and dead.

I tried the driver's side door. It was unlocked. I pushed it closed again and walked around the front of the car, this time to the passenger side door. I put my hand on the door and felt everything inside of me coming up.

Construction had not prepared me for this. None of it. I'd seen guys put nails through their hands and I'd seen guys saw off fingers, but I'd never seen walking monsters or dead cops, mere feet away from me.

I finally threw up, but there wasn't much to eject. I hadn't eaten breakfast and there hadn't been time for lunch. Hell, I hadn't even stopped for water, and suddenly I realized I was dying of thirst *and* hungry as hell. I felt neither like eating or drinking now, though. Not when I was about to do what I had in mind.

The cop was dead. One way or the other, she was dead. It was at least 85 degrees out, and the car's interior would heat up to crazy temperatures inside in a half hour, never mind a couple of hours. I pulled on the handle and the door swung open. I stood there, the stench blasting me in the face, the creature's hungry growls audible to me now, and the dead cop's bullet wound to the head clearly visible.

I ran three feet away from the car, took a deep breath, and turned and ran back. I leaned in and peeled the gun from the female cop's stiff, dead fingers, and I stepped back again, kicking the door closed behind me.

Sticky wetness coated my hand, but I refused to drop the gun. I needed it. I knew I would need it. And more of them, wherever I could get them. Had I known where cops kept their extra magazines or ammo, I would have gone back, but I didn't, and I didn't feel like searching anywhere near the dead woman or the live thing in the back seat that should be dead. At least it was trapped in there. Maybe it would die from the heat eventually. In any case, I didn't need to waste a bullet.

Suddenly I had the strong desire to call Lisa. As I pulled the phone from my pocket, it rang.

I pushed the button and shouted into the receiver, "Lisa! Are you okay? Did you find mom?"

"Oh, Dave, you have to hurry!" my sister cried into the phone, tears in her voice.

"What's wrong, Lisa? Are you still in your room?"

"I am, but mom was screaming, Dave! Right after you hung up before I heard her screaming! She was screaming like she was being murdered!"

I gripped the phone. "Lisa, why didn't you call me then?"

"I couldn't!" she said. "I tried, but the recording kept saying the circuits were busy!"

I knew what it meant and I had to calm myself down. Lisa had essentially just told me my mom was dead. I'd seen enough to know what had probably happened. Still, I asked the question: "Do you hear her now? Have you heard her in a while?"

"No," she said. "Not for a long time. It was far away from my door. At first she was screaming at me to stay in my room ... then she ... screamed like *that*." She burst into tears.

"I'm coming, Lisa. I had to stop to get a gun and some gas, but I'm coming. Don't move, and don't leave your room. Don't look outside anymore, Lisa. I don't want you to."

"I already stopped, Dave. I ... just hurry."

"I love you, Leese."

"I love you, too," she said. "I'm glad you're alright. Hurry. I need you."

"Me, too. Call me if you get scared. I'm on a bike, but I'll put the phone on vibrate so I feel it."

"Okay. Hurry."

"I will," I said.

I hung up the phone, opened the backpack, and rummaged around for a shirt. Then I looked at the mini-mart. Fuck it. I'd just grab a tee-shirt and maybe a jacket from inside. I held the gun in my hand with the sticky blood still there. I'd wipe that off inside, too. On one of the shirts I didn't take.

45

As I approached the storefront, everything was still. I wondered what I would find when I opened the door.

It was a Sunday. That was good. Most people slept in on Sundays.

And right at that moment, I didn't want to be around most people.

*****

I stood by the door of the QuickShop mart, scanning the distance. I saw a man running full steam down the middle of the highway about a quarter mile away. A few moments later there were three of the slower moving things following.

Everywhere.

I ran back to my bike, got on and kicked the stand up, rolling it toward the pump stations. This gas station was powered – I could see by the numbers glowing on the digital readouts – and I thought I should fill up. I was lucky the pants I'd thrown on that morning had my wallet in them from the night before, because I had hoped to use my debit card to access the fuel.

I rolled up beside them and kicked the stand down again, the smaller revolver in my left hand. I'd decided this was a .22 caliber revolver. I had only handled one years ago when I was about fourteen years old. A friend of mine with a propensity for theft stole a .22 revolver from the house of a seasonal resident, and we went shooting it over one weekend. That friend was in jail, last I heard. Some people just never grow up – or at least they grow into something different than I did.

The other gun was probably a .45, as the rounds were quite large, and removing the magazine, I discovered that only the round that had killed the cop was missing. It made me wonder why she hadn't tried to take some of the things out before killing herself, but I hadn't searched the car or beneath her body, so this may have been the second magazine she'd put into the weapon.

Judging from the condition of the creature in the cage behind her, she might have already discovered that the things did not die easily after firing a few rounds.

I decided to save the .45 to use for dire situations – at least the six rounds that remained. The .22 seemed to be effective enough if used accurately, so I'd resort to the bigger pistol only if I wasn't putting down my attackers with the revolver.

I put the .22 on top of the pump and opened the gas cap. I pulled out my wallet and removed my card, inserting it into the reader. To my relief, it asked for my PIN, which I entered. I selected premium, because I figured I might not have a hell of a lot of opportunities to use the card, and inserted the nozzle into the BMW's tank.

When it was full, I was hesitant to flip the handle back down. I needed backup fuel, and the only way I was going to get a small gas can was to go inside that minimart and get one.

The unknown. I was becoming adverse to the unknown. The unknown sucked these days and that pretty much started today.

"Leona," I said aloud. "You can hear me now, I know you can. You're not what you were when I put you out of your misery … now you're an angel or a spirit or whatever you always knew you'd become."

I paused to wipe the corners of my mouth and scan the immediate area again. "So what I'm saying, baby is that I *need* you. Just like I needed you every day for the past five years and like I needed you for the rest of my life. I'm going in now. Just be there, okay?"

Dumb. Maybe. But it made me feel better and that's all that mattered then. I stuck the nozzle back into the open filler on the bike and rested it there. I was going to fill at least a gallon can and have it on that bike with me come hell or high water.

I walked to the door, tucking the .22 away this time and pulling out the pistol. I looked at the side of it and saw that it was indeed a Ruger .45 ACP. I wanted to wipe the blood from the grip, but I'd get to that. It would fire okay, and that's all that mattered.

I was scared shitless. I didn't want to go in that damned store, but I needed some food, some water, some gas and a new shirt would be a nice topper.

I stood there, took two more glances behind me, and pulled the door.

The store was locked.

I looked around for something – anything – to throw at it. There was no auto repair attached to this station, so I didn't find any camshafts or crankshafts lying around, but there were some pavers bordering a small garden off to the right of the store.

That would do. I ran over and grabbed one.

By the time I ran back, there was a face staring back at me where I had intended to chuck the paver. It was a weird, dead-looking face with those strange, pink eyes. This one seemed to be emitting the vapor like Denny had been. I didn't know what it was then, but I imagined it was toxic, like vaporized battery acid or something, and I did not want to breathe it in.

If you've followed these chronicles, then you know that gas would knock me out and make me available for an immediate snack or allow the dude to save me for later. Its hands clawed at the glass, and as I moved side to side, it followed me. This fellow was on the shorter side, and appeared to have been from somewhere in the Middle East. The skin around his eyes, while nothing like it must have been in ordinary life, was darker and sunken, and his hair was a flat black.

But ignoring all of that, the thing that used to be a man wore a plastic name badge that said Amal, which is all I really needed to look at, I suppose.

"Amal, you're gonna want to step back from that glass, my friend," I said, more to make me feel like I was comfortable enough to be a smart ass, more than I felt like being one. This was the old *fake it until you make it* strategy.

It's that awkward moment when you're trying to psych yourself into doing something and even *you* see through your own bullshit.

My plan came together in my mind. I figured that had there been any others like him in the store, they probably would have made their way over to the window to gawk at me, and they hadn't. It was time, because there were clearly more of them out here with me than there were inside with Amal. I stepped back and raised my arm, the paver held firmly in my hand.

Aiming directly at Amal's face, I threw it as hard as I could. The glass exploded as it hit, throwing crystalline cubes of tempered glass in every direction, peppering the creature standing there, but not fazing him in the slightest. All he knew was the restaurant was open. He stepped through the mess, tripped over the lower frame, and fell on his face.

I leaned down with the .45 in both hands and pushed the gun into his skull.

Seriously. My gun sank into his skull. I pulled the trigger anyway, and the kick jacked my arms back into my shoulders as I staggered back two steps.

"Wow!" I said aloud. "Wow," I said again, in case I didn't hear it.

Amal didn't move, and nothing came after him through the shattered window. I moved inside and went immediately to the front counter to grab some shopping bags. I pulled two of them, rushed down the aisle to the water and threw four bottles in. Then I grabbed two more.

Fucking Zephyrhills. Crap tasted like rust. But it was better than what was going on in my mouth at the moment.

I took a bunch of pepperoni sticks and threw them in the bag, too. There were some Lunchables there, and I remembered Gem's chronicle. I swear my journey was like hers. I suppose there were only so many ways to eat your way to safety, and convenience was crucial.

Lunchables were the perfect on-the-go food.

I rounded the corner and saw oil filter wrenches, cloth gloves, Little Tree air fresheners and plastic gas cans. I guessed a gallon of fuel might get me around 40 miles with a bike like the BMW, and the tank on it looked like it held just under five gallons. So with an extra gallon, I'd be able to ride about 220 miles or so before I had to fill up again. I still had over three hundred miles to go easy.

Then I saw bungee cords and some two gallon cans. Screw it, I thought. I grabbed one can and a four-pack of bungees. Even if I had to stop again, the farther I could get the better.

Then I saw a siphon hose kit and it hit me.

The fact that I'm an idiot hit me, that is. It was all I needed. There would be plenty of cars around when I started getting low on fuel, so I'd take the kit and focus on sustenance. I dropped the can, kept the bungees and took the siphon.

What a waste of brain power. It was that very moment that I worried internally that I did not have a ton of mental fortitude to spare in a crisis like the one I faced.

Screw it. I was who I was, and I'd gotten that far. I quickly moved down the aisle and grabbed a large bag of

Cheetos. As I stuffed that into my bag, I moved toward the Red Bull and pulled an entire six pack out of the cooler.

I was good on food and water – at least by my standards – so I moved back to the front of the store to keep an eye out. Nothing out there was moving. I ran to the bike, pulled a Red Bull, a water, and a Lunchable out of the bag, and put them on the ground. I then wrapped the bags and strapped them behind the seat. Not perfect, but stable.

I pulled the nozzle out of the BMW's tank and flipped the handle back down, turning off the pump. Nobody would be charging crap on my card if I had anything to say about it.

I snapped the cap back down and fired the motor.

Then, as I caught a glimpse of my own nipples out of the corner of my eye, I realized I was still shirtless.

I laughed and cursed myself at the same time. I had seen the rack of stupid shirts inside and had run right by them.

I bent down, grabbed the Red Bull and popped the lid. I guzzled it down and tossed the can, then grabbed the water and the Lunchable. Peeling the plastic off, I took the entire stack of mini turkey slices and stacked them on top of the tiny stack of crackers. I stuffed the entire thing into my mouth and uncapped the water. Then I ate a whole stack of cheese.

Washing that down, I quickly polished off the remainder of the Kraft treat, including a Reese's Peanut Butter Cup that somehow made its way into the package, and chased it all down with more water.

If you knew me better, you'd know that Reese's are my favorite food, and you know I was in a hurry to rush through it.

When I was done I felt some energy streaking through me that I did not think – for the first time in a while – was adrenaline related.

I dusted the crumbs from my chest and gunned the motor, jamming up to the storefront where I kicked the stand down and left the bike running.

I was in and out in under fifteen seconds, and as I jogged toward the bike, I pulled the black, cap-sleeved shirt with "Pretty Young Thing" written in rhinestones across the chest over my head.

I looked down at myself and I actually laughed out loud.

It turns out I needed a good laugh, but at that moment, I realized I did not want to stop again until fuel required it. Despite the three staggering creatures I noticed down by the exit driveway, there was also an incapacitated cop car right there, and if I were to leave any ammo on the table in a world such as this one, I was a fool.

I ran back to the car and took a deep breath, holding it as I opened the driver's door again. I reached in, searched for the trunk release, found it and popped it.

Slamming the door and breaking into a run, I saw the creatures that had been in the driveway were now fifty yards away. I lifted the trunk lid and saw a leather bag. I fumbled with the zipper on top and finally got it. Inside there were several spare magazines, which I tucked into my pockets. All were full and heavy. Another 50 round box of .45 ammo was in there, so I grabbed that, too. It would do. It would get me to Lisa and maybe get us out of the house.

Where we'd go from there I had no idea. It was impossible to plan that far ahead. Right now it was just get to the people you love and figure it out from there.

Just like Flex and Gem and Hemp.

Charlie's story had been different. When she left those she had loved, they were all dead and she was on her own. I'm glad she found Hemp.

Hell, I didn't know it then, but I would ultimately be glad they found us, too. Without a doubt, after Serena and I do what we have to do in California, I intend to get us back to where they are. Because they're my family now. I hope to bring my Uncle Brett back with us, if he'll come.

Back to my journey to Knoxville and my younger sister. I'm sorry I get sidetracked, but so much has happened, I'm sure you understand.

Anyway, I hauled my stash back to the still running BMW bike, tucked as much of the ammo as I could inside its seat and hopped on. I tucked the .45 into my waistband, and the .22 between the seat and my crotch.

I turned the handlebars and rolled the bike smoothly toward my three new friends who seemed too intent on meeting me up close and personal. When I drew close, I stopped the bike, kicked it into neutral, and put my feet down.

The .22 revolver in my right hand, I held it out. The closest one was fifteen feet away. I held out my arm, utilized the sights, and fired.

Hit him in the cheek. The side of its face sank in, probably crushing the bone a bit, but it kept coming. Now I was not feeling extremely comfortable. I raised it again. He was at about nine feet. This time the report sounded and the thing went down. I didn't see where the hole appeared, but I had been aiming for its head, so that seemed to be the sweet spot.

I remember thinking about the old zombie movies I'd seen then, and in some of them a shot to the brain worked, and in others, like Return of the Living Dead, the damned pinky finger could live on its own, and they were impossible to kill.

It was kind of a relief to know a shot to the brain could do it. I fired at the other two, who were still about ten feet from me. By the time the gun clicked empty, I had them resting in peace.

I tossed the .22 away and touched the .45 with my hand before pulling the clutch, putting the Beemer into gear and turning left, back onto Highway 431.

I rode for two straight hours, dodging this, shooting at that, and almost crashing at least four times.

I didn't. Maybe Leona was with me after all.

The trip wasn't without tears. After many of them, and another full tank using my stolen siphon, I arrived at my mom and Lisa's house.

The neighborhood had gone to shit.

*****

Eric A. Shelman

Chapter Three

I pulled onto my mom's street, not wanting to think much about what Lisa had said about her screams. I'd seen more of the transformed people as I worked my way through the neighborhood, but they had been occupied with other tasks.

I won't say what tasks – I don't really think I need to at this point. Not anymore.

As I pulled up to the house, I saw three bodies; one on the sidewalk, another sprawled in the gutter, and the last dead center of the lawn next door. Their bodies had all been hollowed out, just remnants of their clothing identifying them as men or women – mostly the shoes.

These things did not seem to gnaw on feet very much. Tearing at the clothing seemed natural, but removing shoes was clearly not a task at which they were proficient.

I saw the creatures that I suspected had done the handiwork; four of them walked toward me presently. I didn't have any idea at that time if they were coming at me or not, only that they were moving in my general direction. Either way, the .45 was in my hand and it had a full magazine. There were two more in my front pockets. On the way I had learned how not to miss, and better, how to clear a jam.

In a hurry.

My mind turned back to Lisa and my mom.

My mom, who was most likely dead already. I knew from my brief experience that nobody could be ready for something like what had happened today, and if Matt had turned, Tammy Rowe, who liked to sleep in, would have been his first target.

You have to remember that when I left Panama City, I knew the things attacked and chewed. I didn't realize that they actually fed on human flesh until I worked my way 500 miles across three states. The truth hit me before I left Florida.

So me getting away from Leona had been a matter of being lucky. I was *lucky* I had been lucky. Leona could just as easily have sunken her teeth into me had it not been for the horrid physical changes in her that had repelled me from her for the first time.

I'd thought about that during the ten hours the trip had taken me, all told. The GPS had initially estimated eight hours, but with my stop at the QuickShop for gas, food and water, and my extra two stops for siphoning fuel, it was still light when I arrived, but fading fast.

Anyway. Back to my mom, Tammy Rowe, formerly Tammy Gammon. My dad, also David Gammon, died years ago. He was a heavy drinker who worked construction, only he was the guy you saw at the 7-Eleven in the morning buying a twelve pack. He was good to me and my mom and he wasn't an angry drunk. It just turns out he couldn't drive all that well under the influence of a twelver, no matter what he thought.

So one evening, on his way home in his beat up Chevy pickup, he fell asleep on the I75 northbound, hit the center guardrail and somehow flew over it. He hit a mini-van with a mom, dad, grandmother and three kids ranging in age from eight months to four years, killing every last one of them and himself.

My mom was devastated, and I became morose. I was fourteen years old and hated everything and everyone. I started skipping school regularly and stayed out all night without calling home.

Mom wasn't much better. She was only thirty years old, having had me when she was just sixteen, so she and I fought, made up and did our best to face the world alone ... together.

Time rolled on and Tammy was working at a dead-end job as a receptionist at a glass company, making just over minimum wage with no benefits. I had dropped out of school and started working construction myself, so she was ready to be rescued from her lonely existence.

My mom always had her eye out, so when a man named Matt Rowe came into the shop with a crack in the windshield of his new Corvette, she noticed there wasn't a ring on his finger. She made sure her hands were visible, and she smiled at him, finally unveiling the beauty that had been tucked away for so long.

He noticed.

When he asked, she said yes. I sure as hell wasn't leaving Florida for Tennessee, so that was that. She got pregnant with Lisa almost immediately, which explains why she's 18 and I'm 36.

So that's my early story. I was a hard worker and made good money, being assigned as foreman on most jobs. I'd go up to see Lisa and my mom regularly enough that Lisa and I became very close, and I liked Matt a lot. He was good to my mom and I hadn't seen her happier since I was a little kid.

Now I stared at the house of Matt and Tammy Rowe, the sunlight waning as the hands of my watch wound around past eight o'clock. I'd parked the BMW in the driveway with about a quarter tank of fuel left, and saw the fucked up neighbors coming closer, but not yet appearing to do more than drift in my general direction. I was vaguely aware that the wind was blowing from them toward me, so that could have had something to do with it.

And there was a stench in the air. A stench of death.

I ran to Lisa's window and tapped on it.

I looked behind me to make damned sure I was alone. I was. The curtains moved, and I saw Lisa's face appear as they were swept aside. She quickly unlatched the window and slid it sideways.

She was crying before she said the first words. "Davey, God."

"I'm here, Leese," I said. "Here, take this and move back. I'm jumping up." I handed her the .45, barrel down.

She took it and stepped away from the window as I hefted myself up and onto the sill. I threaded my left leg in, then my right, dropped to the floor and closed the window behind me.

"Any noise out there?"

She threw the gun onto the bed and wrapped her arms around me, holding me tighter than I think she had since she was six years old and I was leaving her yet again, heading back to Florida. She sobbed against me.

"Shh," I said. "You've been looking outside, haven't you?"

I felt her nod against me. She pulled away and looked into my blue eyes. Her eyes were a deep brown, as were Matt Rowe's, and they were even more dark and sunken that her father's. "What are we going to do, Davey? Where can we go?"

"You might have to think of something, Lisa," I said. "This is your territory. Where would people go in a crisis around here? To hide?"

She shrugged. "The church, I think. There's a small Baptist church. Even people who aren't Baptists go there. It's that friendly."

"I hope it still is," I said. "Leese, I don't have much hope, but I have to go out there. If Matt's there, and he's … different … I'm going to shoot him."

Her eyes went wide. "My … father?"

"He's not *him* anymore, Lisa. Not if he's changed like those people out there. What you heard … I can't see that it means anything else."

"I have to see, Dave," she said.

"That's not a good idea," I said.

"He's my dad," she said. "I'll hate you if I don't."

"You might anyway, Leese. I wouldn't make you do it, though. So you'll have to get over it."

"We're jumping to conclusions, Dave. We don't know yet. I only stayed in here because you told me to, and —"

"Did your dad come to the door and check on you after you heard mom screaming?" I interrupted. "Did mom? No, right? Neither one did. They aren't blind, and they could have seen what was going on outside just like you, so either one or both of them are like those people out there."

She just stared at me.

"You've got to face it, Lisa."

"I still have to see."

I picked the gun up from the bed and checked it again. Walking to the door, I put my left hand on the knob and said, "We do it right now, then. If it gets dark, getting out of here's going to be worse."

*****

When I opened the door with Lisa behind me, I scanned the hallway. The light switch was just beside me, so I flipped it up. I miss those days, thinking back. These days, without a generator, you're in the dark or relying on a fast-dissipating supply of batteries. It's not that there aren't a lot of them, but survivors take them first, so they are becoming scarce in even moderately populated areas.

Back to me and Lisa. I turned to her. Her brown eyes were wide, her bangs a bit too long and in her eyes. My little sister's expression was dead serious. "Looks like the door down there's cracked open," I said.

"I thought I heard metal crashing. Like pots or something," said Lisa. "They might've been in the kitchen."

"First things first," I said, wishing I'd held onto that .22. It had been empty, but I might have been able to find more ammo for it, and it would have been perfect for Lisa. Then I thought of something.

"Leese, did Matt keep guns?"

"Yeah, but just for hunting. Rifles and stuff," she said. "Nothing like what you have."

"Do you know how to use them?"

She shook her head. "I've only used the small one. The .22 rifle."

"Where are they?" I asked.

"Straight ahead," she said. "In their closet."

"No gun safe?"

She shook her head.

"That's good. Think you can handle it?"

"I'm not shooting dad or mom," she said, her mouth fixed when the words came out.

I shook my head. She was saying things like this, and I don't think she really grasped the reality here. I'd been out in the world; I'd seen what was happening close up, not just from a bedroom window.

It got very real when you had to slaughter them. You felt dirty, like some kind of sick psychopath, and you had to keep reminding yourself that it was them or you.

I put a hand on her shoulder and squeezed. "I told you, if it's what we suspect, I'll do it. I like your dad, Lisa, and you know it. But he's not my blood, and ..."

She looked at me. I couldn't say the words.

"What, Dave?"

It was like it all flooded back to me at once. What I'd already done, what I was about to do. I found myself fighting back heaving sobs, and I knew that while I was crying like this, I wasn't protecting anyone, much less my sister. I pushed her into the room and eased the door closed behind us, my back pressed against it.

"Davey, what?" asked Lisa, rubbing my back, then holding my shoulders and she stared up at me.

"I killed Leona," I said. "I had to. She was ... one of them. She would've attacked me, and I don't think she knew me anymore at all. I could've been anyone."

The sobs wracked me again. Snot and tears were running down my cheeks and my mouth and chin, and I wiped them on my tiny shirt sleeve.

Lisa took a step back and looked at me. "What the hell is with that shirt, Davey?" she said, and I looked up to actually see her smiling through her own tears.

I'd forgotten about my Pretty Young Thing, rhinestone-encrusted girl's shirt, and when I looked down at it, I laughed, too. I looked at her, considered explaining, and gave up. I might have spit on her, I laughed so hard all of a sudden, but she was right there with me.

Clearly we were both ready to lose our minds, and laughter, at times like this, could make you feel that much more nuts, but it could also help you chase away some of the crazy and focus – at least when the laughing spell passed.

I shook my head, my smile fading, wiped my nose again, and said, "The .22 rifle is so you not only feel safer, but so you are safer. There are a lot of them outside Leese, and I need you to be able to stop them if I'm preoccupied. What kind of shot are you?"

"With the .22, pretty good. Bigger rifles, not so much."

"The .22's enough, if you hit them in the head. It *has* to be the head. The brain, I think. Not sure, but it seems to be."

"Why?" she asked.

"I don't know," I said. "I don't know anything. I know I'm alive and you're alive, and beyond that, I know mom's probably …"

In my mind I was asking myself what we were going to do. What in the hell were we going to do if the entire country was like this. If the world was like this.

So I just stopped speaking then, because it was speculation, and I was talking out of my ass. My mother could've run outside or into the garage, or locked herself in the car. What Lisa heard might not mean anything. I hoped. Maybe Matt and Tammy Rowe were just fine.

Just as fine as wine, as my dad used to say, even though he was a beer man.

I went to the closet and slid open the door.

"Other side," said Lisa, sliding the other door toward me. She leaned in and pulled out two rifles. It turned out that one was a double-barreled shotgun and the other wasn't what I expected.

"You know how to use this one?" I asked, taking the .22 with a pistol grip and magazine. "I was picturing something that looked more like a BB gun."

"Dad doesn't like reloading. There's ammo for it in that box there," she said, pointing.

I thought to myself, *If my suspicions are correct, your dad wouldn't know the difference between this gun and a popsicle stick right now.*

I leaned in and took the metal box out, placing it on the bed and opening it. We heard a sound in the hallway, just behind the closed door.

Lisa screamed. I held my finger up to my lips and shook my head. "Load that magazine," I whispered, my ear against the door. "Hurry."

Lisa, crying again, got to work following my instructions. I heard scratching through the hollow core door and with my hand against it, I could feel whatever was on the other side … moving.

What I can only describe as wet sounds accompanied an unmistakable presence on the other side of the door, and I pictured Matt Rowe out there, looking just like all the others, gnashing or doing whatever it is they do when nobody's looking.

Then I thought to myself that perhaps Lisa had gotten it all wrong, and what was on the other side of this veneer and cardboard barrier was my mother. Tammy Rowe, hungry and ready to eat her children, come hell or high water.

I looked at Lisa. If it came to that, it would be hell for her, and a different kind of hell for her daughter and me.

A living hell. I think we were already there.

"I got it," she said, standing again."

"Okay," I said. "It's here. I don't know what or who, but it's right on the other side of the door."

"Dad?" Lisa called, rushing forward and knocking on the door. I held the .45 in one hand and pulled her away from the door by her shoulder.

"If either one of them were out there," I said, "one of them would answer. Whoever it is, they're not the same anymore."

"I need to see him before you do anything!" she shouted, and as she was mid-sentence, the door strained in its frame as something pushed it, slamming it and testing its strength. We could hear moans over the scratching and pounding.

I pressed the gun barrel up to the door, and Lisa said, "No, David!"

"Lisa!" I shouted, then forced myself to calm.

People always told me I had a soft, soothing voice and a way to break tension with stupid jokes and an easy tone, but right now I wasn't finding any of those qualities.

"Leese," I said, "we can't do this all night. We have to find out what the situation is, deal with it, and get out of here. I'm opening the door."

She stepped back to the far wall, the .22 in her hands. She kept the barrel pointed toward the ground, but as I stepped aside, my .45 aimed toward the door, she raised the smaller gun.

I unlocked the door. Very slowly, with my left hand, I turned the knob. The wet noises continued from beyond our line of sight, but the scratching and banging had stopped.

I stepped back, the knob in my hand, and let the door open inward, silent and revealing.

Revealing a gray-faced, pink-eyed Matt Rowe. He was holding my mother's hand. More accurately, he was eating it, *tearing* at it with his bloody teeth as he gripped onto her severed arm. I knew it was hers at first glance.

"No!" croaked Lisa, her voice barely audible as she stared at the monster that had been her father, wearing his pajama bottoms and his shirt, the buttons all popped open.

His skin was as pocked and heavily veined as any of the things I'd seen, and he clutched the horrifyingly familiar extremity in both of his destroyed hands, gnawing and biting into the fleshy part of the wrist.

He was quite involved and had not seen the door open just half a foot away from him – which is *probably* a terrible way to word that, but since I'm writing this longhand, it's going to have to stay that way.

As he worked his way up to the fingers, both of us watching in sheer terror, he tore the second finger from its socket with his bared teeth and turned his head up to allow it to fall deeper into his ghastly throat. Before this happened though, the gold and diamond ring that had once been on that finger dropped, clinked against the tile floor and rolled across the room straight toward Lisa, as though it were meant to convince my sister that it was all true.

Lisa stared down at the ring that lay just a few inches from her feet. It was our mother's wedding ring.

She looked at what was once her father again, then at me. "*Kill it, Dave!*" she screamed.

The creature turned toward me as Lisa's voice shattered the sound of flesh being devoured. Her cry was shrill and clearly acknowledged by Matt Rowe, for he looked up just as I raised the .45 toward his head.

Pink mist began to pour from his eyes as I pulled the trigger and staggered out of its cloud, sputtering.

Nothing. The gun had failed to properly chamber a round. I had no backup plan, and this dead fuck was advancing on the door.

With a guttural scream I charged him. Dropping my head like a linebacker, I rushed the feeding creature, slamming my head into the dead thing's midsection. I hadn't expected my *own* reaction, so it took the thing completely by surprise and he toppled backward into the hall, falling and sliding another three feet on its back across the hall floor. My momentum carried me clear over him, and I rolled as I hit the floor, coming to rest against the wall next to Lisa's room.

I recovered quickly, trying to clear the jam from the gun. I quickly discovered it was good and stuck.

"Close that door, Lisa! Close it now!" I shouted, and scrambled back to my feet just as Matt did the same, only a bit more slowly.

I watched until the door slammed before pounding on the wall to get his attention and running down the hall and into the dining room. I threw the .45 down on the dining table, grabbed a hefty chair – the end chair with arms – not a side model – and waited.

I heard him coming up the hall, the chair raised high over my head, and timed my downswing so as his head appeared, the chair slammed into it.

One of the stiff, wooden legs punched through his skull and kept going, exiting beneath his chin. I pushed at the chair then, and knocked him down, his body kicking and almost spinning on the floor. I grabbed another chair and raised it high over my head, bringing it down onto his twitching head and neck. More damage, but it was still trying to get up.

Jumping backward, I grabbed the .45 and yanked on the top of it, seeing the jammed bullet, but unable to clear it. Another try. I pulled it back and the round ejected.

I spun and fired between the embedded chair legs and directly into his head, which exploded onto the floor behind him, the white tile floor turned red-black, spattered all the way to the corner leading to the kitchen. At the sound of the gunshot, I heard Lisa's shrill scream.

My stepdad's deformed body seemed to deflate as it lay there, settling in with a squishy sound as his lifeless corpse sank in and molded to every grout line in the floor.

I leapt over him and ran back to the bedroom. Careful not to frighten her, I called, "Lisa! It's me. It's safe now."

Nothing. I opened the door and saw Lisa sitting on the bed. She had dropped the gun, which lay on the floor in front of her, her expression as dead as the zombies we sought to escape or destroy. If any emotions at all dwelled on her face, horror and fear would be counted among them.

We needed to wipe those emotions away and replace them with one: fierce determination. After all I'd already been through, I knew it was the only way we would survive.

I knew how she felt. I slammed the door again – just in case – and tucked the now functional .45 away. I went to Lisa and pulled her hard into my arms and held her very, very tight, trying to absorb her shudders and take away her trembling.

I pulled away, leaned down and picked up her gun. I lifted her arm and put the rifle in her hand, closing her fingers around it. "Hold onto this, Leese."

She obeyed me exactly. I led her back into her room.

"Get changed into some jeans. Shorts won't do. You need your body to be as protected as possible. I'm going back in there and getting a different shirt. I saw some in the closet."

"Don't leave me," she whimpered.

"Lisa, I'll be thirty feet away. You'll be okay. Hurry."

I ran into the bedroom, pulling my darling tee shirt off and finding a long sleeved, chambray shirt. Levis. I threw it on and buttoned it fast, then slid along the wall past my stepdad and back into Lisa's room. She was already in her jeans and was tying her running shoes.

"Perfect," I said. "Is his car in the garage?"

"Yeah," she said, her voice shaky. "He filled it yesterday. He always does on Saturdays."

"Prius, right?"

She nodded. "Keys in the kitchen."

"I don't think you should go in there," I said.

"You check," she said. "If you don't mind. Tell me if it's bad and I'll take your word. If it's not, I need to say good bye."

I knew in my heart and mind that it couldn't be anything but. But I promised her anyway.

"Okay. You go to the garage, and I'll come and get you. I'll walk you there in case you were wrong."

As we walked tentatively down the hall leading toward the kitchen and dining room, I glanced to my left and shielded her face from what was once her father.

As I came to the kitchen door, my eyes turned right, where I saw my mother's bloody barefoot feet on the floor. All of the toes were gone. The rest was red meat. I did not want to look any closer. I couldn't see her once beautiful face in similar condition.

But I needed the damned keys, and I needed to make sure she would not be rising again as one of these … creatures.

"Go," I said. "In the garage. It's bad. I just looked."

"Oh, Davey," she said, her tears flowing again.

"Get in the car," I said. "I'll be five seconds."

She went, and I turned and ran into the kitchen, focusing on the counters, the walls, everywhere but at my mother's prone body.

And yet I had to glance down. Had I not known it was, there would have been no way to identify this female carcass as human at all.

I know there is a lot of barf in these chronicles. But if I'm being honest, let's just say that as my fingers curled around the Toyota's keys, I left pepperoni sticks and Cheetos on the counter as payment.

One more task. I pulled out my gun, squinted my eyes to avoid a good view of my mauled mother, and fired a round into her head. The body jerked and fell still again.

I spat the horrid taste of vomit from my mouth and ran to the garage. As I pushed the garage door opener and it began to lift, I saw two sets of waiting ankles, which became shins, knees, thighs and finally destroyed skin of hands and torsos. I ran for the car, realizing the stuff I'd had in my bike was lost to me. No more snack food.

I got in the Prius, pushed the start button, and threw it in reverse. I threaded the zombie needle that were probably two of their walking dead neighbors, tried to skirt around the BMW, but couldn't. It was parked dead center, and I cranked hard, knocking it on its side and tearing off my driver's side mirror in the process. The Prius bounced into the street after running over the Beemer's rear tire, and I turned on the headlights and threw it into drive.

I drove that hybrid piece of shit through the night like the Devil himself was behind me.

*****

"Where's this church?" I asked Lisa, who was turned around in her seat, looking behind us. Her eyes still held the dull glaze I'd seen there since she watched me kill her father, and I knew it would be a long time until it was completely gone; despite the fact that she had told me to do it, every time she saw me for the distant future, that is the image that would come to her mind.

In a single day, the world had turned into a living horror movie and Lisa had just lost both her parents. There was nothing to say, and I knew my little sister wouldn't ever be the same.

It was fully dark now, and cloud cover was heavy,

She turned back around and fell into her seat, buckling her seat belt. "Take a right on Perry Street."

I know that Hemp said these things lost their ability to hear shortly after their conversion into walking dead cannibals, but for now, even the relatively quiet engine of the Prius seemed to be drawing them toward us as we passed by.

69

They would change direction and turn their creepy heads as we passed by, driving home again and again how utterly fucked the world had become. We were past them by the time they took four steps, but what would happen if they got their hands on us was never far from our minds. I did not need to ask Lisa this to know that it was the truth.

As we rounded the corner onto Perry, Lisa grabbed her purse and pulled out her cell phone. She looked at the screen, and started to cry again.

One eye on the road and one on her, I said, "Leese, what's wrong?"

"It's Stacy Hayes," she said. "I have six missed calls from her. I don't know how I could've – wait." She punched some buttons. "They just came in while we were … well, after you got to me."

Lisa looked at me, her brow furrowed, her expression desperate, even pleading. "We have to go see if she's okay," she said.

I knew it was coming the moment she mentioned the missed call. I wouldn't deny Lisa anything right now. If life had turned from scraping by in a tough economy to battling mindless creatures just to stay alive, then trying to save Stacy Hayes was probably one of the things we *should* be doing.

She quickly hit two numbers and put the phone on speaker. A girl's voice said, "Hello!" Panicked.

"Stacy? Oh, my God, you're okay!"

"Who is this?" the voice screamed.

In my mind, I saw a girl cowered in a dark closet, hiding from a killer and frightened out of her mind. I was positive that I wasn't very far off.

"It's Lisa, Stacy? Didn't my number show up on your –"

"Lisa!" she shouted, interrupting her. "Oh, God, Lisa, where are you? I'm at my neighbor's house. I don't know what's happening.   What's happening, Lisa?   What are these things?"

"Where are your parents?" asked Lisa.

"It wasn't my mom, Lisa! I was … in the bathroom and she … it … I don't know! It was wearing my mother's robe, but it wasn't her! I thought I had to be dreaming – I thought I was having a nightmare!"

"Stacy, I know. It is a nightmare, but it's real. How did you get out?"

Stacy's quiet sobs could be heard across the line.

"Which way to her house, Leese," I said. "Hurry."

"Turn left up on Wick, and make the first right on Thorogood. Stacy, we're coming."

"My mom's still over there!" she said. "She dove at me and I grabbed a towel and pushed her with it. Lisa, I didn't want to touch my own mother!"

"Stacy, it's everywhere," said Lisa.   "My parents changed, too. Where's your dad?"

"My dad?"

"Is he there?"

"No, no! He called me from New York about an hour ago. I told him where I am."

"What did he tell you do to, Stacy? Did he say he'd be able to get to you?"

I watched Lisa's face and listened to the relative calmness that had overtaken her voice. I was amazed at her composure in the face of her best friend's terror. It was as though she instantly put her own personal tragedy aside to comfort her friend and make her feel safe. Lisa had always been a compassionate child, but I was really seeing the woman she'd become for the first time.

Stacy answered the question.   "He's there on business. He said he was in the airport ready to come home, but everything was going crazy. Three planes took off and crashed within view of the terminal."

"Oh, my God," said Lisa.

My sense of dread was experienced in silence as I listened to her friend recount the call from her father.

"He said TSA officers were shooting at people, and there were people attacking everyone. Biting them. I don't think he told me everything."

"We're coming to get you, Stacy," said Lisa. "Which neighbor's are you in?"

"The Palmers. Two houses on the right as you're facing my house. They were away on vacation and I had the key. I check on their house. But Lisa, I can't go!"

"Stacy, you have to! Why not?"

"Because daddy says he's coming, and I have to wait!"

"Stacy, he wouldn't want you to wait if you're in danger. What does the street look like?"

"I haven't looked out," she said. "I'm afraid those things will see me. And I don't think I'm in danger here, I'm just scared."

"What's the food situation there, Stacy?" asked Dave. "If this is short term, we might be better off holing up there until the government gets this under control. Plus your dad knows you're there, right?"

"He does, and there's plenty of food Mostly boxed and canned, but there's lots of frozen meat and stuff in the kitchen and garage."

"We're coming," said Lisa. "We should be there in less than five minutes. Dave, turn right up here. Next street."

"Thank you," said Stacy. "I don't know how to tell you to get in. I won't look out. Call me if you need me to open the back or anything."

"Okay," said Lisa. "I love you, Stace."

"Thank you," said Stacy. "It'll be good not to be alone."

*****

We pulled onto Kennedy Avenue just four minutes later, and I was suddenly glad it was night.

What we could see in the Prius' headlights was a mess. It was as though everyone on the street had turned into one of these things, and bodies were everywhere, torn open by the new predators of the world. Many of them were busily feeding, yet as we passed, a score of them were drawn to the headlights or the motion, and turned our way.

"Get your damned head down!" I shouted. "Or look down, or something."

But Lisa didn't listen. She stared through the windows in horror, her mouth hanging open, her eyes puffy and red from what she'd already been through.

"Why?" she asked, her voice flat. "This horror is everywhere. I might as well get used to it."

"You're an adult now," I said, relenting. "Where's Stacy?"

Lisa pointed to a white house with dark brown trim. "That's Stacy's house, so two more down."

Two cars had made it partially out of their driveways, but another two cars had smashed into them from both directions of travel in the street. The car heading east, before crashing, was a Gold, Scion XB, its front end now smashed against the destroyed passenger side of a white, VW Beetle. The driver's side door of the Beetle hung open and the car was empty.

I could make out spattered blood on the inside of the Scion's windshield, and it appeared, from the way the car was rocking in its crashed position, that a struggle of some sort was happening inside. I didn't want to think about the activity taking place.

Lisa pointed to it at the same time I saw it. "What's going on there?" she asked.

"I don't know, but it looks like the owner of the Beetle survived the crash. Let's get to Stacy."

I jammed on my brake as a man ran into the side of our car, his face a bloody mess and his hands clenched into fists as he pounded on the window. I stared in shock as one of the vein-riddled things yanked back the man's head and sank its teeth into his neck, pulling back with a mouthful of meat and tendons.

Though the zombie apparently did not excrete it intentionally, I saw the pinkish mist drifting from the attacker's dead eyes – the vapor that I had first seen coming from Denny Steele, and then from my stepfather. I had been so close to being enveloped by the mist that last time. Had I not misfired the .45 at Matt Rowe and ducked low to head butt him, dropping below the vapor, I might have been down for the count.

The mist was a phenomenon that Hemp would later describe as a gas with chloroform-like properties; a vapor created as the zombie gas emitting from the earth melded with the decomposing bodies of its very victims.

The vapor was not toxic in the sense that it caused permanent damage, but if you were subjected to it, you would be rendered instantly comatose. If you managed to awaken with all of your body parts, you could recover, but these creatures did not subdue you with it so they could sit back and admire you; they did it so they could eat you at their leisure. As for how this part of the metamorphosis worked out so well for the abnormals, as Flex initially called them, let's just chalk it up to a miracle of nature. Or perhaps in this case, unnatural nature.

I looked ahead at the crashed cars blocking my path up the street, and back at my uninvited guest. I then cranked the steering wheel full left and pushed it, knocking the zombie at my window backward. My tires and rims hit the curb and launched over onto the grass, where I ran over at least four of the creatures I had not previously seen, all feeding on poor Stacy's neighbors. For all I knew, one had been her mother.

I cranked the wheel right to get around two bicycles on their sides in the next driveway, spun the wheel hard left again to avoid a large oak tree, and finally slid the car to a stop in the yard of the house where Stacy was supposedly hiding.

I threw it in park and cut the headlights and engine. If we were being approached, I could not see anyone, but it would be foolish to think they weren't coming. They always came. Always.

"Call Stacy and let her know we're here," I said. "Hurry!"

Lisa punched buttons on her phone. "I just texted her."

"Can't anyone just call anyone anymore?" I asked.

The phone made a *bloop-bloop* sound, and Lisa looked at it. "Okay, she's going to the front door. If we get there and tap twice, she'll unlock it really fast."

But as I looked out my door there were three of the creatures within four feet.

"David!" shouted Lisa, throwing her body toward me. It was the same on her side of the car. There were five of them pressing against the entire passenger side of the Toyota.

"Hold on!" I shouted, pushing the start button again. I put the car into drive, hit the accelerator and turned hard right, knocking three of the five monsters down as I drove for the only gap I could see.

The rear tire of the Prius hit and rolled over something, landed, and did it again. Probably the legs of the creatures unfortunate enough to tumble beneath the car.

This time I left the headlights off and threaded through the melee of the street, silently counting the number of houses to the corner before making my first left.

I then made another left turn on the street behind Stacy's, Roosevelt Avenue.

Things were also bad here, they weren't as bad as on Kennedy. This time I pulled up over the left curb and drove on the lawns, counting up five houses on the left.

The homes in this area were nearly zero lot lines, so there was perhaps five feet between the homes. I pulled the Prius to the appropriate gap between two of the houses and stopped it. Nothing on the street side would be able to get around the car without climbing over it. I threw open my door because it was clear.

"Text her again and tell her we're coming up to the back. Tell her to be there at the door."

Lisa got to work. I looked through the gap at the rear of the house. It was the right one. The house was light blue, so easy to spot, even in the paleness of the night.

Bloop-bloop. Lisa looked at her phone. "Okay, she's ready."

"Unbuckle and jump out my side," I said. "Then be ready to run." I scrambled out and Lisa was right behind me. She was not a small girl, but I was happy to see that she was agile as hell when she felt the dogs of Hell charging after her, as I believe we both did at that moment.

I yanked the .45 out and held it at ready as we tore through the side yards of the two houses behind that of Stacy's neighbor, and when I came upon a small, rabbit fence, I jumped over it, shouting, "Fence, jump!"

Lisa did, clearing the two foot chicken wire fence easily. I chanced a glance back, and saw three of the creatures emerging from between the homes, coming behind us. They had come through the back yard of the home next door, unhindered by the Prius.

"Come on, Lisa," I said. "Almost there."

I entered the yard and we reached the back door. I pounded on it, and a split-second later, heard a click. I turned the knob and yanked it open. Seconds later, the door closed behind us, Lisa and I stood in a brightly lit hallway, breathing hard.

"Leese," said Stacy, pushing around me to get to her friend. She hugged my sister, and they embraced for a long time. I walked into the living room and fell onto the couch, laying back.

I was exhausted, but we were alive.

*****

Chapter Four

Shortly after our arrival at the Palmers' home, we discovered a major cache of food in the garage storage cabinets. There was literally six months of canned goods, and that included beans, corn, beets, peas, chili, Vienna sausages, Spam, and just about everything else you could think of with and without a pull-tab opener.

The power dumped after around four weeks, and I think we all felt lucky it functioned for as long as it had. Palmer didn't have a generator, so we were eating most of the pre-cooked stuff at room temperature and using what propane tanks they had sparingly. Luckily it appeared they liked camping, so they had two cool little two-burner Coleman stoves and a hell of a lot of the two-packs of small propane bottles, which we used early on to cook up as much of the meat and other frozen stuff that didn't lend itself to our next trick.

The Palmers had a food dehydrator, so around the three-week point, when all we could think about was when the power cut out, Stacy had suggested that we start cooking and dehydrating lots of the brisket and other meats that lent themselves well to the process. After that, we sealed it up in the vacuum sealer. The instructions said that meat would last up to a year if the vacuum held.

I was pretty damned proud of us. We were adapting in a screwed up world, and while they didn't have one damned weapon or bullet in the house, the Palmers sure did like to plan for the future when it came to food.

Aside from our worries about the meat going bad, the ice was also a concern. We only left a full tray of it in the freezer at any given time, keeping three ice chests packed full of it at all times. Very little air space. We knew that when the power crashed, all the frozen meat and poultry we hadn't dehydrated would be trash in no time. The ice stock would keep it for at least three to five more days if we didn't open it much, and by then we'd have no power to run the dehydrator or vacuum sealer.

As for why we had decided to stay put, as long as the water kept running, there didn't seem to be much reason to leave.

Keeping consistent with our newfound survival skills, we had filled both bathtubs with water in the event that it should be cut off, and we had cleaned and filled every viable container in the house with the life-sustaining liquid.

It left only one small shower in which to actually get clean, but it was enough. Filling the bathtubs had been Stacy's idea. Turns out it was the best one. The canned goods would've kept us even without the frozen meat and other stuff – the water was crucial.

We'd been there almost four months, and the tubs were almost empty now. Evaporation got us, thirst got us. We still had several bottles, but it was now late September, and the days had been hot for months.

I was worried about Lisa and Stacy, but our host had begun to look very frail of late.

Her hair was dirty blonde, long and stringy, and the nineteen-year-old would fight her nervousness by sitting on the couch, her thin legs folded underneath her body like a greyhound at rest, chewing her split ends, then endlessly picking at them with her jagged, bitten nails.

I had the distinct impression she was wasting away before our eyes. Not long after we'd arrived, the church abandoned as a necessary destination for the moment, I'd seen Stacy cinching her pants tighter and pulling them up when they slid down over her hips. I appreciated that she had allowed us to come and stay with her, and just after dark one evening, while Lisa was taking a much-needed nap, I said something.

"Stacy, you look like hell."

"Thanks, David."

"Dave's fine," I said. "But you know that after what? Four months I guess?"

"Feels like ten years," she said. "Thanks for saying I look like shit, *Dave*."

"You need to eat more, Stacy. There's plenty of food."

She stared at me, her gaunt face expressionless. "Maybe you need to eat less," she replied.

I shook my head. "I'll go out and get more food if things start running down," I said. "If that's what you're worried about. Have you weighed yourself? How much have you lost?"

"Fifteen pounds," she admitted.

"Okay, so you've weighed yourself. Have you looked in the mirror, because you're starting to look scary."

She unfolded and jumped up from the couch. "Well, you can just goddamned leave if it's uncomfortable for you to look at me!" she screamed.

She walked right up to me and I admit I must have pressed myself back into my chair as she leaned in and continued her tirade: "I'm trying to deal here, and I'm trying to stay alive long enough for this fucking government to do something and tell us when we can get back to our lives!"

"Stacy, I'm sorry. I was only saying it because I care —"

"Care about what?" she interrupted. "About the fact that my cell phone quit working three months ago and I never even got so much as a single text from my father after that first day?"

She paced away from me and collapsed back on the couch again. She looked up at me, tears running down her face. "You care about me? What about my neighbors? Do you care about them? They're eating each other, for God's sake, Dave! I saw Jan next door attacking her child in my front lawn! She killed her *six-year-old son* not twelve feet away from my bedroom window before I ever came over here, and she was eating him!"

I sat there and said nothing. Her head drooped for a moment, and she looked back at me, her anger gone, replaced with immense grief. "So I hope you have a huge supply of caring inside you, Dave Gammon, because there is so, so much in this world to care about right now."

There were no words that I could say to her and I knew it. I didn't take it personally. If I were honest with myself, I felt a bit injured inside, but I knew I'd get over it. We'd all have to get over a lot, and there was no way Stacy could really know what was in my heart, especially in her present state.

I got up and went into the kitchen. I got two packs of string cheese out of the very last bit of ice in the best ice chest we had, along with a warm, canned protein shake. She had sunken back into the couch as I shook and opened the warm shake, handing it to her.

She took it and drank. I then peeled open one of the string cheeses and gave it to her. She had downed the entire shake, then took a bite of the cheese and attempted a small smile that immediately turned into a frown, and then sobs.

"David, my mother's out there!" she cried. "I've seen her. She stands with those other things out there, and she … she wants in. She wants to get to us like the others do."

I shook my head. "She's not your mother anymore, Stacy."

She nodded and bit another hunk from the string cheese stick. "I can't see her like that anymore," she said. "It tears me up a little more every time I see her out there. First it scares me, then it rips me apart."

I went to her couch and sat down beside her. I pulled her slight body over to me and put my arm around her. "Tell me what you want me to do," I said softly. "I'll do whatever you think is right."

Stacy leaned away from me and turned to face me. "You … will?"

I knew there could be only one request. All I could do was kill her to stop both Stacy's torture and that of her mother, whether real or perceived in our living, working minds. "Yes, I will," I said again.

At that moment, we heard a sound against the window. It shuddered.

We both jerked our heads toward the sound at the same time, only I was on my feet and she was gripping the empty space where I'd been with both clutched hands.

I went to the window and lifted the rod which, if turned, would open the blinds. I turned it very slowly.

At first I believed it was so dark out that all external light was unable to filter through to the interior of the house. But that wasn't it. I raised my eyes.

My focus turned to the faces of the zombie-like creatures , all in a row, the hands pounding and scratching the glass, the mouths, tongues and teeth pressing into it, seeing me there behind it, and wanting to come inside.

Behind them was another row, all pushing forward.

Behind them, another. They were pushing in against the doors and windows. Pink mist rose from them, and every now and then, I saw bright red eyes flashing in the distance, like devilish beacons in a distant hell.

Stacy screamed behind me and I spun the rod in the other direction, closing the blinds again. I ran to the back of the house and did the same with the sliding door verticals.

It was another solid mass of walking dead bodies, pressing against the house hard, sensing the food source within; the only sustenance they now wanted – Lisa, Stacy and me.

In another five minutes, I had confirmed that the house was entirely surrounded, pressed in on by the creatures, who were tireless and determined.

I went into the bathroom and closed the door after making sure Lisa and Stacy were in a walk-in closet – one of the only places with a door they could close that didn't have windows. I went in there to be alone, because I didn't want the girls to see me break down. I could lie to them, but I could not lie to myself.

I was scared to death. After four months, we now had to get on the move. But first we had to find a way out of there.

*****

"You guys stay in here," I said after my man cry. "I'm going to pack some food and supplies into whatever I can find, and we're going to blow this firetrap."

"How?" Stacy cried, her crying and shuddering making her slight body appear that much more impossibly tiny. Lisa had lost weight, too. I saw a hollowness in her cheeks that I'd never noticed before.

"I don't know yet," I said. "Do you know where the attic hatch is in this house?"

"How's that going to help?" asked Lisa.

I thought about it. Then I realized it was a dead end idea. I was stupidly thinking I could somehow access the roof from there, but that wasn't even possible. And I was supposed to have been in construction.

Doofus.

"Forget it," I said. "I have another idea."

I closed the door and ran into the garage. There was an aluminum Little Giant ladder. Perfect. I grabbed it, and realized instantly that my own strength had dwindled over the last few months. It wasn't that the food at the house wasn't nutritious – it was that we weren't hungry. Fear had a way of fucking with your taste buds.

I hoisted it up onto one shoulder and threaded it through the door into the house, through the laundry room door, and inside the hall. I moved down the hallway and opened the ladder beneath the skylight. It was about a 9' ceiling and the ladder would get us to 8'.

I locked the legs in and ran back to the bathroom, pushing the door open.

"Okay, you guys. I hate to do this at night, but I can't have one of these freaks breaking a window while we're sleeping. If that happens, they're all pouring in, and we aren't enough to stop them."

They both stared at me. "What?" I asked.

Still, they stared.

"Hey! Snap out of it and grab what clothes you need. While you're at it, grab some of Palmer's clothes for me. His stuff fits me about right. Don't take much, just enough for a couple of changes. Stuff it all in a backpack or something else easy to carry."

They ran off, and I hauled ass back to the living room. I could practically feel the weight against the glass, and with every creak and groan of the house, I just knew something was going to give way and we would be flooded with the walking rotters.

I climbed to the top of the ladder and saw there was no crank. No way to open the skylight. It screwed down from above into a flange that inserted from inside.

I shimmied back down the ladder, and scanned the living room. I ran over, took a lamp off a small side table, and threw it aside with a crash. I grabbed the small, wooden table and hauled it up the ladder with me.

Holding it with both hands, I smashed it into the Plexiglas skylight until a crack formed. Then a chip. With the next slam, the leg of the table poked through, and I knew I would have it in short order.

I dropped down one rung, grabbed the table by the very top, and rammed it as hard as I could into the skylight with my eyes squeezed closed, hearing and feeling, rather than seeing my success, by the crashing sound and the shattered plastic raining down on top of my head.

I threw the table aside and scrambled up until my head poked through the skylight. I pushed my shoulders through, clearing a space large enough for any one of us, and knocking the rest of the plastic out of the way. I then climbed up to the top of the ladder and stepped onto the roof.

As quietly as I could, I crept to the front of the house. The pitch of the roof was mild, so there was no fear of losing my balance and toppling off the roof. I reached the edge and looked down.

It looked like fucking Woodstock around that house. I looked at the neighboring homes.

Wide open.

This meant they could sense us. In a sea of their own stink, through walls, they could smell us – the living.

I went to all sides of the house and it was the same. Then I went back to the west side of the house. Below, the area between the two homes was packed tight with the zombies, but their faces stared straight toward the house –

they did not look upward at all. I moved back anyway. Taking chances was stupid.

Then I looked at the roof of the home next door. It was no more than six feet away. A gap that with a running start, any one of us could manage, but not with a gaggle of zombies below. They'd play hell with a living, breathing person's concentration.

Then I had it. I moved back to the opening and dropped back through the sunroof and onto the ladder.

The girls were there waiting for me.

"What's the plan?" asked Lisa.

"Up here," I said. "On the roof. Then we take the ladder, put it between the houses, and we use it for a scaffold to cross over to the house next door."

"And what do we do over there?" asked Stacy.

"We keep moving. As far from here as we can until we can get off the roof, into a car and get the hell out of here."

"That's a good idea, Davey," said Lisa.

"It's all I got. Got the dehydrated meat in those?" I asked, pointing to the three backpacks.

"Yes, and as much water as I could disperse between them," Stacy said. "They're heavy."

"I don't think we're going very far," I said. "We need to find a good vehicle. That's it."

"The guy four houses down has a Forerunner SUV. It's in the driveway last I saw," said Stacy.

"That's perfect," I said. "Reliable and decent on gas. Okay, this is kind of sketchy. You ready?"

"Listen to that," said Lisa. "I'll take that sketchy over this sketchy any day."

We all grabbed a bag and threw it on our shoulders. "Stacy, you go first, then just take two steps up on the roof and wait."

She went. In less than 45 seconds she was out of view. Lisa went next. She was faster. I crawled up after them and turned, leaning down into the hole. I grabbed one end of the ladder, opening it wider, and as it ratcheted open, I pulled it out as a straight, sixteen-foot ladder.

I was still amazed it could expand to that length and be as light as it was. I nodded to the girls, and we moved as quietly as we could to the edge.

"I'm bound to make a little noise when the other side hits the other roof," I said. "When it happens, I'll just jump out of sight. I don't want them to see me."

I stood the ladder up and walked my hands down the rungs, but as the angle became sharper and sharper, the ladder became impossible to hold onto.

It fell the last four feet and hit the other roof with a heavy thud. I scrambled away from the edge and hung beside Lisa and Stacy for a moment.

In another minute, I went back to the edge. No eyes looking up.

I waved the girls over to where I stood. It was time to cross.

"Okay, I can toss the backpacks over after you two make it to the other side," I said. "Who wants to go first?"

"I'll go," said Lisa. "If I make it over, we know it'll support string bean here."

"Ha ha," whispered Stacy, nudging Lisa. "Okay, go."

I took Lisa's back pack from her. "Okay, sis. Hands and knees, and just shimmy across the rails. And be careful."

As I looked, the six feet suddenly stretched until it appeared to be twenty. Lisa crouched down and put her hands on the first rungs that stretched in the open gap above the heads of the human creatures below, situating her knees on the rails. There would be no more discussion, for now that she was exposed, we all had to be as quiet as church mice.

The ladder appeared to be stable, but I held my breath anyway. Stacy watched, and in the faint light of the night, I saw the watery glaze grow more pronounced as she worried for her friend.

Lisa was now almost to the halfway point. The ladder teetered ever so slightly as the ends of the rails rocked in and out of the not-quite-identical slopes of the two roofs.

Three-quarters. Lisa lifted one hand off the right rail and shook it out. I saw her eyes staring downward, but I did not move any closer to the edge, for I did not want to draw their eyes to me, and in all honesty, I didn't want to see what Lisa was forced to stare at as she crossed.

She raised her eyes to the other roof now as she drew to within a foot of it. With two more moves, her hands fell to the shingles, and from there, she seemed to double her speed as she clambered to safety. Lisa crawled up two more feet and scooted off to the side, looked at us with a relieved smile, and nodded. She gave a thumbs up to Stacy and mouthed the words, "It's easy."

Stacy leaned to me and said, "Sure, it's easy if you're not shitting yourself and throwing up at the same time."

I patted her on the back, and motioned for her to hold on. I waved at Lisa and picked up one of the backpacks.

She stood and moved closer to the edge of the roof.

One, two, three – I tossed each backpack across, and she caught them, bobbling the last one twice until I felt sure it was going to drop and tumble onto the monsters that waited below.

She got it under control and rested them all away from the ladder. She wiped at her forehead in a relieved gesture, and shook her head, sitting again. Using her feet, she steadied the ladder and waited.

"Go," I whispered. "Your turn."

Stacy looked at me, the fear now more prominent. She didn't move.

"You saw what Lisa did. You can do it," I said. "Slow and steady. It's like six feet."

"Might as well be six hundred," she said, moving toward the ledge.

She was so light that I didn't foresee any issues with her crossing. I watched as she crouched down and took the first rungs in her hands. Stepping to the side so I could watch her and offer any tips I felt I could chance whispering, I saw her eyes were squeezed closed.

I was about to say something, but looked down and thought better of it. If she took her time, she could feel her way across – and if that made her feel better about it, then who was I to correct her style points.

Her body had just cleared our side, but she had moved her feet up an extra rung without moving her hands. Now her butt was raised in the air, creating a high center. As I watched, she opened her eyes and stopped. Her bottom teetered from side to side, and she let go her right arm to attempt to grab the rail farther ahead.

I held my breath and took two fast side steps back to where the feet of the ladder rested on my roof, and glanced up at Lisa, whose expression was horrified.

Stacy screamed as she felt the ladder tilting, and I threw my leg forward, trying to hold the rail flat. Even as I came in contact with the aluminum, I knew I'd been too late. It slid away, even under Stacy's minuscule weight.

The things below now *did* look up, followed by their arms reaching, reaching skyward for the girl; their meal. I watched helplessly as Stacy's scream again reverberated through the night and she fell completely off the right side of the ladder, clinging to the single rail with both hands, dangling down within reach.

The things moved in on her, pulling hard, and as her screams grew more shrill they were joined by Lisa's as she watched in terror and shrieked, "Stacy! Stacy! Pull up! Hurry, pull up!"

Then the ladder flipped completely over and slid down on top of the creatures who engulfed the girl's body, their faces no longer looking up, but now burrowing into the sweet flesh of the nineteen-year-old girl who would welcome death as soon as it would take her.

I wasted no time. Stacy was gone and Lisa needed me. I got back, realizing it was tricky to run on a downhill and leap six feet, but as I said earlier, the roof's slope was mild, and I wasn't worried.

Three heavy clops along the roof and I launched off my right foot, realizing mid-flight that I was barely going to reach the other ledge. I screamed, "Lisa, grab my arm!" as I felt my foot touch the fiberglass shingles, and she did take it as soon as it came into her reach. She fell backward, pulling me forward, and I collapsed atop her and into safety.

Breathing insanely hard, I stared down at her, and then I dropped my face to hers and held her to me. "I'm so sorry, Leese," I said. "I'm so sorry."

Feeling the wetness of her tears against my cheek, I did not expect an answer. I took one quick glance back, saw my feet were just six to eight inches from the ledge, and got to my knees and stood. I held out my hand to my sister and she took it.

We got to our feet and I helped Lisa work her way into one of the backpacks filled with supplies, followed by me slipping my arms through the straps of another one. The last one – that had been Stacy's – I slung over my shoulder. Lisa allowed me to lead her across the roof to the opposite side, her sobs wracking her body with each step. I worried that she would stumble.

As I approached the opposite eave, I immediately noticed the house next to this one was smaller, therefore the roofs did not extend as closely to one another as on the opposite side. Knowing Lisa could not avoid noticing it, too, I held up a hand and walked up the peak and looked down the other side.

I breathed a sigh of relief. A large oak that should have been trimmed to keep out what everybody always told me were inevitable roof rats, grew massively between the houses, heavy branches extending easily over each roof.

I moved back down until I reached Lisa. "We're in luck, sis. Big tree. We can climb across on that."

"I'm not feeling very agile right now," she said, her voice paper thin.

"You won't need it. I'll get the backpacks across and you can just take your time. I looked. Heavy branches, you can walk almost straight across."

"Okay," she said. "Lead the way."

I took her hand again and she allowed me to lead her over the peak. As we stepped over the ridge vent, she said, "You're right. Even I can make that."

"Exactly," I said.

We were across in two minutes. She didn't even ask me to take her backpack. We then skirted across that roof and when we got to the other side, I had her wait on the rear slope as I went to the front of the house. It was all clear. I moved closer to the front eave and looked down the street. The zombie horde was still concentrated around the Palmer house, though I did not think of the crowd of them in that way back then. I was scared of them, but I hadn't called them zombies out loud – perhaps only in my mind.

Some stragglers still moved along the street, but clearly did not smell us, because they moved toward the larger group. I knew Stacy's meager body could not provide a distraction for long and that soon, they would crash through a window or two in that house and realize there was no food to be had. I didn't know what would happen for sure, but I imagined they would disburse and go where the breeze revealed fresh meat. I did not want me or Lisa to be anywhere in the vicinity when that happened.

Moving to the front of the house and looking down, I saw the silver Toyota 4Runner, just where Stacy said it would be. Now we had to get the keys, get in it and go, assuming the battery wasn't dead after four months.

I went back to Lisa. "We might have to drop off the other side of the roof. Looks like it's only about eight feet at the rear corner, and there's a small tree there. It's worth a try, 'cause I don't want either of us twisting an ankle."

"Let's go," she said. "I think it's going to feel pretty good to be moving again."

"I agree," I said.

The tree turned out to be too small for our purposes, but Lisa found a 2 x 2 trellis attached to the rear of the house with ivy growing on it. We were able to get down that way, and it took less than three minutes.

We got down and I pulled out my .45 again and tried the sliding door in the rear of the ranch style house. It was locked, so I tucked the gun back inside my pants and put my palms flat against the glass, pushing hard and sharply upward. Once. Twice. On the third try, the lock popped and the door slid open.

I pulled my gun out again and immediately realized the only thing we hadn't gotten from the Palmer's house was flashlights.

"Fucking dark," I said.

Lisa reached in her pocket and withdrew a small, LED flashlight. "Not so much," she said, turning it on as she nodded at me to go first.

There was no smell of death in this house, which made me wonder where everyone was. Maybe they'd been at church or something – it had happened on a Sunday – and this was not the vehicle they drove. Or the gun range, or bowling alley. Whatever. They weren't here, I could smell they weren't dead, and that was all good news.

As it turned out, we did not have to linger long. We checked the pantry, since we would only have to haul anything from here to the 4Runner, and found several worthwhile grocery items. They were a big fan of canned, beef tamales, and had eight of those. There were three cases of snack sized fruit cocktail – the kind with cherries – and also pudding.

I realized I was starving. They also had a full case of bottled water, and the crap wasn't Zephyrhills. It was Smartwater.

We found their stash of plastic grocery bags, filled what we could as fast as we could, and went straight out the front door. I hesitated in the hallway. They had some sort of thick, wooden, ceremonial spear that looked like it had been made in Africa. It was roughly six feet long and had an amazing stone tip attached to the end that looked sharp as hell.

I couldn't imagine leaving it behind, and couldn't imagine not needing it at some point. I remembered pushing the gun barrel nearly through the skull of the one creature, so it might not take much to poke through with that weapon.

I hit the unlock button as we hit the front porch, and the flashers flashed and the horn chirped. If the bastards – and bitches, of course – could hear, then it was game over if that battery didn't have enough juice to fire the starter.

We got inside, dumped all our shit into the back seat, except the spear, which I leaned between us. I jammed the key into the lock and turned it.

The engine roared to life.

"Lisa, get us to the church on time," I said, releasing a huge breath I had no clue I'd been holding.

*****

I backed the car out fast and threw it into drive. I used my high aim steering, just as I had done on the bike. It had me turning the steering wheel in advance of the crap I'd be needing to dodge around.

"Do you still want to go to the church?" asked Lisa.

I looked at her. "Do you know people there?"

She nodded. "I do."

"Do you want to see if they've set up any kind of shelter or ... I don't know. Anything?" I asked.

"Where else can we go?" she asked.

"Your guess is as good as mine," I said. "Lisa, this is everywhere, so ..."

Her shoulders slumped as she thought. "They do have a big food bank. They had giveaways twice a week, so I'd think they'd be set up, depending on how many people made it there."

"I hate to say it," I said, "but there don't seem to be many like us."

"Why did mom and dad change when we didn't?" asked Lisa.

"Why did anyone change?" I asked. "Natural selection? I guess it's like a doctor treating a highly contagious disease and not catching it himself. It had to happen a lot back in the old days, before hazmat suits and oxygen masks."

"I suppose now we have to earn the right to be alive by doing the right thing," she said. "So we go to the church. Either they'll need our help or we can use theirs."

I looked at her and forced another smile. "It's that awkward moment when you first have to choose between feeling guilty for surviving or feeling lucky," I said.

"Guilty, maybe," said Lisa. "Whether we should feel lucky is another story. Kind of depends on what happens from here. How much gas is in it?"

I looked, then looked at her. "How far is the church?"

"About five miles."

"We'll make it," I said.

We got to the church. It was nice for a while, and we met three women we would come to know pretty well over the next few months, Vikki, Victoria and Kimberly. We met many others for the first time, too. We also met a shitload of zombies, but we'd been there for a while before that all went down.

I'd recount it all for you, but this is where we were finally discovered by the group that would become our family. Flex Sheridan, Gem Cardoza, Hemp Chatsworth and Charlie Sanders.

My family. All that's left, except maybe Uncle Bug. Brett Ulrich Gammon might still be out there in his self-made fortress, likely running his own mini-country there in northern California by now.

That church was where we first learned of the new defense system called urushiol. The zombie melter, indeed.

So once they talked us out of that tiny office, and pretty much in the nick of time, you know what's happened since. You'd also think that I'd just give up on my uncle and figure he was where he was and if he was alive, then good for him.

You have to remember that Lisa died right in front of me, and I felt powerless to stop it. And while I didn't know exactly where my uncle was, I had a good idea that he was as immune to this new apocalypse as I was.

So that's my story – mine and Lisa's. It took a lot longer to tell than the others, but you have to remember that they all found one another pretty fast, and they didn't cross our paths until months after the beginning of this apocalypse.

And as I said at the beginning of this, Serena has agreed to come with me. We'd been through a lot already in Concord and Shelburne, and in my heart I already knew I loved her. A month was like a year in this world. You can see how fast your heart might connect and imprint on someone else's these days.

It's happened to us. I want to be away from Serena as much as Hemp wants to be away from Charlie – as much as Flex wants to be away from Gem and his little boy.

Serena feels the same about me.

We're still not sure why Nelson wanted to go.

It might just be that the land of fruits and nuts has drawn one more nut.

Either way, off we go, on the road to California.

*****

Chapter Five

Late August, 2013:

Serena and I left before dawn. We had no idea the surprise waiting for us as we made our way outside to hop on the two bikes we'd found at neighboring homes over the past months. We figured the bikes, both Hondas, would get us to a Harley store eventually, but they definitely weren't of the comfort level that we would need to travel almost 3,000 miles to Dunsmuir, California.

We found it odd that Hemp wasn't letting us go into his workshop, but we never knew what he was up to in there anyway, and gave him his privacy.

We sure know now.

It was like Christmas morning. Serena wore her leathers because she felt safe from road rash and zombie bites in them, and damn, she looked good in them, too.

We both intended to wear helmets, too. If we could make it all the way to the west coast without laying one of those damned bikes down, it would be a miracle.

Anyway, back to the surprise. It was kind of ridiculous, walking out to two, 2013 Harley Davidson Sportsters with custom Corbin Fleetliner bags, along with dual touring saddles and matching helmets, both with radio communication setups.

Each hard shell saddlebag was packed with travel pillows, small blankets, non-perishables and water, and Hemp had fabricated a cool little teardrop trailer behind what I assumed was my bike that matched the Harley line for line. I unclipped the latches and lifted the lid to see that there were two five-gallon fuel cans filled and ready to go inside, along with several pressurized canisters of the urushiol blend, plus several ammunition boxes – all filled, of course.

And that wasn't all.

Almost dead center of the handlebars was a modified machine gun, which looked to be at least part Uzi. Big and deadly, it tucked toward the rider so that it wasn't in the way, but if you needed it, all you had to do was push it out and it pivoted forward and up and panned with full range from left to right just over the headlight. When you had to change the magazine, you lifted the stock up and it soft-locked into position for quick mag release, out and in, back down and you were firing again.

I wanted to run back inside and kiss that man.

I turned to Serena. Up until *that* point we'd both been speechless. "It's that awkward moment when you have a really strong desire to kiss a man – even standing by a beautiful woman in a leather cat suit."

"You *are* a man," she said. "Calling this a cat suit."

"You're hotter than Julie Newmar," I said, walking around the small trailer. "I'll peel ya outta that thing later."

"Think the trailer be stable?"

"Hell yes. Hemp built it. It's no wider than the bike, and look at this little hitch. Awesome."

"Maybe they should've been black," said Serena. "Better for night riding."

"Headlights, though. Even if they're deaf they'll see us."

"Not so fast," she said. She turned the key and the light went on. "This looks custom." She hit a switch, and the headlight and taillights went out. She hit the switch again, and they went back on. "Override," she said, smiling.

"Kissing him. It's on my mind again."

She checked her watch. "Sweetheart, it's five o'clock. I think we've admired the rides long enough. Let's put them to use."

We turned on the Bluetooth and our helmets paired. We could now chat as we rode. If I had a hard on at that moment, you're not going to hear about it here.

Talk about awkward moments.

So we hit the road, and we didn't bother rolling the bikes out of the driveway – they might as well hear us going if they were awake. I wondered if Hemp heard. If he did, I'll bet he smiled.

Our route was planned out. Dunsmuir was a long ways off, but it all began by hopping on Interstate 26 to Asheville, North Carolina, then into Tennessee. We'd be passing through Kentucky, Illinois, Missouri, then skirting the border of Kansas into Nebraska. From there it was Wyoming, Utah, Nevada and finally, into California.

And yeah, I only know that from looking at a map as I write this. Recall like that is pretty much a Hemp thing.

As the sun began to rise, we had not yet found a need to use the Uzis.

"It's pretty right now," I said.

"Peaceful," came Serena's voice in my helmet. She looked over at me with a clear highway ahead for the time being. "Trailer's great."

"It is," I said. "Can't even really feel it back there."

We had been keeping it slow. Unexpected things, either moving or stationary, could be around any corner, and we didn't feel the need to rush. We had plenty of time to get to Dunsmuir before winter set in, and if Bug was there, he wasn't going anywhere.

"Let's pull over and have some breakfast," I said. She nodded, and we hit a nice shady spot off to the side of the road. Both of us had on thigh holsters, each holding one of my Walther PPKs. You *knew* they were coming with me.

The first meals would be the best. Serena had prepared homemade corn tortillas the day before our departure, and using fresh eggs and meat from our stock of pigs – I say this and I'm wondering why the hell we left – she made a nice, spicy chorizo-kinda thing. A thermos of hot coffee was in her backpack, and it was just like being at the Hilton's breakfast.

We kept our eyes peeled and saw nothing. Eager to get back on the road, we stood, and a sound met our ears.

My hand went to my gun, as did Serena's. We both backed off the highway, which didn't do a hell of a lot of good because the beautiful Harleys were right there, big as life.

The sound grew louder. A buzzing. The buzz turned into a *putt-putt-putt* sound, and as we watched in amazement, here came Nelson Moore over the crest of a hill, barely pushing to the top. He saw us and a smile spread across his face as he raised his hand in a sweeping wave.

I was shaking my head and Serena's mouth was turned up into a smile. He finally made it to us, his dreadlocks entirely gone, just wispy, tangled, blonde hair down to his lower back, and the skinny bastard still smiling.

He drew to a stop and took off the bike helmet he wore. "I saw you guys pass me back there."

"Pass you?" I asked. "Where were you?"

"About eight miles back," he said. "I left way before you guys did. I mapped it out and everything. It was all part of my diabolical plan. I'm going with."

"No, you're not," said Serena. "Nelson, it could be dangerous."

"I've got Subdudo and my stars, so no worries," he said. "You guys might need me."

"You can't keep up on that thing," I said. "Nelson. If you wanted to come, you need a bigger bike. Period. If you'd have said something, we could've done something about it. Now it's too late."

"I've had time to think about it while I rode," he said. "You guys aren't going very fast. I don't need a gas hog like these. Most bikes are more energy-efficient than cars, right? Or maybe I can find a Nissan Leaf or something."

I laughed out loud and immediately felt bad. Hell if I didn't like this kid a lot. "How are you going to charge up your Leaf? Were they making solar versions before the zombies came along?"

"Yeah, right," he said, chewing his lip. "I brought weed."

I looked at Serena and laughed again, shaking my head. "That is a plus."

He wore a backpack which I guessed contained maybe another shirt and pair of pants, his weed, stars and not much else.

"Did you bring any provisions?" I asked.

"I brought weed," he said again, smiling.

"We got that," said Serena. "Food? Water?"

"You guys have that, right?" he asked. "I can keep up, I swear. I'll take care of myself, but I want to go with you."

"Why?" I asked.

"Why what?" asked Nelson.

There was a sudden rustle in the trees behind Nelson. We didn't have line of sight from our positions, but he did. He calmly reached into his pack, withdrew a brass star, drew his arm back, and flung it, almost with a snap.

As the completely naked, female rotter put her right foot on the pavement from the trees, her vein-riddled arms outstretched toward Nelson, the 3" diameter star buried itself 2-1/2" into the creature's skull, right between its eyes.

She fell backward, her knees bending in two. Nelson casually put the kickstand down and went to her, deftly pulling the star from its temporary home. He had a rag, already stained with blood, in his back pocket. He pulled it out like an old man with a snot rag, wiped off the star, and tucked it back into his pack. The rag went into his back pocket again.

"Ha ha!" he said. "Blew your minds just then, huh?"

"Did you fucking hire her?" I asked, smiling.

He looked serious for a moment. "No way, Dave."

"I'm kidding. Serena?"

She looked at me and nodded. "He has to ride with me for now. The scooter stays here."

"Okay, we'll get him his own bike when we see something that will work."

"You guys rock!" he said. "But I'll miss my scooter."

"You'll adapt, Nel," said Serena. "Hop on."

He did.

We went.

I was actually happy to have him along, and I wasn't even sure why. Then I figured it out.

I liked the skinny kid a lot, and I think it was his innocence that did that. A world filled with Nelsons would be a pretty entertaining place to live, if not a very productive one.

*****

We got back on the road, and every time I looked over and saw Nelson with that little bicycle helmet on, his blonde hair whipping behind him, I had to smile to myself.

I had been looking forward to lots of alone time to get to know Serena better, but it looked like that idea was out the window.

We pulled into Knoxville around noon, and we expected trouble.

I couldn't shake the fact that is was where Lisa and I had been trapped when the Sheridans and Chatsworths had stumbled upon us, and it had been pretty overrun back then as far as I could tell. Hemp made a list of the approximate populations of each larger city we'd be passing through, and we'd checked Knoxville on our last rest stop.

The population was around 179,000, so worse case scenario, there were roughly 161,000 zombies living there.

If you can call *that* living.

So far we'd stayed on I40, but now got off at I75 south to head over to Lovell Road where the Harley shop was located. If you're wondering how we pulled that off, it's only because we were in possession of a handheld GPS, part of the package put together by Hemp. It was an awesome add, because it also had the points-of-interest feature, and that's how we found the store.

The Harley shop was almost right there when we got off, and I just hoped it hadn't been stripped of inventory already. As soon as we pulled into the parking lot, Serena pointed.

Several rotters, all singles, milled aimlessly about the surrounding streets and sidewalks. When they saw our movement, their motions became more focused.

We cut the motors and put down the kickstands. Once our helmets were off, Serena shook her hair out and stared at them, her expression sad, but contemplative.

She said, "Strange how when there's no single point of interest for them, they just wander around alone."

"It kinda makes sense," I said. "They've got no intelligence or logic telling them to do anything more than eat. No food source, no reason to group."

"Yeah," said Nelson, "but if they see us moving and come to check us out, then why don't they go to each other when they see that movement?"

"Nel, grab a couple of canisters of urushiol, would you? You can use that or your stars."

"Or Subdudo," he added.

"Sure, if you feel like touching them," said Serena, her nose wrinkling. "And that's a good question, Nelson. Why don't they go to each other when they see that movement?"

"Instincts?" I said. "Maybe they know their own kind by sight, just like a dog seems to know another dog, no matter what the breed."

"The shit that stays with you after you're dead," said Nelson. "Crazy. Hold on."

Nelson walked twenty-five yards to his left and sprayed the urushiol in a quick blast to a man with one arm and a missing left foot. Prior to that, the creature had walked toward us in the strangest gait imaginable. Think of how a woman walks when she loses a heel off her shoe. Now exaggerate that by like ten.

The zombie's head quickly dissolved and half his chest melted as he dropped.

"How much WAT-5 have we got?" asked Serena.

"There's a baggie of it in my bike seat, and I keep one in my pocket for quick access," I said. "But I didn't want to waste it unless we really need it. All in all, somewhere around twenty-six doses, which should carry us through."

"Good," she said, taking my hand. She smiled at me, and turned to watch Nelson Moore, the smile lingering on her lips. "But we have another person now," she said. "So I hope it's enough."

Nelson worked his way to another female that was closing in. None of these had much in the way of the pink eye vapor. Food had apparently been scarce, and they hadn't been able to eat enough to generate it.

It was a good sign for us. We would have to keep an eye out for the red-eyed women, though. And obviously pregnant females. They were a game changer.

Nelson blasted this girl in the face, too. Even from twenty-five yards, I could see her facial features dissolve into themselves and run down her chin and neck. Her body took three very clumsy steps before falling forward and remaining still.

"Nelson!" I called. "I got this one."

I pulled the Walther out and held it out. Sighting in on another man who staggered toward us with a machete embedded in his clavicle, I lowered the gun for a moment.

"I know that guy, "I said, as Nelson walked up to stand beside us.

"You know him?" asked Nelson?

"I … well, he was at the church before everything went to hell. He came, ate some of the food and proclaimed his intention to go the lean and mean route."

"Now he's focused on the mean," said Nelson.

"Yeah, eating us is pretty mean," said Serena. "So kill it already."

"Somebody clearly already tried," I said. "It's just proof that you can be immune to the thing and still end up one of them." I raised the PPK, sighted him in – now at only fifteen yards – and dropped him in his tracks. As he fell, the machete flipped out of his shoulder, the metal blade ringing as it hit the macadam.

"Jesus, let's get you a bike and get back on the road," I said. "Killing these bastards is like picking up an entire bag of spilled rice one grain at a time."

"If we don't do it," said Serena, "it falls to someone else. As a group, we decided we all do our share."

"I know, I know," I said.

This was a large Harley Davidson store, but it had been over a year since the apocalypse struck, and I hoped it still had a decent selection of bikes.

As we approached, we saw the front window was shattered. Serena looked at it, moved to the left and tried the door. It was unlocked. Of course it was. You broke a window to get in. You left by the door.

I kept my gun in my hand, as did Serena. Nelson had the urushiol canister, which he held in his right hand like the weapon that it was.

Almost as soon as we walked inside, a partially rotted digger with nearly black skin and Donald Trump hair emerged from behind a row of fallen motorcycles, almost stumbling toward us with each jerky step.

I raised my weapon and unceremoniously shot him in the head, spinning him clockwise and then putting him down on his face. When the bullet blew through his skull, it almost looked like clay dust blew out the back, he was so dehydrated.

Another female in a pair of leather shorts and a leather, zipper-front vest was stuck beneath two of the bikes, its arms clawing at the chrome, plastic and rubber but lacking any cognizant strategy to get out from under the machines.

Nelson walked to her and shook his head as he put the tiniest splash of urushiol on the top of her exposed skull. A hole formed, acting like a sink hole. All the tissue around it began to fall into the hole as it grew larger, and before long, her limbs fell still. There did not appear to be any more of the creatures in the immediate area, but we'd been surprised before.

The skeletal remains of at least eight victims lay around the room, and there were at least five other zombie cadaver remains that we came across in there.

It was easy to tell them, because the head trauma was a quick, visual diagnosis.

"Let's pick you a bike and get back on the road," I said to Nelson. "We have a lot of riding to do before daylight and we haven't gotten very far today."

"Smaller is better," said Nelson. "What's small in a Harley?" he asked.

"That one looks pretty small compared to the rest," said Serena. "I wonder if it's okay?"

It was one of the bikes that had fallen in the row, but she was right. It was a Sportster 1200 Low.

"Here, help me lift these other bikes off it," I said. Serena and Nelson joined me at the bike that had clearly caused the domino effect, and together, we stood the five bikes ahead of the Sportster back on their stands and after righting the 1200 Low, I rolled it around a skeleton and put its stand down. I looked at it, and didn't see anything bent or broken. The mirror was tweaked, but I was able to makeshift it back into position.

The key was in it. I turned it and pushed the auto start. Another beautiful battery. It started right up and fell into a rumble-purr. I smiled at Nelson. "Ever ride a bike this big?" I asked.

"No," he said. "But I rode dirt bikes when I was really young, and they were much heavier than I was, so I get the concept." He looked around at the other bikes at the dealership. "Yeah. It's the smallest. I'll take it. How is it on fuel?"

I shook the bike, and heard it splashing. "We'll top it off with our extra fuel. We'll need to fill those cans tomorrow."

"I need something else," said Serena. "You guys get the bike ready, and top my tank off, too."

When Serena walked back toward us, she carried a nice helmet. She thrust it at Nelson. "Be careful and do *not* need this," she said.

"No worries," said Nelson. "I bounce."

We got back on the road. We would drive to Cookeville and stop for the night. That would put us at around 320 miles for the day. That was enough.

*****

"It would be nice if Nelson could keep up a bit better," I said in Serena's helmet. I hadn't really thought about it, but we were able to have any conversation we wanted to as we rode, and Nelson was blissfully unaware.

"He's not doing bad, considering his lack of experience," said Serena.

"I know," I said. "He really hasn't slowed us down that much. It's all these damned cars. The way they're facing every direction on both sides of the road makes it pretty hard to figure out where they thought they were evacuating to."

"Not everyone has a plan," said Serena. "Sometimes it's just *run.*"

"Don't I know it," I said, immediately thinking of Lisa. Without her, I would not have had much direction, either.

"Let's pull off here," I said. "There's a little motel there. Maybe we can find an unaffected room."

"Let's stop here, where we know it's clear," said Serena. "We should have a standard plan."

They pulled over, and Nelson managed not to run into them as he rolled up and stopped. His helmet had a clear half-face shield, and he was smiling big as he looked at us.

"I am embarrassed to say this," he said, "But I really like this. I just give that thing a little gas and I jam!"

"Live to ride, ride to live," I said, pulling my helmet off. "Glad you're enjoying it."

"I still won't use a gun," he said.

"We'll keep working on you," said Serena, smiling as she pulled the ponytail from her hair. "We're just going to this motel, Nelson."

"That Knights Inn?" he asked, pointing.

"Yeah," I said. "It's right off the exit. We don't need a lot of in-town driving."

"Hope they don't have a zombie infestation," he said.

"We'll handle it," said Serena. "I'd say a sweep's in order no matter where we stop. And in case there are any of the red-eyes around, I suppose we should stick to the quieter methods of eliminating them."

"They can hear?" asked Nelson.

"Hemp says their eardrums were pliable and alive," I said. "So we're assuming it's part of the advantage they have over the others. Problem is, when they detect sounds, they can lead a battalion of the bastards to us."

"So urushiol it is," said Serena.

"And stars – and Subdudo if necessary," added Nelson.

I shook my head, smiling. "If it gets that close and hand-to-hand, by all means use your Subdudo," I said. "But urushiol the others, and if you see a pregnant female or a red-eye, tell us, because a bullet is going to be necessary. Are you sure you won't carry a gun?"

Nelson shook his head. "Guys, I got to where I am now without one. I'm good. Plus, you should *not* handle a firearm when you're stoned. I was taught this by my dad a long time ago."

"Did he have guns?" I asked.

"No," said Nelson. "Just common sense."

"Are you stoned now?"

"I ate a tiny bud, but I've got a good tolerance," admitted Nelson. "It's like my Xanax."

I glared at him. "Nelson, you can't afford to be compromised out here. No more of that shit until we're in and secured for the night, okay?"

Nelson looked shocked. "Dave, I don't think you've seen me when I'm not stoned," he said. "This is my normal. You want me to screw up, then make rules like that one."

I looked at him, and realized he was probably right. If he functioned with weed every day, he probably felt more in his right mind under the influence than not. I liked weed in the old days, but it had mostly been a weekend release for me.

"Okay, Nelson," I said. "But if you get fucking eaten out here, I'm never going to be certain whether it was the weed or just bad luck. It's on you."

"Dude, if you're worried that I'm going to use it all, don't. I brought like a half a pound."

I couldn't help myself. I laughed out loud. "So that's what's in your backpack."

Nelson smiled and shrugged. "It's a long trip, right?"

"Okay, are we ready?" asked Serena.

*****

Each of us donned a strap-on headlight from the seat compartment of Serena's bike. Light was fading, and the rooms would be dark.

The Knights Inn might have looked alright at first glance, but as we passed the pool area, we saw one female creature inside, moving along the fence line, watching us. She was not pregnant, and only a portion of her bikini bottoms remained on her ravaged body, so this was not a guess. No baby bump to speak of.

The pool was now down to about half full, what with evaporation and whatever rain the area had endured over the last year. The water was a murky greenish-black, and if it was zombie algae, then it looked just like all the rest.

I wondered how many sets of bones could be found at the bottom. I knew from Flex's story that if not injured, they were not afraid to venture into the water, so even if those who had been by the pool thought to escape that way, it would have been their folly.

Around the pool there were eight chairs with towels, now as black and molded as the pool water itself. There were several water bottles bunched up against one corner, and many floated in the water. Wind, rain and just plain nature moving shit around.

Serena walked up to the creature behind the fence and unceremoniously squirted her in the forehead with the urushiol. The thing clutched at its new wounds with both bony hands, clawing into the hole created by the poisonous oil before collapsing in a hissing, popping lump.

Serena turned. "Another one bites the dust," she said.

"Queen!" shouted Nelson. "Remind me to get an iPod."

We walked to the lobby and peered in through the closed door. It was not automatic. Nelson pulled it softly and it opened about an inch. He let it close again and looked at me and Serena.

"I don't see a need to go in there," I said.

"Agreed," said Serena. "I'm tired. No sense in looking for a fight."

"Okay, then … looks like the rooms are around this way," said Nelson, pointing to the left side of the building. "How are we going to get in?"

"Break a window?" asked Serena.

"Then we're vulnerable," I said. "Maybe kick a door in and hope the flip-over lock still works?"

Nelson approached the first door. "I know we're trying to be quiet, but maybe just shoot out the jamb?"

I thought about it, and realized if the entire door trim piece came off, we wouldn't be able to lock it once we got inside. Just one shot to mess with the latch itself might make more sense. "Yeah. Get it over with, I guess." I pulled out the Walther and aimed it, when the curtains just beside us flipped aside, and two rotters' faces pressed against the glass, snarling and clawing. It was apparently a mother and son – or daughter. The younger one was almost skinless, completely nude except for a hint of some sort of underwear, and the mom had on a robe, held on by a knotted belt.

We all jumped back, and I put a hand to my chest.

The monsters continued to scramble at the window as we stared. "Holy shit," I said, breathing hard.

"Double that," said Serena. "This is like living in a B horror movie."

"Quick vote," I said. "How about we let these guys be. I don't see it's worth the noise to break the window to kill them, especially since the red-eyed ones can probably hear. So let's not waste the ammo."

"Fine with me," said Nelson.

"I'm good," added Serena. "We just need to get the hell in a room and out of sight."

We walked three rooms over and the curtains were open. The room was empty. Beds made, everything in order.

"I got a good kick on me," said Nelson. "I don't use it in Subdudo, and I guess you know why."

"Be our guest," said Serena, smiling at me. "I suppose it'll be quieter than a gunshot."

Nelson took four steps back, then kind of skip-trotted to the door. His left leg came up to place a perfectly landed kick just beside the doorknob. It splintered and the door flew inward, slamming against the wall.

"Holy shit," I said. "Now I know why you don't use that. Wow."

We all turned on our headlights and walked inside, and I inspected the door frame. It had split, but the hook latch at the top was still intact, attached with very long screws, apparently. We were able to push the door closed and flip it over so that the door could only open two inches.

Beyond that, we angled a chair beneath the doorknob, and we felt pretty secure as we settled in.

"Long day for me," said Nelson. "I'll be out in just a few seconds after a quick bowl. You guys?"

I waved it off. "Not tonight, Nel. Night, man. Glad you're here." I meant it.

"Night, Nelson," said Serena.

He stripped down to his underwear, and I was glad he stopped there. He checked the sheets for something – roaches or bedbugs, I presumed – and slid in, putting the pipe back on the nightstand, removing his headlamp, and putting it beside the pipe.

"Night, guys."

His soft snores came in less than a minute. As soon as he was out, as tired as I was, I put my hand on Serena's shoulder.

"Hey," she said. "Tired?"

"I am," I said. "Nice not to hear the roar of the bikes for a bit."

"I know," she said. "The silence of this new world is eerie and peaceful at the same time. If only it was without … them."

"Thanks for coming with me," I said. "I don't know if I'd have come if you didn't.."

I heard her soft laughter in the darkness, and I leaned forward to kiss her lips, finding them as though guided by radar.

"I wouldn't have said no, David. Not in a million years. I think I fell in love with you in that little cinderblock prison we shared for a while."

The prison she spoke of was a small block building that we got trapped inside, half surrounded by the hungry dead. If not for some ingenuity on both our parts, we likely would have perished there.

I had just witnessed the killing of my sister, and was a mess, ill-equipped to dig deep enough on my own to think of a way out.

"That's funny," I said. "That's where I fell in love with you. You saved me."

"You showed me your heart, David," she whispered, and I realized she was crying. "Your sister meant everything to you, and you weren't afraid to show me that. I've known many men in my life, mostly the type who didn't show their emotions because they didn't want to look weak. But that is not weakness; to me it's a strength I'm drawn to."

"I worry about you," I said. "It's that awkward moment when you realize you're not Flex Sheridan, and you hope to God you can protect the ones you love."

"Flex isn't a superhero," she said. "He's just a man who loves his family and friends and fights for them, just like you."

I felt her hand touch my chest. "In here," she said. "It's where Flex's strength comes from. Yours, too."

"Yeah, and I'm not all hairy there," I said. "Pretty sweet, huh?"

She laughed now, moving in beside me. While it was warm in the room, I didn't care. I wrapped my arms around her and embraced the human contact, throwing the sheet off us and lightly caressing her back.

Serena must have felt some movement from a bit further south, because she said, "Tomorrow night he gets his own room." Her tears long gone for now. There was a smile on her lips that I could hear.

"Deal," I said. "If I have to build the motherfucker myself."

"Maybe you do have a little Flex in you," she said, laughing.

Nelson snorted and rolled over, moaning something unintelligible.

"Night, Serena," I said.

She didn't answer. I felt her steady, warm breath on my cheek and closed my eyes.

*****

Chapter Six

When I awoke, Nelson stood at the window, staring out. Serena still lay beside me, covered by the light sheet. Light shone in from outside, but disturbing shadows broke up the purity of the light. Nelson turned to look at me, his face grim.

I didn't say anything. I slipped out the other side of the bed and padded over to the window, peering out beside him.

"Shit," I said softly.

"It's full time work," said Nelson. "Gramps would tell me I'm up for it, though."

"From what I've seen, you are," I said. "But there are a lot of them out there."

"How," Nelson asked. His face held worry like I'd never seen. Normally the kid was excited at the prospect. I wasn't sure what was different.

"It's been a while, Nel," I said. "Makes me wonder if they're developing heightened senses. There are three of us. We have to combine for some good smells."

Nelson shook his head and scanned the horizon. It looked insurmountable. Then I grabbed his arm and pulled him away from the window.

"WAT-5, Nel. Fuck this, we'll just take some WAT-5 and we're good."

A smile spread across Nelson's skinny face. "Shit, Davey, how come I didn't think of that?"

"I can't believe I got there so fast," I said. "Okay, let's get that done, like now."

I went to the bed and touched Serena's shoulder. "Serena, wake up," I said softly.

She stirred and rolled toward me. Her eyes opened into slits, and she smiled. "Good morning." Then: "What's wrong?"

"You do know me," I said. "Thirty guesses, first twenty-nine don't count. There's a hint in my hint."

"Thirty of them?" she asked, her face horrified.

"Give or take," I said, pulling the WAT-5 out of my cargo shorts pocket. "Wanna trip the light fantastic?"

"I wondered when we'd need it," she said. "Sure."

"Okay, Nelson, you first," I said. "Sit down on that beautiful, striped couch from 1987 and take this." I held out the wafer, and he took it from me, popping it in his mouth.

"I feel like this is an invisibility pill, dude," he said, chewing it.

He slid over onto his side, a smile still on his face. Out cold.

"Okay, you," I said.

"Shit," said Serena. "I just woke up. I don't feel like going back to sleep."

"Look out the window, and you will," I said.

She rolled her eyes and held out her hand. I dropped it in her palm and she sat on the bed, then reclined. "They better not be anywhere near my bike," she said.

In another ten seconds, she was out cold. I went over to Nelson and nudged him. He groaned, but didn't stir. I immediately wondered if the pot had any effect when mixed with the wafers. I wasn't sure we'd ever really mixed the two.

I nudged him again. Still nothing. Finally, I leaned down and took him by the shoulders, and lightly shook him.

When he awoke, his hands started flipping around in Subdudo moves, but there was nothing behind them. Two seconds later, his eyes focused on me. "Whoa, Davey, I'm sorry! I was out, man. Did I hurt you?"

"Buddy, you were so ineffective, I was just trying not to laugh," I said. "You really should test a few moves before you get in the mix outside. You seem rusty."

Nelson got unsteadily to his feet, and stood in front of me. Before I knew it, his right hand touched my neck, his left foot hit the back of my left knee, and his right hand knocked me off balance.

I was on my ass in a split second and I was laughing. In fact, I was almost hysterical. It had happened so fast, yet while I was going through it, it seemed like slow motion. Nelson was stoned and groggy from his WAT-5 nap but I was still putty in his skilled hands.

"Help me up, you prick," I said, shaking my head and holding out my hand. "I don't have any idea how you do that, but you gotta teach me."

"Years, bro," he said. "That would take years of intense training."

I was back on my feet, checking myself. I was fine. No soreness, nothing. I'm sure I was blushing a bit. "Okay, Chuck Fucking Norris, let's wake up Serena, and I'll take my dose."

"Allow me," said Nelson. He went to her bed and sat beside her. He reached down and brushed the hair away from her face, then lightly slapped her cheek. Her eyes fluttered open.

"Hey, Nel," she said. I thought it was strange that she shortened his name, but she never shortened mine to Dave. I think she looked at him almost like a pet or a child. She had a genuine affection for the kid.

"Okay, sunshine," I said. "My turn." I pulled out a wafer and re-zipped the bag, sitting on the striped sofa. I popped the wafer in my mouth, therefore cannot chronicle the next minute or so.

*****

When I awoke, Nelson and Serena were standing over me, smiling. I stared up at them. They stared back, still smiling. "Yeah?" I said. "What's so funny? Did I fart in my sleep or something?"

"No," they said, turning away. "We're good to go when you are," said Serena.

"I have to pee," I said. "You guys should go if you need to. How's the toilet?"

"It *was* sanitized for our protection a year ago," said Serena. "Not so much now that Nelson got through using it."

"Holy shit," I said.

"Exactly," said Nelson, smiling meekly.

"Maybe I'll go in the sink. Pardon me, Serena," I said.

"I won't watch," said Serena.

As I walked toward the mirror, both Nelson and Serena followed me, laughing.

"Seriously?" I said, staring at my reflection in the mirror. They stood beside me admiring their work.

Obviously while I was out, they had split my beard into three twisted points and secured them with rubber bands. My hair was done in two kinky braids and then ponytailed high on my head, like a Rob Zombie-Pippi Longstocking hybrid.

I whirled around and tried not to smile. "Really? You're so comfortable with Hemp Chatsworth's little wafer

119

that you thought you could fuck with me while I was out? What are we, fourteen?"

"We are just children in this crazy, new world," said Nelson, holding out his hands. "Babes in the haunted woods, as it were."

I rushed toward him, and he shouted, "Hey! Subdudo!"

I pulled up short and held my palms up. "Okay, okay. Now I really have to pee."

I went back to the sink and considered leaving the hairstyle in place, but knew it would not feel good under my helmet. The beard work, however, might actually minimize tangling. That would stay for now.

I decided to use the bathtub rather than the sink. It was more civilized, and I was used to it. I went in, said a prayer of thanks that Nelson had closed the lid of the toilet, and slid back the shower curtain.

I know what you're thinking, and no – nothing jumped out at me. Just a tub and a fiberglass surround. I peed for a long time, all the while wishing Serena wasn't in such close proximity.

Walking back out and closing the door behind me, I grabbed the bathroom bag from the counter and held it up. "Brush, or you'll both have rotter breath."

"Are you stalling?" asked Serena.

"Nope," I said. "Complete faith in WAT-5, and the situation outside is exactly why we have it."

Nelson worked on his front teeth and walked to the front window. He pulled the curtains apart and looked out. "Wow," he said. "Half as many now."

I spit into the sink and rinsed again with a small drink of water. "Really?"

Serena finished up and we put our brushes and the toothpaste away. Nelson came back over and did his final rinse. "Really. WAT-5 works fast," he said.

"Yeah, but they're not all gone," said Serena. "Right?"

"Let's be careful, but let's get going," I said. "We're gonna try for another 300 miles today if nothing goes wrong."

We tucked everything into Nelson's backpack, which he then shrugged into. "I'm ready for Freddy, man," he said.

"From the looks of it, I hope it's Freddy Kruger," I said, pulling the chair away from the doorknob. I stood there, one hand on the swing latch and the other on the knob. I flipped the latch free and took my gun from my drop holster. Serena followed suit, and Nelson held up his hands in fighting position.

I smiled. "Nelson, get a star or something. You don't need to be touching these bastards. Too risky."

"Good call," he said, pulling two brass Ninja stars from his cargo pants pocket. He raised his eyebrows twice fast, smiling.

Serena and I, despite the situation we were about to walk into, both smiled. Genuine smiles. Nelson was nuts.

"Alright," I said, opening the door. We all stepped back.

*****

The rotting, former men and women shuffled inside the room as the door opened wide. Not all of them; some walked right by the open door and toward the office around the corner. Others just stood in front of the window as if they hoped the smells they had detected earlier may return if only they were patient.

A skeletal man with leathery skin that hugged protruding ribs and pelvic bones barely brushed me as he moved by, and I held my breath; not so that he wouldn't smell me, but so that I did not have to take in his odor.

I had grown used to the smell of the walking dead things, but in close proximity it was still overwhelming. Decay was an odor that could never be completely accepted by olfactory senses, nor did I want it to be. I would resist it until there was no longer a need to do so.

"Let's move," Serena whispered.

We moved. I went first, walking through the door slowly, my gun held with the barrel facing upward. With a slight turn of the wrist I could put a bullet under the chin and through the brain of any one of them.

Serena came directly behind me, and Nelson, walking backward – I wasn't sure why – followed her. I kept glancing back, but he seemed pretty surefooted, so if he chose to walk like he was The Sundance Kid following Butch Cassidy out of a saloon full of bounty hunters, it was his call.

"Dude, they're following us," he said.

"What?" I said, turning. Then I saw exactly what he meant. The group was back, only they now numbered forty or more. They did not appear to be focused on us, but they were definitely staying *with* us, as though they had taken on a pack or flock mentality.

I didn't like it at all.

"I wish they would back the hell off," I said. "It feels like they're boxing us in."

Serena leaned toward me and said in my ear, "There have to be red-eyes around, David."

I nodded. "I agree." I turned and said, "Nelson, keep your stars handy, but grab the urushiol canister. You might need both."

Because we were concerned the bikes would draw ill-intentioned strangers to our exact room at night, we decided not to park them right outside. The bikes weren't far – just on the other side of the pool fence – but it was impossible to see exactly how far we had to go with the flesh-hungry creatures bunched so tightly in front and beside us. There was no view beyond their filthy, rotting bodies.

I jumped up in the air to see over the mass of zombies. "We're about twenty feet now," I said to Serena. I turned around and told Nelson, "When I duck down and push through, I want you to start spraying that shit for all it's worth, Nel. Something is up with this crowd."

"Okay, chief," he said.

"Serena, get ready," I said. She nodded.

"Go!" I shouted, ducking my head and throwing my arms out in front of me. I pushed between their rickety legs and head butted them out of the way. They fell aside, unsteady and taken by as much surprise as they could be taken by.

Three seconds of full running and we were completely clear. I heard and saw in my peripheral vision the zombies melting behind me as Nelson sprayed them with the killer zombie repellent, and as I reached the bikes I saw how this had happened.

The female stood, completely nude, her lower jaw broken or rotted away. Only her black, rotted tongue flapped and licked the inside of what was once her mouth. Her eyes were a vivid red, even in the brilliant light of the morning.

The swell of her belly would have been enough to tell me she was pregnant; the small hand that had broken through the skin, just below her belly button, drove it home. The little fingers clawed at her skin, and had apparently been doing so for a long time, for the skin was raw, rotted meat where the unborn infant's hand scratched incessantly.

She charged toward us at speed. I raised my gun and she stopped and dropped down immediately, apparently unaware that Serena held her gun on her too, and fired when she reached the bottom of her crouch.

But the instinctive, female monster had jogged sideways as well, and fast, causing Serena's bullet to ricochet away, ineffective.

The speedster shot back to full height like a piston driven up by a crankshaft. She was now almost alongside Serena, as Nelson directed a stream of urushiol in her eyes.

The thing let go a muffled scream-cry of some kind, its bony palms slapping its eyes, and I felt a lightning bolt shoot down the back of my neck as the creeps came on full strength.

Nelson then sprayed the tiny hand. It erupted into spasms instantly, melting before our eyes, and dripping away until no more of it protruded from her. The zombie then clutched at her stomach and shrieked as red-black, bubbling, foam and goo erupted out of the hole in her abdomen, dripping into a puddle of gore at the thing's feet.

"Drop, Serena!" I screamed, and she did so immediately. The second she was safely out of my way, I fired two rounds into the red-eyed creature's face and she flew backward off her feet, landing flat on her back.

With one last hiss-pop, her stomach flattened and she lay still.

Nelson breathed hard as he helped Serena back up and pulled her away from the zombie's body. I kept my eyes on her as I walked backward, even though I knew she was dead.

The creatures that had been following us disbursed now, spreading out and moving without direction, nothing left to guide them toward us.

Their leader was dead. The once-pregnant, enhanced female had gone down, and we knew we had to get the hell out before another of her kind showed up. We mounted the bikes, put our helmets on and wasted no time. First stop would be fuel. The next, after we put some miles between ourselves and this bad experience, would be food and rest.

As I started the Harley, I realized with some level of dread that we had just begun our 3,000 mile journey and were only 10% there. With the estrogen enriched females out there, with highly tuned senses that could obviously detect the whereabouts of human flesh and blood, we would find it difficult to locate truly safe havens along the way.

She had obviously sniffed us out in the night, so by the time we took the WAT-5, it was already too late to mask our presence. I wondered to myself why she hadn't unleashed her horde of walking dead minions on us, ripping us to shreds when we were in their midst; could it have been her selfish desire to have us to herself?

Perhaps this one had no prior knowledge of weapons, only sensing the danger our guns posed as we emerged from the crowd and aimed them at her?

I pulled out, preparing to roll the bike around a male rotter wearing a tattered Hard Rock Café tee shirt.

"Serena," I said into my communication headset.

"What is it?" she asked. I saw her eyeing all the zombies that were now milling aimlessly around the parking lot, some of them converging on another of the hotel room doors.

"Let's try out these machine guns," I said. "Spin it around."

I got Nelson's attention and pointed toward the street, then pointed at Serena and myself, the gun on my bike, and the zombies.

"Go at it," he yelled, starting his bike and riding toward the street.

"You take left and I'll take right," Serena said, and that sounded just fine to me. Holding onto the right handlebar and using minimal gas, I rolled toward them and grabbed the modified Uzi with my left hand. "Ready?" I asked Serena.

"Ready," she said. "Got about ten lined up right here."

"Have at 'em," I said, and pivoted the machine gun side to side at near perfect height for my first time firing it. The rounds met their marks, chopping caps off skulls sending the coagulating blood-goo spitting into the air with biohazard-filled chunks of decayed meat and brains.

The windows of the hotel rooms behind them took several rounds, shattering and crashing inward, and rows of holes punched through the doors and the stucco walls.

Serena was having similar success. My gun fell silent, now empty. Because there were only three creatures left on my side, I reached down to my drop holster and withdrew the Walther. With a careful bit of steering around the muck and piles of bodies, I carefully aimed and sent those three walking dead amigos to their final resting place, which turned out to be the parking lot of a Knights Inn.

I had to remember the cardinal rule, and not make decisions that went against it no matter how *done* I was with the process or how tired I was of doing it.

Kill them all.

The world would not recover if they were allowed to roam it forever. Serena had clearly been more efficient with her weapon, for she had been able to take down the entire rotter crew assigned to her with her bike-mounted gun.

"Nice job," I said.

"You, too," she said. I looked over at Nelson, who gave me a thumbs up sign.

"Let's hit it," said Serena, and as we both started rolling our bikes toward the driveway, we heard a voice calling over the Harley engines.

"Hey! Wait!"

It was a man's voice. I turned back toward the hotel, and saw a man and what appeared to be a female child standing inside a hotel room just four doors down from the room where we had spent the night.

The window of their room was shattered, and the curtains now blew inside. They stood there, the female with a baseball bat in her hands, and the man with what looked like a rope. I could see what appeared to be a holster on his waist. Maybe two.

"Hello!" I called, scanning the lot again before turning my bike toward them. "Cover me," I said to Serena, who stopped her bike with the front pointed toward the pair, lifting the customized gun up. Her expression was fixed and stern as she eyed the two.

"Hold on a second, David," she said. She put the kickstand down and got off, opening the seat. She took a spare magazine out, ejected the empty one from the gun and put a new one in. "Okay," she said, getting back on the bike. "You're good."

Our experiences had been both good and bad with strangers – mostly good – but taking chances and counting on goodness went out the window quite a while ago.

I motored toward them and pulled the Harley as close to their room as I could get before cutting the engine and putting the kickstand down. I removed my helmet and called to them. "Were you here last night?" I asked.

"We were," said the girl, whom I could now see was a woman. She was a very short woman, but the baseball bat she gripped in her hands gave her a very serious edge. Her face was neither frightened nor aggressive, but I could clearly see she was harrowed. She was so thin I wondered if these two had eaten very much in the last few months.

"I'm Dave Gammon," I said. "Serena Casteneda is on the other bike, and the guy down by the street is Nelson Moore."

"So Serena's the one with the gun pointed at us?" the man asked.

"She is," I said. "You'll excuse us if we're a little jumpy." I called to Serena. "We're good. Come on over."

She tilted the gun back down and parked her bike. I turned back to the couple.

"Jumpy?" said the man, suddenly angry as he pulled off his cowboy hat and slapped it against his leg. "Well, you damned near killed both of us," he said. "You shot out that window and let these pieces of shit almost crawl through. Not like we were asleep with all that racket, thank God, so we took 'em out."

I put my helmet on the seat of the bike and walked toward them, my palms held up. "Just coming over to talk," I said. "I'm sorry – oh. I see what you mean now."

When I got closer, I saw there were two dead rotters just inside their room. They must have made their way in after Serena or I had shot out the glass of their hotel room.

The fluttering curtains covered a foot that hadn't quite made it over the sill of the broken window, and on the other side of the window, a hand was impaled on a shard of glass jutting from the window frame. It did not move.

Now I knew why the two strangers had been standing so far back from the window. I couldn't see further into the room, because the curtains were only open about four feet and I was standing toward the door.

"Sorry about that, guys. I really am," I said. "We didn't know you were in there, and we were basically just doing cleanup. It's one of our personal directives not to leave any of them alive. Anyone else with you?"

"Just us," said the woman. She must have been significantly less than five feet tall, maybe 4'8" or 4'9". The baseball bat she held casually over her shoulder removed any perceived vulnerability I might have automatically attributed to her because of her size. She held it like she had used it often, and indeed, the Louisville Slugger was darkened and splotchy with stains I did not wish to consider at the moment.

Her hair was long, wavy and brown, and her deep, brown eyes were a match. Freckles adorned her tiny nose, and I saw suspicion and exhaustion in her expression. She wore what appeared to be khaki pants and a white, v-neck tee shirt, and I estimated her to be somewhere in her mid-thirties. This didn't mean shit, because I sucked at guessing ages anyway and everybody in a zombie apocalypse tended to look slightly older than their actual years.

The man had put his straw cowboy hat back on his head. Before he did so, I saw that he had a full head of mostly grey hair, accompanied by a full beard and mustache. He was a big man; probably 6'3". He was on the thinner side, but his arms showed zero sign of weakness. His muscles were pronounced, and I guessed he was somewhere in his early sixties. The rope he held was actually coiled and over his shoulder, attached via some sort of strap sewed into the shirt with a metal snap. The rope looked stiff, like a rodeo cowboy's.

I turned and saw Nelson hold his hands out and give me an exaggerated shrug, so I waved him to come up. He immediately started his bike and rode toward us, stopping with a bit of a jerk beside my bike. He got off and removed his helmet. Serena was beside me first.

"Did I get here in time to warn you about his awkward moment jokes?" asked Serena.

I shook my head and held out my open hand to the man, because the woman was currently eyeing Serena and did not look willing to relinquish the grip on her baseball bat just yet. "It's good to meet fellow survivors," I said. "Sorry for the almost killing you thing."

I clasped his hand in mine and shook it.

"Don Weston," he said. "This here's my friend Rachel Reed."

I held out my hand to Rachel. She gave Serena an almost imperceptible nod, then released the bat and clasped my hand and shook.

Her grip was strong and her handshake brief. I estimated her to be somewhere in her late twenties or very early thirties, but she was very fit, at least at first glance.

She looked me directly in the face and offered a tired smile, and I realized she was very pretty. I was sure to smile back. Smiles were a nice thing to see when terror was a more common facial expression. I thought I saw a sense of relief in her eyes. Perhaps because we did not seem to be a threat. Weston and Rachel then said their hellos to Serena and Nelson.

A horse suddenly whinnied. It was loud and sounded as though it were mere feet away from us. I whirled around, pulling out my PPK, expecting to see someone on horseback directly behind me.

"Get your hearing checked," said Serena, pulling the curtain aside and looking inside the room. "Wow," she said. "Beautiful animals."

I reholstered my gun, feeling like an idiot. I moved beside Serena and looked deeper into the room.

One horse stood between the dresser and the end of the two queen sized beds. He was a gleaming, almost red color, with a shining mane and alert eyes. Another smaller horse, this one pure white with an almost silky mane, stood directly in front of the double vanity in the back of the room.

"The big male's Duster," said Weston. "Lucky he was behind the door or you'd have shot him for sure."

"The white one's Snowball," Rachel offered.

Weston gave a sad smile. "My daughter Sally named her Snowball as a foal" said Don. "Dang horse was white, so that's what five-year-old girls do," he said, the smile that had formed on his lips when he'd said Sally's name fading away quickly.

"You've been riding them since this started?" asked Nelson.

Yep," said Weston. "Came out that Sunday morning and the damned corral was a mess. The neighbors on either side of me had a lot of hired hands and a few sons, too. They weren't all out there, but the ones I saw were either face-deep into the belly of my dead horses or stumblin' after these two."

"After Snowball and Duster?" asked Nelson. "How'd they get away?" He looked like a child being told a fairy tale.

"My most skittish horses," Weston said. "No way to get near 'em. Not even me. I could see Snowball was tirin' out by the time I killed the rest of those freakshows and got the rope on her, but Duster never woulda got caught. He could outlast anyone."

"You can rope?" asked Nelson? "Like a cowboy?"

"Since I'm six years old," he said. "Rope like a sonofabitch."

"Cool," said Nelson, pulling a brass star from his pocket and holding it up. "I throw Ninja stars. We should team up sometime."

"Not much call for a wild west Ninja show these days, son," said Weston, looking at me, a question in his eyes. No doubt a question about Nelson. I shrugged and smiled.

"I lived next door to Don," said Rachel. "But I was temporarily stationed at the Bolling Air Force Base in Washington, D.C."

"You're military?" asked Serena.

"I was," said Rachel. "Until this."

Serena asked, "Are they doing anything there? I mean, were they? Is there any functioning government that you could see?"

Rachel shook her head. "It was chaos when I was there. Just the same as everywhere else I've been. Most of the men and women at the base changed into those ... things. The zombies. I had to kill a whole bunch of them before I got out. The surviving MPs were killing anything that moved." She raised her tee shirt sleeve and showed me two, round scars. "Here's where they hit me."

"They shot you?" asked Nelson, incredulous. "Their own kind?"

"I assume you mean Navy, and yes," said Rachel. "They were panicking, shooting anything that moved. I'm lucky, in a way, that there were more of those things than us, because while they just wandered around in the open, I was able to keep under cover and out of sight until I was able to commandeer a truck and get the hell out. Blew right through a gate."

"Wow," said Nelson. "How'd you meet this cowboy man?"

Rachel actually smiled at Nelson. Nel's eyes were wide, and he was listening intently to every word Rachel spoke. "I was career Navy, and my assignment at Bolling was temporary," she said. "Jess, my husband, needed to stay to take care of our small ranch. It had been in Jess's family for a century, and there was nobody else, so I went and he stayed."

"What kind of ranch?" asked Nelson.

"Mostly goats and other livestock, a few crops," said Rachel. "Anyway, Jess stayed. After everything started, I wasn't able to get him on his cell phone at all. They did something in DC to jam them."

"Typical government," commiserated Nelson, shaking his head.

"Anyway, long story short, I traveled the almost five hundred miles back home through some things I can't even describe. It took me two months to get there."

"Don't bother going into it," said Serena. "It's not necessary and we know how painful it can be."

"That we do," I said. "And when you think you're past the worst of it, you realize you're not."

Rachel's face acknowledged our compassion, but she seemed intent on finishing the story. "When I got back," she continued, "Jess was nowhere to be found. Just gone. His clothes were still there, wallet, everything. Even the keys to our vehicles. But he was gone. All our livestock had been mutilated. I heard gunfire, so I got in an ATV and rode over to find Don shooting at another straggler that had wandered onto his property."

"I almost shot her," Weston said. "My fence needed fixin', but I hadn't gotten to it. I felt pretty good about stayin' at my place indefinitely, but for that damned fence. I had plenty of food. Lots of oats for the horses and troughs of water that I could cover to keep it from evaporatin', for a while anyway. Had other storage tanks – not the cleanest water, but in the end we could drink it if we had to. So we did. Eventually that ran out."

"That what drove you to leave?" asked Serena.

Rachel nodded. "I wanted to wait for Jess," she said. "I just knew he'd come back."

"I told her," said Weston, "He probably hightailed it to DC when all this came on. I never saw him, I was so damned busy killin' my other neighbors, but he wasn't among 'em."

I thought I saw something pass over Weston's eyes for a moment, but could have been wrong.

"But you guys made it," said Nelson. "So you've been riding Duster and Snowball for like ten months now?"

"Pretty efficient way to travel these days," said Weston. "We all need water, and so far, that's not a problem. When there's nothing else, graze on grass. If I come across bales of hay, I get 'em that," said Weston.

"And we're up high enough that it's easy to keep an eye out for the neighbors."

"That what you call them?" asked Nelson.

"It got to be a habit in the beginning," said Weston. "I didn't like my neighbors much anyway, so when they turned into those things that wanted to eat us, the name still made sense to me. They were just a worse annoyance."

I laughed, despite myself. "Well, again, we apologize. For what it's worth, if you were going to stay here, upstairs looks untouched."

"We're only here for the night," said Rachel. "We mostly gather supplies and find new places to get comfortable while this situation blows over."

She looked into my eyes. "As for the personal directive you mentioned, it's killing every one you come across, right?"

"It is," I said. "We don't think it makes sense to let them go. If they do find food, it's people like us. Letting them go can be a death sentence for someone else. That doesn't work for us."

"Same here," said Weston. "There were so many of 'em outside our room when we woke up, we just figured we'd bide our time, but it didn't look like they were goin' anywhere. Not sure they'd have ever left if you didn't do what you did."

"Do you know about the pregnant females?" Serena asked.

"What about them?" asked Rachel.

"They control the others," she said. "You can tell them because their eyes are red, unlike the others. The others have a pink mist – are you familiar with that?"

134

"I've seen what it does," said Weston. "Never got caught in it, though. Knocks you out, right?"

"Yes," said Serena. "It does, but if you're of birthing age – and you appear to be, Rachel – don't let one of the pregnant ones blast you at any cost. It gives them a form of mind control over you. They can order you to do things against your will."

"It got my sister killed," I said. "Almost got more of us killed, too."

"Thanks for the advice," said Rachel. "Where are you headed?"

"California," said Nelson. "Looking for Dave's Uncle Bug."

"Uncle Bug?" asked Weston. "What the hell's an Uncle Bug?"

"Brett Ulrich Gammon," I said. "Bug to his friends. Lives in a kind of remote spot in northern California."

"What makes you think he's okay?" asked Rachel.

"Don't know for sure," I said. "But he's immune to urushiol, that much I do know."

"What the hell's urushiol?" asked Weston.

I realized we needed way more time to talk all this stuff over than we'd likely have standing in the parking lot of a Knights Inn surrounded by piles of dead zombies.

"It's a poisonous oil, and the chance that you and Rachel are immune to it is 100%," I said. "Look. We woke up in kind of a pickle and had to move. So that means we're hungry, and we're going to have to dig into our food supply before we hit the road anyway. If you guys want to, we can kick open another hotel room door, move your horses, have a bite and go over some of this stuff. We have a lot to do today, but we can take that time if you think it'll help you."

"I recon we made it this far with a bit of luck on our sides," said Weston, looking at Rachel. "What do you think? Have some breakfast, see what they know?"

She nodded. "Yeah. I love you, Don, but it is really nice to run into other people to talk with for a while."

"Don't worry 'bout offendin' me," said the cowboy. "I'm tough like leather."

*****

"That's right," said Weston. "I've got caught in the middle of poison ivy and poison oak a bunch of times. Never got anything from it."

"I have no idea whether I have or not," said Rachel.

"According to Hemp," said Serena, "This immunity can go away. We haven't experienced it among our group yet, but all that means is you have to be watchful and diligent. If someone gets a bad headache, just dab some of the oil on their wrist. If –"

"If that dude starts to sound like a bowl of Rice Krispies, run like hell!" interjected Nelson.

Serena couldn't help but smile, but continued: "I was going to say that if a rash appears, you've got a big decision to make, and it's not going to be if you kill them, but how and when. They should definitely be isolated and restrained immediately. Everyone should know it so it's not a surprise."

"Wow," said Rachel. "That's pretty intense."

"Good word!" said Nelson. "That's exactly what it is. I hate intensity, and I'm not a big fan of tension, either." He swiped his hair behind one ear and prepared to listen intently with it.

"What's your plan?" I asked.

"Didn't have one besides what's gotten us from a year ago to now," said Don Weston. "Got room in your expedition? That is, if you want to go, Rachel."

I heard the words and my heart sunk. It wasn't that I didn't like them; I did. It was that in this world, if we had learned one thing, it was that less is more. I already knew I would not turn them away, though. If they thought they might like to go to the Golden State, and they intended to adapt as necessary, my answer would be yes.

"We can't keep up on the horses," Rachel said. "They've been good to us."

Weston looked at Duster and reached up and patted his rump. In response, Duster's tail swished and he snorted. "Before we go rackin' our brains about that, what's the answer?" He looked at me.

I looked at Serena, and saw in her eyes what I'd already wrestled with. We both knew that the bigger the group was, the more pain in the ass it was to be versatile, but at the same time, Flex, Gem, Hemp and Charlie hadn't hesitated, so neither would we. We couldn't.

"Look," I said. "I have a specific mission to accomplish. If you think where we're going might be someplace you'd like to settle in for a while, then yeah. You both look capable, and it's still a free country, as far as I know."

They looked at one another.

"And let me add that everyone needs to pitch in with everything – that means finding food, water, defending, all of it." I looked at Rachel. "I take it you're good with the bat. Do you shoot?"

She reached behind her and pulled out a Smith & Wesson .38 revolver from somewhere. "Crack shot," she said. "Can't say I was a year ago, but I damn sure am now."

"We've been doin' everything you said since this began," said Weston. "Rachel here likes the bat-to-head combat and yeah, she's good with that revolver, but she can also use a rifle like Lucas McCain."

"Who's Lucas McCain?" asked Nelson.

"The Rifleman," said Weston. "Chuck Connor. Only Rachel's prettier."

"I'm Air Force," said Rachel. "Or I was, when there was still that free country you were talking about. There's a base nearby where we've been stocking up on MREs. Meals Ready to Eat."

"I might not know who Lucas McCain is," I said, "But I do know what MRE stands for."

"No offense," said Rachel. "Anyway, Don and I have been to the base quite a few times since this shitstorm started. They may sound crappy, but they're good to eat on the road, they have all the necessary vitamins and they keep for a century."

"I have a question," said Don.

"What?" asked Serena.

"I know what it is," said Nelson. "You want to know how we walked right through that crowd of stinkers."

Weston pointed at Nelson. "There's more under that blonde hair than I thought."

"Tons more," said Nelson. "It's WAT-5. Also known as Walk Among Them, five-hour. Invented and perfected by one Hemphill Chatsworth."

"He still alive?" asked Rachel.

"He's about to be a new papa," said Serena with a smile. "Charlie looked about to pop."

"Baby could kick like it was doing Subdudo in there," said Nelson, his eyes twinkling.

"Okay," said Weston. "So how do we convince you to share this stuff with us?"

"It's a matter of need," I said. "If we pull back those curtains and there are fifty more, we dose you guys."

Nelson went to the curtain. "Drum roll, dudes," he said, a big smile on his face.

Rachel actually made the sound with her mouth, and we all smiled. She was having trouble keeping it up, because she was trying to fight off a smile, too.

Nelson ripped the curtain back. Two more rotters stood among the bodies in the lot, but they would be easily handled in conventional ways.

Rachel went to the door and peered through the peephole. As she reached for the knob, Nelson let go of the curtain and ran to her side. "Hey, one for me, one for you. Let's show each other what we got."

Rachel raised her eyebrows, smiled, and pulled the door open. "Which one do you want?" she asked.

Nelson reached into his pocket and pulled out a 3" diameter star. The teeth alone were over 2".

"I'll take the woman. She's about what, thirty feet away?"

"About."

"Thirty two, to be exact," said Nelson. "I'd prove it if you had a tape measure." He took two quick steps, drawing his arm back. With his left arm extended for balance, he whipped his right hand forward like a major league pitcher. The brass rang through the air like the constant peal of a bell and sank into the side of the thing's skull, just above its left ear.

It stopped mid step and fell over sideways.

"Shit!" said Weston.

Rachel shook her head and stepped forward to pat Nelson on the back. "Now me."

Her target was initially about sixty feet away, but had closed the distance, smelling its meal. This was a teenager, for he wore a *Gary Hoey: Guitar God* tee-shirt.

139

She pulled back the hammer of the Smith & Wesson raised it and fired the moment it stopped rising.

A fine spray, accompanied by larger chunks of hairy skull, flew behind it, and its heels left the ground as the emaciated flesh eater landed flat on its back.

I hadn't even seen her aim. Gun up, fire, dead.

"Okay then," I said. "Invitation extended."

"Rachel," said Nelson. "You can ride on the back of my bike until we find you something for you to drive, if that's cool."

Rachel looked grateful, but in seconds, her expression turned to worry. In another second, her eyes filled with tears. She looked at Don Weston and it was clear he did not need an explanation.

"Come here," he said, his arms open.

She tucked the gun away and stepped into his arms, which he folded around her. She returned his hug like a daughter hugs her wise father. Serena walked up behind her and put a soft hand on her shoulder.

"She just made her decision," whispered Weston.

"Yeah," said Nelson. "To come with us, right?" His face was awash with confusion.

"Yes, but that's not it," said Weston. He pushed her back by the shoulders and said, "Look at me, darlin'."

She did.

Don Weston nodded, and she nodded back, letting go of him and wiping at her eyes.

Weston took a deep breath and let it out slowly. "She's givin' up her search for her husband, Jess."

"Oh, my God, Rachel," said Serena. "I'm so sorry."

Rachel shook her head. "I've been clinging to hope since I got back home, and I've made Don go with me back to the ranch every month or so, just to see if Jess is home. He never is. So at this point, I guess I'm ready."

"This is really heavy, dudes," said Nelson. "I'm really sad right now."

"Don't be," said Rachel, forcing a smile in his direction. "This needed to happen. Life goes on, and I suppose mine should, too."

There was a sudden thunder crack outside, and Nelson nodded at Rachel and went to the window. "Wow," he said. "Where did that come from?"

"Since we're on bikes, it pretty much came from Fuckoffville," I said. "Damn it."

"How far is the ranch, Rachel?" asked Serena.

"Why?" she asked.

"Because it's about to pour from the looks of it, and you need to check for Jess one more time before you leave. Right?"

Rachel's eyes brightened. "The base is on the way. Both are within five miles, and the roads are usually clean except for a few stragglers here and there."

"Then we go," I said.

"Rachel," said Weston, "what say we let Duster and Snowball go over by the ranch? Some good woods and pastures over that way. As long as they got lots of room to graze and run, these dead fuckers won't ever catch 'em."

"Perfect, Don," she said. "Nelson, until I get a bike of my own, I'll take you up on your offer."

Nelson's face turned beet red. It was then that I realized he never, not in a million years, thought she would get on the back of his bike.

His smile stayed with him. He couldn't take his eyes off her. I did not believe she had a clue she'd just made his day. Scratch that. His *year*. Nelson practically skipped among the bloody muck in the parking lot to retrieve his Ninja star from the dead zombie's skull.

*****

Chapter Seven

The rain started, and to our relief, the main storm clouds were still miles to the south of us. The sprinkles wet us and our gear, but the rain was not so heavy as to be blinding.

We took it easy on the bikes and let the horses and their riders follow us. We figured they didn't need rumbling engines behind them and the walking dead in front.

Rachel was right about stragglers. Serena took out two rotters along the way, and Nelson stuck with his urushiol canister to take out about three more of them. On a personal note, I only had to deal with one who almost got hold of my left handlebar, and I was happy to see Rachel's batting skills displayed for the first time as Nelson intentionally left two for her to take out.

I made sure I had a clear path and slowed down, looking behind me.

With no hands on the reins and Snowball in a full gallop, she spun that bat in her right hand like a mallet and shattered the top of a naked digger's skull.

In one fluid motion, she flipped that bat in mid-air over to her left hand. Her right hand snatched the reins and with a quick snap, she had Snowball jog sharply to the right. This left her plenty of room to bring the bat crashing directly down on the skull of a former woman in a tattered, bloody nightgown. The hardwood club drove clear through its skull, then through its face, finally stopping at the clavicle before Rachel relaxed her arm and dragged it out behind the now dead monster, that collapsed like a jellyfish.

Rachel reached down to a large towel connected to the saddle, and wiped the muck from her weapon before again tucking it in beside her.

"Woo hoo!" shouted Nelson, who wasn't sure enough on the bike to catch the entire show, but who saw enough to make him happy.

Weston seemed pleased just to let everyone else do the work. I couldn't blame him. We got to the naval base in another mile. We slowed and let Weston and Rachel take the lead. Most of the uniformed bodies scattered around were long dead, and just like everywhere else where there wasn't a red-eyed, pregnant female, there were only scattered, shambling walkers. High concentrations of the creatures meant either the red-eyed females were consolidating their troops or there was a major food source nearby.

We got to the building where we assumed the MREs were kept, because Rachel and Weston dismounted.

We pulled a short distance away and cut our motors.

We approached the metal building, and Rachel withdrew a small key ring that held only two keys. She chose the smaller one and inserted it into a padlock on the door.

"You lock it, huh?"

"I did up until now," she said. "When we leave, I guess we'll let anyone in. It's kind of been our food source. All kinds of jerky and other canned stuff too, but like I said, the MREs are compact and easy to handle."

"There are canvas bags over there on a hook," said Weston. "All told, we should be able to carry plenty enough to get us to California."

We shopped until we dropped. Nelson wanted popcorn. There wasn't any. Not in an MRE. Needless to say, the kid wanted to Subdudo somebody. I didn't need the laughter or the embarrassment, so I'm glad it wasn't me.

After we finished stocking up on what I felt would be enough to get us through the rest of our journey, I said, "Fuel, Rachel? We've got a good siphon setup."

"Good," she said. "You got extra cans, too?"

"Yeah, in the trailer," I said.

"Right around the corner," she said.

We had the bikes and cans filled in another twenty minutes and tucked everything away. We were ready to roll. Unfortunately it was now 10:30. We'd really pissed away the day, but it was time well spent.

"Okay," I said. "Let's get these horses where you want them and get going."

Serena nudged me, and I remembered immediately. It wasn't just the horses we were taking care of. We were allowing Rachel one more time at home to see if the love of her life had returned. I instantly thought of Leona. Then I thought of Serena. I'd die before I'd walk away from Serena, and I'd do anything to protect her.

It was a short ride to the ranches. Don's was a good distance away from Rachel and Jess's. When you live in Florida, it's sometimes hard to put an image to a story. Needing to ride an ATV from one house to another in Florida just means you're lazy. Here it means you don't have an hour to waste walking there.

Since Rachel took her Slugger and her Smith & Wesson inside the house with her, we stayed outside and let her take her time. After fifteen minutes passed and she didn't come out, I held up a hand to the others and went inside.

I walked up to her. She was sitting at the kitchen table, staring out the dirt-covered window. In front of her was a note, written in her near-perfect handwriting:

Jess,

I'm okay. I'm telling you that right up front, because all I've done is worry about you. It's almost September of 2013 now, and Don Weston and I have met some others. We're going to California. Dunsmuir, I think it's called. I waited as long as I could, Jess. I miss you so much it hurts, but it's been a year, I guess. Not sure. But this place was our home, and it will be my point to come back to, Jess. If I don't stay in California, then I'm coming back here before I go anywhere else. So if you come home – God, please come home safe – I'll either be in Dunsmuir, or I'll come back here and leave a new note for you. Please don't give up on me. I'm alive. I'm okay physically, but my heart is a mess because you're not with me. I'm thankful that I'm not one of those things and I'm not sick. But Jess, all I'll ever be is just okay without you, so please be alive. I love you. If you come back within thirty days of me writing this, come for me. Come to Dunsmuir, because Dave, Serena and Nelson said it's a small town, and if it's worth staying there, it should be easy to find us.

I can't end this note. If I do, I'm so afraid these are the last words I'll ever say to you. So no goodbyes.

I love you, Jess. Either wait for me or come for me.

Rachel.

I couldn't help reading her note. Her grief, just as mine and Serena's and everyone else's was part of our history, and it helped all of us to know one another, and even more, to care. So as private as it was, I knew the pain in Rachel's heart, as well as the hope to which she still clung.

"We have to go, Rachel," I said, touching her on the shoulder.

She jumped a little, and her tears came. She struggled to her feet and I pulled her to me and hugged her. Her muscles were stiff and tense at first, and as her sobs grew in intensity, her muscles relaxed, and soon I felt her almost collapse in my arms. I supported her slight weight and held her until she was cried out.

When she finally finished, she slowly let go of me and wiped at her eyes. She reached into her pocket and pulled out a rubber band, and pulled back her hair.

Two more swipes at her eyes, and she looked at me. "How do I look?"

"It's that awkward moment when I'm about to lie to you and you know it, but you look good."

She patted my arm and managed a smile. "Thank you, Dave. I've been holding that in for a long time."

"We're not Jess," I said. "But we can be good friends."

She nodded, wiped at her eyes once more, and headed for the door, me behind her.

Neither of us knew at that moment that Rachel would never return to her ranch again.

*****

"Over by them trees there," said Weston, holding his hat in his hand, pointing with it. "It's about a half mile away."

"It's a nice pasture," said Rachel. "They'll have plenty to eat, and they can use the trees for shade. There's a lake over there, too. It's about the best we can do for them."

"Nervous, honey?" asked Weston.

"Yeah," said Rachel. "And excited, too. If Jess comes back, he'll know where I've gone. No reason to stay."

I wondered if I had made it clear, so I thought I'd reiterate something just in case.

"I want you to remember that we're not necessarily staying in Dunsmuir," I said. "I'm playing some of this by ear, but if it's just as big a mess there, and there's no benefit to it, I'm going to do my best to get my uncle to come back with me, and we're going back home – to our family."

"We got a good family," said Nelson. "My Gramps is there. He's a doctor."

"Looks to me that you have a good family right here," said Weston. "Serena, where you from? You Cuban or something?"

"Spanish," she said. "My parents were first generation immigrants from Spain. They lived very near Gibraltar, in a village called San Roque."

"Why'd they come here?" asked Rachel. "Isn't Spain beautiful?"

"It is," said Serena. "My parents took me back several times to visit relatives, but they came here for the same reasons so many others do. Opportunity."

"Let's do this," I said. "We're burning daylight."

They took off, and we fired our engines and rode along behind them. When we got to the top of the hill, I realized they were right. It was beautiful up there. The pastures, despite the hot weather, flourished, and the lake had plenty of water. There were trees on three sides, and plenty of room to run.

They dismounted, and we all took off our helmets and watched. Rachel and Don unstrapped the saddles and slid them off, then pulled the blankets off of the horses. Next came the bridles. Before long, the horses stood there as God had intended them to.

Rachel went around and took Snowball by the face, nuzzling her nose for a moment, before putting her cheek against the side of the horse's head. She whispered something – I guessed a thank you – and walked away. Snowball followed.

Weston was less sentimental. He patted Duster twice on the rump, and with a "Hah!" he slapped the stallion hard, and the big, red horse took off in a gallop.

With that, Snowball followed, and they watched the horses make their way toward the taller grass.

"Who am I ridin' with?" asked Weston.

"You're on with me, Don," I said. "We'll find you two something soon."

"I've been outside a while," he said. "Kinda ready for a car if you don't think that would be too big a drag on your convoy."

"Depends on the car," I said. "It gets tight out there sometimes. Is there a dealership row around here?"

"Yeah," said Don. "There definitely is. I can get us there, and it's about ten miles in the right direction. Toward Nashville."

"Nashville about three hours from here?" I asked. "It's what we calculated."

"If everything's clear," he said. "But we don't expect that, do we?"

"Never. Hop on," I said, and he did. "I don't have a helmet for you now. I'll be careful."

"If I bust both my legs, just be sure to put a bullet in my head before you leave me," he said, and I don't think he was joking. There was no humor in his voice.

Nelson had given his helmet over to Rachel, who had her arms wrapped around his waist. I immediately hoped he would be able to focus on the road, because while he could really do some things well, I suspected that being close to women wasn't necessarily among them.

Serena must have sensed it, too. "Sure you don't want her to ride with me, Nel?" she asked.

"I'm good, dude," he said. "Didn't even smoke any weed today. I'm gonna be extra careful with this cargo."

"So I'm cargo?" asked Rachel, smiling.

"It's an expression," said Nelson, serious. "Ready?"

"I am," she said. "Surprisingly, I really am."

Don called the directions into my ear, and we worked our way back to the main highway and on toward Nashville.

After we were on the road for a couple of miles, Serena spoke in my headset. "David, did Donald say they wanted a car?"

"Yeah," I answered. "Not sure about that, though. Some of these roads are pretty congested."

"Maybe a smart car or something," she said. "Tiny. Good on gas."

"That would work," I said. "Or a Cooper. They might be more reliable. Not sure about the Smart Cars. They might be stupid."

"They might be," she said, and I heard the smile in her voice. I loved that I could hear that.

We rode in silence. Don did not put his arms around my waist, and for that I was glad. I glanced at Nelson occasionally, and without his helmet, his hair was ponytailed and twisted into a little bun so as not to whip into Rachel's face.

From my angle, Nelson looked like a skinny, little old lady with his pointy nose and bone-thin face. But he was smiling. Let me just assure you of that. I'd never seen him having so much fun, and I was sorry that Rachel and Don would ultimately end up in a car.

As we moved into downtown proper, I was beginning to get a bit uncomfortable. There were abandoned cars that we could easily get around, but the streets were empty.

Dead empty.

"Don, what are these buildings?" I asked as we came to a spot where we had to stop and figure out a detour.

"Hospitals, mostly," he said.

I looked at him. "So then, where is everyone?" I asked him. "This is a big city. Where the hell are all the dead ones? And the survivors?"

"Beats me," said Weston. "I didn't know what to expect. We pretty much stuck to rural areas outside of town, killed off a few stragglers at the AFB, and any we saw on our property when we went back."

"David," said Serena, her voice thick with tension.

"Wha – " I began, but the word caught in my throat as I followed her gaze. If I would have screamed like a six-year-old girl at what I saw, I don't think anyone would have blamed me. The deserted roadway I had looked at just seconds before was in the process of being filled from both sides of the street with the walking dead.

"Jesus. Did we reload the Uzis?" I asked.

"I took care of it," said Nelson.

As I watched the shambling, undead creatures moving into the street from between the buildings, my heart sunk.

We had never before faced so many at once that I could remember – perhaps not even in Concord – and worse yet, there was a method to their madness. This could mean only one thing.

Zombies didn't have methods. They were now stationed there, an army of them. A solid wall of the standing dead, numbering in the hundreds. Quiet as a graveyard.

I felt a presence to our right and slowly turned my head.

And there she was: A perfectly preserved, naked creature with eyes that glowed as red as those of the devil himself. She was no more than fifteen feet away and appeared to be staring directly at me, but could have been watching all of us.

"David, we need to back out of this mess," said Serena.

I didn't want to take my eyes from the creature. "I know." Our bikes were facing the wrong direction to use the machine guns, and I had the distinct feeling that by the time we changed position it would be too late.

"What's happening?" asked Rachel. "Where did they all come from?"

Weston was quiet. I swore he was holding his breath behind me.

"Nelson, I want you to very slowly turn your wheel hard right. You've got room. Use your gas a little and balance with your feet, but when you get turned around, you need to go like a motherfucker."

Nelson didn't ask any questions. He started to do what I said, but when I looked behind me, I realized that would not work, either.

"Wait, Nel," I said.

Behind us were five more red-eyed females, almost arms length apart, walking toward us. They were still forty feet away.

When she saw me watching them, one crouched low, preparing to spring. We'd seen their speed and ability before, but now, as we looked back at them, we heard the motion of hundreds of dead, yet animated legs, dragging, stepping, and shambling toward us.

Nelson apparently saw the female crouching, too, and he had heard the stories from the prison in Concord.

Straddling his bike, he shook out his right arm and reached into a pocket. He withdrew one of his stars, and without thinking and barely aiming, he drew his arm back and flung it at the crouching red-eye just as she began her launch, or whatever it was. I saw him adjust mid-throw, and with a ringing-buzz, it flew toward her at speed, hitting the dead, pregnant fiend in the center of her forehead.

She stopped mid-motion and her hand went up to the star immediately, pulling it back out. Black ooze ran down her face and her gaze found Nelson Moore.

As her red eyes stared toward him I held my breath, but a split-second later, her intense, red eyes faded to black, and she crumpled to the street.

I almost shit my pants. I had, for a brief moment, believed they had become invincible.

With the cars blocking the road and the solid wall of walking dead ahead of us, we didn't stand a chance. Even if we exhausted all the rounds in the machine guns, we'd just die a little bit later. I had to make a quick decision – something I wasn't fond of. I liked time to consider options, but it seemed most of them had flown out the window. So I acted on instinct.

"Follow me!" I shouted. I gunned the engine of the Harley and let out the clutch, spinning my rear tire and sliding around toward the building.

"Hold on, Don!" I shouted. "And tuck your head down against my back and close your eyes!"

I rode toward the glass doors of what I assumed was a hospital. As I got to the curb I gunned it and pulled hard up on the handlebars, lifting my front wheel in the air in a low wheelie. With my left hand, I grabbed the Uzi and fired at the glass front, panning the machine gun as low and high as it would go.

I prayed the others would be able to maneuver behind me and keep up. I knew Serena could, but Nelson wasn't as experienced, and poor Rachel probably had no idea what to expect.

I rode across the threshold into the building, bounced three times over the debris and slid the bike sideways, slamming into the opposite wall. The foot pegs had protected my right leg from being crushed beneath the motorcycle, and I felt Weston bailing off just before impact. He landed on his tailbone on top of the small trailer, which was now flipping sideways as the bike went down. Weston rolled off and skidded along the marble floor, coming to rest about six feet behind the bike. He jumped to his feet immediately and reached for his gun, a large caliber pistol.

Serena came through next, and as soon as she rode over the debris, she braked hard, turning sharply left, then gunned the accelerator. She shot free of the debris, pulled her bike to an easy stop and hopped off, letting it fall to the marble floor. I crawled out from under my twisted bike, disgusted that Hemp's innovative work on it was now trashed. I saw everything had spilled out of the trailer, including the gas cans, some of which had had popped open and were now the source of the odiferous, flammable fuel that poured onto the floor around us.

Nelson brought up the rear, and I saw immediately that Rachel had doubled her grip on his waist. His front tire punctured and popped the moment he hit the glass, throwing his handlebars sideways, the bike going down hard.

It landed atop my fallen trailer, preventing the heavy machine from landing flat and crushing their legs beneath it. I ran over to help Nelson to his feet, seeing that Weston had already recovered and had begun helping Rachel. We pulled them and they staggered after us, both apparently without serious injury or broken bones.

I looked outside, and the five females were on the move, along with their shuffling horde. They had closed in fast, and now threatened to block any way out.

"Run!" I shouted.

"Wait!" said Serena. "There has to be a back way out of here. You figure a path. I want to let some of them get in, at least a few feet."

"Nelson," I said. "Run up and see if that fire exit door is unlocked."

Nelson nodded and said to Rachel, "Come with me!"

She did. Weston also followed. Nelson ran thirty yards down the hallway and pulled open the door.

I kept one eye on the walking rotters pushing closer to the door of the hospital, and one on Nelson, Rachel and Weston. As Nelson held the door open, watching us, something came out of that door.

"Nelson!" shouted Rachel, and whipped her six-shooter from her pants, raised it and fired in a quick motion.

The hands that had curled around Nelson's neck fell away and the body lay on the floor in front of the door. Rachel yanked Nelson away from the opening, the door automatically swinging closed, hitting the zombie on the floor.

"What are you waiting for, Serena?" I asked, frantic. "Let's just go!"

"Grab the ammo box and the urushiol canisters at least, David. Hurry!"

She was right. I was in panic mode; not thinking properly. We were screwed right now, and we'd need our weapons and ammo to put in them. I dove to the floor and pulled out a half-empty can of fuel, throwing it toward the shattered door. The ammo box was on the bottom, and my fingers curled around the handle. I pulled it out and slid it away from me across the floor. Then I reached in and grabbed all four of the canisters.

"Nelson!" I shouted, and he ran back toward me, holding out his hands. I tossed them to him one by one and he caught each of my wild throws, quickly placing the last caught canister on the ground, emptying his hands for the next.

The WAT-5! I had less than half my supply in a baggie in my pocket, but the majority had been in the bike seat compartment, which had popped open.

I searched frantically, and saw it. The baggie had dissolved and the scattered wafers were in the process of melting into mush on the marble floor, soaked in gasoline. I stared at them for a brief moment, then at our pursuers moving toward us. I could do nothing ... they were destroyed.

I then scooted clear of the fuel, grabbed the ammo box and stood, taking Serena's arm, pulling her away.

She yanked her arm from my hand and said, "Not yet, David. Your pants are soaked with gasoline. Get over there with the others, for God's sake!"

"Serena," I said, but she was pulling a Bic lighter out of her pocket. "Go, David! I'll be a second!" Her face was stern and set.

"Serena, will you listen to me?"

"David," she said, glancing from me to the advancing horde. "I'm certain there are other exits from this building, so I intend to put this gas to good use. *Please* go over there and wait for me."

I put my hand up and carried the ammo box toward the stairwell door. The four of us stood in silence and watched her. I thought my heart was going to jump out of my throat if I opened my mouth again.

Serena stood there and waited, but the females she wanted did not come inside. No doubt using their strangely powerful minds, they sent their minions inside, dozens of them flooding in toward their certain deaths, driven there by the smartest of their kind.

"Serena, they're too aware!" I yelled. "They know you're up to something, so just do what you can and get over here!"

She looked frustrated. "Fine. Just stay where you are."

She ran and pulled another of the leaking cans out. With one eye still on the advancing zombies, and one on her work, Serena removed the cap completely and threw the open gasoline can toward the door, splashing the legs of several of the rotters.

Dozens of them were now inside. Six feet from Serena. She moved slowly backward, watching the floor. She had gasoline on her feet, and I was freaking out that she would go up in flames herself.

She stood clear now and put her thumb in her mouth. After a moment, she peeled her thumb away, then took something from her teeth. She struck the Bic, lighting it, stepping backward at the same time. Whatever it was in her fingers, she worked at jamming it into the lighter. She held the flame up in front of her for a moment, took one more look at the zombies, now just three feet away, and tossed the lighter at their feet.

Flames ignited in a fifteen-foot high plume as she retreated toward us, and sure enough, the soles of her shoes were flaming as Serena reached the door where we waited.

"Jesus!" I shouted, and Weston thought fast. He ripped the shirt off his back in a split second and dove to the floor, snuffing out Serena's burning shoes.

The zombies moved through the flames, and burning brightly, advanced toward us.

"C'mon dudes!" shouted Nelson, and yanked open the fire escape door. "Mind the zombie!"

Mind the zombie?

156

At first I wasn't sure he'd said it, but if Nelson was proving to be anything more than an amusing stoner, it was that he was more astute than we'd ever given him credit for.

We all stepped over the dead creature, and being the last one in, I put the ammo box down, bent down and spun the dead thing's legs free of the door, and yanked it closed behind us.

We ran up the fire escape. I knew we needed to find a secure place to ingest some WAT-5. Beyond that, I didn't have much of a plan. I found myself asking:

What would Flex do?

*****

"Hold on!" I said, and we all stopped, breathing hard. "I've got a mix of ammo in here, but mostly 9mm. There are some .45 rounds, too, and I think a box or two of .38. If you've got a gun, load it up. If you've got extra mags, load them up, too."

The fire must have caught quickly outside the stairwell, because I could hear a deep roar. In my mind it grew hotter, and sweat poured from my face and arms. It might have been my imagination.

Within less than a minute I slammed the lid of the ammo box closed again and grabbed it. We took the steps two at a time.

One, two flights.

There was a click down below us, and I stopped, as did everyone else. I went slowly to the edge of the stairs and peered over.

Red eyes peered back at me. The rotter's clothes were half burned gone, and her hair was singed completely away, but her eyes were unaffected; they were bright red and if the thing could have smiled and patted her decomposing baby bump, I believe she would have.

Behind her came more and more of the half-burned dead walkers, flooding into the stairwell and mounting the steps after us.

"Run!" I shouted, and pulled out my Walther. I held my shaking hand over the rail and fired once, missing. The ricochet sounded more frightening than the echo of the shot, and I was sure it would bounce from a block wall into my own skull. Rather than fire again, I charged up the steps with Serena, Nelson, Weston and Rachel Reed.

We reached another landing. "Keep going?" asked Nelson. "Or try this floor?"

"Do they have exterior fire escapes on these buildings?" asked Weston.

"How the hell do we know?" asked Serena. "We're not from around here."

The noise from below grew louder – the sound of shuffling feet behind us, and to all of us that was the sound of death.

"What about that WAT-5 shit?" asked Don Weston. "Can't we take that?"

"We're already on it," said Serena. "It won't work against them – not with the pregnant females around. Don, what kind of hospital is this, anyway?"

"It's a pretty popular women's hospital," he said. "Good trauma center and the busiest maternity ward in Knoxville. My boy was born here."

I didn't ask what had happened to his son, but what he had just said couldn't be worse news.

"That's fucked, Don!" I said. "I think when we filled you in we mentioned the pregnant female factor, right?"

"I didn't tie it together," he said. "Sorry. I don't listen too well sometimes. So my wife always told me."

"Let's go up," said Rachel. "If there's a trauma center, I'm hoping there's a surprise on the roof for us."

"Like what?" I asked. Then I knew. "You fly helicopters?"

"It's what I did in the Air Force. Trained for it anyway. Ended up mostly admin, but I was a hell of a pilot."

"Then the roof it is," I said. "Everyone cross your fingers, but only if it doesn't slow you down."

We ran. There were eight stories all together, and when we reached the door marked roof, Weston got there first and pushed the mechanical bar.

It opened outward, and almost immediately, a rot-faced man in a button down short sleeved shirt smacked square into Don, who was still without a shirt. The older man straight-armed the zombie in the face, and the creature went flat on its back.

"Move!" shouted Rachel, and ducked low between Nelson and me. She pulled out the revolver and fired almost at the same time, capping the former Medevac pilot in-between the eyes.

I looked up and saw a pristine medical evacuation helicopter sitting squarely on the pad in the center of the massive roof.

"Nelson, pull that door closed, and hurry!" I shouted, and he did.

Weston held his right hand with his left, and I went to him immediately and took him by the wrist, pulling it toward me. "Shit," I said. "Don."

Serena looked at the situation and said, "This is a big roof." She pulled out her PPK. "I'm going to walk the perimeter and make sure we're alone up here now," she said.

"Be careful," I said, looking at Don's hand and knowing what I was seeing was horrible news. A tooth was embedded in the heel of his palm, and blood ran from the wound.

"I was just tryin' to push the big bastard away from me," Weston said. "Musta caught him in the mouth."

"You gotta aim low, man," I said. Then: "Nelson, I hate to keep bossing you around, brother, but bring me urushiol. I need the one you've been using and a full canister."

"Not a problem, dude," he said, already going for the requested items as he answered. "It's why I came. I want to be a help."

The canister Nelson had been using was in his backpack, which had been on his back, therefore was not left behind with the bikes. He set his pack down and unzipped it, and quickly yanked out the cylinder. "Okay, what do you want me to do?"

"We need pure urushiol for Don's hand, Nel," I said. "Unscrew the lid on that one slowly – let the pressure out."

"Gotcha, dude," he said.

I did the same with a full bottle. "Okay, Nel. Give me yours."

Nelson handed it over and I slowly poured the contents of the full bottle into the three-quarter empty bottle. This was a blend of oil and water, so it needed a good shaking to thoroughly mix. There was a chance I could get enough pure oil out to kill any infection the rotter's tooth may have introduced into Weston's bloodstream.

As I had hoped, the water drained into the other canister, leaving almost pure oil behind.

He held his hand out to me, and the tooth was still stuck there. "Crap," I said. "Don, can you get the tooth out?"

"I might look tough, but if I touch that mother-piece-of-shit, I'll pass out, I swear."

Rachel started running toward the chopper and shouted, "We should find what we need in there! Hold on."

She climbed inside and I saw two cushions fly out of the back. Then she was out and running, a small, white box in her hands. From the red cross on the outside of the container, I could see it was a small, portable first aid kit.

She dropped down beside us, unsnapped the latches and flipped the lid. There were tweezers in a sterile package, and she tore it open with her teeth and reached up to take Weston's hand.

"Grit your teeth, Don," she said. He did. She unceremoniously jammed one side of the tweezers under the canine, and clamped it down. She twisted it once, blood squirted out from the side, and she yanked it out.

A shot rang out and I jumped up, searching the roof for Serena. She appeared from around the air conditioning equipment. "I'm okay! We're good now. Just one."

She came over and watched as Don's blood poured from the newly released bite wound.

"Get some of that gauze, please Rachel," I said. Jesus, I was no damned doctor, but I actually felt like I knew what I was doing, I'd seen Hemp in action so many times.

I realized as she gave me the gauze and I pressed it against the wound, that my heartbeat had settled down from the run up the stairwell. Any other time in my life I could only imagine this kind of crap accelerating it, but *Dave Gammon was actually handling this shit right now.*

I'd think about that later, because for now I had to focus. I applied pressure to the wound for five hard seconds, then said, "Clean gauze, Rachel."

She gave it to me, and I pressed it to his hand. Then I positioned his injury right over the top of the urushiol canister's mouth and pressed it down, upending the bottle.

"Shit! That burns like a motherfucker!" shouted Weston.

"Good!" I said. "If it hurts, it's working."

"That's wives tale bullshit, and you know it," said Weston.

"Yeah, but somebody somewhere said no pain no gain, and there had to be a reason."

"My ass," he said.

"Hang in there, Don," I said. "We'll wrap it in a minute."

Serena had gotten a bottle of drinking water out of Nelson's backpack, and tipped it to Weston's lips. He drank as fast as he could swallow.

"Hold that on there until it doesn't hurt anymore."

"I'm going to inspect that bird," said Rachel. "Nelson, would you help me get the body out of the copilot's seat?"

Nelson hesitated for a brief second. "What?"

"C'mon," she said. "It's mostly bones now."

Nelson looked at me, and I did pity him. Talk about putting away your childish things. Nelson was going to mature like no tomorrow during this journey – I just had a feeling.

I thought I should help. "Serena, will you hold this bottle here? Just keep it inverted. Another couple of minutes and you can wrap it up."

"I got it. Go help them," she said.

We jogged to the chopper and saw that a skeleton rotted in the passenger seat, dried chunks of the meat that could not be gnawed from the copilot's bones, clinging to them in dark, dried knots.

Rachel reached inside and pulled out a box of nitrile gloves. "Here. Snap these on."

We did. It made pulling the human remains out as horrid as hell, but not nearly as horrid as it would have been had we been required to get it on our hands. Pieces of his pants were matted to the seat cover, so in the end, we just snapped our gloves inside out and spread them over the seat.

"Hope the battery's still got juice," said Rachel.

"Is there a key for these things?" asked Nelson.

"It's right there," she said. "They must have been taking off, because the back's empty. No patient."

"So full tank?"

Rachel went around, opened the door and hopped into the pilot's seat. She was so small that she looked like a 12-year old sitting there. She turned her freckled nose toward us. "Say a little prayer for me," she said, turning the key.

The control panel lit up and the gauges bounced once, then settled. Except for the fuel gauge. It settled at 4/4.

"Bastard's full," said Rachel. "Glory, glory."

"I like the way you talk," said Nelson.

"Why thank you, Nel."

He just nodded and smiled. "Will this carry all of us?"

"We should dump some of this equipment, but yes, easily. Not sure of the range, but the lighter the better."

"I can't believe it," I said. "We lost all our food, but if you can fly this, it's not going to be a hard trek to California. We won't need near as much, right? We can take this all the way there?"

"I don't see why not," she said. "But remember. We haven't actually started it yet. There's battery, but whether it's enough is anyone's guess."

"Should I pray first?" I asked.

"Is that something you ordinarily do?"

I shook my head. "No."

"Then I will," she said. "I practice multiple times a day. With Jess gone, I've gotten pretty good at it."

Nelson looked confused. "But how good?" he asked. "Jess isn't back, so why do you think God's listening?"

Rachel smiled. "I don't know what's happened to Jess, Nel. It could be that God doesn't want me to know. I accept that."

"That makes sense," said Nelson. "So what are you waiting for?"

"I'm gonna have to close my eyes for this prayer," said Rachel. "Ya'll go get Don and Serena."

*****

We helped Don to the chopper and sat him in the co-pilot's seat beside Rachel and the three of us worked on removing excess weight, pre-approved by our pilot of course. That included a rescue basket that could be snap-clipped to a hoist cable. There was no easy way to dump the hoist and cable though, so that would stay.

Rachel seemed to know what wasn't essential, but made some good suggestions as to some items we might want to keep in the event the landing did not go as smoothly as we hoped. Oxygen tanks and other medical apparatus, for example.

"That's good enough," she said. "It'll carry up to nine passengers – we're only doing what we're doing so we squeeze better mileage out of it. You guys put on those headsets right there so we can talk."

"How are the prayers going, Rach?" asked Nelson, reaching for his headset and putting it on.

"We'll see in a sec," said Rachel. "You guys strapped in?"

"Please start," whispered Serena. "Please, please start."

I patted her knee and she smiled at me. I could see in her stressed, brown eyes that she was nervous as hell. I didn't blame her for a second, but we had been through some pretty tough spots together and she always pulled through.

"We're ready back here, Rachel," I said. "Fire it up."

"From your lips to God's ears," she said. Rachel hit a switch and the rotor on top of the helicopter began to turn. A sonic noise accompanied it as though a jet engine powered it. I had no idea how one of these things worked; I was only relieved that Rachel seemed to.

I don't know why, but my eyes went to the small tower in the center of the building, and at the moment I focused on it, the door burst open and rotters began to flood onto the roof. Nobody else had noticed, because none of them had reacted yet.

"Rachel," I said, keeping my voice calm. "We're now officially in a hurry," I said. "They're here."

She looked. "Shit," she said. She held a check list and was going through it as all good pilots did I assumed, but she would have to settle for mediocre pilot and get us the hell out of there.

"You set them on fire, you go up stairs … is there anything these jerks can't get past?" said Nelson.

"With the pregnant females guiding them," I said, "They push through their pain I guess."

I knew it to be true, but it was illustrated for us again as the main group of diggers and rotters flooded through the door. Alone, they wandered around with little focus. In terrified amazement, we even watched two of them approach the edge of the building and topple over the low wall, falling to what must have been their final deaths.

But next, what I'd come to think of as the job foremen showed up, as politically incorrect as that term might be for the two, half-burned and pregnant females who stepped onto the roof from the stairwell. I remembered their horrific faces from out in the street, but now, after the fire burned what clothing she had been wearing away, one of them was nude, her belly showing a pregnancy of seven months or more.

She moved toward the helicopter at quadruple the speed of the others, but as she bee-lined toward us, the rest of the reanimated corpses became a focused, surging river of bodies, flowing toward us with no stragglers and none with a seemingly different agenda.

"Is it ready to climb yet?" I asked. "Lift off, whatever these things do?"

"Not yet," said Rachel, her face intense and her teeth gritted. "And if too many of them … shit. Shit!"

They had now reached us and they surrounded the helicopter, clawing at the doors and pressing against every window. We could not see their feet, but knew that several of them must be standing on the skids of the bird.

"If too many of them hold on, we're screwed," said Rachel. "We can only carry so much weight."

"Now?" I asked. "Can we go now?"

"Not yet!" said Rachel. "We're still ramping up to full speed. We need another thirty seconds or so!"

"Alright, this is driving me nuts," said Weston, still holding his wrapped wound. "Get this son-of-a-mother off the ground, would ya, Rach?"

"I can't speed up the process, Don," she said.

Seconds later, a green light flicked on in front of Rachel. "Yes!" she cried. "That's it! Hold on, guys … here goes nothing."

She means here goes everything, I thought. *Fly or die.* I hated to be morbid, but I was pretty used to calling a spade a spade.

This is all shit I kept to myself, of course – the calling a spade a spade thing. I didn't need to freak everyone else out with my insecurities. All the same, I was pretty certain that my bloodless face and the fact that I was almost chewing a hole in my lip wouldn't have tipped anyone off that I wasn't the most confident man in the room.

The helicopter lifted from the roof, then dropped back down. The red-eyed female – one of them, anyway – had moved around to Rachel's door and I hoped to God it was locked. Red vapor began pouring out of her eyes and I feared it would somehow leak in and engulf Rachel, making her this creature's slave as another of her kind had so effectively done to my own little sister.

"Too much weight!" said Rachel. "We need to shake some of them off!"

I looked at the door, and suddenly, the other red-eyed female slammed into the side next to me. I involuntarily drew back and reached for my Walther.

"Don't fire through the glass!" shouted Serena.

I looked at her. "I have to do something, or we just … Jesus!"

I looked at the other side. It was just as packed. Serena was in the middle, between me and Nelson. I looked at the doors on each side. They both opened outward.

"Get ready, Nelson," I said. "Serena, give Nelson your PPK. Hurry."

Serena pulled it from her drop holster, chambered a round and put it in Nelson's hand, who looked at it as though confused.

"Okay," I said. "Nelson, you are going to have to fire the damned gun, because I don't think you can throw your stars fast enough. When I give the word, I want you to pull the handle and slam your shoulder into that door so hard you knock as many as you can off the skids. Then just point that gun right at the heads of the ones forward of the door and pull the trigger until you hear clicking."

"I'll try hard, dude. I promise," he said.

I patted his shoulder and turned back to the window, where the other red-eyed bitch stared at me. This one did not pump the vapor out – I suppose she had the basic awareness that I was male and not susceptible to its properties.

"Now!" I shouted, and we simultaneously pulled the door handles and shouldered them hard outward. On Nelson's side, five of the creatures fell away.

"Red eyes!" shouted Serena. "Nelson, shoot the one in front with the red eyes!"

I was focused on my side, where four of them, including the pregnant female, had toppled from the skids at the impact of my door. Apparently they could not read *our* minds yet, for she didn't anticipate what I intended to do.

As I heard Nelson firing on the opposite side, I leaned out and aimed my gun down where the pregnant one had dropped, but I only saw her feet as she skittered beneath the chopper. I returned my hand up and fired three times fast, blowing the brains out of another trio that had been perched on the helicopter skids.

"You got her!" shouted Serena, and I turned to see Nelson slam his door closed and look over at me, a nervous smile on his face.

"Close your door, Dave!" shouted Rachel, and I did. The chopper rose from the concrete, and this time it did not drop back down. We moved three feet, then four, then five feet above the roof.

"Unbelievable job, Nelson," I said, reaching out with my left hand to clasp his shoulder. "I'm proud of you, man."

"I'm proud of me!" he said, smiling even bigger than before.

Two more of the rotters still held to the front part of the helicopter, too far for Nelson and I to handle, but they fell away one by one as she climbed and the wind rocked their emaciated bodies.

Rachel then picked up speed, straightening the airframe out as she moved the joystick forward. I raised my arms in the air and laughed out loud.

Everyone else began to cheer.

Until a hand slapped the window next to my head and turned my laugh into a scream. As I watched, the door beside me opened a crack and fingers curled around the edge.

The wind pressed hard against it, preventing the door from opening further, but clinging to the door and standing on the treads was the estrogen-charged female whom I'd lost beneath the helicopter. I fell back against Serena as I reached for the Walther, but now she had somehow worked her way around to the edge of the door and one of her arms hooked around as she tried to pull herself inside.

"Hold on!" shouted Rachel, and she pushed the joystick hard right, turning the chopper almost sideways. The door flew open as my body, held only by the nylon restraints, hung over open sky. Below me the eyes of the female met mine as she clung with the dead fingers of both bony hands, struggling to hold on. Her feet dangled in air, but she did not kick them or move them at all. She simply stared at me with her crimson, knowing eyes, her gnashing teeth hungry for my flesh.

I pointed my gun at her face. Without taking her eyes from mine, she let go.

She just let go.

"She's gone!" I shouted, and before I knew it, the helicopter turned sharply left, and the door slammed closed again.

My heart could not have beat any faster. Not if I had just run a 10k obstacle course filled with the walking dead.

"Did you see that?" I asked Serena. "She chose her death."

"I'm not sure what I saw," said Serena. "Maybe she believed she could survive the fall."

"But not the bullet," said Nelson. "Weird."

I could not think about it too much. There were no answers. All I knew is that we were now in the air. Since this entire apocalypse had begun, none of us had ever been safer than we were at that very moment.

Completely out of reach of the hungry dead.

*****

Chapter Eight

"We're going a lot farther as the crow flies that taking the streets," said Rachel. "Not sure of her range, but we'll probably easily do over three hundred nautical miles on this tank."

"What's the difference between that and a regular mile?" asked Nelson.

"Nautical miles are essentially knots," said Rachel. "Based on degrees, the planet representing 360 of them. Divide a degree into 60 minutes, and a minute of arc over the planet Earth is one nautical mile."

"Never mind," said Nelson. He was not smiling. No biggie. I didn't get it, either, but I wasn't going to tell Nelson that. Or Serena, for that matter.

"When we get close on fuel," said Rachel, "I want to try to set her down somewhere we can refill her. The nice part is we can recon the area first to make sure it's relatively safe."

"Oh, glory," said Serena. "That will be a nice change."

"Got a goddamned headache," said Don.

I looked at Serena.

"What kind of headache?" asked Nelson.

Serena nudged him and he said, "I'm just asking, because in that First Aid kit there are aspirin that say they're for tension headache and others that say they're for arthritis and inflammation."

"Oh," I said. "So Don, which is it?"

"The worst kind," he said. "It's pounding."

I searched my memory. Had we told him about the migraine symptom preceding the conversion to flesh-eating zombie? Had he figured it out on his own, or perhaps once knew and had forgotten about it?

Either way, he didn't hesitate to share the information with us, and I was pretty sure it wasn't because he was subtly alerting us to his potential, future transformation.

I eased my Walther onto my lap and lay my hand over it.

Serena noticed.

*****

We had been flying for just over an hour and a half, and Rachel told us that we were flying at around 134 knots. Translated, this meant that we had gone well over 200 miles. Rachel had passed a chart back to me, and gave me a quick rundown on how to figure it out. Some of what she told me I remembered, and I tried to fake the rest.

"Rachel," I said. "It looks like we should make it into the southeast corner of Missouri before we have to put it down. How's it running?"

"Perfect," she said. "Not a glitch. But with the weight we dumped, and the fact that we're not carrying anywhere near a full load, we're good for at least that. I'm thinking we can go another hundred miles beyond that."

Rachel had located the package with the specifications on the helicopter, and the American version of the Eurocopter EC145 T2 would cruise at 134 knots, which equated to about 152 miles per hour.

172

Serena pored over the book at advised Rachel that she should be able to travel a distance of 356 nautical miles, which Rachel – to put in plain English for us – told us was just over 400 miles.

"Hey," said Serena. "Would a heliport have fuel or just landing pads?"

"Most heliports have landing pads, fuel, the works," said Rachel. "Why?"

"Because there's one in Jefferson City, Missouri. Do you think you can make it that far?"

"Where exactly is it?" asked Rachel. "It should show the latitude and longitude there. Read them off to me."

Serena read them off and Rachel entered them into something that might have been a GPS, but I wasn't smart enough to make that call.

Rachel gave us a thumb up. "Okay, yeah. We can get there, and still have enough fuel to circle around and recon the area so we know what we're getting into."

"Bird's eye view," said Nelson. "Speaking of being high, I'm so glad I didn't lose my weed."

"You a pot head?" asked Weston, without turning.

Nelson shrugged and held up two fingers about an inch apart. "Little bit, yeah. Keeps me mellow."

"If you were much mellower, you'd fall asleep."

"I remind you," I said, "That he saved our asses back there when we couldn't lift off. Your ass is included in that grouping."

"I know, I know," said Weston. "I'm just grumpy because of this damned headache."

For the most part I watched the back of Weston's head for any temporary unconsciousness. I didn't know what he would be when he awoke again. Serena nodded off, as did Nelson. I occasionally talked to Rachel to keep her company, and before long, we were hovering over Jefferson City, Missouri. I looked out the window as she brought the chopper to within a hundred feet of the ground and nudged Serena and Nelson.

"We're here," I said. "Keep an eye out for anything unusual, Nel, okay?"

"Got it, dude, "he said. Then: "Hey, are those people?"

I moved over to his side and knelt on the floor in front of him, looking out. Every now and then, two or three people with guns ran from one concealed location to another.

Everyone on the ground in Jefferson City knew we were up there, because it wasn't every day you saw a helicopter or a plane. Occasionally one did fly over, but it was always a small craft. Nobody fired at us, so we assumed immediately they didn't begrudge us our mode of transportation.

"They look like they're trying to stay out of sight," I said. "See any of the dead ones?"

"Gotta be somewhere," said Nelson. "We have enough fuel to cruise a few minutes and see?"

"We have plenty, actually," said Rachel. "Say the word, and I'll swoop in a bit."

"I'm okay with it, but I wouldn't take any unnecessary chances," I said. "It's not like we can conduct a rescue mission of any kind, and no matter what happens, we could only carry a couple more people."

The group of survivors we'd seen was several blocks from the heliport, so we could be fueled up and in the air again by the time anyone figured out where we'd gone. If they'd survived a year, then they had enough knowledge and skill to survive pretty much anything.

Rachel brought the helicopter around the backside of a four story building, and we spotted a small army of the walking dead. They were on the move, filling a street that was thick with stalled and wrecked cars, the rag-tag, flesh hungry group threading between the vehicles as thick as a river of molasses, moving steadily in the direction of the people we'd seen. There would be no way for them to know what was around the corner unless they had scouts over that way with radios.

"Rachel, bring it around," said Serena. "We have to warn them. How low can you fly this?" she asked.

"As low as I need to," said Rachel. "But no matter what, they're not going to be able to hear you. Just use hand motions as best you can, but see if you can get the point across that they need to run in the opposite direction."

"That's not going to work," said Serena. "No broadcast loudspeaker or anything on this thing?"

"I hadn't even thought to look," said Rachel. She looked up and found a handset. "Hey, maybe," she said, following the cord and finding the box to which it was connected. "Well, what the hell do you know?"

She brought the chopper back over the building and began dropping the skids straight down toward the street until she was no more than fifty feet above it.

"If you can hear me," she said, holding the button down, "On the other side of this building there are approximately 100 or more of the creatures coming your way. We suggest you retreat for a good distance and find cover in a building with a back way out."

"Good point," I said. "Get trapped by this many and you might as well be dead."

As soon as she had announced, several of them ran in the opposite direction. I counted fifteen people, and I was glad to see another independent group of survivors. Two or three of them waved up at us in thanks before joining their comrades.

"Good," said Serena. "Maybe we saved some lives just then."

"I'm heading to the heliport," said Rachel. "We need food, fuel and more water."

"All of the above," said Nelson. "and I need to smoke a bowl."

"Pothead," admonished Weston.

*****

Regretfully, there were no other helicopters at the landing pad, and the heliport turned out to just be a single pad on the ground outside of St. Mary's Health Center. There was an in-ground fuel pump though, and Rachel suspected it was capable of working if we could arrange some temporary power.

When the rotor blade slowed to a stop, we all pulled off our headsets and stared at one another. I knew we were all glad to be on the ground again, but not without a solid awareness of the dangers that lurked there.

"Wow," said Nelson. "Quiet."

"Nobody happier than me," said Weston, holding his head. "I need quiet."

"You doing alright, Don?' asked Rachel, her frown bunching up the freckles where her brow furrowed.

He shook his head. "I need an ice pack and some shut-eye."

"Sounds like a migraine," I said, looking at Serena. "You have a history of them, Don?"

"Not that I know of," he said. "Not like this."

I whispered in Serena's ear, "He needs to be restrained or someone needs to keep an eye on him every second."

"Rachel has a gun," said Serena. "But I'd still rather not leave him loose in case she's distracted, working on the helicopter or something."

"I agree," I said.

ric A. Shelman

Nelson leaned in. "What's up, dudes?"

"We'll tell you later," I said. "Let's step away from here for a minute."

We walked out to the street and looked down it in both directions. The road where the hospital was located was in an older section of town. In the distance we saw some ambling, hungry souls, but none of them were in groups, so we concluded there weren't any of the red-eyed women around.

I knew we needed to replenish a number of things since we'd lost our bikes. We had no machine guns. We had no more fuel. No portable radios, and no damned food. It reminded me of Robert Heinlein's quote: *You do not truly own anything that you can't carry in both arms at a dead run.* He was right on there.

Don't get me wrong; I wasn't smart enough to read Heinlein. His writing was for really smart people, and I much preferred that my science fiction be dished out in short, vague Star Trek TV episodes where Captain James T. Kirk was busily making out with a woman who looked to be half Smurf.

That said, I could comprehend a clever quote by a genius, so long as it was in plain English. Here's one from me. You can write that shit down and put a squiggly line next to it with my name:

It's that awkward moment when you realize that the only nearby food is you.

I made a decision then. I'll tell you about it in a minute. We needed decisive action and we needed it yesterday.

Rachel looked at us and I waved her over. Don made no effort to leave the helicopter. He sat there with his head resting in his hands, looking miserable.

She approached, smiling. Rachel spoke first. "I really want to thank you guys."

"For what, Rachel?" asked Serena.

"It might sound silly," she said, "and I realize that nothing you've said or done really seems as though it should have triggered any major revelations relating to my life, but you've definitely inspired me to get out of my funk, quit feeling sorry for myself, and do something."

"You just finished flying us out of danger and over three hundred miles closer to our intended destination, so I think you're confused on who should be thanking whom," I said.

"Yeah," said Nelson. "You're helping us. I didn't like that bike all that much anyway. Too much power."

"Well, Rachel," said Serena. "*I* know what you mean. When Dave and Charlie – maybe you'll meet her someday – found me in a boarded up house in Shelburne, Vermont, I might have sat there day after day just surviving with the people there. Since the day I decided to go with David and his group, I came back to life, too. So I get it."

"Exactly," said Rachel. "I was as dead as those things out there – only difference was I still had a heartbeat. So yeah. Anyway, I'm sorry for changing the subject. What did you need to talk to me about?"

Serena nodded toward me, so I said, "Don's headache. You know how the sickness starts, right?"

Rachel nodded. "It's been a year since I saw a lot of it, but it's not something you forget. Scary dreams and headaches. I thought about it when he was bitten, but you used that oil stuff, so I didn't worry."

"True," I said. "And it could be that he has nothing more than a bad headache."

"But you don't *really* think so," said Rachel.

"Coincidences aren't always coincidental," said Nelson with a knowing look.

I stared at him for a moment and added, "Like Nelson said, it could be a coincidence, but you can't bank on them these days."

Nelson pointed at me, then at her, smiled and nodded. "Yeah."

I shrugged. "So I'm saying we can't take the chance of leaving you alone with him unrestrained. If he turns … it's not worth the chance."

"But Dave," said Nelson, "You put like pure urushiol on it. It worked for Gem, right?"

"I know, Nel, but it's different," I said. "From what I heard, Gem was bitten on her thumb, and when that happened I think they actually cut her wound open more, trimmed away excess skin tissue and soaked it in urushiol for hours, or overnight or something."

"Did she ever get the headache?" he asked.

"I don't think so," I said. "I wish I knew more."

"Don's taken care of me," said Rachel, tears beginning to leak from her eyes. "Or he *thinks* he did, really," said Rachel, laughing through her tears. "It's funny. If I actually remember back, it was me taking care of him. He has this fatherly way of talking that makes you believe it's the other way around."

"I've known men like that," said Serena. "David is a wonderful exception."

"And me," said Nelson. "I'm a wonderful exception, too."

"I'm certain you are," said Rachel, smiling.

I saw that Nelson's eyelids were heavy, and concluded that he took a couple of quick hits of pot on the other side of the helicopter. I also noticed he held one of the brass stars in his hand and his fingers played gently over it.

Stoned, but focused and ready. That was our Nelson. I knew he'd be on target, too.

179

"Anyway, Rachel," said Serena. "What David is saying is we can't leave Don unrestrained."

"I can't be the one to tell him," said Rachel. "I'd feel like I was jamming a knife in his heart. Like saying I didn't trust him."

"It's not a matter of trust, dude," said Nelson. "The guy could flip any time."

"Any zip ties in the helicopter?" I asked.

"They got those cuffs like on the cop shows," offered Nelson. "In packages marked Flex Cuffs. I almost tossed 'em, but since they had Flex's name on them I thought it would be cool to bring him back some. They looked pretty light anyway."

"They probably kept them on board in case they had to restrain any meth heads," said Serena.

"Look," I said. "I'll do it. C'mon, Nelson. Show me where they are. Why don't you guys hang here until it's taken care of. He'll need a friendly voice by then, and I don't think he's going to be very happy with us."

Nelson and I walked over together. I took a package of the cuffs from the box he showed me and opened it. I stepped aside from Nelson and offered up my plan.

"How much longer we flyin' today?" asked Weston from the front. "I could sure use a bed."

I walked casually around and signaled to Nelson to climb inside from the back door. He did. We were ready to execute our hastily thought-out plan.

I reached the front door, opened it and leaned in. "Hey, Don. I have something that might help your headache."

"What's that?" he asked.

"It's a therapy thing," I lied. "Grab this bar here with both hands and grip it as tight as you can. Then lean back and close your eyes."

"I don't go for shit like that," he said. "Too damned old to try Yoga crap."

"It's not yoga," said Nelson. "It's marshal arts stuff, and you're never too old for that."

Weston rolled his eyes and gripped the horizontal bar mounted on the control panel in front of him. I supposed it was for the co-pilot to steady himself on in the event of heavy turbulence.

"Okay, hold it tight, close your eyes, and lean back like you're trying to pull it off the dashboard."

Nelson crept closer to him, but Don was distracted, looking at me. As soon as he leaned back and closed his eyes, Nelson's hands shot out and he squeezed his hands tightly on top of Don's.

I reached over and zipped on one Flex Cuff, then the other, securing both of his wrists to the grab bar.

"What the mother fuck!" Don Weston shouted, and tried to pull his hands back. I'd gotten the cuffs closed securely, and he couldn't free his hands, nor could he break the plastic.

"Sorry, Don," I said. "We had to do this because of your bite."

"But you put that oil shit on me!" he shouted.

"Which we're not certain will work, and you have the symptom – the headache."

"Damn it!" he said. "I do *not* want to turn into one of those fuckin' things."

"Well," I said, "It goes without saying that we don't want you to. And what you have could just be a headache. Have you slept at all since we took off?"

"No," he said. "Head hurts too bad. Why?"

"Has to do with dreams," I said. "Horrible, vivid dreams. Another indicator you're infected."

He looked hopeful. "So if I go to sleep and I don't have any crazy dreams, there's a chance I'm alright?" He turned to look at Nelson on his left. "And you. You have a pretty good grip on you for a stoner."

"Subdudo," said Nelson. "Keeps me conditioned. Sorry I had to do that, but Davey told me to."

"You do everything he tells you to do?" Weston asked him.

"Pretty much, yeah. Except go home. It's the only thing he's told me to do that I told him no."

Rachel came over and put a hand on Weston's shoulder. "I'm sorry, Don. I have to defer to them, since they've been through a lot more than we have. You can't be trusted until that headache goes away."

"At least," said Nelson. "Do you need a drink of water, Don?"

"I am a bit thirsty," he said. "But give me just a minute, would you?" he asked. "I need a minute alone with Dave here."

"Sure," I said. "Guys?"

"Me, too?" asked Rachel.

"Just Dave," said Weston. "Thanks."

They stepped away, and I stood close to Don Weston. "What's up, Don?" I asked.

"It's not good, what I have to tell you," he said. "I feel like shit about it."

I wasn't sure I wanted to hear it, but I nodded. "Go ahead, but why now?"

"Because I've never had a headache like this," said Weston. "My brain is doin' flip flops. I don't know if I'll have enough sense to tell you later."

"Okay."

"I killed Jess," he said. "Well, I shot him, anyway. When I came out that first day, he was one of the things in my corral attacking my livestock. I knew Jess and Rachel real good for a few years, and I liked both of 'em. He was a good guy. He almost got the better of me out there, 'cause I didn't want to shoot him."

"You know you had to, right?"

"I know that, but it didn't mean I could tell Rachel. I knew she'd hate me, and she was all I had. Everyone else I knew was dead 'cept her."

"No family?"

"Not close, no. So that's it. Maybe if she starts goin' on about Jess and finding him, you'll let her know the truth. I can't."

I nodded. "Thanks, Don. I'll pick the right time to let her know, and I'll try to explain why you couldn't tell her."

"Bottom line is because I love her like a daughter, and I couldn't take it if she hated me." His eyes squeezed together in pain as he moaned.

I patted him and motioned Nelson back over. He went into the back of the copter and brought back a bottle of water. "Only four left back there," he said, uncapping the water. He tilted it to Weston's lips, and the older man drank half of it down.

Nelson jumped out of the bird and stood next to me.

"Thanks Nelson," Weston said, with a sigh. "Okay, then. You guys get whatever you're gettin' and let's get back in the air. If it happens to me up there, you can just cut these ties and kick me out the door."

"If you turn into a zombie in mid-air, I'm pretty sure that's exactly how it will go," said Nelson, turning and kicking his right leg straight out.

I was in shock.

Nelson went on. "I kick pretty good with my Subdudo, so that will likely be my job. Please allow me to apologize in advance."

I elbowed him in the ribcage and he stepped back and threw up his hands in his Subdudo stance. Despite the tension with Weston, I couldn't help but laugh, holding my palms outward. "I don't want to take you on, Nelson. It's just that a little decorum might be in order, that's all."

He looked at Don and couldn't suppress a smile himself. "Dude, I'm just being honest!" Then he looked at us. "When did honesty become a bad thing?"

"Kid, you are something," said Weston.

"Okay, we've got lots to do," I said. "Don, just try to relax. Sorry it was necessary to secure you like that."

"I get it," he said. "Hurry back."

Nelson patted Weston on the shoulder before he joined me and Serena.

"I'm not sure he gets it yet," said Serena.

"Oh, I'm pretty sure he does," I said.

Serena walked on my left and Nelson on my right. Out of the blue, Nelson elbowed me sharply in the ribcage. It produced a quick pain, and I looked at him and said, "Dude!"

It was a catchy word.

"See how that feels man?" he said, eyebrows raised and his smile still in place.

I think he poked me harder than he intended, because the pain lingered. I just rubbed it and gave him a smile and a shake of my head. "Sorry, Nel. My bad."

"No problem, dude."

It was time to gather supplies and get our asses back in the air. I longed for isolation on land as complete as that we had while airborne.

We picked up our pace and I checked my pockets for extra magazines for the Walther.

*****

As we rounded the corner, we were on Missouri Boulevard. Just from the corner there was a Conoco Gas,

Missouri Blvd Pawn & Gun, and to top it off, we saw a place called Vince Kobb Auto Sales.

First things first. I saw Nelson tense as Serena pulled out her Walther. She immediately pulled out another magazine and put it in her front pocket

I was similarly ready. We had begun to draw kind of a crowd, though in a world teeming with souped-up, pregnant abnormals, it wasn't nearly as bad as it could have been. We were drawing their attention in drips and drabs, and that's how I liked it.

But watching Serena preparing to take action, and seeing Nelson feeding off her preparedness, it became clear to me that a plan – even a shitty plan – was better than none at all. We had to focus on making better, more well-thought-out plans. Contingencies, if you will.

Up until that moment, I hadn't felt like a leader. I hadn't, in my opinion, acted like a leader, either.

Fuck both of those statements, because they don't tell the whole story. The truth is, from that morning Leona first turned until then, I hadn't intended to be, nor did I want to be a leader. That was the honest truth of it. I liked hanging back whenever it was possible, and letting someone else do the heavy lifting.

Flex. Gem. Hemp. Even Charlie, though I had, for a time, felt about her the way I feel about Serena, so with her, other emotions had kicked in, and I'd have done anything to protect her. I don't think it was any secret; in fact, I'm pretty sure Hemp knows I was smitten with her.

But I digress.

It wasn't that Dave Gammon was a lazy man, because I wasn't. I was just on the more passive side. If goaded into something, I might join in; but if things were being handled by others who were perfectly happy to take that role, I wasn't one to fight them.

But now things were different. This was *my* journey, and there was no getting around it. I was fine when it was just me and Serena, because I knew I would step up like a beast when it came to protecting her – whether a strong woman like her needed my protection or not.

But subconsciously, I realized that even when Nelson insisted on coming along, that I shrugged off just a little of the weight I'd carried before.

I felt myself shedding some of the responsibility onto his bony shoulders. Uh huh. Not anymore.

The only damned reason anyone was heading west right now was because I had this notion to find Uncle Bug. It was all by my design, so damn it, I would start to be the man they needed me to be. Even if they didn't realize that I hadn't yet felt like that man.

"Okay, here's the plan," I said, already impressed with the tone with which I spoke the words. "We hit that little auto dealer there."

I pointed to the medium-sized lot with several cars and trucks sporting fake balloons on window flag mounts that had gathered a year and change worth of dust.

"If any of these rotters get within twenty feet," I continued, "we take them out. I'll hit the office and grab a handful of keys, and hopefully they're marked. All we need is battery and even an 1/8th tank of fuel, and we're good."

"Good," said Serena.

"What next?" asked Nelson.

"Next we go to that Pawn & Gun right there. We grab guns that would make Flex and Gem have instant orgasms. If it's picked through, we grab the most powerful weapons with the most plentiful ammo. After that, pretty much whatever else we can throw in the car. Next, we hit that O'Reilly Auto Parts there and see if we can find some big tanks."

"Like gas cans?" asked Nelson.

"Yeah," I said, "but it doesn't matter whether they're made for gas. Just the largest tanks we can find. What was the capacity on that Eurocopter, Serena?"

"Almost 250 gallons according to the spec sheet," she said.

"We'll need an open bed truck then," I said. "And big tanks."

"How we going to power the pumps at the Conoco?" asked Nelson.

Luckily I'd already thought of that, so I didn't have to scramble for words. "We grab some sort of siphon kit at the auto parts store, like we had before. I don't think this is a big farming area, so they won't likely have the hand-crank tank pumps, but if they do, we grab one. We'll get a length of hose and pump directly from the in-ground tanks."

"I'm crossing my fingers, dude!" said Nelson.

"Ready?" I said.

Three rotters were coming at us from two sides. "I got this one," I said, and I raised my arm, aimed and fired. The dead stinker in torn jeans and one Nike collapsed five feet from me.

By the time I looked back, Nelson's arm was drawn back like he was skipping a rock. When he spun it away from him, the big, sharp star entered the bald digger through the right eye socket and ended up sticking out of the back of its head. As it began its topple backward, I realized it was devoid of clothing and so deteriorated that it was impossible to tell the sex. Where its genitals had been looked like rotted meat, so knowing if it had been an innie or an outie was not apparent, nor was it important.

Nelson walked toward it and with two fingers, yanked on the tip of the star until it popped free with a sucking sound. He wiped it on the shirt of my zombie and tucked it back in his jacket pocket.

I had initially wondered why I hadn't heard a gunshot from Serena, but she apparently had decided to save her rounds. Instead, because the creature that approached her did not have any arms at all, she just conked it in the noggin with the butt of the Walther, and it dropped like a water balloon that had come untied.

"We are really stupid," said Nelson. "We have those damned bottles of urushiol in the helicopter."

"Double stupid," I said. "We don't have near what we started with, but there's still some WAT-5."

"No use in wasting it," said Serena. "We don't know what we'll run into at your Uncle's place."

"Let's go."

Stragglers came at us from here and there, but as they did so, we took them out easily. We ended up getting a Dodge Ram Pickup with a half a tank full of fuel. It was a 2011, and the battery still had enough to crank the motor, though it was a grueling first couple of cranks until the motor loosened up and the engine fired.

"Yes!" shouted Serena, shooting another male abnormal, this one pumping some significant pink vapor from his eyes.

"That one had been feeding," she said. "Let's get in."

We climbed inside the truck. I was in the driver's seat, but motioned to Serena. "Here, let's swap. You go over."

I slid across the seat and she crawled over me. "Why?" she asked.

I pointed. "See that down there, near the station?"

"What?"

"Tanker," I said.

"You know how to drive it?"

"No fucking clue," I said.

"So?" asked Serena.

"I know how to drive it!" said Nelson

I turned around and stared at him. "You do?"

"Heck yes," he said. "My pops made me go to trucker school."

I shot a glance at Serena. "Trucker school?" she asked.

"He said there'd always be work," said Nelson with a shrug.

I had to ask the obvious question. "So, were you ever a trucker?" I asked.

"Heck no!" he said. "Me? Blowing out that pollution? Never gonna happen. I did it to make my pops happy."

"You have to tell us about that later," said Serena. "You still remember how to drive one?"

"I don't know if I've ever told you guys this, but I have kind of a photographic memory."

My mouth fell open and I tried to close it. "You're serious?"

"Yeah, I know. Seems kinda far out with me enjoying the herb like I do. But I find that it actually improves my ability."

I shook my head. "Nelson, you are like Forest Gump's box of chocolates."

"You never know what you're gonna get, right?" he said.

"Right," I said. "Serena, get us over to that tanker, babe."

"Nope," she said. "I'd feel better if we go to the Pawn & Gun first."

"Six of one, half dozen of the other," I said.

"I'd rather have a half dozen AK-47s or Uzis," said Serena, putting the Dodge into gear.

She drove. I felt good. Like I was doing what needed to be done.

WWFD?

Just what I was doing, I was pretty sure.

*****

Missouri Boulevard Pawn & Gun was closed. I could tell because of the closed sign on the outside.

The door was locked, too.

"Wish Hemp was here," I said. "He could pick this lock."

"So could I," said Nelson. "If I had a lock pick kit."

"How?"

"Hemp taught me," said Nelson. "Photographic memory, remember?"

"Now I do. Mine isn't what yours is," I said.

"He showed me another trick that might work, though." Nelson looked around.

You have to understand that in a world like the one in which we now lived, there were certain, everyday fixtures that we'd gotten used to and that we don't necessarily write about in these chronicles. They were so commonplace that to read about them again and again would become monotonous. They were the dead uninfecteds that pretty much littered the streets.

When I say this, I now mean skeletons. Animals had begun venturing into the asphalt jungle shortly after the infection had begun to spread and fresh bodies were everywhere. The zombies ate their share, but the sharp teeth of wild animals were better suited for really cleaning the bones.

Anyway, to make this long story short, the skeletons were still there. They still wore pants, and those pants pockets often had keys in them.

Nelson knew what he was doing when he held out his hand and said, "Gun."

I pulled it from my drop holster and put it in his hand. He trotted about twenty feet away on the sidewalk and bent down over a body, patting the pocket. Then he patted the other.

He stood up and shook his head, and looked around.

"There's another right there," he called. Serena and I nodded, and he ran another fifteen feet and bent over another body. After patting, he reached down and just tore the material open with his fingers, removing the set of keys. He held them up, inspecting them.

Then he ran back. When he arrived, he was not winded at all. "Got it. Hemp showed me another trick. It's called bumping."

I'd heard of it, and had even tried it, but after several tries, I had begun to believe it was just some stupid joke meant to make guys like me look lame.

"Have you tried it?" I asked.

"Yeah," said Nelson. "I had it down. Not sure if one of these keys will work, but if I can put it in, I can probably get it open. I need a screwdriver or something else to hit the key with."

Serena looked around. There was a rock sitting against the curb. "Will that work?" she asked, pointing.

Nelson nodded. "Sure. Anything hard and a little heavy. Grab it."

Serena did, and Nelson trotted up to the door. He tried one key, but it would not slide into the lock at all. "This is a Schlage key," he said. "The lock is a Kwikset." He flipped. "This should work." He smiled and gave me the gun back.

Fucking Hemp Junior, I thought. *Love it.*

Serena gave him the stone. Nelson took it and slid the key in the lock. He tried to turn it, and it wouldn't budge. Then he tapped the key five or six times and tried again. Nothing. He jiggled the key and tapped simultaneously, and to my surprise, the key turned and I heard the deadbolt retract.

"Seriously," I said.

"Totally," he said.

Nelson tried to pull the door, but the bottom knob was locked. "Gun," he said, holding out his hand.

I assumed he was going to use the butt of the gun as his rock, but instead, Nelson raised the Walther and fired right behind the jamb, splintering the wood.

I jumped, not expecting it. I might have screamed a little. "What the hell, Nelson!" I scolded.

He laughed. "I might have gotten lucky a second ago, and I didn't want to screw up my perfect lock bumping record."

"Why didn't you just do that to the top?" I asked. Serena was laughing, and I knew why. I had jumped like a foot off the ground, and she didn't even twitch.

"You can't just shoot a deadbolt," he said. "Knobs are easy. They just latch onto the jamb plate."

"More Hemp teachings?"

"Sure. Who else?" he asked, handing me the gun. "Here. Shooting bullets at moving things are your department."

I shook my head and stepped aside, pulling the door open. Serena stayed to the left of the door, and Nelson got behind me.

"Hello! Is anyone there?" I called.

Nothing.

"No damned headlights, either," I said. "We have to hit a pharmacy next."

"We should have made a list."

"You don't need a list. You got me."

"Oh yeah," I said. "Mr. photographic memory."

"Make fun, dude," he said. "It comes in handy."

I wasn't making fun. If anything, I was jealous. I'd heard of people with that gift, and I always wished I had it.

I squeezed his shoulder and smiled. He knew what I meant. I moved inside, the light from the late afternoon illuminating the interior of the store. From the looks of the place, nobody had been inside since this thing began. There were no windows from outside that weren't barred, and the metal door looked imposing. The locks just weren't as good as they apparently needed to be.

"Guitars!" said Nelson, and rushed over to pull one down. He turned it over, smiling. "Do you know what this is?" he asked.

"A guitar?" Serena said, pulling the door closed to within a foot, still allowing light to stream inside the large room.

"It's an Elvis Costello signature model! This thing's almost five grand!"

"You play?"

"Since I was a punk," said Nelson. "I'm taking it. How long's it been since you heard live music?" he asked.

Serena smiled, big and genuine. "Too long, Nelson. You sing, too?"

"I do," he said. "You?"

"She does," I said. "Didn't you ever hear her at karaoke over at Three Sisters Bar?"

"Never did," said Nelson. "I'd remember that."

"Ha ha," I said. "Gun time, then go time. We've been gone forty minutes already."

"Jesus," I said. There were tons of what appeared to be automatic weapons, but I only knew what I knew. I supposed I could figure them out. I moved along the wall and pulled three identical guns down that looked pretty military. I held one up to catch the light of the door.

"AR-15," I said. "Hell yes, we'll take all of them."

Serena came behind the counter with me and moved along the case, looking down at the stock. She leaned down to slide open the back door. "Shit."

"What?" I asked.

Too late. She turned away from the case, raised her boot and kicked the glass. It shattered.

"There," she said, leaning inside to remove a very cool looking, engraved stainless steel handgun.

"Nice little Sig Sauer," she said. ".380 ACP."

"Grab as many as you can carry," I said.

Nelson leaned against the door and was busy tuning the guitar. I wanted to say something, but the kid needed a moment or two of peace. He wouldn't know what guns to grab anyway. I let him be.

"I'm running these out to the truck," I said. "Serena, would you help me grab some of this ammo?"

"I got it, dude," said Nelson. He slung the guitar over his back and double-armed a bunch of the ammo boxes. "This .223 stuff?"

"Yeah," I said. "And the .380 ACP. And the 7.65 mm for the Walthers."

We loaded up and hit the truck. Two more straggler rotters saw us and headed over, so we had to wait for them to make their way up before Serena and I took them out with double double-taps. Nelson was putting his guitar in the truck and was preoccupied.

"Okay, let's get back in there and see what's what. Serena, if there are any more of the .380s, let's grab as many as we can carry. They're an easy little gun for anyone to handle. A few of the .22 revolvers, too. Ammo's everywhere, plus they hold a bunch of rounds. Some speed loaders, too."

"You learned a lot in a few runs to the store with Flex and Gem, didn't you?" asked Serena.

"Shitloads, to quote them," I said.

The gun shopping was uneventful. Now we had to hit the auto parts store, the pharmacy and then the big one: We had to see if Nelson could get the tanker over to the helicopter.

The reason for the pharmacy was just the radios, but they were important. We would definitely run into more situations like this one, where Rachel was alone, back at the helicopter.

"Don't suppose anyone saw a CVS or a Walgreens, huh?" I asked.

"Nope," said Nelson. "Schnuck's."

"Schnuck's?" I asked.

"Yep. We passed it on the way to the gun shop. In that big center."

"Okay, Schnuck's it is," I said. I turned the motor over and put the Dodge in gear. It felt good to have gotten more weapons, but there were two, maybe three more important jobs to finish before we could go back. Splitting up significantly wasn't a real option, because I did not want to lose anyone. And by that, I meant to the rotters.

I drove into the center, and noted that the O'Reilly Auto Parts was there, too. "Perfect," I said. "Two birds with one stone."

"I'll run to the pharmacy," said Nelson. "If you want to go to the parts store. But why do you still need to go there if we can use the tanker?"

"I want to get a siphon," I said. "We lost ours, and we're going to be back to bikes or cars eventually. Once we get to California."

"Makes sense," said Nelson.

"Want a gun?" asked Serena. "There's plenty."

"Nah," said Nelson. "Got my Subdudo and my stars."

"How many stars do you have left?" I asked. "You've left some behind, right?"

"Yeah. I have four."

"Where do you get something like that?"

"I sent off for them on the Internet. Maybe a martial arts supply, but no big deal. I have my martial arts in case I get into trouble, but it's been a year, so how many can be inside there?"

"Be careful," said Serena.

Against my better judgment, Nelson jogged across the parking lot and Serena and I went into the auto parts store.

I was hungry and exhausted, and remembered that we also needed some damned food. Wow. So much to remember and so much to do.

We found our siphon in a hurry. It was the type with a battery powered pump, so we scooped up a few bags of D-Cells, too. I grabbed some tire filler and patches, too. Just in case. The store was dead empty except for the expected deteriorated corpses and because the front door was smashed in, we didn't have to worry about it being locked.

We bagged our stuff and got back to the truck, then drove the truck across the lot in time to find Nelson staggering out of the Schnuck's Pharmacy with a full-sized, yellow plastic baseball bat in one hand and plastic bags hooked over his arms. He was spattered with blood and he looked exhausted and shaken.

We jumped out and ran to him.

*****

"Dude, have you ever tried to kill a zombie with a plastic bat? Much less three of 'em?"

"What?" said Serena. "Three of them?"

"There were six!" he said. "I don't know what they were doing in there. Maybe they've been in there for a year, but I found three dead people – well, bones, anyway – and I was kinda spacing out, I guess, checking out the different radios. They were real skinny and so dang quiet! All wearing rubber-soled tennis shoes, like some kind of uniform or something. I never heard 'em."

"So ... you grabbed a plastic bat?" I said.

"They were too close for the stars by the time I saw them behind me," he said. "I reached down in this cardboard bin and grabbed two of these pieces of shit – excuse me, Serena – and I was two-hand swinging the things, but it takes a heck of a lot of pounding to make a dent with a bat like this." He held up the toy bat.

To be honest I was on the verge of a laughter attack. Nelson was so damned serious but what he was telling us was just absurd and even funnier in my mind's eye.

Serena had taken the grocery bags from him and as he spoke, he waved around the yellow, plastic bat, darkly stained from the grip to the tip, with several reddish-black chunks clinging to the end of it.

"I ask you again," said Nelson, "Have you ever tried to kill something with a plastic bat? It's insane! I mean, you're swinging and connecting, and you feel like some kind of ... I don't know, some brute or something, but nothing's happening! Even I don't have enough energy for an all day beat down."

"I'll say with pleasure that I haven't been put in a situation where I had to use a plastic bat on a zombie," I said. "Serena?"

"No, but the apocalypse is young," she said, and I saw her trying to suppress her own smile. Luckily, Nelson was staring at the ground, breathing hard. "Did you kill them at least, Nelson?" she asked.

He shook his head. "Nah, almost. Most of them are dead, I think. I started poking at them, 'cause the bats work pretty good as pokers. I reeled back and put some kicks on four of them, and when they were down I ran into the aisle behind them and pushed the whole shelf over on top of them."

"Wow," said Serena.

"Jesus," I said.

"Yeah, right! So while I'm jumping up and down on the rack trying to crush them underneath, I was just poking at the other two while I grabbed my bags and ran out here. I was so damned tired!"

"Did you get the headlights and batteries, Nelson?" I asked.

He stared at me in amazement. "Dude, did you miss the entire story I just told you?"

I patted his shoulder. "No, buddy, I just have to know if I need to go back in there. You weren't bitten or scratched by them?"

Nelson held his arms out, the yellow bat skyward. "Hell no! Check me out, man. I want you to be sure so you don't freak out or anything."

"I trust you," I said. "I'm glad you're alright, brother. Seriously. Thanks for doing that."

Nelson nodded. "I need to go sit for a bit," he said. He held out the bat. "Need this?"

I pulled my gun from my holster, and Serena did the same. "Nope, we're good."

"Shoot that jerk in the bow tie," he said. "I don't like him very much at all."

We nodded and he went to the truck. We looked at each other and smiled. "Maybe Nel tired them out for us," I said.

"They're right there," she said, pointing at the door. Sure enough, both zombies, the man in the bow tie – which was very intact – and a dead-eyed woman who was probably in her mid-fifties before the scourge struck her, stood at the door, clawing at the glass. There appeared to be several dents in their faces, and as their gaping mouths gnashed aimlessly, I saw yellow plastic in the teeth of the man. Nelson had been beating him in the mouth, obviously.

We walked toward the door and I put my hand on one door handle, with Serena doing the same to the other.

"God, I wish we had video of that fight," I said. "On three?"

"You're funny," said Serena.   Then: "One, two, three."   We opened the doors, raised our weapons and placed clean, point-blank shots through the foreheads of each of the creatures. They crumpled to the floor at about the same time the spent cartridges rang off the concrete behind us. We walked inside and immediately heard more sounds from the other end of the store, so moved along the front counter to where Nelson had pulled down the rack.

An arm was clawing at the ground from beneath the fallen shelving unit. I walked to it and stomped on it, then held my PPK through the two shelves and fired.   The fingers quit twitching. I don't even know if it was a male or female. Didn't matter.

"Let's get the headlights and batteries, then get the hell out of here," I said. "This is all taking too long."

"Food, David," said Serena. "I don't know about you, but I'm starving, and I'm sure everyone else is, too. And water."

"God," I said. "I am a terrible leader."

"Just preoccupied," said Serena. "Can't understand why."

We took our time and loaded out as much of the canned food as we could. Nelson even got up the cajones to come back in and help us.   Cases of water, canned vegetables, tamales, chili, beans, bags of Top Ramen. Anything that didn't look spoiled went into the back of the Dodge. This would easily sustain all of us until we got to California.

*****

Chapter Nine

Five rotters were shuffling toward us in a group from the east. I turned and saw three or four stragglers coming from various directions on our west side.

Being comprised of flesh and blood, I suppose we were enough to entice their sense of taste. I again worried about Rachel and Don Weston, alone at the chopper for well over an hour now.

We pulled alongside the stalled big rig, but I did not get out of the Dodge, nor did Serena, because after a good fifteen minute rest, Nelson said he had recovered enough to handle it.

He climbed out of the pickup truck and pulled open the door of the diesel's cab. Nelson screamed, and Serena and I jumped, our guns out.

"Sorry," he said. Serena had her window down and stared up at him. I leaned over so I could see, too.

"Roll up your window, Serena," he said.

The moment it was up, Nelson dragged a skeleton, still wearing a tee shirt and jeans, with a Peterbilt cap on its skull, out of the truck. It fell into a hundred pieces and the dust and hair blew all over the window where Serena looked out.

"Glad he warned us first," she said.

"That would have been a mouthful," I said.

Nelson gave us a thumbs up and climbed inside the truck. The trucker likely would have turned the truck off to preserve fuel while he waited for whatever it was he was waiting for. There *was* an overturned car in front of the tanker, but it was clear behind him. I wondered why he would have succumbed inside the vehicle, but I didn't expect Nelson to concern himself with that detail, plus we'd seen enough cases of suicide in the face of this apocalypse that it did not pay to dwell on such things.

Nelson situated himself in the seat and seconds later, we heard the sound of an engine cranking.

It turned fast, winding three times before stopping. A second later, again, it turned, turned again and stopped.

The next time the engine cranked, it was slower. Nelson looked over at us, frustrated. He paused and motioned for Serena to lower her window, which she did.

"I may only have one crank left," he said. "I need to see if you can pull off one of those Rachel prayers, Serena."

"Of course," said Serena. "But I've been praying the whole time. It's kind of a natural background activity for me," she added.

"Good. I'll beg the Universe," he said. "That's how I work it. If God's out there, he'll hear me."

I didn't say anything. I figured these two had it.

Nelson closed his eyes, bit his lower lip, and turned the key again. The motor turned once, twice and caught, clattering to life, rough as hell. It sounded as though it would shudder and cut out, but as the entire cab of the rig shook and rattled, it finally settled into a smoother, quieter idle.

"Yes!" shouted Nelson. "Wow! Got it!"

"Okay, let's go, Nelson," I said. "You'll have to back it up. Can you find reverse?"

"Duh," said Nelson, rolling his eyes. "Trucker school? Photographic memory? Any of this ringing a bell?"

I waved at him, smiling.

I was starting to wonder when Nelson became such a smart ass, but on him it was charming, because everything was accompanied by his thin-lipped, goofy smile. Still, all this talk of his photographic memory made me wonder why he hadn't mentioned it before. Oh, well.

Nelson focused again and we heard the gears grinding. They ground. On and on, they chewed at one another, and finally, with what appeared to be a good push with his right arm, the grinding stopped. He looked over again double-pumped his left fist, then eyed his rear-view mirror and the truck lurched backward.

"Follow us!" shouted Serena.

Nelson nodded and we pulled hard left.

"Stop," said Serena.

"What for?" As soon as I asked the question, I knew. The five zombies that had been approaching from the east were now seven strong, and had gotten to within fifteen feet and still closing.

The ragtag bunch looked as though they came from a retirement home. They were all trudging along in the bodies of expired senior citizens, blood-soiled, torn clothing and even a hospital gown on one of the men. Wispy hair clinging to dried-out scalps, some completely bald, missing eyes and some noses, too.

In all cases their gnashing teeth were more than exposed, and pickings in this part of town must have been pretty slim, because no vapor emitted from their tear ducts.

Chalk up an advantage for us.

Their dead eyes saw us, but did not really see anything at all; still, Serena and I knew that their reaching arms would find us if allowed to try.

Serena unrolled her window and held out her Walther. She aimed and fired once, then twice. The first shot had missed its mark and had struck the neck of the man on the far left. The second bullet took the creature down in a dry spray of rotting, biological matter. Serena was right on with her third and fourth shots, so three down, four to go.

Her fifth bullet cut through a bald man's ear. Of course he did not go down, instead drawing to within five feet of us alongside the others.

I reached into the back seat and pulled out a fully loaded AR-15 that I'd been preparing while Nelson recovered from his Tee-ball inspired zombie fight.

"Here," I said, handing her the weapon. "I disengaged the safety, and there's a round chambered."

"Hold your ears," she said, raising the weapon. She fired six shots in rapid succession, missing once. The advancing creatures danced momentarily like marionette dolls on a demonic puppeteer's string, then fell to their eternal positions of final decay.

Serena brought the gun back inside, leaned it against the seat between us and rolled her window back up, winking at me. She did not have a smile to offer at that moment, and having known her for a while and falling in love with her, I knew why.

To pose a comparison, Gem Cardoza had a big heart, but she was also a wise-ass who fully accepted that these human beings-turned-zombies died long ago, when the infection set in. Gem therefore looked at what she did as a service, not only to surviving mankind, but to the zombies themselves.

Kill the zombies, save the world.

Both things, in Gem's mind, were reasons for celebration and joy. I tended to agree, but we all dealt differently.

Serena processed things differently, and she had expressed it to me on many a quiet night as we lay together, talking. She told me that as long as the creatures had even the most primal consciousness and desire – even if that was for human flesh – that they were worthy of our compassion and our mercy.

She fully acknowledged that our mercy was in their killing. That is where she and Gem agreed: Killing them was merciful, and none should be left walking if they were even semi-convenient to kill.

Nelson stayed behind us, and as we pulled back up to the hospital and the helicopter landing pad, we saw several zombie bodies scattered around the chopper, leaking deep red ooze into puddles around them. Rachel sat on the ground outside, the revolver hanging limply from her hand.

She was crying.

*****

I threw the truck in park ten feet away from where Rachel sat, grabbed the AR-15 and ran. When I reached her, I dropped to the ground, rolled onto my stomach and fired beneath the helicopter, where two zombies had crawled from behind to within three feet of Rachel, who sat unaware.

She screamed and leapt to her feet as I fired, but I hadn't had time to issue a warning. I saw them closing in on her and couldn't even find any words on such short notice.

She stood there, all 4'10" of her, her hand on her chest, breathing hard. She turned around and saw the two dead abnormals beneath the helicopter and said, "Oh, my God. Thank you. Thank you."

The revolver was in her hand, and I noticed that it was open, the cylinders all empty. The spent shells were on the ground around her feet.

"Rachel, are you alright?" Serena asked, running from the truck.

She shook her head. "No … Don," was all she could manage. Serena's eyes shifted to where Don sat in the Eurocopter, but she did not leave Rachel's side.

I hadn't even looked at him since we'd arrived because of the unexpected company. I ran to the chopper and opened the door. His hands were still cuffed to the dash-mounted bar, but his eyes were wide open, pinkish-white and blank. There was a bullet hole in his right temple, and the window on the driver's side was spattered and shattered from the blood spray and the exiting bullet that I knew Rachel had fired.

The poor woman had been forced to kill a man whom she saw as a father figure, and even though I now knew what he had done, I did not yet know whether I would ever tell her about it.

Nelson knew to focus elsewhere. He was already connecting the thick hose to the tanker. Now we would have to figure out how to get it from that huge hose into the chopper's fill spout.

A little at a time. That's how we did it. A crack of the valve. A dribble of fuel.

Like everything else. A bullet here. A bullet there. A dead abnormal here, and one there. It was the process until we were once again able to walk the streets without fear.

After some serious usage of alcohol swabs and gauze, we had the helicopter cleaned up and in the air in another forty-five minutes.

We left Don's body behind, on the macadam.

Just then I decided that I had actually liked the man quite a lot, and I realized I would miss him.

*****

We made it as far as Salina, Kansas on the next tank. We decided, since we had some fuel to spare, that we'd set the chopper down in a more remote area on the outskirts of town.

We were exhausted, and found what appeared to be a grouping of model, manufactured homes. We were stoked to find them locked, and full propane tanks in locked cabinets on the outside of each unit.

We chose a nice, three bedroom. We were able to use the stove, and an attached generator also ran on the propane, so we actually had lights and water, pumped from the clean water storage tanks.

Fucking showers. Hot food. Model home beds, actually made up and as comfortable as hell.

I felt bad for Don. He would have really relished the bed.

I don't know if I need to say any more than that. This was Heaven in the middle of Kansas, and believe me – if you've ever been to Kansas, that is really saying something. I'm pretty sure we wanted to stay here for a few days.

So that's what we did.

Fuck it. That's actually what we said. It had been over a year since the damned zombie apocalypse or whatever you want to call it had screwed the planet, and from our periodic tests, we knew the bubbles were still flowing, so it wasn't going to end anytime in the near future.

This meant that if Uncle Bug was there, he would still be there in three more days. Plus, we needed the rest – yeah, I know we'd only been on the road for two days, but the last day had been an awfully long one – and we intended to take whatever time we felt we needed without worrying about some schedule I had invented.

That first night, Serena and I waited until the propane heater had the water nice and hot, and we got in the shower. I held her in my arms as the water cascaded down onto our bodies, rinsing away the unthinkable residue of a contaminated world.

Her arms wrapped around my waist, I leaned back to take in her perfectly rounded breasts, cupping them in my hands as I leaned in to kiss her neck. She arched her back beneath my touch and I smoothed her long, brown hair down against her back as I pressed my cheek against hers, my eyes closed.

I know hers were, too.

I believe we could have remained there, beneath the clean, warm water for hours, but the supply wasn't limitless, and we had the entire night ahead of us in a clean, soft bed.

But as we finished rinsing off and I watched her squeezing the water from her hair, I knew that the intense connection we'd shared for that brief moment of immersion, both in the water and one another, had created a permanent bond between us.

Loss has a strange way of shining a spotlight on what is important, and that did not just include your own loss; it included seeing the anguish and pain of someone like Rachel, who watched the only friend and companion she had known over the last year turn into something horrible and unrecognizable. Worse, she had to pull the trigger of the gun that ended his life.

Serena had seen and felt it deeply. Rachel was the only other woman with us and no matter how we men like to think we know how women feel, it truly takes another woman to know that.

It's that awkward moment you take a break from your chronicle to see if you're growing breasts ... and are relieved to see you're not.

So Serena cried in my arms that night. She cried for Rachel and for Don Weston. While I believe many of her tears were of compassion and sorrow, I also believe, as we made love and held one another, than a good bit of her emotion was joy.

Yeah, I cried too. It's catchy, that crying.

I love Serena. I still miss Leona, but I see a lot of her in Serena. Goodness. Caring. Beauty.

So, anyway. Hot food and showers, air conditioning, soft beds. We deserved it, and we stayed a while. A few straggling zombies arrived here and then, but for the most part it was quiet on the edge of Salina, Kansas.

*****

Before we left, refreshed, well-fed and clean, Rachel performed the necessary maintenance on the helicopter, making sure all the fluid levels were up to snuff. On an adjacent property, there was a storage garage that contained spare parts, oil and coolant for the farm equipment maintenance.

We didn't know what else was in there, and it was locked. I pried open the door with a crowbar, and as I pulled it open, one of the creatures came barreling out, directly into Nelson.

The skinny kid acted fast, and this time, I saw what his so-called Subdudo could do if he did away with the light touches and just went for it.

Nelson's first right-handed chop to the neck of the thing wearing overalls and black work boots clearly broke its clavicle, for its head immediately fell sideways onto its left shoulder.

The other came out and staggered at me, and I had the crowbar in the air and down on the center of its skull by pure reaction.

Had to change my shirt on that one. A spatter of blood and chunks of rotted brain shot out at me and sprayed me from forehead to waist. I spat the disgusting crap from my mouth and kept spitting until the taste dissipated. I did not like the hand-to-hand fights, because it was dangerous, and it was a horrid mess.

The one crack did it for me. Nelson had the bastard who was on him down in another two moves.

He balanced on his right leg and shot his left leg out like a piston, snapping the right knee of the creature. Before it could crumple, Nelson jumped to his left leg, kicked with his right, and broke the thing's other knee.

It was disgusting, watching its legs bend the wrong way. I shot it the moment it hit the ground and Nelson nodded to me.

He wasn't breathing hard. When it was over, he said, "Thanks," and walked into the shed, turning on his headlight.

Inside was everything they would have needed for perhaps a week of survival. Sterno cans for cooking, a bucket they had probably gone to the bathroom in, and some small pieces of cookware. Gallon bottles of water.

Only two of the bottles were empty, and whatever was in the bucket was so dried up it no longer even stank.

Just the smell of rotting zombies. Nothing else. They had probably transformed before the second day, and from that moment on, it had just become an eternal waiting game.

We ended their eternities for them.

You're very welcome, zombies. It's what we do.

Also inside were the supplies we'd actually been looking for, as I said before.

So the helicopter was fully fueled, thanks to several gas cans and our little, battery powered siphon. It took us several hours – clearly, we missed our tanker – but we got it done.

We spent a total of three nights at that little slice of Eden, and when we left, it felt as though we'd had a much-needed vacation. When the chopper skids left the ground, I think all of us were smiling – even Rachel.

It was funny, too. Nelson had taken to riding up front with Rachel, and they played these memory games. It was like the old color game, Simon. Sometimes they used numbers, other times, letters and colors. Rachel would say, 1, 6, blue, A, 12, yellow, 5. Nelson would repeat it back and add another color, number or letter.

Nelson won every time. Serena and I never played.

"What's that town down there, Rachel?" I asked.

It was 1:30 PM, and Rachel had begun to hint that we'd need a fuel stop soon.

"According to the chart," said Rachel, "it's Deer Trail, Colorado. Or thereabouts."

Serena had continued to work with the map, and based on our flying speed and direction, we were probably close to there, anyway.

"I'm going to fly around a bit," said Rachel. "I'll drop down low. Keep an eye out for places with lots of farming equipment. We'll be able to siphon fuel."

"It's all farms down there," I said.

Nelson stared down for a while, then said, "I used to think the wide open spaces were all gone. Just takes a trip across the country to see that's not true."

"Look there," said Nelson, pointing. "Are those … are those *them*?"

Serena and I looked. Below us was an enormous group of people, filling a street and the grassy shoulders along the road, moving northwest, toward Denver.

"They only group like that when there's a pregnant female with them," I said. "Or more than one."

"Fly low overhead, would you, Rachel?" said Serena. "We need to make sure of what we're seeing."

"I think they're what you think they are," she said. "See how tightly they're grouped?"

Nelson nodded. "Yeah. Not worried about fresh air. Just following the orders of the red-eyes."

"Then we need to kill them," said Serena. "We have the weapons. Rachel, do we have enough fuel?"

In answer, Rachel turned the helicopter sharply away from them and buzzed low over some farmhouses on the southeast side of the group of rotters.

"Let's find where we're stopping," she said, "and I'll be able to answer that question. Then we can go back and take care of them."

A minute later, we saw a large, fenced yard, easily big enough for the chopper to land. Inside the fence were several tractors and backhoes.

"Bright colors, too," said Nelson. "Newer."

We'd made mistakes in the past where we'd believed the amount of equipment meant fuel sources, but discovered that the equipment was dilapidated and out of use. No fuel, no sense in stopping. Relatively bright colors meant newer tractors and combines that had good-sized fuel tanks that were probably topped off.

"That's going to work," said Rachel, turning the helicopter back toward the mobile horde of abnormals. "Now grab some of those new guns of yours and we'll set this baby down about two hundred yards ahead of them."

"This might take a while," said Nelson, again looking down at the large group that moved along Highway 36.

"Should we take out some from up here?" asked Serena.

"Yeah," I said. "If we can fly over and find the females leading them, it'd go a long way toward disorganizing them."

"Dude," said Nelson, "I think we know that if those females are down there, they're hiding right in the middle of the crowd. We'll never find them."

"Good point," I said.

"Plus, you'll waste a lot of ammo," said Rachel. "I'll set it down and we'll leave the doors open and the engine running. All I'll do is disengage the rotors, so we'll be able to take off fast."

"They're a slow bunch," I said, "But land three hundred yards ahead of them. We can always run toward them to give ourselves more kill time."

"You got it," said Rachel, angling the chopper and easing it down in the center of the road. "Get ready."

We were, and we weren't. But we went anyway.

The fight was afoot.

*****

The four of us were equipped. It was broad daylight and the road was dry. I had an AR-15 with the largest magazines we took from the gun shop. Nelson and Serena had identical weapons strapped on their shoulders, but Rachel preferred handguns, and carried with her at least three that I had seen.

"Got your plastic bat?" I asked Nelson, poking at him a bit as we ran.

"Hilarious, dude. Someday you'll know what that was like."

"I don't think so," I said.

As we drew to within a hundred yards of them and they stopped dead in their tracks – no pun intended – I think we all got a chill down our spines.

"The freaks on the outside aren't smart enough to know what we represent," I said. "So how did the females see us?"

"If they're in the middle, I'm not sure," said Nelson. "Sensed us?"

"You know how women just know things," said Serena. "Let's just carry out our plan. As many as we can take out."

We all carried one of the four canisters of urushiol we had in case they got too close. These were strapped on our belts.

When we could see their dead eyes, we began firing. All of our guns were on single-fire mode. With four of us going, and an estimated hundred of the creatures or so, it would be a while before we finished. At least in their stationary state, they weren't moving any closer to our escape vehicle.

We advanced on them, firing as we went. The front row dropped and we took out the next. Pretty soon it was fairly scattered, and the front line was no longer a solid wall, but more staggered and out of order.

"This doesn't make any sense," I yelled to Serena.

She called back, "What do you mean?"

"They never just stand there and die," I said.

As the words left my lips the horde broke into what I could only describe as a run.

No. A sprint. They were coming at us like a mudslide of undead, swift and almost silent. Their whitish-pink eyes and gnashing mouths grew clearer as they drew closer.

I fired my last round before needing a reload, and yelled, "Turn! Run!"

I hoped it wasn't too late, but as I glanced to my right, I saw Rachel, Serena and Nelson pacing me. I looked behind us, and amazingly, the creatures were gaining on us, as though energized by the powers of Hell.

Out front, breaking free were three females.

I stopped and turned, pulling my Walther.

The three immediately slowed and were swallowed by the advancing crowd, that had not appeared to slow one iota.

I turned and ran again. I was now fifty yards behind the others, who had not stopped.

I did not look back again. I watched as my friends reached the chopper, and I heard the rotors engage seconds later.

Rachel wasted no time, and already had the chopper six inches off the ground, only waiting for me. I ran. I could clearly hear the hundreds of dead feet beating the earth behind me, and as I reached the helicopter, I dove inside and felt it spin beneath me and take flight almost immediately.

"I'm circling around!" said Rachel. "Kill as many as you can from the air. Kill those females first!"

I rolled onto my butt and got in position as she angled the chopper over the crowd, just thirty feet above their heads. The wind kicked up a dust cloud around them, and Nelson, Serena and I lay side by side on the floor of the Eurocopter and fired down at them.

"I can't see the females!" said Nelson. "Screw this. Can I use a bottle?"

"Urushiol?" I asked.

"Yep," said Nelson.

I thought that I'd rather save it for when we were in immediate danger, but we needed to land and the horde below was a threat. "Go for it," I said. "Rachel, if you can, drop to like ten feet above that crowd, and Nelson, shake the bottle really good and uncap it. the rotor blades ought to disburse it pretty well, so just sprinkle it out."

"Got it," said Nelson, reaching back for the canister. He began shaking it hard.

"I'm going to keep firing," said Serena. "We might get lucky that low and get a direct hit on the females."

"Wow," said Nelson. "This is crazy."

As the chopper zigzagged just over the heads of the creatures below, I saw two of the three faces of the red-eyed, pregnant females looking up. They were like beacons in the darkness, their ashen gray faces contrasting to all the sameness below as they watched us in the sky.

And just like that, as though they saw me spot them, they sank into the crowd.

"Right there!" I shouted. "About midway back in the center, Nelson! Rachel, get right over that area. I saw them."

Rachel spun the bird around again and hovered just over the place I had indicated.

"Now, Nelson!"

He shook the bottle side-to-side and in the whipping wind of the rotor blades, it became a mist that we could not see. Serena kept firing her weapon as the urushiol canister emptied and Nelson brought it back inside.

Rachel hovered for perhaps thirty more seconds without moving, and we saw a kind of steam hissing off the group below. Seconds later, like dominos, they began collapsing from the center outward, revealing the three females who had been our focus. But only briefly, before they once again found cover among their minions.

So many of them had fallen that others were tripping on their dissolving cadavers, but as they fell they scurried back to their feet again and moved. Our little trick appeared to have taken out as many as a third of them – which still left a lot.

A red-eye's face appeared below. Just one this time. As I stared down at the female, the crowd behind her split in the center and became two groups. They skirted around the piled bodies and came together again once past the melee.

The other two came into view. "There they are!" I shouted. "All three of them!"

"Oh, my God," said Serena. "We didn't kill *any* of them." She began firing directly at them, and they dropped down, the crowd again closing in on them like a hive protecting their Queen.

Their *Queens*.

"Fuel ready to be an issue," said Rachel. "We have maybe twenty minutes of flight time left before we're burning fumes."

The helicopter angled sharply east and I turned to look behind us. I got a chill.

"Rachel," I said.

"What is it, Dave?" came Rachel's voice in my headset.

"They're following us. Turned in our direction."

"Then we touch down, fuel up and go," she said. "What other choice do we have?"

"None. But take us farther away. We'll just have to find another place to do that."

We flew low toward the house we'd spotted, when Nelson spoke up.

"Whoa, dudes."

"What?" asked Serena.

"Look down there," he said, pointing. See those three there?"

"Yeah, so what?" I said, seeing the three walking stiffs moving along the street.

"Okay," said Nelson. "Now look over there." He pointed to another street and there were two more, walking more or less together, in the same direction.

"Can you get a bit higher Rachel?" asked Serena, her fingers clutching the AR-15 she still held even tighter.

"Sure, but what's going on?" she asked.

"Hold on," I said. As the helicopter gained altitude, we now took in several streets, and uncannily, what was happening.

Nelson turned to look at us, swiping his long, blonde hair behind his left ear. "They're all going to the same place," he said, leaving his mouth hanging open when the words were out.

"But where?" asked Rachel.

"To the group," I whispered. "To the females. Holy fuck."

I didn't cuss a lot. You might have noticed that. Oh, there were moments – like right now – that I felt fuck to be the perfect word, but mostly I could internalize that stuff.

"What does this mean?" asked Serena. "Do you think it's a kind of telepathy? Like what that female used on Lisa when she hit her with the red vapor?"

It wasn't like I'd forgotten about how my sister died, but it also wasn't something I thought about much. Serena didn't bring it up either, but this was clearly an exception to the rule. We had to figure out what was happening, and if straggling zombies about town were all walking in the same direction, there was damned sure a reason for it.

"Dudes, those red-eyed-bitches are assembling their troops," said Nelson. "Using their damned minds." He looked at Rachel. "It's a mind fuck," he whispered.

The laugh erupted from me involuntarily. "No, no, Nelson. That's something else completely," I said. "What this is is mind control, and they can clearly do it from a good distance. Rachel, do you have enough fuel to fly a bit farther away?"

"I have maybe ten minutes at this altitude and these kinds of turns before I need to set her down," she said. "If I fly farther away, then it needs to be somewhere we have hope of finding fuel."

"We'll fucking siphon it with that measly pump if we have to," said Serena. "What are you trying to figure out, David?"

"I need to know how far they can reach," I said. "How far away they can control. What are we right now, like half a mile, as the crow flies?"

"Three quarters," said Rachel.

"Okay, just fly for a bit – I guess east. Everyone, keep your eyes peeled for abnormals."

"There's one," said Nelson. "He's not moving toward the group."

Serena spoke next. "One there, too. See, right there by that house?" She pointed again. "And there. On the street, by that blue mailbox."

"They're wandering," I said, adding, "How far away are we now, Rachel?"

"Just about a mile," she said.

"Okay," I said. "So they can call them from approximately a mile radius, or thereabouts. A mile in all directions."

"How do you figure, dude?" asked Nelson.

"Because like I just said, Nelson, they're not moving toward them, right? They're milling around like they do when there's no food source nearby that they can smell or sense."

"Good to know, I suppose," said Serena. "But what are we going to do about it?"

"It's about what Nelson and I are going to do," I said.

Serena's eyes flashed. "David. Don't start pulling that male chauvinist shit with me now."

"Serena," I said, my voice calm. "What I'm thinking about doing *is* risky, but that's not the problem. You or Nelson – you both have the necessary skills to do what I need. It has nothing to do with the fact that you're a woman."

"So leave Nelson behind."

"I could," I said. "But it's my idea and I want Nelson with me. You don't even know what the plan is."

"Neither do I, Davey," said Nelson. "Mind if I make the call?"

"Screw it," I said. "Fine. Here's what I want to do."

I told them. They stared at me like I was nuts.

"I'm going," said Nelson.

"You could use me," said Serena. "There are three of them down there – at least. Maybe more by the time you get this crazy shit plan ready."

I saw a small neighborhood just below us. Nothing roamed the streets in plain view.

"Rachel, set it down right here, anywhere."

Rachel did, dropping the helicopter down to land gently on its skids. She had come to know the characteristics of this machine as deftly as I had ever seen anyone learn anything. When the woman had first lifted off, I could feel her testing the joystick, figuring out the controls and rotor tilt. Not any more. She had it down as though it were an extension of her own body.

"Okay," I said. "You guys work on finding a place to fill this bird, okay? This is going to take us a while."

Serena's face was solemn, but not angry. I went to her. "If anything happens, someone needs to be able to get Rachel back to Flex and the others. If it all goes wrong, that's where I want both of you."

She nodded. "I hate you." Her eyes wouldn't meet mine.

"Nah, you don't. You love me."

Serena shook her head, looked at me and reached out, putting her arms around my neck and pulling me close to her. "Hurry," she said. "Hurry, be careful and get back to me fast."

"I will," I said, fishing inside my pocket. I pulled out the baggie of WAT-5. "Nel, you ready for a quick catnap, brother?"

"Let's do it," he said.

*****

We talked about the plan more extensively before taking the wafers. We didn't want to waste a minute of the protection they would provide in case something went terribly wrong and we needed all five hours.

After we were both nudged awake by Serena and Rachel, we put together everything we'd need in Nelson's backpack, emptying it of the items that would not serve us.

"How many rounds do you have, and in how many mags?" asked Serena.

"We have a hundred fifty rounds in fifteen 10-round mags, plus what's in the guns."

"How many spare guns?" she asked.

I humored her, because I knew why she was so concerned. I didn't even look the slightest bit impatient, I'm pretty sure. "Serena, we are on a time schedule now that we've taken the WAT-5, but we have a spare gun each."

"It's in case of a jam, so it's not for nothing that I'm asking," she said.

Maybe I had looked a bit impatient. "I know, baby. I'll be fine. Promise."

She hugged me again and I hopped out. Nelson came toward the door to get out, but Rachel called after him.

"Hey, Nelson, come here for a sec." She unbuckled and crawled out of the pilot's seat, stepping into the passenger compartment.

"What, Rachel?" he asked, smiling his innocent, crooked smile that hid such talent and brainpower behind it.

She opened her arms, smiling. "Come in for a hug, buddy," she said. "You're gonna need some love to get you through this."

"Hell yes," he said, and put his arms around her, squeezing her tight. He pulled away. "Thanks, Rachel."

"Love works," she said. "Makes you want to come back."

Nelson leaned forward quickly and planted a peck on her lips. Rachel pulled back, surprised, though there was a smile on her face. "Wow!" she said. "What was that for?" she asked.

"You and me," he said. "You because you needed a kiss for luck. You have to find fuel. Me, because it couldn't hurt."

"Get out of here," she said. "You guys are going to take a left on this street and work your way northwest. Be goddamned careful."

*****

We moved into the street and stayed alongside the roadway. There was a small neighborhood of homes nearby, and that's where we headed. We needed some supplies that seemed pretty easy to find in most homes – but it might take a few tries.

We reached the street and hit the lawn of the first home. It had a two car garage, which was promising, and the house looked nice.

"Come on, Nelson. Around the side."

We walked to the side and tried the hinged door to the garage, but it was locked.

"Allow me," said Nelson.

I remembered. His Subdudo. "Go for it," I said.

One swift kick, and the jamb splintered and we were in. "Nice boots," I said. "Gotta get me a pair."

"Yeah, dude," he said. "Steel toe, but I didn't use it that time."

"Headlight," I said, and we switched them on. The garage was empty, but on the WAT-5, we didn't care anyway. We'd blend right in with 99% of the abnormals. It was the other 1% that we were concerned about.

"Bingo," I said, walking up to the bicycles. One was a an old Huffy beach cruiser, and the other was stingray with mini-ape hanger handlebars. I shone my light on the tires. Rotten, cracked.

"No good," I said. "Tires are gone."

"Shit. Fire extinguisher?" said Nelson, walking toward the door to the house. Sure enough, one hung there. He shone the light on the gauge and it showed the stainless steel canister was drained of pressure. "Good," he said. He pulled the tank down and inspected it, and sure enough, he found a fill valve, identical to that on a bicycle tire.

"Got a good Bingo this time," he said. "One down."

"Okay, let's get out of here and into a garage with bikes owned by healthy people."

It took us three more homes and some tense moments working near the walking dead before we manually raised the garage door and rode out on two fifteen speed mountain bikes, probably from Wal*Mart, with our jury-rigged backpack fire extinguishers on our backs, two empty bottles stuffed with torn tee-shirt strips and a barbeque lighter in each of our pockets.

"Let's fill these and get changed," I said. "We've already burned through half an hour."

Each bicycle had a small bike pump mounted to the crossbar. Nelson's was a girl's bike, but he didn't care. We filled the flat tires and were now riding in relative style. We'd also chosen two nice baseball bats, and had screwed nylon straps at the grip and midway down its length to create a weapon that would sling over our shoulders like a rifle.

"I'm feeling pretty damned good about us right now," said Nelson.

"So am I, but we need to find them yet."

"Check the radio," he said. I stopped the bike for a second and unclipped it from my waistband. "Rachel, Serena? Come in."

"Hey," said Serena. "You on your way yet?"

"No," I said. "Almost. Just have to change now."

"Yuck."

"I know."

"Hurry, and be safe. Got everything you need?"

"Totally. Good bikes, bats, extinguisher canisters with fill valves."

"Don't blow yourselves up," she said.

"We won't, mom," I said. "We'll check in when we can."

"Smart ass. I love you," she said.

"You too, Serena."

I put the radio away. At the end of the street we saw a straggler. The ones we'd seen earlier were in such a condition of half-dress, that they would not serve our purposes. The one at the end of the street looked to be well-covered.

"Those duds are mine," said Nelson, standing on the pedals and pumping toward the creature. When he got there, he dumped the bike, jogged to the abnormal and stood in front of him for a second.

The zombie nudged him lightly with his shoulder as he attempted to walk around Nelson, and just as the rotter passed, Nelson swung his bat, cracking open the backside of the abnormal's brittle skull. He spun a half-turn and went down flat on his back.

I rode up and Nelson smiled at me. "Perfect position for undressing," he said. "Good part is, he didn't smell me."

"That's comforting," I said. "Get it done, then."

Ten minutes later, Nelson had pulled the creature's loose clothing over the top of his own, and the pustule-riddled body of the dead zombie lay nude on the ground at his feet. Apparently, zombies preferred commando style.

Once he finished buttoning the gore-splattered, filthy and tattered long-sleeved shirt, he looked at me, tried to smile, then bent over and threw up in the street.

When he stood again, his face was green. "Fuck, dude," he said. "They really stink when you're in their clothes."

"I don't want to think about it," I said.

Nelson recovered a bit and pulled his arms back through his various gear and weaponry. He adjusted all the magazines in his nasty pockets and the backpack, picked his bike up, and got on.

The moment he was on, he pointed down the street. "There!" he said. "That's one with some wearable clothes."

"No way. Let's keep looking," I said.

"Dude, you can't be choosy, and we don't have much time. We've still got to get gas and get to wherever they are."

Nelson was right. It's that awkward moment when you realize the stoner has more sense than you sometimes, damn it.

We rode down the street. I killed me a zombie and changed into her clothes.

*****

Chapter Ten

I had to hike the filthy, ankle-length dress up onto my thighs while I rode the bike. It was loose enough at the bottom that I didn't think it would impede my ability to run if necessary, so that was okay.

We'd used the siphon to get gasoline, so with the full fire extinguishers, we were riding pretty heavy. As I rode, I pulled out the radio.

"Rachel, come in."

"Hi babe," answered Serena instead. "Rachel's filling the chopper with gas."

"Cool," I said. "It's been an hour and ten minutes, and we're on the way now. I wanted to see if you guys had enough fuel to get airborne for a few and tell us where they are."

"Hold on," said Serena.

She came back on a second later. "We can do it, but the startup uses a lot of fuel, so it'll set us back. Worth it, right?"

"Hella worth it," I said. I'm not sure why.

"Where are you guys?" she asked.

"We rode northwest like she said, but we've been zigzagging, so I just don't know how close we are," I said. "We've passed by a few rotters walking, but if we followed them it would take all damned day."

"Okay, give us like ten and we'll get up. Stay in the middle of the street. If you're on bikes, Rachel says she can find you."

"We are," I said. "Tell her to hurry."

"Duh," said Serena.

I tucked the radio away.

"There's another," said Nelson. "I got it." He rode his bike over to where the rotter walked. It was a female in the same, deep reddish-brown clothing that they all seemed to wear, if they wore any at all. Stained from over a year of blood, mud and God knew what else. Nelson pulled his bike ahead and parked it, then put the kickstand down.

He walked up to it, cautious at first. "Got pink eyes, but they're not red," he said. He looked at her stomach. "Nothing showing, either."

"Nelson, just take it out."

Nelson looked at me. "Pardon me if I still like to marvel at the capabilities of WAT-5." He raised his bat and twirled it three times as though waiting for the pitcher windup. Then he swung the bat hard, catching the abnormal just above the ear.

The bat disappeared in the left side of her skull and came out the other side, like cutting the top off a soft boiled egg.

"Oh, shit," said Nelson, disgusted by his own handiwork. The rotter fell onto her right side and lay still.

I had been circling, but rode over and stopped, putting my feet down and pulling down my skirt over my jeans.

"You think you're used to it, huh?" I said, knowing what he was feeling. "Then you remember they used to be people."

Nelson looked at me, his face unreadable, tapping the business end of his bat on the asphalt. "It was really hard at first," he said. "I remember standing there, still thinking of them as sick people. They'd come at me and I'd dodge them, like I was some stupid kid playing tag, and I wasn't it."

"I never thought about it like that," I said.

"So I'd just jump back, playing keep away with my body until I realized they'd never give up until they had their teeth in me. So it got easier, but never easy."

We heard the sound of the helicopter, and saw it just off to the southeast. Nelson slung his bat back over his shoulder and ran back to his bike. We started riding in big circles in the middle of the street and waving. It wasn't long before our motion caught Rachel's eye and she angled the blades toward us. The bird followed.

My radio clicked, and I grabbed it. "Yeah," I said.

"You're not far from them," said Serena. "They're two streets over. You head straight to the next corner and turn right. Two blocks and you're there."

I could barely hear her, but I got what she said. "Thanks, Serena."

"Want us to stay airborne and cover from here?"

"No, go back and see if you can fill that gas tank. If this works out like I planned, we're gonna burn our way to the bitches," I said.

"I hate to sound like a broken record, but be careful," said Serena.

"Nothing less," I said. I waved up toward the helicopter and then motioned them away. It turned back toward where it had dropped us off.

"Did you hear what she said?" I asked Nelson.

"Yep," he said. "Straight down this way. I'll follow you. So when we get there, what's the deal? I cut left, you cut right?"

"We'll just approach them that way," I said. "Remember. We've got the nozzles dialed in for a fine stream, so just douse the ones in front and then spray high over them so you rain it down on the crowd a bit. We need them good and soaked."

"Got it," he said. His smile was completely gone. Determination replaced it, and I liked what I saw. I'd seen him determined before, and when he was that, he was good.

I pulled down my dress again. We rode.

*****

"Stop," I whispered, and we both pulled the bikes up onto a lawn and peered around the corner of a house. They had moved from the street – which was not good for my plan – and were now pressing in on a house in the middle of the block. It looked like all the other houses, so I couldn't tell what was special about that one.

"Nelson," I said. "If they go inside, we just burn the whole thing down and get runners – so to speak – when they come out."

"Works for me," he said.

But we waited, and in about seven more minutes, they shambled back into the street, moving as one unit. The roadway was perhaps thirty feet wide. The group of shuffling infecteds almost filled the street, curb to curb, with maybe three feet on either side, between the houses. They were longer than they were wide, though. I guessed their numbers somewhere near 200 now. They had definitely been collecting more bodies as they made their way toward where the girls and our helicopter waited.

How they knew where to go I didn't want to think about, but I didn't have to, did I?

It was the red-eyes. Sixth sense. Telepathy. How much didn't we know?

Long distance telepathy. That was new. I wondered if Hemp knew about that yet.

"Okay," said Nelson. "We have to go eventually."

"Get the lighter in your front pocket," I said. "We'll need to strike at the same time before they start to scramble, then we start shooting."

"Is this gonna work, dude?" asked Nelson.

"Hope so. WAT-5 should help as long as the red-eyes don't see us."

"Then we ditch the bikes for stealth. Speed's not as important," Nelson said. "They're not fast. The bikes got us here, but we don't need them to do this, plus we're sitting up so high on these damned things they might see us above the crowd and set their robots onto us."

I stared at him. "Dude," I said. "I feel like I'm talking to Flex or Hemp. What happened to you?"

"Some of my shit's a put-on," he said. "People tend to be protective of me and they give me stuff. I kind of got used to it before I met all of you. It got me to my Gramps."

"Now that I know," I said, "I won't forget. "Good idea. Let's do it."

We laid the bikes down and crouched low. When we reached the outside of the group, I pulled the extinguisher off my back and took the handle. We'd pressurized the hell out of both of them with the bike pump, and the gauges read FULL.

I detached the nozzle from the clip and held the hose in my hand, looking at Nelson. He did the same with his. We nodded at one another and took off.

I started spraying as I ran, soaking the perimeter zombies with gasoline, and then wagging the hose high and low. I glanced behind me and saw Nelson doing the exact same thing. We'd practiced it, and it was working exactly as we thought it would.

The creatures walked on. The smell of gas obviously did not alarm them. It wasn't flesh and blood, so they weren't alerted and our WAT-5 made us a couple of walking nothings to those who did see us.

I reached the front of the crowd and saw Nelson disappear behind the rear. The canister in my hands still felt full, and the arrow was still in the green, so I continued running and spraying, sure to get it over and deep into the crowd. I stayed ahead of the advancing group and rounded the next corner, now running parallel to the curb, dousing them on the other side.

I saw Nelson come around, and when he saw me, he could not suppress a smile. He ran toward me, and I ran toward him. When we reached one another, I said, "Keep going. Double up, wet 'em more."

He did. I felt my tank reaching its bottom now, so I sprayed more on the outer creatures, and raised the nozzle as it began to sputter. Nelson was out of sight, likely in the same position as me, but on the other side of the crowd.

I pulled out my radio, which was on channel 16.

"Nelson," I said.

"Yeah."

"Light 'em up."

I reached into my pocket and pulled out the barbeque lighter. I moved right next to a particularly wet zombie who was about two bodies from the outside perimeter of rotters, and I lit him on fire.

Then I ran back and pulled out my Walther. The crowd caught quickly, the fire spreading in a huge circle, and I saw the bodies begin to stagger and fall. As they fell, more of them tripped, stumbling on top of the others, catching fire themselves.

A sort of hiss-pop-screaming began to rise from the crowd, but I wasn't sure they were zombie voices I heard, rather the sound of gasses escaping rotting pockets within their bloated bodies, and the smoke and smell that started to flood out of the collapsing horde was choking me.

I shot one who broke free. I heard Nelson's gun from somewhere, so knew he was okay.

Where were the females? Ten deep had fallen in, and I still did not see them. The smoke was now thick, and the heat caused them to waver back and forth like macabre mirages.

Then I spotted her. She stared toward me, her eyes burning red as torches through the smoke, and I raised my gun and fired in her direction. She pushed through the burning bodies directly toward me and I calmly ejected my magazine and slid another into place.

I lowered my arm and watched her. My other hand instinctively went for the bat, so there I stood, a Louisville Slugger in one hand – my right – and my Walther PPK in the other.

She caught fire. I was the only one in a dress here, but I'm sure she got no amusement from it. I stood there, staying clear of the flames, watching as her clothing ignited even further. I was amazed to see her pants and blouse burn completely off of her, but the garments were probably nearly rotted before the flames even touched her.

Either way, by the time she was ten feet away she was nude, stepping over the creatures, her skin bubbling and cooking over her skeleton.

And still her eyes glowed. Had I not been flammable myself, I would have walked into that crowd and emptied the magazine into her brain, but instead I waited for her, my hands trembling.

I stepped back. Glanced behind me to make sure she wasn't giving silent commands to some out of my line of sight. There were none.

I still did not raise my weapon. In fact, I moved my hands behind me so as not to reveal them to her. She knew what could harm her, but she had no defense against fire.

I was now about eight feet away from the nearest burning zombie. She drew to within four feet of me when I raised my Walther and fired six shots into her face.

She stopped, her eyes going instantly dark. I don't know why, but I dropped the gun, double-fisted the bat and swung as hard as I ever had, knocking her horrid head cleanly off of her spine, sending it deep into the burning madness.

I watched her body become fully engulfed and burn for a few moments until I was convinced it would not rise again, and when I believed it would not, I reached down and took the Walther back in my hand. Then I ran around the rear of the crowd, looking for the other one.

I did not see her. The pyre had consumed them all now, and it was a horrid scene reminiscent of some terrible, Holocaust footage.

"Davey!" I heard Nelson shout, and I ran toward his voice. As I reached him, I saw another of the red-eyes on the ground in front of him. He had no doubt had a rerun of what I had been through play out on this side.

And he had been victorious.

"Did you find two?" he asked, his breath ragged as he took in the smoke and fumes of rotting, burning flesh and gasoline.

"No," I said. "I don't know where she is. Maybe she burned."

Nelson pointed. "There! Over by that house!"

I turned, and sure enough, she was there, her blood-red eyes turned toward us. Suddenly, she walked in the opposite direction.

"The fucking bikes!" I shouted, and Nelson fired two quick shots at a zombie who had emerged from the mess, laying it down. Nothing else moved.

I kept my eye on the female. She was six houses down now. I noted that she was between a yellow and a blue house, then ran toward the bikes alongside Nelson.

"We have to get her," I said as we picked the bikes up. It was much easier now without the extinguishers filled with gasoline.

We rode across the grass, for the street was filled with smoking, and in some cases, squirming rotters in the throes of a high-Fahrenheit death. Rounding the corner, we could no longer see the female.

Our legs pumped. The apocalypse had ensured that we were in good shape – more fit than either of us had been before all this crap went down – and we cranked those pedals for all they were worth.

"There she is!" said Nelson. I saw her at the same time.

Then we heard crying. It came from a house to our right. I looked over, and saw the figure of a woman drop out of sight behind a broken window.

"Jesus, Nelson! There's a woman over there! In that house!"

Nelson looked. "Where?"

"Blue house. Go! I'm going after the red-eye!"

Nelson peeled to the right and I stood on those pedals and pushed them hard. When I reached the corner of a brown clapboard house, I turned right, and saw her eyes glowing. She stood there. Still. She did not run.

I recognized her as the tallest of the three who had been manipulating the large group we had just dispatched by fire.

Vapor began pumping from her eyes and she began a slow, deliberate trek toward me. I stopped and watched her. If she knew what her vapor was capable of, perhaps instinctually, like a porcupine or a skunk – to use some of Hemp's examples – then she must know they were ineffective on me. It was about mind control with these monsters, not about knockout vapor.

In the end, it was everything but anticlimactic. She spewed her vapor, her eyes big, her hair almost healthy-looking. As she drew to within five feet of me, she seemed to bend her knees, and I didn't realize her plan.

It was good I had the gun in my hand, because even as I began to raise it, she sprung off those bony legs and leapt six feet in the air – in my direction.

Even as I fell backward, two hands on the Walther, firing round after round, I believe I was just lucky to put one through her right, red eye and one into her frontal lobe.

I rolled quickly off to my right and her body splatted down where I had been moments before. I looked at her, raised my Walther, and fired two more shots into her head.

I lay there for at least five minutes, never taking my eyes from her. I didn't move. Not until I heard Nelson's voice.

"Davey, you alright?" he asked.

I waved my arm. "I'm resting," I said.

"Get up," he said. "You need to meet Lolita Lane."

I rolled over. Nelson stood beside a harried-looking blonde girl of perhaps twenty-four, who raised her hand in a shy wave, a canvas pack slung over her shoulder.

*****

We'd gotten Lolita inside the helicopter with Rachel while Serena, Nelson and I finished siphoning nearby cars until the chopper's tank was full and ready to go. Everything we had done had taken us just over four hours. It was almost 6:00 PM.

It had seemed like a lifetime. We were all exhausted and nightfall would be coming soon. Even if we flew just a short distance to a remote farmhouse or something, I wanted to get the hell out of whatever damned town we were in, and I kinda wanted to locate our night's resting spot in daylight. We didn't have a hell of a lot of time.

"I'd ask you how you came across the name Lolita Lane," said Serena, "But I've always thought it was the stupidest question ever. Of course your parents gave it to you."

"Flex has had his share of that, I'd imagine," said Nelson.

"Guys, we're taking off. Get your headsets on and you can chat in the air."

"Is this thing safe? Do you know how to fly it?" asked Lolita.

"Rachel's a pilot," said Nelson. "She's gotten us all the way from Knoxville, Tennessee."

Lolita Lane stood about 5'7", her figure thin, but her arms and calves muscular. Her eyes were brown, and when we found her, her long, blonde hair had been dirty and matted. Her clothing, worn over her obviously diminished frame, appeared to have been changed recently, for she wore a relatively clean, blue and white striped spaghetti strap tank top and black cotton capris pants. Her shoes were suede hiking boots that my dad used to call waffle stompers because of the pattern the soles left in the mud.

When we'd first brought her to the women, Serena had agreed to give her body the once over for bites or scratches. Lolita seemed reluctant at first, but we explained all we knew about the creatures out there, and that if she did not agree, she would not be welcome to stay with us.

It was even tougher because Rachel held her revolver at ready the entire time. When it was done and we were allowed back inside the helicopter, we came in to find the filth cleaned entirely from her face and arms, and her hair combed through.

She was pretty cute, and I thought that Nelson might be a little shy around her, but that just proved to me I didn't know Nelson very well. He was unfazed and just like he always was.

"We used your brush from your backpack, Nelson," said Serena. "Hope you don't mind."

Nelson looked at Lolita and smiled. "Nah, not at all. She's my first rescue. You're kind of special to me that way, Lolita," he said.

"My friends call me Lola," she said. "One less syllable. Rolls off the tongue easier."

"Well, around here," said Nelson, "if someone's not trying to eat you, they're your friend. So it's Lola then."

She smiled and nodded as the rotors reached their maximum RPM. The helicopter lifted off and as I knelt down in front of our new charge, I steadied myself on the back of Rachel's seat.

"So you're bite free," I said. "No scratches, either. Do you have a weapon?"

"I'm mostly a runner."

"Wow, a runner," said Nelson. "So you've just been running from them?"

Lola shrugged, then nodded again. "I can run a long time, as long as I'm hydrated. Hours. I haven't had any need to stand and fight as long as there was a path to get away."

"So Lola," I said. "What happened back there? We saw the abnormals surrounding that house you were in."

"Abnormals? You mean the biters?"

I nodded my head. I guess we all had our names for them. "Yeah," I said. "Biters, diggers, rotters, infecteds, abnormals ... zombies."

Lolita looked at me and nodded. "That's what they really are," she said.

"Yeah," I said. "So tell us what happened. Do you mind?"

She shook her head and uncapped a bottle of water we'd given her, taking a sip. As she screwed the cap back on she spoke: "They came to the house and I was watching from the window," she explained. "When I saw them go by, I was confused, because I watched them pass by earlier, you know, and I was glad to see them keep walking. I couldn't figure out why they were coming back."

"What did they do?"

"It was pretty sudden," she said. "You saw there weren't any curtains in that house, or blinds or anything, so I was afraid to run out of the front room thinking they'd see me – like you guys did from your bikes."

"So what did you do?" asked Nelson, his mouth hanging open.

"I dropped to the floor," she said. "Carpeted." Just tucked against the very front corner below the window and prayed. They broke the glass out, and the next thing I knew they were just gone."

"What do you mean?" I asked.

"I mean I woke up and they were gone."

"What do you mean, you *woke up*?"

"I don't know, I just … one minute they were there, like a hundred of them, and the next they weren't. I don't know. I guess I fell asleep, because how else could that happen?"

I thought about this. The regular, pink zombie vapor could make you fall asleep, but you wouldn't awaken on your own, so I wasn't convinced that was what had happened.

"Lola, do you remember seeing any pink or red vapor coming from their eyes?"

"I know what that is!" she shouted, her eyes wide. Nelson winced as her voice boomed in his headset.

"It puts you to sleep. They drag you away when you go out, or they just eat you right there, but it's like a weapon. I've seen it a few times, especially in the beginning when there were a lot like me."

"Where is everyone?"

"Mostly dead," she said. "But we're off the subject, right?"

I nodded. I wasn't sure I wanted to get back on the subject, because it wasn't good news no matter how we sliced it.

"Lola, this is very important," I said. "How old are you?"

"Twenty-three," she said.

"Can you have children?" I asked.

Her brows furrowed together, and she said, "Not that it's any secret, but why do you ask?"

"It's important," I said. "And don't worry, we're not looking to use you in a baby factory to repopulate the world or anything."

"I hadn't even thought of that," she said, looking at Serena for help.

Serena smiled kindly, and said, "No, we don't want to kidnap you to be a baby maker. The vapor from the females with red eyes," she said. "It's dangerous to women and girls of child-bearing years. It can put you under their control."

Lola stared at her. "Are you serious? How?"

"There's a telepathy thing going on with them," I said. "It's real, and they can apparently use it for a significant distance. And for different things."

"Like *how* different? Do you think I've been sprayed?"

"He doesn't know, and neither do I," said Nelson. "You were wide awake when we saw you."

"Lisa didn't fall asleep when she got doused either," I said. "The red gas doesn't knock you out, remember."

"I don't feel any different," she said.

"The red-eyes are all dead, and we're up here in the air, so you wouldn't," I said. "And we don't know how long it lasts, if it's permanent, or it acts similar to the pink gas where it goes away in time and leaves you normal."

"So tell me what they can do with this ... control," said Lola. "With the red vapor."

Serena answered. "The telepathy and the vapor are two separate things, we think. With their mind power, one thing they can do is call their minions, the dumber ones, to come to them from a distance of about a mile radius."

"No shit?" she said.

"None," said Serena. "But even the dumb ones have some innate abilities, like recognition of things that can hurt them, like firearms, swords, knives."

"I've seen stuff like that, but I could never give them that much credit!" she said.

"We probably wouldn't have put it together except for our scientist buddy, Hemp," said Nelson. "But the red stuff is way different," he said. "If you're doused with that stuff, they can make you do stuff. They think it and you just start talking out loud and next thing you know, you're doing what they made you say, like a command."

"Guys, there's a nice spread below us," said Rachel. "Looks like a good place to stop, and we're getting near sunset." Rachel pointed below and we all looked.

"Fenced, with plenty of room to land," I said. "Go for it, Rachel."

"To answer your question – and I'm sorry for the runaround," said Lola, "Yes. I can have children."

I nodded. "Okay. We'll talk more when we get inside and settled," I said. "You'll find it all very interesting, I'm sure. Plus, we have some special wafers for those of you who can bear children. I don't know how well they work if you've already been hit with the vapor, but to me, it's worth using one to make sure we can sleep without worrying."

Serena looked at me. "You have the red-eye wafers?" she asked.

"Just a few," I said. "They were in my pocket, separate from the others. I thought you knew."

"No, but that's good," she said. "I haven't had any close encounters with them yet, but if I do, one of them is on the menu."

"There are six," I said. "But believe me, if it gets hairy and there's any chance you'll come face-to-face with them, I'll force that damned thing down you."

"You sure know how to give a girl the tingles," she said.

"Always been one of my strong suits, and you know it." I stroked my beard and smiled. I'm not sure Lola knew what to make of us just yet.

The helicopter dropped, and settled into a dirt yard. The six-foot fence around us appeared to be made of galvanized, corrugated steel, and you could not see through it.

Privacy.

From prying, red eyes.

*****

The front door of the house was wide open, which we hadn't seen from the air, of course. There were two bags of bones in the house; one in a bedroom, which was badly stained with old, dried blood. This one had been badly ravaged, either in the throes of death or just after. Looked like a multi-pronged attack of the zombies.

Some of the bones were not there. I always pictured an infected walking across a field holding an arm like it was a goddamned turkey leg at a Renaissance Faire. Just one of my visuals that I couldn't shake.

The other deteriorated corpse was in the front room. A fireplace poker lay on the ground near its outstretched arm, and dried, brown smears decorated the brass handle.

I went to it, gathered the material around it and brought all the torn corners together. I was able to lift the bones, aside from the skull, which had fallen off and rolled against the couch, to the back door, where I dropped them in a metal trash can and put the lid on.

Nelson carried the skull out as though it was smeared in dog shit. I lifted the lid again and he dropped it in with the rest of the fellow.

Two more bodies were in the front yard. They would be resting in peace. Perhaps they said to any visitors, we're all dead here. Move along.

We ate food from the helicopter. Lola did not act strangely that evening, but before we went down for the night, I asked her to chew up one of the special wafers and she agreed. I'd call it WAT-5 Special, made from the vapor of the red-eyed females but we didn't know how long its effects lasted. We'd not encountered any more pregnant females until this road trip, so Hemp had no reason to keep in touch with Rebecca Dovorany for the purposes of monitoring her.

Either way, the wafers were all magic stuff.

Serena and I didn't make love that night, though I wanted to. Instead, we both fell asleep instantly and slept like the dead.

I hope like hell we smelled better than the dead. I was sure that we were no longer equipped to judge, one way or the other.

*****

When I awoke, I lay there for a while staring at Serena, then quietly got out of bed, trying not to wake her.

I went into the garage and searched the shelves, locating a small, propane camping stove with three spare canisters of gas. In the kitchen pantry, I found an un-pierced can of Folgers medium roast coffee.

I pierced it.

Powdered creamer would have to do but it *was* Coffee Mate, and I can tell you the house smelled like Starbucks and the coffee tasted like dry roasted Heaven in a cup.

"Morning," said Rachel, walking out with a yawn. Serena was still sleeping, and I didn't like to wake her up until she was ready; primarily because she was so damned beautiful when she slept that I could watch her for hours.

"Hey," I said. "Morning. Hot coffee, there in that tin camping pot."

"Are you kidding me?" she asked, going to it and filling one of the mugs I'd left beside it.

She added nothing, just held the steaming cup in both hands and took a sip. "Wow," she said. "Don and I kind of put all these good things away," she said. "Seems we ate MREs and drank water and let go of all the things that used to make a crappy day better."

"Well, just remember my new rule to live by," I said.

"What's that?" she asked, taking another big sip of coffee.

"Survival is a state of mind," I said. "It's what you make of it."

"I'm getting that now. I miss Don," she said. "I really grew to love that old guy."

"We need to have a little service for him before we go," I said. "He deserves that, wouldn't you say?"

"Yes," she said. "And I know you didn't really know him, but he was a good friend to me and Jess and he really did his best to take care of me while we were together."

242

"From what he said, you did your share, too."

"It was a partnership. Every time I wanted to go back and see if there was word from Jess, he'd agree without any hesitation. Even after a year."

I nodded, wondering when I would say something. It wasn't now. She did not need to have any confusion about her feelings for Don when we had our little ceremony, whatever it ended up being.

Nelson came in from outside, and we were surprised to see him, because we thought he was in one of the bedrooms sleeping.

"Mornin', dudes," he said, smiling.

"What's that you got there?" I asked.

"Pop Tarts."

"Shit, I forgot about those," I said.

"I love Pop Tarts!" said Lola, padding in from the hallway. "Where did you get them?"

"Pharmacy," said Nelson. "I had to pummel six zombies with a plastic bat for these, so if you want any, I'll have to challenge you to a plastic swordfight battle to the death."

"You're funny," she said. "I'll take a pack."

Nelson smiled at her, his eyes narrow slits, and threw her a foil pack that she caught easily.

"Did you sleep out there, Nel?" I asked.

"Nah, I went out to smoke a bowl and grab the Pop Tarts."

"Want some coffee?" I asked him.

"Nah, thanks," he said. "You got your morning medicine, I got mine."

"I can't smoke weed in the morning," said Lola. "I'd be tired all day. I'd never wake up."

"Ditto," I said.

"I smoked before I got into the military," said Rachel, "but there's nothing like a relentless enemy to convince you to stay on top of your game," said Rachel. "Assholes never take time off, it seems."

"Evil never sleeps," I said. "That said, we had some hilarious evenings with Flex and Gem – sometimes Charlie, never Hemp – where we got high and played games. Laughed our asses off."

Nelson handed Lola a pack of Pop Tarts. She held the package in her teeth while she poured herself a cup of coffee. She put in five packs of sugar and the amount of powdered cream she added almost overflowed her cup.

She pulled her blonde hair into a ponytail and sat on a barstool, her knees pulled up to the seat as she sipped the coffee and pivoted back and forth.

Nelson slid onto the stool beside her and chewed his Pop Tart, looking stoned.

"We're going to have a little memorial service for Don before we leave," I said. "We already almost have a full tank of fuel, so there's not going to be a lot of prep today."

"Where's Serena?" asked Lola.

"Here," said Serena, walking into the room from the hallway. She wore gray sweatpants and a blue, ribbed cotton tank top. Her feet were bare. Serena's straight, dark hair was also in a ponytail and I loved the way she looked in the morning.

I'm not sure I was aware of my smile at first, but when she looked at me and returned it, I knew I must have looked like a love struck goof.

"I smell the coffee," she said. "How's it holding up?"

"Good," I said. "And God, it tastes fresh, too."

Serena got her cup and sank into a couch in the middle of the family room, just in front of the kitchen.

"You know what?" said Rachel. "While everyone's relaxed and we've got a bit of peace, I want to say a few words about Don."

244

She started to cry, then just stopped talking and looked down for a couple of moments, biting her lip. She looked up again. "He died, and I know I don't have to tell you that. I wanted to do something for his memory, but I just wasn't ready until now."

We all nodded. She carried her coffee slowly to the front of the family room and stood facing us.

"Don was our neighbor for six years," she began. "He took a lot of stress off Jess when I deployed by offering his help. His wife had died a year before my last deployment, and since his kids were all moved out and living in other states, he was pretty much alone with his own hands full. But that didn't stop him offering. I appreciated it."

She started to cry, took a sip of coffee, and wiped her hair away from her face. "When I finally made it home, after a crazy journey that I was lucky to even survive, he was there. He'd put a sign on my door telling me he was at his house and he'd left an ATV right there ready for me. There was a gun taped to the seat and a flashlight. That's how he took care of me before he even knew I was back."

"Good guy," said Nelson. "Cared about you."

"He did, Nelson," she said. "We were partners for a year. I knew he saw me like his own daughter, and I loved him like a father. But my parents were in Japan. My father has been top brass in the Air Force for years, and he was in Misawa with my mother when all this started."

"Did you ever hear from them after everything began?" asked Serena.

She nodded. "The first day I got a call on my cell. It was crazy on the other end and I could barely hear him, but I got the picture. Within a week of that phone call I knew I'd never see them again. You guys know what a long week that was, and how much realization we all came to."

"Hell yes," I said. "It was eye-opening. I didn't really expect to be alive today, over a year later."

"None of us did," said Lola. "When my whole family was killed I just ran," she said. "I haven't stopped running since."

"Wow," said Nelson.

"Anyway, back to Don," said Rachel, holding up her coffee cup. "Here's to Don Weston. A good man who put me above himself until the day he died. The kind of man we need on this earth for this time and for all time. Rest in peace, Don."

"Rest in peace," we all said together.

Rachel shrugged. "It wasn't much, but Don would be tickled," she said.

"He'd be honored," I said. "As would any of us." I checked my watch. "It's 9:00. Let's say we get the hell outta Dodge by 10:00."

"We should do some ransacking," said Nelson. "See if there's anything else here we can use."

"There are a bunch of 1-gallon bottles of water in the garage," I said. "That means we've got plenty if you guys feel like a quick sponge bath."

"We just had a nice, hot shower at that model home," said Nelson. "Lola, been a while for you?"

"It has," she said. "Serena? Help me out?"

"Absolutely," said Serena. "And since it looks like this was a family with a daughter, there are men's, women's and about a fifteen-year-old girl's clothes here, too. Rachel, those ought to just about fit you. No offense."

"Check that," she said. "None taken."

*****

Serena helped Lola in the bathroom with her sponge bath, and everyone else began searching closets and

246

dressers for changes of clothes. Nelson and I were extra ripe, having worn the disgusting zombie wear, but we felt it necessary to blend in with the crowd to avoid being spotted by the red-eyed females from a distance. Whether it had played any part in our success, we did not know, but we had no regrets other than our foul odors.

I found a fresh pair of jeans that were only a waist size too big for me, and just the right length. There was a ZZ Top concert tee shirt from 2005 that suited me just fine. Nelson settled on a Foreigner concert tee shirt from 1999, and Rachel found a nice button-down khaki that she looked comfortable in. She also wore a pair of rhinestone-emblazoned jeans from the daughter's room and a Margaritaville baseball cap with her own ponytail sticking out the back.

Rachel and Lola emerged looking clean – with Lola wearing makeup she had obviously found in the bathroom. She looked very cute, actually, and I realized I hadn't seen a woman wearing makeup for a long, long time. She wore light yellow pants and a black tank top. Serena had on a pair of cargo shorts – I didn't know whether they were men's or women's, and she kept her ribbed tank. She looked great in it, so I didn't mind in the slightest.

Everyone was primped and ready. We were out of there by 10:00 in the morning as planned. As the helicopter rose above the fence line, I got chills down by back, eyeing the crowd of walking dead that pressed against the exterior of the fence.

Fifty or sixty of them. Two deep, side by side, all along the fence, wearing their bloody-drab clothing, clawing at the metal with no hope of penetrating the barrier.

As I looked down at them, I remembered Rachel's tribute to Don Weston, and then I pictured what Don must have seen out in his corral that Sunday. His neighbor Jess Reed, biting into the underbelly of one of his finest calves, and turning his face up to stare at Don with no recognition; only hunger and determination.

I tried to push the image out of my mind. We rose higher into the air, and as the entire property came into view below me, we saw that the fifty or sixty we'd seen was actually over a hundred. I immediately knew the meaning of that line in a poem I'd heard a long time ago.

Good fences make good neighbors.

"Fall," said Lola.

I had barely heard it in my headset, and I hadn't been looking at her when I heard the words, so could not be sure. I looked at Serena who stared between Lola and me and I then looked directly at Lola, seeing the look of confusion and fear in her eyes.

"Fall to us," she said again, then screamed a shrill, ear-piercing shriek. Nelson had spun around in his chair now, and I saw that he had one of his Ninja stars in his right hand. He was not smiling. Rachel glanced over her shoulder every now and then, but remained focused.

Lolita Lane started crying. "What's happening?" she said, staring at me.

"You're okay Lola," I said, reaching over to take her hands. "You are. They must have doused you in the house before Nelson got to you. You're kind of a portal for them," I said.

And immediately after I said it, I realized that I not only took her hands to comfort her; I also took them to make damned sure she did not use them to harm us in any way.

I did not let go of them again until we were miles from that house.

And the creatures below.

*****

248

We'd been flying an hour and no more strange words had come from Lola's mouth. She had been alternately crying and staring out the window since the event, and I thought it was time to fill her in.

"Feel like talking?" I asked.

She nodded, swiping at her red eyes. Serena looked at me and nodded her approval, too. "We've seen it before," said Serena. "It's not dangerous like this. It could've been."

"What stopped it?" she asked.

"The wafer we gave you as a precaution," I said. "We didn't know for sure if you were gassed in the house, but since you didn't remember where a huge crowd like the one we saw had gone, I had to go under the assumption that you were. It wouldn't have knocked you out, but might have affected your memory. We experimented with a girl named Rebecca Dovorany in Concord – she volunteered to take it and be sprayed."

"Brave," said Lola. "But it works in the opposite order? After you're sprayed?"

"Now, I suppose the answer is yes, unless you had an urge to attack Rachel or pull open the door. Did you? *Do* you?"

She shook her head. "No, and I never did. Not even when I heard those words coming from my mouth."

"So that's language," said Serena. "Basic, but language. I don't think I was around to see what happened when Rebecca was tested."

"You were preoccupied," I said. "Me, too. Hemp worked on it during what would have been our last hours if not for Tony."

We *had* been about to die – a bar filled with every survivor in town was either going to be overrun with zombies and burned, or the same thing in the opposite order. We were lucky – so damned lucky – that Tony Mallette from Shelburne, Vermont picked that damned day to move to Concord. He's living near my old friends now, and I know I'll see him again if we make it out of California.

I patted Lola's hand. "I don't know how long this ability lasts," I said. "You were a portal back there, and I don't think anything more than that. You might keep the ability, you might not. Either way, it could serve as an early warning system to us. If they're nearby."

"Do you think they're broadcasting those commands all the time, David?" asked Serena.

"You mean just blasting out commands in case one of their gas victims is around?" asked Nelson. "Like you guys said Hemp's radio was doing in Alabama?"

"Yeah," I said, looking at Serena. "Hemp looped a message on a Ham radio telling everyone they went to Concord when they left, which is how Carville found him. Hope that battery died already."

"Yeah," said Nelson. "Town's a dead end now. Probably burned to the ground, surrounded by crispy critter zombies."

"But to answer your question," I said, "I guess it's a maybe."

Rachel chimed in from the pilot's seat. "They're dead," she said. "How do they have words at all? Language skills."

"I didn't hear any voice inside my head," said Lola. "I don't remember that. I just remember the thought originating and coming out. Like from mush to words."

"It's like how they call the other zombies, dude!" said Nelson, his eyes wide for a change. "Talk about dead, those dudes are freakin' deader'n dead. They can't hear shit, so words wouldn't work. Maybe just like a draw, like a magnet. A pull."

"A telepathic command?" I asked. "Well, I guess that's what it is anyway," I said, answering my own question.

"Whatever," said Nelson. "I think that when it's dead to dead, like from the red-eyes to the others, it's just what you said – a pull. When it's picked up by Lola here or Rebecca back in Concord, it's converted into words that they can understand, but not sent that way, just like converted by these chick's brains."

"That makes sense," said Serena. "If by *these chicks*, you mean Lola and Rebecca. The intention of the command is clear, like a woman giving her husband or boyfriend a look. He'd know what that look means, and could act on it as surely as if words were spoken."

"You got looks like that?" I asked, smiling.

Serena said nothing. She just gave me a look.

"Got it," I said. "But I think we might be thinking we're smarter than we are," I said. "It makes sense, but I can't fight that imposter complex. You know, that I'm not smart enough to have figured it out."

"Dude, you can drop that worry, because I figured it out and I damned well know I'm smart enough" said Nelson. "Ha ha! It's an intellectual switcheroo."

I had to laugh. Nelson had already told me his goofy stoner game was largely an act, and while I didn't believe it completely – if only based on the amount of weed he smoked – he was a hell of a lot smarter than I'd ever given him credit for before this road trip.

"Touché," I said. "Rachel, how we doing on fuel?"

"We've got another hour and a half. Based on the chart Serena marked, we're looking at stopping in Limon, Colorado. That way we can just fly right over Denver. Too many people, right?"

Serena nodded first. "Fine with me," she said. "I'm getting like Gem. Small, tight group. Scent to a minimum."

*****

We got there in just about an hour and twenty minutes, and Rachel spotted a landing pad near what appeared to be a small hospital. It was empty, so Rachel set the Eurocopter down smoothly right in the center. As she cut the engine and the rotors slowed to a stop, sweet silence ensued.

Rachel looked out her window. "Guys! Fuel tanks and a crank pump out there!" she said, gleefully. "Oh, shit. Something else, too."

In the silence of the Colorado afternoon, even the zombies that approached us were silent. Ears gone, several with one eye. We were so taken with their level of decay, we almost did not take action.

Mesmerized. All but Lola, who said, "Anyone want to handcuff me or anything?"

"Why?" asked Nelson. "Feel like you're getting any signals?"

"No," she said. "I want to run, though."

"Don't run, dude."

"I won't. Kill them, though. Okay? Like ... now?"

I looked at Nelson, then back at the seven or so rotters who were now within fifteen feet. I then got out of the helicopter and ran around it, checking in all directions. I ran back to the open door. "Just them," I said.

"They look fucked up, bro," said Nelson.

"Really rotted," said Serena. "We're in Colorado, right? Maybe the winter did this?"

I thought about it. Good point. Rachel confirmed.

Eric A. Shelman

"Extreme cold would do this," she said. "I've seen frostbite and what it does to living humans in no time. These things start out cold. Not far to go to frozen."

"And still moving," said Nelson. "No pain to stop them, no sleepiness, right?"

"Right," I said. "Like that one there. One arm and walking on a stump."

"I'll feel like I'm doing them a favor," said Nelson.

"Let's do this so we can figure out the fuel situation and get some food down us," I said.

Nelson walked toward the tail of the craft and I went to the front. Serena grabbed her gun, but I waved her off. This would be easy, and I preferred she stay with Lola Lane. I did not know the status of the females who approached – even the tiniest remnant of a fetus and something could happen that I just did not trust we were protected against yet.

Serena nodded and sat on the floorboard of the chopper while we went to do our thing.

I approached two women, one with stringy, brown hair, matted with blood and the other missing all of her toes on both feet. My eyes were drawn to this one, her condition was so dreadful. Her pants were practically torn from her body, and huge strips of dried, jerky-like skin hung from her exposed right leg as she staggered toward me, her teeth gnashing in her exposed skull. What remained of her skin began at her cheeks; it was gray and cracked like the Sahara desert landscape.

I raised my AR-15 and shot her once in the face, said a silent *I'm sorry*, and shot her in the cranium. I had apologized for missing her brain the first shot.

The other one held up and stopped, her eyes staring at me and my weapon. After Flex, Gem, Hemp and Charlie got to Knoxville and started confronting the creatures, I'd seen a bit of that amazing behavior, but most of the time I fired too quickly to observe it.

They *did* recognize a threat – this time being the gun. I dispatched the internalizing and shot her in the brain – the first time. She fell backward and lay still.

When I turned to take out another two who were now within five feet of our transportation, I turned to see all of Nelson's three brass Ninja stars in the heads of three downed infecteds. No twitching, all good.

"Get your stars, Nel," I called. "I got these others."

This time I pulled my Walther and walked up to each of them, fired a single shot into their brains and down they went. All of them were trashed the same, and I had to attribute it to the blistering cold they no doubt had endured during the Colorado winter.

Let the process of turning to bone, then dust, ensue. Seven more of them could now ascend to Heaven or descend into Hell. Far be it for me to make that call.

The thought lingered as I walked back to the helicopter. I didn't know what kinds of people they were when they lived, whether they were good or bad, respected or reviled by others.

Then I wondered something unique to that moment and especially unique for Dave Gammon: *If there is a God, had he taken their souls already?*

Then a horrible thought hit me, and I pondered how the uninfecteds – me, Nelson, Flex, Serena, Gem, everyone. How had we gone from ordinary people to the kinds of people who could kill these things instinctively, with no guilt or reservation.

One final question about God nagged at me as I offered a smile to Serena, meant to tell her everything was just fine: *Had he already taken our souls, too?*

*****

Chapter Eleven

"There's a ranch or something just down this road," said Nelson. "Maybe we walk there, let Rachel get some rest before we hit the breeze again."

"I could use it," said Rachel. She carried her cap in her hand and ran her hand over her hair.

"Sounds like a plan," I said. I carried an AR-15 strapped on my shoulder and a bag of various food and supplies. Serena had her AR-15 at ready, and Nelson carried the other one and another bag of supplies. We never knew when we were going to get somewhere and decide it was a comfortable enough place to settle in for the night, so we went prepared.

We'd need to scavenge for fuel again before we hit the air again, too. There weren't a ton of vehicles around, so we hoped the in-ground fuel tank at the helipad was full. We'd look for a bolt cutter in the garage at the ranch, because there was a hefty padlock on the hand-crank pump.

Lola looked like she had something on her mind. As we made our way to the ranch, she kept glancing in my direction. I saw Serena noticing, and finally smiled and asked, "What's up, Lola? You look like you have a question."

"Yeah," she said. "I'm wondering what happens when we get to California."

"It's pretty simple," I said. "I know pretty much where Uncle Bug lives, so we just have to get there and play it by ear. I'm not positive, but if he's got things well in hand, we might decide to stay, at least for a while. I know he has provisions for years, so it might be the best bet for me and Serena. Maybe you, if he's cool with it and that's what you want."

Nelson walked over and fell in beside us. "What about Flex and Gem and everyone?" he asked. "You can't just not go back."

"I'm not saying I'll never go back, Nelson," I said. "Yeah, they're like family to me, but they knew when we left that there was a chance they'd never see us again. That's just the way of the world these days. It's not like we can send them a postcard."

Nelson was more upset than I'd ever seen him. "I'm going back!" he said. "I'll go to California with you, but I'm going back to our friends. Dude, they *are* like family, but my real family's there, too. My Uncle Jim."

I was beside myself. I hadn't asked Nelson to come, and I'd already discussed all the possibilities with Serena, who was the only person in the group I owed any explanation to anyway.

"Nelson," said Serena. "David talked to me about it long before we left. You might remember you joined us on the road, and there was no talking you out of it."

Nelson looked somewhat ashamed, but said, "I didn't think you'd leave your family behind. Not for good."

I stopped and took him by the shoulders. "Dude, look at me."

He raised his eyes. "What."

"You're like family to me, too. Okay? I don't want you to be pissed at me, Nel. I guess all you knew was we were going to California, and I suppose if I'd have told you the entire plan when you rode up on the scooter, you might have turned around."

He gave me and Serena a crooked smile. "Probably not. I really wanted to come. You're like my family, too."

I hugged him, and our guns clacked together.

"It's that awkward moment," I said, "when you hug another man and find something hard between you."

"Dude!" Nelson said, pulling away. "Correction! It's that awkward moment when the awkward moment joke itself is what created an even *more* awkward moment!"

I laughed. "Good point. Nelson, don't get too upset, okay? There are multiple possibilities, and at least three of them send us right back home. One, we don't find my uncle at all, and it's homeward bound. Two, we find him, he doesn't want me there anyway, and we leave. Home we come. Three, he wasn't immune, and it's the same result."

"There's four," said Nelson. "The one where everything's hunky dory, he's got a guestroom all set up with a big screen with Playstation and Blu-Ray, and solar-powered cars for getting around town."

"You left out the hydroponic weed garden."

"Yeah, that," said Nelson. "Then I'd stay, too."

We both laughed. Nelson turned and we started our trek toward the house. It was about an eighth of a mile away now.

Suddenly we heard a distant report, and Nelson flew backward, landing hard on his back and sliding along the gravel road. His eyelids fluttered, and his arms and legs jerked and twitched as spasms shook his body.

We all stood there with our mouths open, staring at Nelson, except Serena, who screamed, "Down! Gun!"

I dropped down beside Nelson. His shirt was torn and smoking just over his heart, in the center of his pocket tee. It was bulging out, pointed on both sides of the smoking tear, and I realized he had a Ninja star in there. One of the stainless steel 2" stars. I pulled it out and saw a dent in the center of it.

It had stopped a bullet, like the badge of a lucky cop.

Nelson's obsession for Japanese martial arts had saved his life. And I remembered that he had just wiped that one off after killing the zombies at the helicopter and put it back into his shirt pocket.

More gunshots, and puffs of gravel and dirt near me.

"Stop fucking shooting at us!" I shouted, trying to lift Nelson's head off the gravel. I put my face beside his, and I heard and felt his breath, coming in and out of his mouth in rapid, shallow puffs.

I felt a wave of intense relief wash over me. Nelson was alive. Trying to stay low, I shrugged out of my weapon, I wormed my way out of my own tee shirt, balled it up and tucked it beneath his head.

The shots had stopped for the moment.

"Can you tell where they're shooting from?" I asked.

"No," said Lola. "You said get down, and I did. I don't have a gun, remember."

"Serena?" I asked. "Fuck, I hate this!"

"It's coming from that way," she said, pointing toward a cluster of more dilapidated farmhouses ahead of us, off to the right. The house we'd set our sights on was straight ahead.

"Is he okay? Is he bleeding?" asked Rachel.

"He's breathing," I said. "No blood. One of his stars stopped the bullet."

"Thank God," whispered Serena.

"Okay, guys. Because of my training, this is where I take over, if you don't mind," said Rachel. "Slide me that AR-15. We're going to drop down in this ditch here, to our left. Once we get in there, we're going to crawl until we put at least fifty yards between where we are now and where we end up."

I pulled Nelson's weapon away from where he lay and pushed it over to Rachel. She took it and chambered a round expertly.

"Back toward the chopper, right?" I asked.

"No. They'll be expecting it. Look up there. If we can make it to the bend in the road we can cut straight down, across that grassy area and make it to the fence line of the ranch house." She stopped and bit her lower lip, looking behind us. "Wait," she said. "Maybe we should go both directions. That ditch extends all along this road, so if you can get Nelson back to the helicopter there are medical supplies there if you need them. Plus, you'll have cover."

"I'm not going to know what to do if he's seriously hurt," I said, realizing I was the only one strong enough to carry him over my shoulders, or in my arms if necessary.

"There's a cold pack, Dave," said Rachel. "Just break it and put it on the wound. Could be broken ribs or even his chest plate, so be as gentle with him as you can."

Another gunshot rang out, and I felt rocks hit my right foot. They were close.

"Lola, Serena, and I can draw their fire from farther ahead, give you a clear run. You can fire a shot or two from back there."

More gunshots, and a nearby ricochet.

"Now," said Rachel. "Serena, you're stronger than Lola or me. Help Dave drag Nelson into the ditch. I'm going to cover you."

Rachel, lying flat on the gravel road, turned her AR-15 toward the source of the gunfire and said, "Now!" She began firing the weapon. Single shot bursts, two that we heard ring off the distant barn. Another quick shot. She swung the gun far to the right and fired off two more, then quickly back to fire another pair of shots.

Lola never stood, rather she put her arms straight down by her sides and rolled like a cylinder into the ditch. Once in, she moved over to where we'd come in.

"You two go!" Rachel shouted, ramping up the gunfire to automatic, spraying bullets from left to right. Serena and I got to our feet and bent down, taking Nelson beneath the shoulders. We dragged him toward the ditch as fast as we could. It was about four feet deep, but it was enough. As his shoulders crested the edge of the embankment, Lola took over, dragging him the rest of the way in as we jumped down inside the crevice.

Rachel fired two more shots and dove toward the ditch. A split second after she was in, the gunfire started again, this time multiple weapons firing.

Seconds later they were silenced. We were obviously out of their line of sight, and they were like us in that regard; they did not like to waste ammo.

There was a little mud in the bottom of the ditch, and since I needed to drag Nelson much of the way in order to stay out of sight, I was glad. It would make the job easier.

"You killed our fucking sentries!" a voice shouted.

"What did he just say?" I asked, looking at Serena.

"Sentries?" she said. "What? The zombies?"

"Must be," said Lola. "Who else? They're the only ones you guys killed."

Rachel looked ahead and behind us again. On the north side was the ditch and beyond that, a steep hillside. On the right side of the road was a drop-off, and we could see the top of a fence.

"We killed some infecteds!" I shouted. "They were coming at us!"

"Yeah!" said a different voice. "To keep you out! Thieves!"

"We'll barter!" said Serena. "We'll trade you things. We have things you don't!"

"What the hell can we trade, Serena?" I asked.

She looked at me, her face grim. "Urushiol, right? The new gold?"

I shook my head, then looked into her eyes, then down at Nelson. I nodded. "You're right. They don't have to know the limitations with the red-eyes."

"No," she said. "They don't."

"You're going to want to know what we know!" she shouted, then smiled at me. "I feel like I'm on a cop show."

"I'd rather be on a fucking cop show," I said.

Nelson began to stir. My heart started going like a metronome on meth. I got down to him and when his eyes fluttered open, they rolled for a couple of seconds before staying still. He blinked a few times before a look of recognition swam back into his eyes. "Dude," he said. "What'd you do to me?"

I slipped my arm under his neck and head. "Nelson, I didn't do anything, man. You got shot. Well, you almost got shot."

"Dude, where's my weed?"

"Nelson, don't worry about that right now. Your Ninja star saved your life, buddy. Bullet hit it dead on."

Nelson took a breath and winced. "Ouch! Crap," he said. "I can't take a deep breath."

"It definitely knocked the breath out of you. I think you're going to have more of that," I said. "I'm just glad you're alive, my friend."

"Put your hands up and come out!" yelled the first voice.

I squeezed Nelson gently on the right shoulder. "Hey, rest here a second. Just relax. We're trying to talk our way out of this shit. The guys who shot you."

"Dude, people should be nice to one another. What is that, anyway?"

"I know, Nelson. It's like Shelburne all over again. I'm borrowing my shirt back."

I took the shirt and put it on the end of my rifle and raised it up high. A ZZ Top flag of surrender. Who could resist that? I swung it back and forth.

"Climb out of the ditch!" the first voice – apparently the leader of the two – called again.

Making sure I was below the ridge of the ditch, I carefully removed the PPK from my right leg drop holster and tucked it into the back of my pants. I slowly put the AR-15 just outside the ditch so they could see me do it, and pulled my shirt back on, making sure it covered the pistol.

Raising my hands, I looked at the others and said, "I'll go, guys. You guys just wait here and I'll try to calm them down."

"That's not going to happen," said Serena, following my lead, tucking her Walther into the back of her pants, too. That was my girl. She moved the other AR-15 beside mine and crawled out alongside me, raising her hands in surrender.

"Okay," Serena called. "What now?"

"Just wait!"

"If I thought there was really a brain between them, I wouldn't have come out," I whispered.

"I know," said Serena. "They just sound stupid, don't they?"

I nodded. As we stood there, our hands in the air, two young men – they could not have been more than twenty-two or twenty-three – emerged from behind the corner of a farmhouse off to our left, one holding a small rifle of some kind, and the other holding a pistol. They both wore the type of workout tank tops that weightlifters often wear, presumably to show off their massive pecks and guns.

As we watched, another three – a woman and two men – came out from behind a barn just west of the others. They were all scrawny in comparison to the other two.

"See?" I said. "Three stooges and two meatheads."

"If they kill us, you're going to feel like an idiot," she said, smiling.

"Then embarrassment won't be the worst of my problems," I said. I wasn't sure what had gotten into us, and I was willing to bet Serena didn't know either. It had just been so long since we'd faced an enemy that we could actually communicate with that this felt like a game show challenge more than any real danger.

"Tell those chicks to come out of the ditch." said the girl, waving a shotgun at us.

"Lower your weapons, and we will," said Serena. "I don't know who the hell you are or why you shot at us, but we don't kill living human beings."

"Well, bitch," she said. "You just killed our watchdogs, so I guess you just made it more dangerous for all of us. It's the same damned thing."

Now that they were closer, I could see their clothing was in relatively good condition. None of them looked to be starving, so it appeared they had provisions and food. I saw a retention pond in the distance, and aside from the gas bubbling from the earth and sending its zombie-making element into our atmosphere, we'd found the water to be drinkable in most places.

The girl had short-cropped, red hair and was probably five and a half feet tall. Her eyes were set close together, her nose small and straight, and her lips thin.

I notice these things because I've always found it fascinating. Looks define us in many ways. If you're average looking, that neither helps nor hurts you. If someone is extremely attractive, advantages go along with it. If one is unattractive, the reverse applies.

Let me interrupt this thought by saying that the zombies could give a shit about any of this.

Back to my thoughts: Personality comes into play immediately, no matter the level of beauty. We've all met those who were extremely attractive to us at first glance, but the moment they reveal the ugliness within, the physical beauty disappears and our visual assessment also shifts in that direction.

I was withholding judgment on the girl for now. We were all under stress. At that moment I would neither describe her as attractive nor unattractive. She could drift in either direction and that now largely depended on how her personality unfolded.

I saw what appeared to be a Superman logo tattooed on her right arm and below that were a series of letters, beginning with X. Below that was an L, followed by a C. They were clearly not professionally done.

They reached us and stopped in front of us now, and I was glad to see that as they approached, their weapons, while definitely still in hand, were no longer pointed at us. The two twenty-something men who had been off to the left together appeared to be brothers, if not identical twins. Their faces were not evil; they were scared if anything. Both appeared to have shaved heads beneath their baseball caps. One hat had a Colorado Avalanche logo on the front, and the one was embroidered with the words, *It's Beer-Thirty*. Both had intense, azure blue eyes, and if you ever hear me describe a man's eye color in a similar manner again, slap me and call me Nancy.

I'm just shooting for precise.

"Where did you get that fuckin' whirlybird?" the girl asked. She spat rather than said the words, her attitude aggressive and nasty. My internal beauty scale needle decidedly shifted closer to the unattractive side.

My eye, however, was on the kid beside her. He was a couple of inches taller than her, and his hair was ginger like hers. His face was festooned with freckles that rivaled those on Rachel's nose and cheeks, and he appeared to either have no eyebrows, or very lightly colored ones. The kid was maybe eighteen or nineteen years old and he was staring at Serena's breasts.

I felt a sudden anger well up inside me. I ignored the girl's question and the gun in the kid's hand and said, "Do you fucking mind?" I said, looking directly at him. "She's with me, and even if she wasn't, you're being a disrespectful dick."

The girl followed the young man's gaze, then she punched him hard in the arm. "Frankie, you jerkoff," she said, then looked back to us. "He's my brother and he's a damned pervert."

"Good to know," I said, feeling she had redeemed herself just a tad.

"Just a warning," said Serena, matter-of-factly. "If you come too close, Frankie, you'll never want to look at another pair of tits again."

"I'm sorry," he said. "I've been holed up here for like a year with my damned sister. I guess *that* makes a little sense?"

He looked at me. "Then *you* come flyin' in here with three women like some fuckin' sultans or somethin'."

"Three *hot* women," said one of the twins.

Lola smiled a little.

"Yeah," said Nelson, popping his head up from the ditch, holding his chest. "That's us. A couple of King Tuts."

"He was a Pharaoh," said Rachel. Ignoring our pseudo-captors, she turned her back on them, walked over to him and knelt down. "How are you feeling, Nel?" she asked.

"I'm just glad they were so far away," he said. "I'm fine, I think. Just sore." He crawled out and got to his feet. An angry red mark in the shape of a Ninja star adorned his bare chest. "Which one of you shot me?" he asked.

The man who hadn't spoken yet, raised his hand. He had shaggy, dirty blonde hair and a scraggly beard and mustache. He was the thinnest of the group, but still not emaciated. His brown, button-down shirt was clean, and his jeans looked dusty, but new. He stood about an inch over six feet. "Me, but I didn't want to," he said, pointing to the girl. "She told me to shoot, and I didn't even aim."

"We're not used to shooting from that kinda distance," said the girl. "We were just trying to scare you guys off."

"Plus we were pissed because you shot our guards," said the other twin.

"Why do you call 'em guards," wheezed Nelson. "They're abnormals, zombies."

"Glad you're alive, man," said the shooter. "How *are* you alive?"

Nelson pointed into the street where he'd apparently spotted his Ninja star. "Right there! I had a Ninja star in my shirt pocket. It's gonna be my lucky charm from now on."

"Look," I said. "We're not here to kill anyone who breathes. We stopped here to refuel and that's it. Nothing else. If you prefer, we can fly a couple of miles from here and try again."

They all looked at one another, but said nothing.

"Can we put our hands down?" asked Serena.

"Yeah, but you'd better not try anything," said the girl.

"We're headed to California to find someone, and we haven't intentionally hurt anyone yet," I said. "Like I said, we stopped to refuel and rest, and that's it."

"And we made a decision in that ditch right there that'll change your lives," said Serena. "Improve your odds."

"We got food, even livestock," said what seemed like the nicer of the twins. They were both about 5'10", and looked like they spent most of their time in the gym before zombies made weightlifting seem just plain stupid. "So what do *you* have that can make that big a difference to us?"

I looked at him and thought, *It's that awkward moment when the zombie doesn't notice your massive, oiled up pecks and just goes for your jugular.*

I almost laughed out loud. As Dudley Moore said in a rerun of Arthur I'd caught at like two in the morning before all this crap started, *Sometimes I just think funny things.*

"It's called urushiol," said Serena. "And it melts the bastards like butter in a hot pan. Just a touch of it."

"Hemp told me that one drop of urushiol on the head of a pin could give 500 people a rash," said Nelson.

Five pairs of eyebrows furrowed.

"I can probably demonstrate it on one of the dead ones," said Serena.

"Don't bother," said the girl, her tone softened slightly. "I know where more are. Just on the other side of our fence. You see there?" she asked, pointing to a distant fence. "We put that up on the other side of the hospital. We cleared that a long time ago so we could get to medical supplies if we needed them. You landed inside it."

"But why put the infecteds inside the fence?"

The tall, lanky one beside the girl and Frankie said, "We've been attacked before," he said. "And not by the biters. By regular people like you."

"Not like us," said Rachel. "If people like that showed up now, we'd help you fight them."

"Okay," said the girl. "Then follow us."

I saw the tension completely drain from her shoulders and neck.

"Nelson," I said, going to him, "Are you okay?"

Nelson grunted as he leaned over and picked up his bag of supplies. There was a slight wince on his face. "I'm alright. Lola, would you carry my gun? I could probably smoke a little bowl to kill the pain."

"Dude," said both twins together. "You got weed?"

I knew at that moment. We'd keep our urushiol.

We'd share the knowledge with them, but we'd be bartering with buds.

So we *were* in Colorado, after all.

This time, as we followed them down the incline toward the fence, I did laugh out loud.

*****

We went to the fence line, and sure enough, there were at least ten abnormals there, staring with dead eyes toward us as we approached.

"This won't take long," said Serena. "You want me to kill one of them or all of them?"

"Just one," said the girl. "We'll need to let them in as a buffer zone."

Serena walked up to the biggest male. His right eye hung from its socket, but his left one stared down at her, and his skinless jaw revealed all the teeth that remained, gnashing and gurgling whatever bile bubbled up their nasty throats.

His arm shot toward her and she dodged backward, spraying the smallest amount of the urushiol on his hand, and it began.

The fingers dissolved instantly, and the rapid disintegration worked its way up his wrist, then all the way to his elbow. Now that he was safely distant and had not thrown his other arm forward, Serena squirted a tiny bit into the center of his chest, then turned away.

The rest of us watched what Serena did not care to see; the abnormal's chest ate itself away until his black-red insides became visible, then daylight behind him. His chest split all the way up to his neck and his head collapsed into his chest where it also began popping and breaking down into cells of gore.

Moments later he was a bubbling pile of muck.

"Are you kidding me?" asked Lola. I'd forgotten she hadn't seen urushiol in action yet.

Another of the creatures stumbled into the downed zombie, apparently getting the oil on his bare foot. In another fifteen seconds, that foot was gone up to the shin and he toppled over, too, clawing at the gravel path.

"So" I said. "You like?"

"Fuckin' A," said the twins, followed by a high five.

I took it this was not the first time they had done that.

*****

We all sat in lawn chairs around a large camping table near a low window. Seems they liked to keep an eye out.

With the news that Nelson had marijuana, everything changed. Nelson packed a couple of nice-sized bowls and all five of them smoked, laughed and joked with him. I couldn't help but think that if they knew how little of his weed Nelson was probably willing to part with, their moods might have been a bit more somber.

We had gone through everything they needed to know about urushiol, and as it turned out, they all knew where some pretty substantial amounts of poison ivy grew.

"Another interesting tidbit I read in Hemp's lab notes," said Nelson. "Urushiol stays effective and active for up to five years. You can get the rash from dead poison ivy, just the same as when it's alive. So why not plant it all around wherever you set up your place?"

They all nodded. "If we do that, we might not have to worry about extracting the actual oil."

"It's useful to have with you on the road," said Serena.

They had indeed set up their living quarters in the buildings they were shooting at us from, and they did have quite a setup. Full beds, a gravity-fed tank water system where they could even take showers, and they had a storage room stocked with a ton of dry and canned food. They'd clearly raided a camping supply store, for they had a makeshift kitchen set up with every type of propane cooking device you could want. They even had a garden in the back, and whatever they were growing, it clearly wasn't marijuana.

"How long have you been living here?" asked Lola, pulling her hair out of her ponytail and running her fingers through it in an effort to untangle it.

I noticed twin number two, whose name we now knew was Gary McKinnie, the brother of Greg, who went by Plug (don't ask – we didn't) was staring at Lola and smiling the entire time we were together. I thought it was creepy, but Lola didn't seem to notice, and if she did, she apparently didn't care.

"Well, I found the place," Gary said, diverting his gaze from Lola to me for the moment. "After this shit started, we'd all been pretty much just running from house to house trying to escape the biters. Just me and Plug, and we didn't have any guns or anything yet. Didn't even know how to kill 'em. We got baseball bats from home and those were our first weapons."

"Worked pretty good," said Plug. He flexed his right arm. "Some power behind our swings."

Lola reached over and squeezed Plug's muscle, and he flexed tighter. She smiled, nodded and withdrew her hand again.

"We didn't know these guys," continued Gary, "but we ran into this one house and Mila and Frankie here almost shot us in the face."

"They didn't so much run in as slide a window up and sneak in at like three in the morning," said the girl whose name we now knew was Mila Lacour.

Then she added: "Look, I'm sorry at how this started. If you guys came here to rest, then we can offer food and water. Save yours if you want. We have plenty."

"Hey, Mila," I said. "You mind telling me about your tats?"

"Oh, those," she said. "Seems kinda dumb now. Wayne did them, but it was my idea. He was just learning ink before everything went down, and in the beginning I'd count how many I killed."

"So, they're Roman numerals?" I asked.

"Yeah. I don't know what I thought, having the X put on. Guess I didn't realize we'd be doing this for years."

"There's nobody to tell you this stuff," said Serena.

"I know," said Mila, smiling. "I gave up at 100. The C."

"Maybe one day you'll forget what they even mean," said Nelson. "It'll be so far in your past, like a bad dream."

There he was again, showing me wisdom I'd never have initially given him credit for. Not only that, this kid Mila had slid further toward the pretty side of the scale.

I nodded. "We'll leave you some of the urushiol until you get yourselves protected. You guys have any bolt cutters?"

"Tool shed out back has everything you could want," said Gary. "Big bolt cutters."

"Mind if we cut that lock of the helipad pump and use that fuel?"

"Those are fuel tanks?"

Rachel nodded.

"Shit," said Plug. "We never even gave them a second thought. Walked right by and went into the hospital for stuff."

I wondered if they focused on the pharmacy or the bandages, then decided I didn't really care. They were being hospitable now, and everything else was just survival in the way they best wanted to shape it.

"I have to show you something, Nelson," said Wayne Sypes, the tall one who had fired the shot that might have killed him. "And give you something."

"What, dude?" asked Nelson. "Look, I know you didn't mean to hurt us, so don't worry about it."

"I can't use 'em anyway," said Wayne. "Check it out."

He stood, and Nelson did his best to get out of the chair, one hand on his bruised chest. At the end of the room, Wayne opened up a wall-hung cabinet six feet wide by six feet tall, but only about five inches deep.

In it were Samurai swords of varying lengths and blade arcs, along with twenty or so Ninja stars, all bright, stainless steel.

"Dude!" said Nelson. "Wow! You good with these things?"

Wayne shook his head. "The swords, yeah, not bad. It's not like we're fighting the most savvy things in the world, so yeah, I seem pretty good when I spin around and cut their heads off."

"What about the stars?" asked Nelson, removing one from a pin on which it hung.

"Nada. Can't aim for shit."

"You mind?" asked Nelson, palming a 2" star in his right hand.

"Not at all," said Wayne. "Are you good enough to throw it? I mean, with the bruised chest and all?"

"I may not look it, but I'm in great physical shape," said Nelson. "Over there, okay? See that key ring hanging by that back door?"

It was on the other side of the room, about ten feet past us.

Nelson wound up and let the star fly, and it ticked the bottom of the key ring, planting itself deep into the wall just below it. All in all, it was about a thirty-foot throw.

"Jesus!" shouted Wayne, smiling big.

Nelson waved him off and rubbed his chest tenderly. "It's in the wrist, man," he said. "With a little shoulder thrown in."

"They're yours, buddy," said Wayne. "Call it an apology, but I want you to take all of them. I like the swords."

Nelson nodded. "Okay," he said. "I was down to two after the bullet thing, so yeah, I'll take them. Thanks, Wayne."

We raided their pantry. The food was hot and it was good. The bolt cutters were out back like they said, the underground tank was full of fuel, and the pump worked beautifully. It was the easiest fill-up since we'd boarded the helicopter.

We left our strange, partially creepy friends with 1/8th bottle of urushiol blend and a lot of knowledge they did not previously possess.

Nelson left them with about an 1/8th ounce of pot, too. It was more than I expected.

*****

273

Chapter Twelve

The remainder of the trip to California involved only two more stops, and when I saw the tall trees of northern California below us and confirmed by the map that Serena had become so adept at reading, I felt a sigh of relief.

It had been a total of 771 nautical miles past Denver, and even utilizing low, smart flying and with the wind in our favor, we still landed the helicopter with the engine running on fumes.

But we had arrived. Finally. I briefly thought about how much harder the trip would have been had we not been able to get the chopper, and I realized that everything happens for a reason. Meeting Rachel and Don. Meeting Serena. Even Nelson coming along. All of it.

I wondered how Lola would come into play. I had initially believed she might stay with the group we'd met outside of Denver, but ultimately, she may have had no interest in being fought over by four guys. She certainly had more going for her than Mila Lacour, though I had changed my opinion of the girl quite a bit before our visit was through.

I knew Bug lived just outside of Dunsmuir, but I still didn't know where. I hoped we could find some people still alive there. It might be the only way to find Uncle Bug unless he shot at us or something, which wasn't out of the question.

We all sat in the helicopter and kept the doors closed. Nelson had stepped outside to relieve himself when we'd arrived, and we all felt the chill in the air as he opened the door. We were at a high altitude, after all, and from what I knew of the annual temperatures, July was the warmest month of the year, but still crisp in the evenings and at night. According to Serena's watch, we were in early September. In all, we had taken about a week to work our way across much of the country.

We had arrived just after sunset, and the lights from the helicopter, which were a necessity for navigation, particularly without lights below, were a beacon to anyone nearby, and while most of the rotters could not hear – save for the estrogen-charged females – we knew damned well they could see.

We set it down in the middle of a wide highway. There were some cars, but they were in no way blocking the roadway. This was a more populated area during winter when the skiers were crowding to Mount Shasta ski resorts, but in summer it was mostly hikers and the approximately 1,600 regulars who called Dunsmuir their home.

Serena and I knew this because we did plan, believe it or not. We knew we had to have some idea of the number of infecteds we might be facing – if the cold and other factors didn't do them in – and it was all part of our plan.

Which wasn't much of a plan.

Nelson came back in, rubbing his hands together. "It's good to be cold again, but man. It's just September, right?"

"External temp is 59 right now," said Rachel, inspecting her gauges. She cut the lights and darkness fell around the Eurocopter. "Feels good, actually."

"For now," I said. "In a month, this cool will be just plain cold."

"We staying in here tonight?" asked Lola.

"Not if I can help it," said Serena. "I could use a bed tonight, how about you?" she asked me.

"Lots of cabins and stuff around," I said, peering out the window. "Damned moon's zilch tonight."

"It's 7:30," said Rachel. "If we go, I want us all to go."

"That worked out real great last time," said Nelson, smiling.

"This time we take minimal supplies and keep our weapons ready. We got caught by surprise by those guys."

"Yeah, because we're used to having run-of-house on this planet now," said Serena. "Rachel, are we on Interstate 5?"

"Yes, as near as I can tell. Just east of us should be downtown Dunsmuir, and we're probably actually sitting within the town limits. You'd be able to see the lights over that way if there was power." She pointed off to our right.

"Okay," I said. "Headlights on, weapons loaded, extra mags, the works. Just enough food, water and urushiol for the night. We lock this bird up tight and see if we can find shelter. Preferably with a fireplace."

"I'd guess everyplace here has a fireplace," said Rachel. "Looks like that kind of area."

We loaded up and got out. It felt good to have our feet back on solid ground, and we walked south, away from the helicopter.

"It's cold," said Serena, as I walked alongside her.

"I'd warm you up," I said, "but we need to be ready to defend if anything presents itself."

She nodded and we all kept our eyes on the road ahead as our headlights illuminated the area six to eight feet before us.

Suddenly a pair of eyes glowed on the path ahead. They were not red or pink, but white. Bright white.

All of our headlights pointed directly at it, and its form became clear in the night as its outline emerged from the blackness beyond.

It was a deer. More than that, it was a 12-point buck, standing in the road, mesmerized by the many lights on top of our heads.

We all stopped. It stared at us, and we stared back.

"Venison," whispered Rachel.

"A majestic beast," responded Nelson.

"People are majestic beasts, too," said Rachel.

"Sometimes," said Nelson. "If there's one, there's more."

"Nel's right," I said. "As sweet as fresh venison sounds, we're in no position to field dress anything. Let's keep walking."

As we continued walking, the buck snapped out of its temporary coma and leapt off the roadway onto a trail beyond. Beside the trail was a low, rustic looking sign.

"Hey, look!" said Lola. "Creekside Cabins .3 miles."

"Hear that?" asked Rachel. "Sounds like a brook or a creek."

"Follow that deer," said Serena. "And let's get ready to clear out a cabin or two."

I took a risk and dropped my left hand, reaching for Serena's. She took it with her right hand, and as we walked, she leaned in and gave me a peck on the cheek. "This is cuddling weather," she said.

"I'm in," I said.

Less than a quarter mile in, we heard a sound off to our right. We all stopped immediately and raised our weapons, turning our heads to illuminate the area with our headlights.

Out of the brush came the figure of a human, and the moment we saw the pink eyes glowing, either from a meal of human or animal flesh – it didn't matter much to us – we all fired at once, lifting the creature off its feet and sending it into the bushes beyond.

I'm not certain any of us missed. Even Nelson's AR-15 flew into action. Lola still did not opt for a weapon, so she just watched as we took care of the threat.

We all tentatively stepped forward to see what we had killed. As for the eye shine, it was no more; but that was because its head – along with the eyes – was now in little chunks, scattered within a fifteen foot area to the west, south and east of the trail upon which we now stood.

"Let's get a move on," said Rachel. "I'd like walls between us and this crappy visibility."

We did. An easy jog got us closer to the creek, and the rushing water grew louder as we descended farther into the wooded canyon. We found a larger, carved wood sign that said, "Welcome To Creekside Resort." Beyond that, to the left and right were several narrow trails, obviously leading to the cabins.

I stopped everyone. "Okay, we'll clear a cabin at a time, huh? Maybe just one or two for tonight. If we run into anyone, let's just be careful to identify ourselves so they know we're not the walking dead, okay? Be vocal."

"Vocal," said Nelson. "Because zombies don't talk."

"You are a master of the obvious," said Lola Lane.

Nelson replied, smiling and shaking his head. "Thank you, Lola."

"Follow me," I said, turning right up a path.

When the winding, forest path before us grew sharper, and even slight shadows fell off of the trees, I glanced toward the sky and was amazed at the billions of stars overhead, like a celestial artist had swiped a starlit brush across a sheer, black canvas. The clouds had parted, and at that moment, it seemed divinely influenced.

The feeling could have spurned from just how grateful I felt in my heart, I guess. I did not want to lose any of the wonderful people in my company and this gift of nature's own light could seemingly only have come from some divine command.

I tapped Serena on the arm and pointed upward, and her eyes remained turned toward the heavens for a long time as she drank in the vastness of the sky overhead.

We reached the first cabin. It was a classic, log cabin, but it was on stilts, raised over an area covered in gravel. Beneath it we could see an old, rusted quad ATV and a snowmobile that didn't look much newer. The stairs were beneath the building. Nelson and Rachel agreed to stay down below, guarding the perimeter while Lola, Serena and I went up the stairs. When we reached the door, I whispered, "We knock, right?"

"It's what I'd want people to do," said Serena. "You heard how Mila and Frankie almost shot Gary and Plug in the face."

"Yeah," I said. "*Plug*. What's that about?"

"I didn't ask, either," said Lola. "Nice nickname."

I knocked. We waited. I knocked again. We all listened.

"Quiet," I said.

"Try the door," said Serena.

I did. It was locked. I shined my light at the jamb. "It's a push."

"So, can you get enough leverage to kick it?" asked Lola.

"To be honest, I'm tired of fucking around," I said. "You guys go warn them I'm about to fire."

Serena and Lola hurried back down the stairs and I held out the AR-15 and fired into the jamb. The wood splintered and the door flew inward, slamming into a wall on the right side. I waited, turned to look to the bottom of the stairs, and four faces looked back at me. "Well," I said. "Come on. Let's clear this place."

The house was empty. It appeared to be ready for rental, and we had obviously found one of the larger rental cabins available, because this one was a four bedroom with a large, centered living area. The refrigerator door was left open, because the power had clearly been turned off.

After clearing the place, we secured the door I'd trashed with an upper deadbolt that hadn't been in use at the time, so all was well in the security department.

Once we'd picked our rooms, where we found folded blankets and very simple, rustic beds with very soft mattresses, we all met in the living room. A fireplace filled the back of the wall, its wide mouth open, but dark, empty and cold.

We would change that. Nelson and I went back downstairs where I'd seen a stack of logs beneath the stairway on the way in. We both brought an armload upstairs, though I could tell Nelson's chest was still hurting him.

In another twenty-five minutes, the fire roared, sending its rays of heat throughout the main room of the cabin.

A fluffy rug that was supposed to look like bearskin, but was probably polyester, lay spread on the wood floor in front of the massive fireplace, and Nelson had opted to lie on his back in the dead center of it.

Everyone else curled up on cushioned sofas, except I sat in an armchair about one and a half times larger than an ordinary chair, and Serena had crawled in next to me, tucking in, her forehead resting softly against my neck.

Nobody said anything. We listened to the fire crackle and enjoyed the peace surrounding us until we all fell asleep.

*****

I awoke to see the fire had died to a quarter its size, but had no idea how much time had passed. It was still very warm, as the coals glowed red, tiny sparks swirling up toward the flue periodically.

I heard a low whimper and looked over to see Rachel staring at the fire, her eyes glossy and red, crying. She had her knees pulled up to her chest with her arms wrapped around them.

I heard Serena's steady breathing; felt her warm breath on my neck. I relaxed my body and slid out of the chair, easing Serena into the indentation where my body had been just moments before, warm and soft. She did not awaken, but sought her own, comfortable spot and snored lightly.

I stepped over Nelson, who was still flat on his back, out like a light. I saw Rachel look up at me and smile as I sat on the sofa beside her. Seeing Nelson there reminded me that I had told him about Jess and Don. He asked me, and I trusted him a lot by then. I knew he wouldn't say anything to her, and would let me break it to Rachel when the time felt about as right as it would ever be.

"Is it Jess?" I asked her, softly.

She nodded. "What else."

"Rachel, I have to tell you something."

"About what?" she asked.

"About Jess. And Don. It's important."

She looked at me, wiping at her eyes. "What? What could you know?"

"Remember when you left me and Don alone in the helicopter the day he died?"

"Yes," she said.

"He told me something."

Her eyes pleaded in the glow of the firelight. "What, Dave?"

"Rachel, Don loved you like a daughter. He appreciated being able to spend that year with you after this all happened. But there was something about Jess that he couldn't tell you when you got back home and found that ATV and the note outside your place."

"What? About Jess?" Rachel asked.

"Yes," I said. "Rachel, that Sunday – when all this happened. That morning."

"Yes, I know, I know. Please, Dave. Tell me."

"Jess was out there."

"Where?"

"He was in the corral."

Now her expression was one of confusion and realization, combined. I knew Rachel was smart enough to figure it out.

"With ... with the things?"

I nodded. "Jess was ... well, he was one of them, Rachel. He was going after the horses."

"No," she whispered through her tears, burying her face in the palms of her hands. "Not my Jess," she cried.

I put my arm over her shoulder and pulled her to me, and she allowed it. I rubbed her arm and back and rested my head on top of hers.

A moment later she pulled back and looked at me. "Did Don ... kill him? Don shot my husband?"

"No," I whispered. "Rachel, you know it wasn't Jess anymore. Not by then."

Her sobs came then, shaking her entire body and the couch on which we sat together. Off to our left, Lolita Lane gave a quick snort and rolled over onto a corner pillow.

"A whole year and he didn't tell me?"

"I'm sure that after a couple of months of not telling you, it just got harder and harder, Rachel. You know, when a lie or an omission goes on too long and then there seems to be no way to get to the truth. Let sleeping dogs lie."

Now there was no controlling her emotions anymore as she sat up and stared at the fire, swiping roughly at her eyes in anger. "He went back to that house with me every time I asked him to!" she shouted now, and this time everyone did awaken.

"He lied to me again and again, treating me like a weak fool – like the chauvinist fuck he was, thinking I couldn't handle the truth about what he did!"

I let her rage for now.

"What's going on?" asked Nelson.

"It's okay, Nel," I said. "I told her about Jess. And Don."

"Oh," he said. "God, I'm sorry, Rachel. I really am. I know Jess must have loved you a lot. What happened to him wasn't his fault, and it wasn't Don's fault, either."

Rachel nodded at him as she dabbed at her eyes with a sleeve, and suddenly, Nelson got off the floor and on all fours, crawled to where she sat. He got up on his knees and opened his arms, pulling her into them.

I watched him, again marveling at the heart within this young man I continued to think of as a kid.

Rachel closed her eyes and let her tears flow as she returned Nelson's embrace. With his head against hers, he held her tight; he did not pat or rub her back in some lame gesture to make the embrace seem less personal; he just held her in his arms as her shuddering sobs came harder and returned the hug as though helping her cling to her own sanity.

I felt tears running down my face, too, and looked over to see Serena wiping her own face in the flickering, dying firelight.

Among us, only Lola slept through, unaware of this powerful moment of shared sorrow.

Afterward Nelson sat on his legs and held her hands as we listened to the crickets outside and the crackling and popping of the fire within. When Serena announced it was three in the morning, everyone got up and went to their respective bedrooms.

Lola had slept through all of it. It was okay; she could be brought up to speed later on when Rachel did not have to relive the loss of her husband yet again.

*****

Serena and I lay in bed together, me on my back and her on her side, facing me. Her arm was over my chest, and her head was on my shoulder. I could not have imagined I would ever feel this content again after the loss of Leona, but here I was.

This world bred the need to connect; I might have grieved for years in a normal society; started drinking heavily, hitting strip clubs, losing myself on purpose so I wouldn't miss her. But here, in this fucked up world, I was preoccupied with staying alive.

And protecting my friends and my family. And apparently falling in love again with a strong woman who had never really shared her own story with me. I wasn't tired. Serena was still awake, and I could feel her eyes on me in the dark, so I broached the question.

"Serena," I said.

"What?" she said.

Eric A. Shelman

"How did you get to Shelburne? And before you say anything, tell me you'll be up front if you don't want to talk about it."

She was quiet for a long time. Finally, she said, "To answer your question, I had lived in Vermont for years, in a town called Carthage. We moved to Shelburne when I was nineteen. And this might sound stupid maybe, but from the moment you walked through the door of ZFZ-4, I was attracted to you, David."

I never knew what to say – especially when the opposite wasn't true. I was still pretty hung up on Charlie at that time, and didn't really see anything but a bunch of strangers. I decided to be honest.

"I think you know I had a little Charlie crush going on then."

"But you knew she was with Hemp," said Serena.

"I did," I said. "And when he was kidnapped, I don't know … I got this terrible hope that I should never have gotten, because I love Hemp."

"You hoped he'd … die?"

"No, but I didn't know that he wasn't already dead, Serena. It's not that I'd ever hope that. That's not me at all, and I knew how much Charlie loved him. Hell, I love the guy. It was just that if he was gone, I wanted to be there for her. Eventually, anyway."

I lay there in the dark for a while, then said, "Anyway, I interrupted. I just want you to know that by the time we were leaving Shelburne, I wanted you to come. I was so damned excited that you did, I can't even tell you."

"I'm kind of the opposite of Charlie," she said.

"In some ways," I said. "Mostly physically. You're taller, have longer hair, and darker skin. You're runway model sexy, and as for ass-kicking, I'd say it's a tie."

285

She elbowed me in the ribs, and I feigned injury, laughing. "I love you, Serena. You're part of me, like it or not."

"If I didn't like it, I'd be part of someone else," she said, and I heard the smile in her voice. "But now you want to know about my life before, and I lie here beside you, realizing I've known you several months now and haven't shared any of it with you. How many times have we made love?"

"Not enough," I said.

"I agree," she said. "Anyway, it's a bombshell, I guess."

"Really?" I asked.

"I was married, David."

I hadn't expected that. "You ... were?"

"That's not all."

"What do you mean?"

"I had a son, too."

I had no words. I felt embarrassed that this had gone unsaid for so long, and I felt it was my fault. I knew I'd told her all about Leona, and yet, had I asked her about her past? Had I detected some reluctance to talk about it?

I honestly couldn't remember. The last few months since we'd found Serena in that safe house were a blur.

"God, I'm so sorry, Serena. I feel like some kind of selfish prick for not knowing about it."

"Gem's the only one I told," she said. "Not even your girlfriend Charlie knows."

"Very funny."

"Sorry," she said, rubbing my chest and kissing my cheek.

"It's okay. Go on."

"My husband was the son of close friends of my parents, from our village in Spain. I had known they wanted me to marry Enrique since I was six years old. By the time I was old enough to marry, it was preordained. So it happened."

"Did you love him?"

"He was like an older brother to me," she said. "So I loved him in that way at first. I don't think I even knew how I really felt about him until after I gave in and married him. The very night of my wedding was when I learned my true, inner feelings, and none of what came after our nuptials felt ... moral. I tried to accept it, but it felt disgusting. Like incest."

"It must have been horrible for you, babe," I said. "Was it the same for him?"

"Not at all," she said. "I was more to him, which became obvious after our marriage. I was repulsed by the intimacy, but he was aggressive and insistent. I couldn't talk to my mother about it; she wouldn't listen."

"How old were you?"

"Seventeen," she said. "I had my baby at nineteen."

"They forced you to marry at seventeen?"

"It wasn't unusual," Serena said. "He was nineteen, working with my father at our jewelry store. He was apprenticing there, and his family had contributed much to the business. As I said, it had all been planned for years."

"I'm afraid to ask, Serena. About your son. You said you *had* a son."

"I did. His name was David."

"Seriously?" I asked.

"It's a very popular name in Spain, too. Funny, huh?"

"I'm afraid to indulge in anything funny. You want to tell me about him?"

"I do," she said. "He was like you, in some ways. He was gentle, very kind. He was twelve years old when it happened, but before that, a good student, and despite his father, he was kind to people, including the opposite sex."

"Came from your influence, no doubt. Right?" I said.

"I suppose it had to," she said. "Anyway, that Saturday night, before everything happened, Enrique had gone out, which he did a lot. If David wasn't doing a sleepover or something with his friends, we'd do fun things – whatever he wanted. So that night, he said he wanted to build a fire in the pit in the back yard and roast marshmallows. So that's how I spent the last night with my son."

"Serena, you don't have to go on," I said. "I love you. I don't need you to go through this for me."

"It's as much for me, David."

"Is that why you never call me Dave?" I asked. "Did you call him David?"

"Always," she said. "It's a beautiful name – a Biblical name. To shorten it is to diminish it, to me."

"I get it."

"Anyway, so I had a tray with lemonade and we ate too many marshmallows, and when it got to be around ten, of course Enrique wasn't home yet, so I just put David to bed and locked up the house. I felt Enrique come home around three in the morning, smelling like about five different kinds of alcohol. He tried to climb on top of me, but I pounded on him and told him to stop."

"Shit," I said.

"Exactly," she said. "I also smelled perfume on him, and to be honest, I said to myself at that moment – that *very* moment – that I was done. I pushed him off of me and he rolled onto what would have been my side of the bed and passed out."

I knew there was something to that part of the story, and she did not make me wait to find out what it was. I put my arm over her shoulder and she tucked into me again.

"I woke up early, well before daylight, and I pulled my Kindle from the drawer and started reading. I loved it, and with Enrique and David, I didn't get a lot of time to do it. At one point, I suppose I fell asleep again. I was awakened by a snarling and then screaming. It was Enrique, and I heard a loud noise and thrashing, just before I was literally knocked out of bed."

"Did Enrique turn?" I asked.

"No," she whispered. "If he had, I might not be here to tell you this."

She was quiet and I heard her breath filling her lungs, and releasing with a stutter. "Wait," she whispered. "I'm sorry."

"Take your time, Serena."

Another deep breath. "I got up and turned on the light, and saw my son ... my precious David, on the floor with blood around his lips and mouth. Enrique had kicked him and was lying in bed beside me holding his neck, where his blood was just pouring out. I grabbed the phone and hit the power and just pushed 911 and dropped it. I knew they'd come if they saw the number, and then I ran to David. He wasn't facing me at first, but when I turned him around, his eyes ... they were white and blank, and he was making these sounds that I know now, but had no idea about then."

"God, Serena, I'm so sorry," I said. "How horrible. For both of you."

"He didn't know, and you know that, David. He wanted only one thing, and that was from me, too. He threw himself up at me and I caught him by the shoulders – I'll never forget holding him away from me when I'd only ever welcomed his embraces. The older he got the fewer they were and the farther between. But when I saw him, his mouth chewing and chewing, and his eyes gone, I knew he was sick and looking at what he'd done to his father, I also knew he was dangerous."

"What did you do?" I asked the question with full recollection of what had happened with Leona – the same monster coming for me – a monster that I loved just earlier that morning. Such sudden changes turned our worlds upside-down.

"Enrique had passed out," said Serena. "The blood had soaked the top sheet of the mattress. I didn't know if he was dead, but I had to do something with David. I yanked the light cover from the bed and tried to throw it over my son, but he had gotten back up and was back on top of his father now, and he was biting chunks of his ... you know, David. You know what he was doing."

"I know. That's enough, Serena. Shh." I held her there, and listened to her cry for her son.

"I may as well finish," she said in a few more moments. "Anyway, I was horrified, and I screamed David's name over and over, but it was as if he could not hear me. He wouldn't stop doing that horrible thing to his father, and as I watched him, I realized that if I had been on my normal side of the bed, I would have been the one attacked by him, David. My own son."

"No, Serena," I said. "Not your son. Not then. Not anymore."

Her body was racked by sobs and I held her. I was sure the memory of her sweet boy, with whom she had laughed and shared roasted marshmallows just hours before, was a living Hell to remember. Especially considering what he had become, and how fast it had happened.

"I didn't know what to do," she sniffed. "I threw that blanket over him, fought him to the floor and wrapped him in it. Then I carried him into the bathroom and closed him inside. I still don't know how I did it. Adrenaline, I suppose."

"Did the paramedics or police ever show up?"

"No, of course not. It was everywhere by then. I pulled a sheet from a guest bed to wrap around me, and I ran outside to go to a neighbor's house. When I got there, I pounded on the door, but nobody answered. I tried the knob and pounded on it some more – I heard sounds inside, but nobody ever came."

"So what did you do?" I asked. "Where did you go?"

"I didn't even bring my cell phone out, so I had to go back in my house. No keys, either. I went back inside, and I was shocked when Enrique came down the hall and ran at me, screaming like … like he was dying and like he was some insane warrior. And his eyes … they were like David's."

"Serena," I said. In my heart I wished she would stop. I had heard and seen enough of these terrible stories, and they never got any better. I felt this way for a brief moment, then I realized that was selfish. I was being selfish, if only in my heart. Serena needed to tell this story, and she needed to tell it to me. The least I could do was to be man enough to hear what she'd gone through.

I stroked her hair and she continued.

"I avoided his reach and knocked past him, grabbing my robe on the door. I went out the other hall door and got my phone and keys off the hall table and ran into the garage. Enrique stumbled after me and I barely got in the car with the door closed before he was pounding on the window. His neck had stopped bleeding, his skin was ash white, and his eyes were just as dead as David's had been. I got the garage door up and I just drove."

She stopped for a long time. I knew she never saw David again. It was an unceremonious ending to her loving relationship with her 12-year-old son, and she couldn't have comprehended that when she had shut him inside, that it would be the last time she would lay eyes on him. It had to be worse than hearing your child had been hit by a car or that they had vanished. She knew exactly where he was and that he had become a monster.

How fucking horrible.

"The rest of it doesn't even matter anymore," she said. "Nothing mattered from that moment until you found me in Shelburne."

"What about your parents?"

"My father died when David was four. Hunting accident. I went to my mother's house, David. I went there and I stood in the front yard and watched her through the window. She didn't see me, but she was like David and Enrique. She had many cats, and that's all I'll say. I never went inside – I saw enough from outside. If I had gone inside, I would have been forced to kill her, and that was not in me then. Today I'd do it for the mercy I now know it to be, but then ... I just didn't know. I was scared."

"Of course you were," I said, stupidly.

"So," she said, "I've never turned my mind back there since I drove away, except when I told Gem about it. I lost everyone I ever cared for in one fell swoop, and by that, I mean David and my mother."

"What about your husband?" I asked.

"Like I said. I made a decision the night before. I had already lost the Enrique I knew as a young girl; the one I loved like a brother. When he became my husband, he saw it as a license to control me. He tried. He did try. I did not mourn his loss. I mourned my mother and my only son."

"Serena," I said. "I'm so sorry. I had no idea, and I can't tell you how selfish and what an asshole I feel like right now. Telling you about what happened with Leona and never even asking."

"We've been pretty busy," she said. "I could sleep, David. I'm exhausted now."

I knew why. *I* was exhausted. I held her tightly to me and in moments, heard her steady breathing.

I did not hear it for very long. We woke up with bright sunlight streaming through the windows and birds singing in the trees beyond.

*****

Chapter Thirteen

The smell of coffee accompanied the bright sunshine, so I cut my quiet time – which is what I called the ten minutes or so that I normally lie there and watch Serena sleeping – in half.

Creepy, you say? Nah. She's beautiful, even when I can't see her gorgeous, green eyes.

It's funny. I read the other chronicles over a period of time, and I realized that Serena isn't really described in them. There is a moment in Hemp and Charlie's chronicle when Serena rides up on a motorcycle wearing a leather body suit, and that's about all you get.

Let me tell you something: if you want to picture my Serena, picture Julie Newmar in her Catwoman outfit from the original Batman TV series. Now take her mask and ears off (save them and I'll give them back to her later,) give her dark brown, wavy hair down past her shoulder blades, make her curvy sexy and close to six feet tall. Words don't quite cut it, but you get the idea. I'm pretty sure that neither Flex nor Hemp wanted to describe her because Gem and Charlie would kick their asses after reading it.

Believe me, *both* are capable of it.

"Nelson, dude!" I said. "How did I not know you brought that with us?" The propane stove and Folger's

Eric A. Shelman

coffee we'd found along the way sat on the counter and a full pot, minus his cup, sat on the burner.

"I like surprises," said Nelson. "Thought you might like one here and there, too."

"Have your morning bowl?"

Nelson looked at me. "Look at me, dude."

I did. His eyes were slits, and his mouth was formed into a thin-lipped smile.

"Okay," I said. "How'd you sleep?"

"Like a log. How about you guys?"

"We had a good talk last night, then I was out until a few minutes ago. Serena's – "

"Up right now," she said, walking in the room, pulling her long hair back. "God, I love you, Nelson. Coffee smells fabulous."

"You are not alone," he said, smiling. "Davey loves me, too."

"I do," I said.

Serena poured herself a cup and sat in a chair. Nelson had rebuilt the fire, and it filled the room with warmth and a feeling of home.

"You can almost forget all the bad stuff here," she said. "Nice fire, Nel."

We drank in silence, and within fifteen minutes, Rachel came out to join us, wearing a men's tee-shirt that must have been an extra large, because it went all the way to her knees. She scratched her nose and yawned. "Good morning," she said, smiling. Her freckles bunched together as her smile lines emerged.

We all returned the greeting. "Miss Lane must be sleeping in," I said.

Just then, there was a knock on the door and Nelson said, "Man, I almost forgot. She went out for a run."

He walked to the door and opened it, and she came inside, put her hands on her knees and tried to catch her breath. "Wow," she said. "It's brisk up here in the morning."

My mouth hung open. "You went running? Are you nuts?"

"Not completely," she said. She pulled what looked like a Bowie Knife out of her waistband. It was in a leather sheath. "I have this with me wherever I go. Hadn't felt like running until this morning for some reason. Have to wash it."

"Why, dude?" asked Nelson.

Lola pulled the knife out of the sheath, and it was black and sticky. She held it up. "Because it stinks."

I could not close my mouth. "Lola," I said. "Did you have to ... kill one?"

"Three, actually," she said. "Look, it's not the first time. Remember what they used to tell us after a terrorist attack? Don't let them change the way you live?"

Serena laughed. "This is just a little bit different, Lola," she said. "It's not like these attacks happen every once in a while."

"Yeah, dude," said Nelson. "No sleeper cells, man. They all just go after your ass wherever they find you."

Lola said, "Watch."

Her legs came apart as she planted her feet. In three lighting fast moves, she jabbed the knife head-height straight out, cranked her wrist and jabbed to the right, flipped the knife quickly in mid air and jabbed behind her over her shoulder.

"Holy fucknuts!" shouted Nelson. "You told us you just ran!"

"I run, too. But sometimes you get cornered."

"You should get a Samurai sword," said Nelson. "You'd kick ass with one of those."

"I could've talked Wayne into giving me one," she said. "Already had my knife, and it's easier to run with."

"You are hereby tasked with defending the family," said Rachel.

Nelson went and sat beside Rachel. "How are you?" he asked.

She looked at him and smiled. "I'm okay, Nel. I had a lot of time to think after I went to bed last night. I know where he is. He's at peace. He's not somewhere frightened, and he's not somewhere worried about where I am. And now I don't have to worry anymore, either."

"It's a great attitude," said Nelson. "I'm sure you'll have your moments. Be ready for them."

"Is there a little damned Buddha tucked inside your brain?" she asked. "Or whatever's wise? Is that a Buddha? A Gandhi? Maybe a Mother Theresa?"

The gleam in Nelson Moore's eye just then told me more than I believe he ever wanted to reveal.

"I'm just a stoner, Rach," he said. "That's about it."

"You're a fucking liar," I said, laughing and putting down my coffee cup. "I bet you tested off the charts in school. Am I right?"

Nelson laughed, but he did not deny it. "I don't know, man."

"In Concord, when everything was going to shit, Nelson thought to fire up a street sweeper filled with urushiol blend and he saved a bunch of people, Gem included. On the way here, he tells me his simpleminded stoner persona is largely an act."

"Okay, okay," said Nelson. "I did test off the charts, and I was bored as hell in school. I dropped out because I already knew all of the shit they were going to teach me."

"I knew it!" I said.

"Everyone just saw me as *stoner Nelson* and never really gave me any credit for anything else. I discovered I was cool with that. Expectations were low, and no matter what I chose to do – and I wanted to try everything – it was cool. At least I was doing something."

"What about your Subdudo?" I asked. "That is an amazing technique. Didn't anyone start to wonder how you were smart enough to come up with it?"

"Dude, it was all theory until the damned apocalypse," he said. "The first time I used it on anything but a dummy was with a zombie."

"No shit," said Lola.

"And you haven't even seen it," I said.

"It's amazing," said Serena. "I've only seen it a couple of times."

"Yeah, after I realized they didn't care that you were taking them down by humane means, I decided the stars were a better option," said Nelson. "Anyway, enough about me."

"You've got a great story, Nel," said Rachel. "And a good heart."

"I care about my friends," he said. "More since I met all these guys." He pointed at me and Serena. "They kinda taught me how close people that aren't actual family can get. I love them."

A little knife stabbed me in the heart, and I don't mean Lola's. I got up and as I walked by him, I squeezed his shoulder and he smiled. Lola was rinsing her bloody knife in the sink using water from a one-gallon, plastic bottle sparingly.

I filled my coffee halfway to leave some for Lola, and turned around. "Okay. We need to find my Uncle Bug today."

"I brought the map," said Serena. "We might need to pick up a better one of Dunsmuir unless you can figure out approximately where his place is."

"Like I said, we have to find somebody who knows. I have an idea of where to go. It's like the first place I thought of, just because of the structures there."

"What structures? Log cabins?"

"Logs are tough, but steel's tougher," I said. "These are railroad cars."

"That's right," said Serena. "You told me about the resort."

"Yeah, more of a campground, but it's all old railroad cars converted into little cabins. Like cabooses."

"I always liked the word papoose," said Nelson. "I wonder if caboose is Indian, too," he said.

"I think it's Native American," said Lola.

"In your world, maybe," said Nelson. "But I didn't grow up playing Cowboys and Native Americans."

"Touché," said Lola, laughing. "Guess we can toss the politically correct shit out the window."

I shook my head. "Anyway, let's eat what we can and gun up. Then we hit the road. I want to be ready for anything."

"I'll put together a good backpack," said Nelson. "Extra water, magazines, weed, headlights, snack bars."

"I love how you just threw weed in there, right in the middle," said Lola.

"Nobody else smokes, if you don't mind," I said. "Nelson's a natural on the shit, but I don't want anyone else compromised."

"I won't smoke in front of anyone," said Nelson. "Don't want to make you jealous because I'm treated differently."

We got busy. Showers were out, so sponge baths were all we could do. Nelson had Dial deodorant, so all of us smelled baby powder fresh.

By 9:20 AM we were ready to go.

*****

"Nelson, show us your Subdudo," said Lola, pointing up ahead. A grey-skinned rotter staggered toward us, about fifteen yards away.

"Okay," he said, but I'm using mostly footwork. I don't feel like touching them right now."

"Screw that," I said, pulling cloth gloves from my pocket. I'd found them inside the house and had taken them as a provisional tool. I gave them to Nelson. "Go all out, dude."

"Fine," he said, taking the gloves and passing me the AR-15. He approached the zombie from the front and it reached for him when he was about five feet away.

"You see what he's doing there?" asked Nelson, never taking his eyes from the creature. "I call it the hungry reach. Perfect opportunity to do this."

He turned sideways and stood on his left leg, thrusting his right leg out quickly, and high. It hit the creature's right arm, spinning him counter-clockwise. Nelson quickly kicked the same raised leg to the left, hitting the other arm, reversing the monster's spin clockwise. When the zombie faced away from him, Nelson moved in and gave him a quick chop to the back of the neck, two fast kicks to the inner joint of both his knees, and he fell backward, folding on top of himself.

Nelson stared down at him, took three steps away and turned to face us. "He's not really hurt, he just has no bloody idea what I just did to him."

"Bloody?" I said, laughing.

"Got that from Hemp," he said, smiling.

"That is cool, Nelson," said Lola. "I mean, wow."

Sure enough, the zombie crawled to his knees and got back on his feet, resuming his trek toward Nelson.

"Move," said Lola, walking forward.

Nelson stepped aside.

She whipped out her knife and as the creature reached for her, she brought the blade down on its right arm, severing it to the bone near the wrist, then did the same to the thing's left arm. Both hands hung limp, but it kept coming. Lola held the Bowie knife, which had to have a fourteen inch blade, like an ice cream cone, and slammed it into the side of the creature's head, just above its ear.

Down it fell, like a sack of rocks. When it was on the ground, she put her tennis shoe on top of its head and withdrew the knife. She held it up.

"See? Blade's almost clean. The first ones mess it up a bit, but a direct head stab will pretty much clean the blade, like a fork in a just-baked cupcake."

Serena smiled. "We have a cool little group here," she said. "I like us."

Nelson took his gun back – which I was glad he had finally agreed to use – and we continued walking. The air was a bit thinner than we were used to, and it was uphill, so only Lola was handling it well, with her conditioned lungs. Nelson was in second best condition, oddly enough. So much for marijuana being hard on your lungs.

We walked on. A small plane had crashed into the trees off to our right, and several cars had broken through the guardrail, plunging into the canyon far below the road. If they suffered massive head injuries, I figured they were the lucky ones.

If not, they were no longer in the wreckage unless trapped there, and in that case, there they would remain forever. These were the thoughts that crossed my mind. Sometimes I used them to make conversation, but mostly I entertained them for a few moments and discarded them.

Morbid. There was enough of that, but humor was still important. I began thinking about an awkward moment joke. It had been too long, and I told myself everyone was disappointed because they missed them so.

In a half hour, I could just make out a sign ahead, and a clearing on the left. I squinted to read it. "Railroad Park," I said. "Right there."

For some reason, everyone hoisted their guns into the ready position. I saw Lola's hand go to her knife.

We crossed the highway, walked around an overturned Airstream trailer, and all ignored the growls coming from within the silver wreck.

For now we searched for the living. The dead could tell us nothing, and we knew they could wait.

They *would* wait. Forever.

*****

We made our way up the road, and on the way, nothing lurched from the trees or came at us on the road. We were armed to the teeth, and anything or anyone with a functioning brain would likely not stick around if they saw us coming.

A couple of times we heard rustling in the trees, but we already knew this was deer country, so there was other wildlife, too. We knew it could be the walking dead, but it could also be a frightened doe or buck.

"Looks like that was done on purpose," Serena said as we approached a short bridge with low side railings. A bus was on its side, and extended from rail to rail, blocking both lanes. With the zombies' lack of coordination, not to mention their distinct lack of critical thinking skills, it would bunch them up at the very least, should they be following scents to the Railroad Park Resort.

"Look over there," said Nelson, pointing. There was a footbridge off to the left. "Guess that's how they go across."

"Good idea," I said. "Blocking off the main road. Zombies wouldn't look for an alternate path."

I turned around and walked back, searching the grounds on the side of the bridge.

I saw what looked like a pathway beyond where I stood, but no entrance to it. Rachel and Nelson came up beside me, and Rachel swept aside a large plant, and there it was.

"Smart," I said. "Hide the path by letting the plants grow up around it."

"This must mean people are here, like you thought," said Nelson.

"Friendly people?" asked Lola, pulling out her Bowie knife.

"Keep that handy," Rachel said. "Never know these days."

"Okay," I said. "Let's go in, but maybe we should keep our voices down unless we see anyone. Who knows what's gone on here over the last year."

"They could be having battles for food and stuff," said Nelson. "Being where these guys are, the local supplies have to be either exhausted or pretty near gone, anyway."

I turned and looked at Nelson, who sounded nothing like he had when he'd chased us down on the scooter and asked us if he could join us. "We're going to sit down, you and me," I said to him. "I feel like I've got Hemp with us, only with longer hair and no British accent."

Nelson shrugged and smiled, but said nothing.

We approached a clearing, and much of the park became visible. From where we stood, we could see eight or nine railroad cars, a large sign that said LODGE, and some light poles.

"There!" whispered Lola. "Someone just disappeared around that Great Northern Railway car. The green one."

303

"I can still see their feet," said Nelson, pointing. "About mid-car now."

I nodded. The railroad cars, which did look like cabooses, were lined up on the perimeter, placed far enough apart to provide privacy to the vacationers.

Now that we were in, we could see the occupants had put up about an eight-foot, chain link fence around the property. There were fire pits and clothes lines, but nobody else moved except the person Lola had caught sight of.

"I'll bet they had sentries," said Serena. "Maybe using radios. Could be that everyone took cover when they reported us."

"I would," I said. "It makes sense. If we'd had our radios on, we might have caught the warning."

"That last one in could've been the lookout," said Nelson.

"I say we walk on in and just go knock on the car," said Rachel. "We're armed, and there's not too many windows in the cars. We should have an advantage if we avoid the windows we do see."

I shrugged. "Standing here's not going to get us any farther."

We started walking. All of our guns held out, we walked across the bridge over the small canyon that likely accommodated the runoff from melting snow on Mount Shasta in the spring and early summer. Beneath it ran a moderately sized creek with crystal clear water bubbling over smooth, oval-shaped river rocks.

Rachel slipped into what seemed a natural role with her military training guiding her. She tapped my radio. "Channel 16. Keep the volume very low, Dave."

She split us into two groups once we reached the other side of the bridge. Serena, Nelson and Lola moved left and ducked behind a Southern Pacific caboose, and Rachel and I went right, across the street.

There were two windows on that side of the car, though, and we saw the curtains move inside the green car where we'd seen the feet moving.

Rachel and I ducked behind a large tree, then peered around it. We watched the rest of our group cross the gravel road and approach the rail car from the front.

I heard the radio click and put it to my ear. Rachel said, "Okay, run low to the car and stay beneath those windows. They won't be able to see you from inside."

"I saw the curtains move," I told her.

"Yeah, me too," she said. "Okay. Go."

We all ran at once, from two directions. If they had been watching, they would not have known where to look.

Above our heads, we heard a sliding sound.

"For Christ's sake," a man's voice said. "We've got one gun and it's out of ammo. What do you want from us?"

I looked over at Rachel and shrugged. "We're not going to hurt anyone," I said, my voice as calm and soft as I could manage. "We're here to find someone. That's it."

"How do we know that?" the man's voice came again. It was cautious and nervous, and I instantly felt bad for the man connected to it. He sounded defeated.

"My uncle goes by Bug," I said. "Brett Ulrich Gammon. Big guy, kinda strange."

"You're Bug's nephew?" the voice said. "Have you seen him?"

I was confused. I had just told him we were looking for my uncle. "No, sir. We're here to find him. We got here last night."

"In that helicopter?" he asked.

"How did you know?"

"Sound carries out here," he said. "Shit sounded like a damned Boeing coming in."

"Can we meet face to face?" asked Serena. "How many of you are there?"

"Only twelve of us in this camp," he said. "I'm Russell Levenson."

"Okay, Russell. I'm Dave Gammon. We're coming around to the door and our guns will be pointed downward."

"Please don't be lying to us," he said. "That would just take the cake after everything else."

"My name's Rachel Reed, and I'm former Air Force," said Rachel. "If I've got one thing going for me, it's that my word is my bond. I'll vouch for the rest of these guys. They found me along the way, and I'm glad they did."

"Okay, just two of you come up the steps, Rachel," said Russell. "You and Dave. There are only four of us in here. The others are in the other cars. I'll radio them that you're okay once we confirm."

"Fair enough," I said. I nodded to Serena and the others, and Rachel and I mounted the steps. The curtain moved back, and I saw who I assumed was Russell. He nodded and opened the door.

"Come on in," he said. "Please leave the guns on the porch for now, if you don't mind."

I looked at Rachel. Knowing I still had the Walther in my waistband, I put the AR-15 down, and she did the same. We nodded at Russell.

"Thanks," he said, standing aside.

We walked in to find a young girl who looked about ten years old, and what might have been a fourteen-year-old boy. They were clearly siblings; their eyes were almost an identical hazel color, and their noses were shaped exactly like the one on the woman who stood behind Russell.

"So that was you we saw coming back inside?"

"Yeah," he said. "I was fishing. You guys scared the hell out of me."

"Is this your family?" asked Rachel.

Russell nodded. "My wife, Madeline – Maddie – and my kids, Hannah and Russ."

"Nice to meet you," said Maddie, smiling. The look in her eyes told me she had not completely abandoned her suspicion, but I supposed it was to be expected.

"Hello," said the girl.

"Hi," said the boy, holding out his hand. I shook it, noticing his red hair and freckles, just like Russell.

"Nice to meet you, Russ," I said. He was about 5'7" tall, and very lean and muscular for his age.

I held out my hand to Hannah, and she hesitated. I could see her eyes darting back and forth between all my tattoos and my hair and beard, and wondered what she was thinking of me.

"I'm harmless," I said, smiling at her. "Just ask any of the folks I'm with."

She smiled and took my hand. As we shook, I saw that she was very pretty, though her eyes were haunted and tired – pretty much how everyone on the planet was these days – and she was also ginger-haired, with freckles like her father and brother. She wore dull, brown pants and a brown hoodie.

I stood there and stared. I had not seen an entire family that had survived since it all happened. I was amazed, but it made sense. Two immune parents, two immune kids. Luck and smarts allowed them to survive this long.

"Excuse me if I'm a little taken aback," I said. "You're unique."

"I'll say," said Rachel.

"I know," said Russell. "If you're talking about an intact family, believe me, we're the only one we know of."

"We're still blessed, amidst all this horror," said Maddie.

"You are," said Rachel.

"Mind if we let the others in?" I asked. "I want you to meet them. We're just here to find my Uncle Bug, and if we can help you, we will. Anything we can do."

Russell nodded, but something else touched his expression, too, at the mention of my uncle.

Moments later, Nelson, Serena and Lola were inside, introduced, and relaxing in the chairs and on the couches. The walls and ceilings were done in what appeared to be knotty pine wainscoting, highly polished and absolutely beautiful. Several hurricane lamps with large candles lit the room with a dancing light that gave it a warm feeling. A Queen-sized bed sat in the center, and the car felt larger inside than it had appeared from the exterior. All in all, not a bad place to hole up during a zombie apocalypse.

"Any fish in that creek?" I asked.

"Nice rainbow trout," said Russell. "I have four on a stringer down there, hanging in the water."

"Sorry about that," I said. "We were playing things by ear, and we've been shot at once already on this trip."

"They shot at your helicopter?"

"No, no," said Serena. "We were already down and walking to shelter. They almost killed Nelson here," she added.

Nelson withdrew the dented star from his shirt pocket – where I was sure it would now forever stay. "Hit me right here," he said. "Lucky charm, now."

Russell looked it over, and gave it back to Nelson.

"If you're looking for Bug, you're in for a disappointment," Russell said.

I did not want to hear that. "Why?" I asked. "Is he … dead?"

"Nobody knows," he said. "Can't get close enough to his place to find out. You might have noticed a distinct lack of walking corpses around here."

Eric A. Shelman

"We expected more," said Lola. "I did, anyway. I was in a damned farm town and there were a few hundred."

"There are more than that here in town," said Maddie. "I don't know if you noticed from the air, but most of the town burned to the ground right after this started. Lucky for us, the wind blew the fire off to the west."

Maddie was very thin with dark brown hair, cut to her shoulders. Her deep, brown eyes were sunken, too, with dark circles beneath them. Her skin was dry, and her hands looked like those of a farmer's wife.

"Then we got a good rainstorm, and it put it out. Saved a lot of food in town, but most of that's gone. We're on a diet of mostly fish that we catch. Some game, if we get lucky. And creative."

"What do you mean, creative?" asked Lola.

"No ammo," said Russell. "Used up most of it right off trying to kill those biters."

"Russell's killed his share," said Maddie. "So have I. Most of them are still up and moving though, over at Bug's place."

"I'm glad they're there and not here," said the boy.

"I know, son," said Russell, squeezing his boy's shoulder.

I was confused. "Why are they concentrating at my uncle's place?"

"Because over a hundred people headed up there and broke into his place right after this all started," said Russell. "They cut his locks and got into his ground-floor storage and shut themselves in. We were there, but it was too much. We all decided to take our chances here."

"Hundreds?" I asked. "How can they all fit?"

"Have you been there before?"

"When I was a kid, really. Long time ago," I said. "I don't remember it being that big."

"Bug kept going deeper and deeper into the hillside," said Mattie. "Several chambers, from what I hear. Storage, water tanks. I hear the inside lower level is as big as half a football field, all told."

"Bug told us that before," said the boy. "Those zombie things kept coming here, but when the main group left for Bug's, they moved away, too. A ton of 'em. We stay clear."

"He's right," said Mattie, pulling a strand of her hair away from her face. "We get the odd straggler, but they tend to migrate over there."

"Scent is a draw for them," said Nelson. "Happened to us in Concord."

"New Hampshire?" Russell asked. "How far did you guys fly?"

"We came from South Carolina, but we flew from Knoxville," I said.

"Far as we know they're trapped in there," said Russell. "Only one way in and out, and they can't get out. They had radios for a bit, but their batteries went dead, 'cause we haven't heard from them in months. I don't know if they're dead or alive now," he added.

"Jesus," I said, looking at Serena. "How are we going to get to Uncle Bug?"

"If he's even still alive," said Nelson.

"If you ask me, I think he is," said Russell.

"How do you know?"

"Because I smell exhaust once in a while, when the wind is right. Just slight, but sometimes like diesel. Other times I swear I catch a whiff of propane, other than our own."

"He must have vent pipes," said Rachel.

"You guys have any weapons?" asked Nelson.

"Yeah," said Russell, going to a closet in the middle of the rail car. He reached in and withdrew a rifle, holding it up. "30-06."

"I think we have ammo for that," I said. "In the chopper. We didn't carry it all down to the cabin because of weight."

"If we stay here, we only need it for hunting," said Maddie. "The dead ones are stragglers mostly, so we use bats and scrap metal to kill them."

"What do you do with their bodies?" asked Rachel.

"We burn them," said Hannah, surprising all of us, I think. Her voice was not gloomy, rather bright and informative. "We drag them to the north side of the park. There's a pit there."

Life changed. Trina will be just as sharp when she's ten, I thought.

"Good," I said. "Prevent bringing other diseases into the mix."

"So you said there are twelve of you, huh?" asked Nelson. "Where are the others?"

"Oh, that's right," said Maddie. "Should I call them?"

"Not here," said Russell, shaking his head. "Let's go to the Crew Dispatcher cabin. More room."

Maddie got on the radio. "Guys," she said. "Our guests are okay. Let's all head over to cabin 6."

Russell opened the door and led the way outside. The kids followed him, with me, Serena, Maddie, followed by Nelson, Lola and Rachel. I looked back to see Rachel scanning the tree line beyond the park, her AR-15 ready to fire.

What I saw next blew my mind. A tall, young black man in dark blue overalls led the remaining group. He was probably only nineteen years old.

The rest were all young girls. Their ages ranged from five to probably fourteen years.

I didn't say anything until we got inside; I watched them file in, all very orderly and quiet. I noted that as they walked, each of them turned their heads and scanned the distance. Training, I knew. It was necessary to stay alive.

Each of them held a length of what appeared to be rebar. The older ones carried thicker pieces, longer lengths. The younger girls carried ½" diameter pieces, maybe three feet long.

"It makes me want to cry," said Serena in my ear as we followed them into cabin 6. The kids all hopped onto the beds, and there was a dinette set with six chairs as well.

Once inside, two of the older girls went to drawers and removed lighters, then moved around the room lighting the candles on the tables and counters. The light was sufficient.

We numbered 17 all told, and once inside, we pulled the door closed and Hannah turned the lock.

"I'll let the kids sound off so you know their names," said Russell.

The young man who had clearly been in charge approached the table and held out his hand. "I'm Albert," he said. "Brookins."

A girl of about seven sitting on the bed raised her hand. "I'm Frannie," she said.

Another of around ten said, "Cara."

As we moved around the bed, we met Crystal, Linda, Lily, Robin and the oldest of the young girls, Kristin. She was seventeen with dirty blonde hair, just past her shoulders, kind of like Charlie's. She appeared closer to fifteen years old.

"Dudes," said Nelson, looking between Maddie and Russell. "How did they all end up here? Where are their parents?"

"You don't have to answer that," said Rachel, taking Nelson's hand and squeezing it.

Nelson's face said he realized his lack of delicacy. "I'm sorry," he said, shaking his head. "I just meant that I wasn't sure how so many kids ended up here."

"Girl's camp," said Albert. "I was one of several camp counselors. My parents ran it."

The girls all sat around the bed, their hands in their laps. Their faces were expressionless, and no smiles touched their lips. It was not as though they looked sad; instead they appeared to be children waiting for something terrible to happen, but with no idea when or what it would be. At the same time, they did not look frightened.

"I take it all you girls like fish?" asked Lola, with a smile.

"We eat it a lot," said the one named Robin, who was probably twelve years old. "It's okay with seasoning."

"I cook a mean fish," said Lola. "Russell here said there are four down there on a stringer."

"We'll need more to feed this batch," said Maddie.

"We have food in the chopper," said Rachel. "Do you have any fuel here?"

"We actually do," said Russell. "I have at least a full 5-gallon can right now. The tanker had just filled the underground tanks at Manfredi's Food & Gas on the Friday, and everything started on a Sunday, so yeah. We've been able to get as much as we could haul. We're in need of another run about now."

"I can dump that in," said Rachel. "It'll get the chopper from there to here, and I can put it down over by that little pond. All our supplies and ammo are in there."

"Better get it right away," said Russell. "There aren't too many folks around, but you never know who might come across it and try to break inside."

"Has anyone from up there come down here?" asked Serena.

"Only the scary ones," said little Frannie. "Nobody else."

"Did anyone up there know where you were going?" asked Serena. "I mean, do they know you're here now?"

Albert shook his head. "Who knows now," he said. "I believe my parents are still there. I know they *were* alive, because I ran up there with them, along with all the girls that didn't get sick. I got separated from them, but I saw my mom go inside. I lost track of my dad, but last I saw, he was right behind her. I don't think he'd have left her side."

Albert's hair was very short, and his eyes were pale white against his skin, slightly bloodshot, but alert. I saw determination there, too.

"I'm sure that was hard," said Lola. "We've all lost people. I'm glad there's still hope in your heart, Albert."

"Thanks," he said. "Everyone in town thought of Bug first," said Albert. "We knew he was one of those preppers, or whatever they call them. He had an arsenal of guns, lots of food, water and supplies to last forever. Everyone pretty much laughed at the guy for years, but when all this went down, I guess you know what happened."

"Suddenly the dude wasn't such a goofball," said Nelson. "His place looked like a sanctuary."

Albert nodded, scratching his head. "Yeah. Exactly. It was like this mad rush to get up there, just crazy. People coming from everywhere in town, but in the middle of it, people were getting sick and going after other people, so it was pretty nuts."

"Were you still with your parents when you got to Uncle Bug's house?" I asked.

Albert shook his head. "Nah, it was like an anthill getting sprayed. The things were going after everyone, so it was a scatter. Like I said, I was lucky to catch sight of them at all before they went inside."

Albert shook his head, remembering. "When my folks got separated from us, I was watching after these girls and some others. It was quite a trek up there, and by that time I'm pretty sure my parents were up towards the front. Like I said, things were getting nuts, and more and more people kept getting in between them and us. By the time we got there, the bolt cutters were on the ground and I just caught sight of my mom going inside with the crowd."

"I was there," said Russell. "It was like a river of bodies flowing into that garage. Swept inside is right. More like swept away. Lots of people with powerful headaches pushed in there, too, and I'd already figured out it was the first symptom, so I'd changed my mind about wanting to go there."

"When they pulled the doors closed," added Maddie, "we barely cleared them and got the kids away. Hannah's hand got caught in the door. Scared us to death."

Hannah held up her left hand and I saw she was missing her pinky finger. The ring finger was only a nub, severed just above the first knuckle. I was surprised I hadn't noticed it earlier, but when I'd shaken her hand, it was her right.

"I'll go with Rachel to get the chopper," said Nelson. "You going to do any more fishing?" he asked Russell. "I'd prefer some trout to the preservative-laden crap I've been eating lately."

"I normally catch enough for the day if I can," said Russell. "Another couple hours should do it."

"I'd like to watch your method," said Serena. "I love fishing. Can I go with you?"

*****

The girls stayed inside the cabin under Albert's direction. None of them complained, and the older ones took care of the younger ones. They were promised lunch soon.

Maddie and her kids, Russ and Hannah, joined Russell and Serena down at the brook to fish while Nelson and Rachel took off on foot to retrieve the helicopter, both armed and ready in case trouble presented itself. They took a radio and I had mine as well, both tuned to channel 16.

Albert led the way toward the trail.

"It's right here," the nineteen-year-old said. He pointed. "You take this, and it crosses over interstate 5. On the other side, you'll find a narrow trail that eventually goes through a small tunnel. That's not easy to find, either. When you get through it – it's about fifty or sixty yards – you're on the other side of the first hill, and that's where it opens up and you can see some of Bug's place."

"I don't remember it being that hard to find," I said. "From when I was a kid."

"My folks have run the camp up here for twenty years," said Albert. "They told me it didn't used to be. Used to be a driveway right off Mountain Avenue."

"When did that change?" I asked.

Albert shrugged. "I don't know. Since I remember, it's been pretty hidden. But I know how to get there like the back of my hand. I go there once in a while. I can't give up on my mom and dad."

"What do you do there?"

"Mostly stay out of sight," he said. "Like Russell probably told you, we don't have guns. Nobody had many up here anyway – this is California, after all – but I still come up just to see if anything changed."

"Like what?" I asked.

"Like if all the zombies or whatever are gone," he said. "I need to get in that garage and see if Bug ever let everyone further into his complex. Maybe he saved them all and they're just living the good life inside there. Like I told you, I never saw it, but I heard he was set up, man. Had all he'd need for years."

"It's all about your parents," I said. "I get it. You think they might still be alive."

He nodded, then pointed off behind me. "Turn that gun, buddy. Quick." He double-fisted his chunk of rebar, but I turned and saw the thing staggering from among the trees, its skin almost completely black, its eyes blowing pink vapor in quantities I hadn't seen in a long time.

I fired twice, capping him in the skull with both rounds. His head flew backward and his body got the message a split-second later and flew backward, too.

The dead thing lay there on its back and I saw that both its tennis shoes had lost their soles; now his shredded, gray feet were exposed like rotted meat.

"That gun sure is easier than this," said Albert, holding up his rebar.

"That works, though. I imagine you're pretty quick now. You guys know about the vapor, right?"

"What vapor?"

"The stuff that makes their eyes pink. Some of them are red – the pregnant females."

"We've seen it. What about it?"

I looked at Albert, dumbfounded. "All this time and you don't know what it does? Have you ever gotten lightheaded at all after killing one of them close range?"

Albert looked confused. "I don't know … maybe. We're always outside when we come across them, so it's not like we're in close confines or anything."

I thought that might explain it. It also depended on the food intake of the abnormals. The vapor dissipated if they didn't eat for a while.

"Anyway, the vapor will knock you out. The wafers our scientist friend made – we call it WAT-5 – prevents it, but it also makes them not gas you, because they don't see you as food."

"Cool," he said. "Wow. Good information."

A gunshot rang out. Then another. It sounded like an AR-15. I snatched the radio from my belt and pushed the button. "Nelson! Rachel! Come in!"

"Whoa, dude," came Nelson's voice. "No worries, brother. Rachel here just killed one of nature's most majestic creatures with her majestic machine gun."

"A deer?" I asked.

"Yeah," said Nelson, sadly. "Here, talk to her. I've gotta go say a prayer over what's left of the little guy."

"*What*?" I said.

"Dave?" came Rachel's voice.

"You shot a deer?"

"Yeah!" she said. "I wouldn't have, but it was within view of the chopper. Fresh venison today. How does that sound?"

I looked at Albert. "How does fresh venison sound?"

He rubbed his stomach. "I am gonna be so full. Tell them to hurry. The smell of blood draws 'em fast."

"Rachel, Albert said to tell you go get that deer to the chopper fast and get here. We all know what the smell of blood does for our rotting friends out there."

"Oh, yeah," she said. "Nelson finished his prayer. We're good. See you in about fifteen minutes. We'll need a bit of engine warm up."

"Good enough," I said. "Check in before you lift off, would you? I just want to make sure you're okay."

"You'll hear the chopper, Dave," she said. "Pretty sure."

"Oh, right. Okay, bye."

I looked at Albert. "When's the last time you went to Bug's place?"

"About a week and a half ago," he said. "I didn't tell Maddie and Russell."

"You go during the day or night?" I asked, hoping it was day.

"Always in the light. I told them I was checking traps."

"Traps?"

"Yeah, small game stuff we got from the farm supply. Rabbit's good now and then. Any meat we can get."

"What's left of the deer you can cure. I'm not sure how long we're going to be here, but I don't expect more than a couple of nights, so what doesn't go is yours."

"Cool," said Albert. "I'm excited."

I liked Albert. He had a determination and a sincerity about him that told me he would make a loyal friend and a formidable adversary. I'd want him on my side if I lived here.

"Okay," I said. "Today we plan, eat and rest tonight. Tomorrow would you care to join us up there?"

He nodded his head. "Do you want to breach the perimeter?" he asked. "Go inside?"

"I kind of have to," I said, shrugging. "But I need to get deep into the place if I want to find my uncle."

"Okay," he said. "I'll help all I can. I need to answer some questions. Once and for all."

I put a hand on his shoulder. "Hope I can help you do that, man."

"So do I," he said. "My folks' names are Morgan and Ellie Brookins, and if they're alive in there, I need to get them out."

I wondered if anyone could be alive in there after so long essentially trapped. Supplies had to have run out, and if many of them were sick, I didn't hold out much hope.

I said nothing to Albert. He deserved to cling to his bit of hope.

*****

While Rachel had plenty of expertise in field dressing a deer, so did Russell, and he insisted on doing the job.

Albert and the girls built a nice fire in the pit in the middle of the camping area with a large, round grill top over it. The smell of fresh venison and trout cooking was visibly driving everyone over the edge.

We'd brought out some of our extra .22 rifles and supplied the group's adults and the older kids with enough weapons and ammo to defend their home for perhaps a year, at their current level of infestation – I suppose that's the word for it.

In return, they promised to assist on runs down to the gas station to haul enough fuel back to fill the chopper. We all thought that was a pretty fair trade. Plus, we got shelter for the duration of our visit.

The kids all carried their own chairs outside from one of the other cabins, which I assumed was used for storage. We all sat on molded resin patio chairs – the stackable kind – and when the food was done, Russell carved the meat and cut the fillets into halves.

We all sat in a large circle around the cooking fire, our plates on our laps. I took a large bite of deer meat and chewed it. It was amazingly tender, thanks to Maddie's expertise in preparing and cooking it. I drank down a large sip of the Cabernet Sauvignon they'd provided with dinner and I almost felt human again. Beside me, Serena looked at me as she bit off another mouthful of meat and smiled. She looked beautiful, having bathed in the cool water of the creek. It reminded me that I needed a bath, too.

"Have you got any kind of early warning system out here? How do you know when someone's coming? One of them?" asked Nelson.

"We actually do," said Albert. "We have to check on them all the time, but you might have seen PVC poles sticking out of the ground wherever there's a clearing. We mounted cowbells on the tops."

"Cowbells?" asked Lola.

"Yeah," said Kristin, the oldest girl. "There was an antique shop downtown that had tons of them, some painted with local scenes and Dunsmuir, California on them and some really old and rustic. Tourists loved 'em, I guess."

I was glad to see the kids, even with what they were going through, were very sociable and friendly.

"Good idea," said Nelson.

"They are," said young Russ. "Saved us a bunch of times."

"So we're going tomorrow," I said to Russell. "I would say that everyone here should be on alert, because we're going to basically slaughter as many as we can up there. While they don't run from a fight because they're too stupid, some could end up down here, I guess. Just be aware."

"I'll join you," he said, glancing at Maddie.

She did not respond, but broke her eye contact with him and looked back down at her plate. I took that to mean she preferred he didn't.

"Look," I said. "We came here prepared to do what we had to do. We never anticipated help, so if you have reasons – and you clearly do – to want to steer clear of the fight up there, then I absolutely insist that you do that. Stay here and defend your home and family."

Russ glanced again at Maddie, then said, "I have Maddie and my kids to think about. I don't think there are many men who can say that anymore."

"You're right, Russell," said Serena. "As the world begins to rebuild when this has passed – and I have to believe it will eventually be over – you will be one of the original families. It's unique."

"As unique as a hand-painted, Dunsmuir cowbell from Tessa's Antiques," said Kristin, smiling.

"Anymore venison, anyone?"

Six girls raised their hands. I sheepishly followed suit.

After dinner was over and we all pitched in, washing the dishes in the creek, night had fallen. The girls retired to their sleeping quarters and full bed checks were done by Russell, Maddie and Albert to make sure nobody had wandered off.

I guessed it was more of a ritual than a necessity – this was a well-organized group of survivors. A great little community, but a huge responsibility for the generous couple.

After all was said and done, we all reassembled back in Cabin 6 where we relaxed. Nelson slipped outside to burn a bowl of pot, and came back inside, ready to strategize.

"So urushiol oil melts them, huh?" said Russell.

Albert sat up suddenly, his eyes wide. "Russell! Remember that day I told you I was walking through the woods and I smelled something? And I went toward it and found like a whole bunch of rotted meat and bones?"

"Yeah, I do. Three months ago or so."

"Yeah, well there was a whole bunch of low, green plants in that area. I wonder if that was poison ivy. Or oak or something."

I sat up. "We have some urushiol, but not much. Do you have a brewery in town? Or a distillery of any kind?"

"There is a brewery," said Russell. "Not sure how it survived the fire, though. We haven't been down that far. There wasn't a need."

"A brewery will need more modification and we'll need other parts," I said. "I was in on the work done in Concord, so I have a good idea of how to go about it."

"Before we go," said Serena. "If we can get you guys extracting your own urushiol oil, it would be a Godsend to you."

"Sounds like it," said Maddie. "You guys are giving me this sense of hope that I haven't had in a long time."

"And dudes, don't forget. The best part is, you don't have anything to worry about while you harvest it. All of you – even the girls – are immune to it. It's why you survived the zombie gas."

"Whether we need to mess with the brewery equipment depends on what we find up there," I said. "It's not going to be a quick job and it's definitely not top priority for now."

Russell nodded. "Got it."

"Albert, when we go tomorrow," asked Rachel, "do you want to join us?"

I had told Rachel about his parents.

"Oh, I'm going," he said. "No doubt. I already told Maddie and Russell." He looked at them. "You understand, right?"

"Hell yes," said Russell. "If not for the responsibility we have, I'd go, too. But they're right. They're equipped, they know how to use the weapons they have. I might get in the way."

I pulled out the bag of remaining wafers. "These are all we have left of our main protection," I said. "If there aren't any of the red-eyed females around they'll be effective. If there are, these will help some, but in the end, we'll be found out."

"Really?" asked Maddie. "You can take this and just stand right there with them? Like you're one of them?"

"Yeah," I said. "It's pretty freaky at first, and you still have to make sure you don't get scratched or bitten if they fall into you or something. You also don't want it wearing off while you're in the middle of them. You're toast if that happens."

"If we mulch up a bunch of the poison ivy," asked Albert, "and spread it around the perimeter of our compound, think that'll stop them?"

"If their skin is exposed," said Nelson. "and they walk on it, I guess it would. Once the leaves die, only the oil will remain, right Davey?"

"That's what Hemp told me," I said. "As for touching their skin, most of them are barefoot now, even the ones that had shoes on at first. Saw one like that today when I was out with Albert. No soles."

"Ha, good one," said Nelson. "Souls, right? Like in the spiritual sense?"

I hadn't even thought about it, and I laughed at Nelson's connection.

Lola yawned and stretched. Her hand went instinctively to her knife, and she said, "I need to turn in. I'm in the Northern Pacific car?"

"Yep," said Russell. "And Dave and Serena are in the CCT car right behind it. Rachel and Nelson, you guys are free to take either the Cotton Belt car or Cabin 4."

"Oh, we're not together," said Nelson, with an embarrassed smile. "Rach, if you want the cabin, I'll be fine in the car."

"That's fine, Nel," she said, smiling. "Thanks."

Rachel did not seem embarrassed at the implication she was with Nelson. In fact, I thought I saw faint disappointment in her eyes. It was probably my imagination.

"Any special procedure for problems at night?" I asked.

"If you hear cowbells, get on the radio and await instructions. Channel 16. I'm glad we've got the guns now, but that doesn't mean I want their putrid asses in our compound."

"Got it," I said. "Once it's good and light, we're heading up there in the morning."

"We've got chickens that you haven't seen yet, so there will be fresh, three-egg, venison omelets if you want them," said Maddie. "You'll need energy, so don't leave without eating first."

With that we retired to our respective rail cars and cabins. Sleep came fast.

I don't remember dreaming, which is good. I can't imagine my mind settling on pleasant things, considering what task lay ahead.

*****

Chapter Fourteen

Breakfast was good, but I found myself powering through it. I had only one thing on my mind now.

Brett Ulrich Gammon. Uncle Bug.

As we prepared, we saw something very cool and a little strange: Some of the girls were undergoing zombie-killing training. Someone – I assumed Maddie, Russell and Albert – had constructed what appeared to be a kind of a horizontal, turning carousel, like a merry-go-round of sorts. It looked like it was made out of 2" x 2" lumber with bearings and spindles, kind of like a wagon wheel, complete with spokes and supports, along with a series of guy wires.

I could not see exactly how it was designed, but it appeared to have been built utilizing a large flywheel of some kind that connected to other gears. Beneath it, I could almost make out a flat, coil-type spring beneath its base, similar to what you see in wind-up toys.

This made sense when I saw three of the girls rotate the entire device counter-clockwise a few dozen times before letting it go. When released, it slowly unwound, turning the entire upper piece and its attachments. Atop the carousel were ten dummies of varying heights and configurations, dressed in torn up clothing. Some had arms down at their sides, others arms reached outward, and some were missing limbs altogether. Their heads looked like tightly balled and wired balls of straw, which is what I assumed also stuffed the bodies.

When it was all underway, the girls, from the youngest to the oldest, leapt over the spinning base, gauging the time remaining until the next lower crossbar arrived. Their eyes never left the looming, faux zombies, and as one neared, they would lunge forward and jab twice with their lengths of rebar, piercing the heads of each crude, representative mannequin.

I was impressed. I was captured by little 7-year-old Frannie's level of focus, and was mesmerized, unable to look away.

That is, until I saw Cara, the 10-year-old, ram her rebar in the side of the head of one of the dummies, her hands well-placed on the sharpened steel rod, only to yank it out, reposition it, and jam it at the perfect angle beneath the dummy's chin and up into its straw brain.

No grunts, no sounds. All were silent as they killed their makeshift zombies.

I was glad at their level of preparation, but at the same time I thought, *I hope there's room for love in their hearts, along with all that fierce determination.*

Nelson came out of his place, and I was surprised to see Rachel step out behind him a few seconds later, looking up to reveal a slightly embarrassed look. She raised her hand in a wave. I waved back and looked away, hopefully leaving her dignity intact.

She'd been through a lot, and Nelson was a good man. Age differences mattered far less these days, and going by Madonna, Jennifer Lopez and about a hundred other celebrities, there was really nothing unusual about it anyway.

"Ready?" asked Rachel, walking up to us with her AR-15 and drop holsters loaded up with a pair of .45 semi-automatics.

"We are," I said. Serena and I were similarly equipped.

"I get WAT-5," said Lola, coming out of her cabin with an empty plate. "Sorry. I breakfasted alone this morning. I got so used to being alone. Gives me time to think."

"To each their own," I said. "Will you be taking any other weapons besides your knife?" I asked her.

"Nope," she said. "Your wafers and my blade. Along with these feet, it should be all I need."

"Your call, just be careful," I said. I thought again how glad I was that Nelson had finally decided to arm himself. I needed firepower by my side, and as much as I could get.

"Nel, you got all your mags loaded?" I asked. "Extra ammo, too?"

"Yep," he said. "I'm primed, too."

"Comforting," said Serena, smiling and shaking her head.

"For me, it is," he said, shrugging.

"We leaving the helicopter here?" asked Rachel. "Make our way on foot?"

"Yeah," I said. "Albert showed me the trail, and with a group like the one they described, there are going to be a few pregnant females in there. If their ears are working, we need to mitigate that risk."

"Davey," said Nelson. "Mitigate. Good word."

"Saw it on Wheel of Fortune," I said, smiling.

As if on cue, Albert exited his cabin and walked over. He held a .22 pistol we'd given him, and over his arm were a load of jackets.

"Okay, guys. Are we all taking those wafers?"

"Yes, but we need to sit," I said. "What's with the clothes?"

"Russell and Maddie don't want you guys going up there without these on. Lightest leather we could find over the past year."

"It's not that cold," said Rachel.

"Not for cold," said Albert, holding one up. "These are long-sleeved vests. If we're going to be right there with them, we should all protect our arms. Scratches, even bites won't get through it. You guys been hiding under a rock?" he asked, smiling.

I smiled back. "Good idea. We haven't been involved in too much hand-to-hand," I said. "Mostly distance kills. I'll wear one, if you have something that fits."

"There are more," he said. "If you don't find something, we'll grab it from inside."

Albert put the stuff on a nearby mesh table and we sorted through it. He ran back in to find one that was long enough for Nelson's arms and soon we looked like a strange motorcycle gang, looking for trouble.

"We can take the wafers over by the fire pit," Albert said. "I'm ready to go. Let's dose and get out of here."

"Now you're talkin' my language," said Nelson.

I pulled out the appropriate number of wafers, and realized we would only have around seven left when it was all said and done.

Nonetheless, we all took our wafer naps and woke up ready to go see what was up at Bug's compound.

It's that awkward moment when everybody seems to trust your judgment, and the only holdout is yourself.

We said our goodbyes and headed toward the trail to Brett Gammon's place.

*****

329

There we were, finally in California, doing what we had gone there to do. I appreciated the help from my friends, both old and new, but I also worried for them. This was my mission, after all; not theirs.

Knowing that each of them had their skills – including Lola and her awesome blade work – I was put somewhat at ease. Communication would be everything up here, especially if it was anything like Albert said.

Speaking of the kid, he was the wild card in my mind. He'd been perfectly comfortable hoisting a bat in one hand and a .22 rifle in the other.

I hoped he had a plan on how to use both if he needed them. I was on his turf, and he had a mission. As we walked, I called him to the front and because we were already on the trail, it was narrow enough that Serena had to fall back.

"Yeah, Dave," he said. "What's up?"

"Albert, what's up is that I don't know what the hell I'm doing. I don't mount offensives and I don't fight wars. I'm a shitty captain to put your confidence in."

To my surprise, he shook his head with a big smile on his face. "Seems to me you've got a group here who knows you and they're following you. You tellin' me they're stupid?"

It's that awkward moment when a nineteen-year-old puts you in a conversational box that you can't get out of.

"Good point," I said. "And yeah, to a man and woman they're smart and capable. I just might be the only one who's been running off of dumb luck."

"Well," he said, taking a deep breath and a glance at those behind us, "I don't think *they* think so, and I don't either. That said, what is the plan?"

"Is there any other way inside?" I asked.

"Never looked," said Albert. "I've been focused on the place my folks went in."

I looked at him as we walked, occasionally glancing ahead on the path in case something popped out ahead of us. "Seriously? You've never scouted higher up?"

"We can do it today if you think it'll help."

"We don't have enough WAT-5 to waste," I said. "So depending on how things go now, we may need to take advantage of every minute of invisibility this stuff provides us. It might get us into where your folks are."

"Do you think so?" Albert asked, hope in his voice.

The path widened and Serena and Nelson moved up beside us. I looked back and saw Rachel in the rear, her AR-15 ready for trouble.

It was about a 1-1/2 mile hike from the Railroad Car Resort to the narrow trail that led to Bug's place, and another half mile up the winding path to his house, according to Albert.

"Albert here just asked me about his folks," I said to Serena and Nelson. "I was just about to tell him that if we find them, he needs to take them and hightail it back down to the park."

"But –"

"No buts, Albert," said Serena. "You've got quite a responsibility down there, and you're good at it, from what I saw. They need you. If it were up to me – and I think Nel and David here would agree – you wouldn't be here now."

"You don't have a right to stop me," he said, with no hint of a smile now. "I need to find my parents, and I'd have come up here whether you did or not. Now that I have this," he said, holding up the rifle.

At that point, we were about halfway up. Just under a half mile to go. It was fairly steep, though, and the going was sluggish.

It had been so long since I'd been there, nothing looked familiar. It's funny how well we think we remember something until called on to access the information. Then it's gone. *Poof.*

"Davey doesn't bark commands," said Nelson. "Albert, dude, this is your call and it always was, but that doesn't mean we don't have your back. That said, I barely know how to shoot this damned gun."

"Oh, that's comforting," said Albert with a smile.

Albert stopped. "There," he said, pointing. "We should move off the trail. I've gone through the woods here so many times there's a narrow trail now. I get pretty close to them."

He pointed to an almost invisible path. The only indication it was there was what looked like a fallen tree branch with dead leaves packed over it. The trail of flattened leaves and branches wound their way into the forest as far as we could see.

"Lead the way," I said.

He did. We followed.

"How far from here?" I asked.

"Another five minutes," he said. "Shh."

In four minutes I called a halt to our forward momentum and asked everyone to get in a circle.

"Okay, guys. We've got ..." I turned my wrist up to look at my watch. "about four hours and fifteen minutes of WAT-5 protection."

"I feel something," said Lola, looking directly at me.

I was shocked to see her eyes with a red tinge.

"Oh, my God!" said Rachel. "What's wrong with her?"

Nelson put a hand on Rachel's shoulder and nodded toward me.

"Lola," I said. "I need you to stay calm, but your eyes are ... well, they're red."

"What?" she asked. "Like bloodshot? I was just saying I feel a pull. Something pulling me forward. It's … like it's almost impossible for me to just stand here."

Nelson reached into his pants pocket and pulled out a shiny, 3" Ninja star. He held it up and she looked into it.

"Oh." She stared at her reflection in the gleaming, stainless steel and at first, her eyebrows furrowed together. A moment later, her red eyes began to water. "Am I … is this *still* from what happened to me before you found me? I'm like … *them*!"

"That this is from your exposure to them is a definite," said Nelson. "But that said, you don't seem like one of them. You're much nicer."

Despite her fear, Lola laughed, and I was surprised to hear Rachel laugh, too.

Nelson seemed pleased at that. A shy smile crossed his lips. "Don't worry, Lola," he said. "You took one of the wafers made of the red-eye vapor right away. It didn't get to you in the helicopter, and that was right after." He turned and looked at me. "Plus, we don't even know if getting blasted by them affects you long term, right Davey?"

"I *told* you I feel a pull," Lola said, obviously still frightened. "So something is happening."

"What the hell is this about?" asked Albert.

"Sorry," Serena said. "Albert, have you noticed some of the females have red eyes?"

"Yeah, I've seen it a couple of times."

"Okay," said Serena. "If a woman in her childbearing years who is fully capable of having children is doused with the eye vapor from a pregnant female abnormal, she can fall under their control."

"Like psychic stuff," said Nelson. "Magic."

"More like telepathy," I said. "It happened to my sister."

"And what happened?"

It was the last thing I wanted to talk about, but if we ever wanted to move forward, it was necessary. "They essentially forced her to sacrifice herself to them," I said.

"I'm sorry, man," said Albert.

I shook my head. "It's the past."

"So we've got the WAT-5," said Rachel. "Right? We just spot them and kill them."

"WAT-5 doesn't work on them so well," I said. "They see right through the ruse."

"Well isn't that beautiful," said Albert.

"The present bad news," said Serena, "is that if she's feeling the pull, there are probably some red-eyes up here."

"All the more reason to be watchful," I said. "Buddy system. There are six of us, and I don't ever want anyone off on their own. I'd prefer to stay as a group, that way we can ... I don't know ... circle the wagons or something."

"Maybe Lola should hang back," said Rachel. "I'm sorry, babe," she said to Lola, then turned back to me. "I mean, how can we trust her?"

"Because she might be a mouthpiece," Nelson interjected. "She could be an early warning that the females are nearby."

"Hint, hint," Lola said. "They're nearby." She spread her arms apart.

"Listen to me," I said. "the fact that she feels them is good. It's already the early warning system we hoped it would be." I looked the young girl directly in the eyes. "Lola?"

"Yes," she said.

"If anything starts to pull at you, makes you want to do something you know is bad for the rest of us, will you handle it? Run or something? I know you can do that. Just get out of here?"

"If I think I'm going to hurt any of you, yes," she said. "I'll run."

"Don't hurt yourself," said Serena. "Just go, okay? Don't you do anything stupid. We're going to want to see you around later."

"Promise. I still feel it."

"You will," said Nelson. "Focus your mind on us," he said. "Focus is everything." He rubbed her back and nodded, and she nodded back, smiling.

"Thanks, Nelson."

In twenty more steps we laid eyes on what had to be three hundred infecteds milling around a huge clearing. There were so many of them you couldn't see the ground. The zombies pressed against two enormous, closed plank doors that looked as if they were embedded in the side of a huge hill or mountainside.

Above that just appeared to be a rocky, timber-covered slope that disappeared into the massive boulders and treetops. I could not see any other way in besides the two huge doors, but it appeared a substantial trail ran along the north side, disappearing into the woods.

The doors themselves appeared to be made out of rough hewn timbers, thick-looking, like massive, castle doors on the other side of a drawbridge that spanned over a moat. Impenetrable, as though designed to keep dragons out. I wondered how the hell we would get inside to get to my uncle.

Albert whispered, "The bunker itself is embedded into the mountainside. I've never been inside, but I heard there are three main chambers – the one you see here, a middle section, and then the highest section is the main chamber. This garage level in the clearing is where he planned to keep his vehicles."

"How do you know all that?" I asked.

"He wasn't completely recluse," said Albert. "Not until this hit. We all pretty much liked him, we just thought he was kind of extreme."

"*That* he is," I said. "Okay. Everybody ready to put WAT-5 to the test out west?"

"Hope the altitude doesn't mess with its effectiveness," said Serena.

"Seriously," said Nelson. "You had to think of that now?"

"I have something for you first," said Albert.

"What's that?" I asked.

He reached into a large cargo pocket and withdrew several pieces of brown leather. He handed one to each of us.

I unfolded mine, and saw that it had eye and mouth holes, with a protruding area for a nose, complete with nostril holes.

"What the fuck is this?" I asked. "A human-sized falcon mask?"

"We do a lot of hand-to-hand when it comes time to fight," said Albert. "Your arms are protected, but you can't just have your face exposed."

"I think this is a cool idea," said Nelson, resting his gun against his knee and pulling his on. "Do I look like a Mexican wrestler?" His long, blonde hair hung down onto his back, so it would not be an issue knowing who he was.

"Maybe a little," said Serena.

"These are awesome!" he said. "I can see and breathe perfectly."

"Thank Maddie," said Albert, pulling his on. "She worked out the kinks over the year."

Soon, we all looked like we should either be holding a WWE tag team match or playing important roles in The Texas Chainsaw Massacre. Judging from the drab colors, the latter seemed more appropriate.

"So we're all ready to go now?" I asked.

Nobody said anything. They just stood there looking like a bunch of Leatherfaces.

I led the way. We reached the outskirts of the shuffling horde of zombies. The smell permeated my leather cowl.

They paid us no mind. We moved through the crowd tentatively at first, working our way toward the doors. We were able to shoulder them aside and soon, we had progressed the fifteen feet through the crowd. I have to say that the leather protection did give me more confidence.

We stood back and looked up. The doors were more massive than I had expected. Once at the front, we all shuffled sideways until we got to where the two large doors came together. The handles were heavy steel, and no chain or other impediment secured them.

"We can't pull them," I said. "Not with all these things here."

"Right," said Serena. "We have to kill them all first."

"Or draw them away," said Lola.

"How do you propose doing that?" I asked.

"I'm being pulled that way," she said, pointing. "I thought you said you saw Hemp leading one around once."

"Yeah," I said. "He was trying to make us feel safe on the wafers. He just took one by the arm, like this."

I turned and looked at the crowd just behind me. I chose one, and curled my hand around the arm of a male to my right. I turned him slowly clockwise, then took three steps, pulling him along behind me.

Like liquid, the zombies filled the space the man had vacated. Emerging from the crowd, what was once an older man in his living years, turned his deteriorated face toward us. Albert looked at it and screamed.

*****

"Dad!" he said, bolting toward the creature. I was too far away to do anything, but Lola jumped into action, rocketing forward and throwing her arms around Albert. She yanked him away from the reanimated, deteriorating black man whose dead, pinkish eyes stared blankly. Albert staggered backward, stumbled and fell down on top of Lola, who had tripped.

When I looked down, I saw what all of us had apparently failed to notice before; crushed and broken bones and skulls littered the ground wherever our gazes fell.

Lola noticed them too, and her terrified expression showed every level of her shock. Albert still stared up at the zombie that had probably once driven him to little league games, but the rotting man did not return his horror-struck gaze.

Instead, the thing again focused on the doors. They wanted what lay beyond the doors, which meant only one thing: There were still people alive in there. People they could smell and whose brains and flesh they craved.

Nelson pushed his way through the grey-faced, gore-spattered creatures, reached Albert and physically pulled the large young man up from the sea of bones, his feet struggling to maintain purchase among the shifting ground.

Lola got up with the help of Serena, and I went to Albert and took him by the shoulders. He would not look at me; he continued to stare at the thing that used to be his father, now melding back into the crowd of undead and in danger of being swallowed up by its shambling mass.

"Albert!" I said. "If that is your dad, he's been gone a long time. You know that."

"I saw him go inside!" he cried. "I swear I saw him go in!"

"You told us you saw your mother, Albert. There was probably a big crowd trying to get in," I said. "Albert, it's not your fault. He might have fallen, and you just didn't see him."

He tore off his leather mask and shook his head. Tears streamed down his face. "I could have saved him ... I didn't try hard enough. I ran like a coward."

"You saved *your* life, Albert," said Serena. "And look at the reason for that; all those sweet girls your mother and father cared about so much, and now you've stepped in to fill their role. If your father had any awareness of what you've done, he would be nothing but proud."

With one arm, Albert pushed me aside, and I did not fight him. He stepped forward, toward the place his father had last stood. He searched the crowd of hungry dead nearby, and as he spotted the man, so did I.

Despite the fact that the young man's father had been dead for some time, I still saw the resemblance between what he used to be and his son; the profile of the face, his height; the shape of the remaining right ear.

When Albert caught sight of his dad again, he stopped and turned toward me. "Dave ... they really don't see us as ... well, as food? They won't attack?"

"No," I said. "You'd be dead by now if they did."

Albert passed me his rifle and his mask, nodded, then stepped toward his dad. The young man gently put his arms around the thing's neck and hugged it. I could see him sobbing as he spoke some words that I could not hear, and I knew at that moment that none of us would ever ask him what those words were. Time stopped as Albert held onto the abnormal, his eyes squeezed closed, ignoring what had to be a putrid stench emanating from the thing.

I don't know about the others, but I held my breath, my muscles rigid to the point I found it hard to believe blood could still flow through my veins. I didn't want to see anything happen to the kid. I liked Albert and I felt for him, but despite the shielding of the WAT-5, what he was doing was irrational and foolish.

Around the pair milled shuffling feet and gnashing teeth, a stench borne of death and decay, and yet Albert held his dead father, oblivious to it all.

When he was done, he appeared to be focused. He walked back to me, nodded and held out his hands. I gave him back his gun and mask, the latter which he pulled back over his head.

He walked back to where his father wavered, nudging aside the walkers all around him, and stopped three paces away. Albert raised the .22 rifle and placed the barrel against its forehead. He fired two times, and the former Mr. Morgan Brookins stood for another two or three seconds before whatever it was that kept his dead body upright and balanced, resigned its post.

The deteriorated, bullet-pierced corpse collapsed to the ground and the crowd closed in on it, beginning the slow pulverization that would soon render it shredded, rotted meat and one day, dried, crushed bones.

Albert came back and stood in front of us. "My mom's inside. I know it. That's why he never left."

I would've hugged him, but not after the hug he'd just given. Instead, I squeezed his arm. "I hope you're right, Albert."

"I am," he said with resolve.

"Oh, no," said Lola, and we all looked at her. She stared into the crowd at something none of us could see, and as we all watched her, her eyes grew redder, a fine mist now drifting off of them like steam from the surface of a lake.

"*Alive*," she said. "*Eat*."

She turned to us and said, "They're issuing commands. Be careful." Her gaze returned to where she had looked before, and the vapor increased.

Suddenly, the entire crowd of rotters pressed in on us, arms reaching and their throaty groans increasing in volume.

They did not close in on Lola.

"On the ground!" shouted Nelson, and it seemed like a good idea. We all dropped down to our hands and knees except for Lolita Lane, who stood straight up, still staring somewhere off into the crowd.

"On your backs and fire up at their heads!" I shouted. "Watch for Lola!"

"Lola, get down!" I heard Rachel call. Lola did not.

I heard the gunfire start within five seconds of my command, and moments after that, zombies began toppling all around and on top of us. I was thankful for the leather mask, for many of them dripped their gooey black innards down on me as I scrambled to stay free of them to kill more and reload when my magazines were spent.

"Serena!" I shouted. I couldn't see her, but I thought I heard enough gunfire that it had to account for all four AR-15s and the .22 that Albert carried.

"I'm okay!" she shouted, and my heart settled a bit.

"Dudes!" I heard Nelson call. "Work your way back! Away from the doors!"

That seemed like another good idea, because we were all getting buried under the weight of the dead abnormals and it was becoming more difficult to move as each new rotter dropped. Worse, the layer of bones beneath us dug into our backsides, and it was getting harder and harder for me to ignore.

"Rachel?" shouted Nelson. "Did you hear me?"

I heard worry in his voice. I had not heard her say anything in a while, so was glad when she acknowledged him.

"Yes!" she shouted. "I'm going now!"

As I turned, spider-walking backward across the bone fragments to the clearing that lay somewhere beyond the undead crowd looming above us, I screamed "Lola!"

I got to the edge of the crowd and scrambled to my feet. Once up, I saw that some of the biters had spread beyond the horde's edge. I smashed the stock of the AR-14 into the heads of two who came too close to me, crushing their skulls and ending their miserable lives once and for all.

Nelson crawled out to my left, and Serena and Rachel came out at the same time.

I helped pull Serena up, and she immediately ejected her spent magazine and fished in her pocket for a fresh one, latching it in place. I took her lead and did the same.

"Where's Lola!" shouted Nelson, searching the crowd as he pulled Rachel to her feet.

"There!" said Rachel, pointing. "Over by the doors!"

We all looked and saw Lola standing there, but she wasn't as tall as many of the zombies crowded around her. She stared off to what I believed was east, and as I followed her line of sight I saw what had captured her attention.

A female, about ten yards away, walked toward her. It's blonde hair, still intact and straight, with a sheen that did not belong among these filthy, rotted monsters.

The breeze caught it, wispy strands blowing around her shoulders as she walked with extraordinary grace toward Lola.

I realized then that Lola had never followed Nelson's suggestion of dropping to the ground below the closing horde, and it wasn't that she had hesitated; she simply never dropped. I had seen her knife in her hand when I'd last caught sight of her and wondered if she still grasped it.

Then I realized something: she hadn't dropped because they were ignoring her. The command that she echoed had come from the red-eyed, likely pregnant female abnormal, but Lola had still been essentially invisible to them.

But not to the red-eyed female, whose stare never once wavered. She kept disappearing below the heads of the other rotters, but when she reemerged, she was even closer.

"Lola!" I screamed, but she did not respond.

I raised my weapon, and the moment I did, the bitch's eyes turned directly toward me, the red vapor thick and practically leaving a trail wafting in the air behind her.

She dropped from view.

"Shit!" I said, lowering my rifle. "Lola, run!" A zombie got too close to my left side so I pulled out my Walther and shot it in the head. A substantial chunk of its skull, along with the remainder of its brain and its right ear, flew from the corpse and the thing tumbled away from me, down toward the trail on which we had come in.

"What's going on, David?" asked Serena, her face terrified. "What's she doing?" Then she called, "Lola! Come here, please! Come to us!"

"Oh, my God," said Rachel. "What's wrong with her? It's like she's in a trance."

"She's going to die," said Nelson. "I can't see the thing anymore."

And then we *all* saw it. The red-eyed female shot up straight and tall, with speed that should have been relegated to the living. She was three feet from Lola when her arms went out and hooked around our young friend's neck.

I could not hear what Lola said, for I don't believe she actually vocalized anything. I did see her lips move. I saw her mouth form the single word.

Die.

The moment her mouth closed again, her arm was in the air and the Bowie knife came straight down toward the creature's head.

343

One of the thing's dead hands caught her wrist when the blade was less than an inch from plunging past her thriving hair, through her skull and deep into her advanced brain.

What happened next would have to be replayed in slow-mo before I could ever figure it out.

The knife flipped through the air, the source of its propulsion unknown to me. Lola caught it in her left hand, and in the next split second, the hilt of the knife slammed against the zombie's head, the blade penetrating everything between its ears.

Black liquid flowed from the gash as Lola withdrew it, yanked her wrist free of the waning grip of the red-eyed female, flipped the blade yet again and caught it in her right hand. She plunged the hardened steel through the she-bitch's eye socket and pushed upward and kept pushing, until she had nearly severed its head in two. Lola withdrew the knife and the thing fell away.

So did Lola, suddenly dropping from view. We heard a scream and Nelson almost ran into the crowd, but I grabbed his shirt. Two seconds later, Lola stood again, only this time, another female zombie, this one with gleaming, brown hair, hung from her blade, and Lola twisted it into the center of its forehead, and kept rotating, alternating with both of her hands.

A cry still emitted from the abnormal. Its mouth was open, and the horrid shriek echoed off the canyons, seemingly for miles. Lola suddenly withdrew the blade and double-gripped it in both hands, slashing lightning-fast from right to left at the female's neck, silencing her mournful howl.

In a move worthy of Nelson Moore, the amazing Lolita Lane leaned back and threw her right leg up in a piston-like kick. The monster flew backward, her severed head spinning forward before falling at Lola's feet. The headless zombie smashed into the massive horde of shambling walking dead behind her, taking several of them down as well.

When Lola was done, she looked at us, and an almost embarrassed smile touched her lips. I saw her once crimson eyes were now almost clear again.

She walked back to us. "That was intense," she said.

"You fucking saved us," I said. "I mean, really saved us. We couldn't have killed them and kept reloading at that pace."

"You saved *all* of us," Lola said. "That wafer saved us." She looked back and forth between all of us, as though she did not want us to miss what she was about to say.

"I drew her to me," she said. "When I heard her thoughts, I pulled her to me. I thought the word *come*, and I just said it over and over in my head, and every time I looked, she was closer. Same with the other one."

"Lola," I said, finally pulling off my mask. "You're telling me that you were controlling *them*?"

"Did you see the one grab my neck?" asked Lola.

"Yeah, dude!" said Nelson. "I was freaked out! Thought you were a goner."

"She was pissed," said Lola. "I felt her anger. Emotion, raw as it comes. I forced her to me, and she lashed out."

"Holy shit," I said. "I wonder if Hemp's figured this out yet."

We looked around us. With the two females down, the crowd was now a mess, moving in all directions, no focus and seemingly, nothing drawing them to the doors anymore.

"What's happening?" asked Albert.

"I don't know," I said, lying to the young man. Because I thought I might know.

"Stay here for a moment," I said. "Serena, I need to talk to you."

"Okay," she said, following me. I moved about ten steps away.

"I think this means ... Jesus."

"What, David?" she asked.

"If there was anything alive in there," I said, "They'd push that way, toward the doors. Look at them. They have no focus. Some are moving toward the forest. Animals I guess."

"So ... the females?" asked Serena. "They directed this group to your uncle's place?"

"They know something," I said. "But if there are people alive in there, they're not behind these doors."

"We still have to go in," said Serena.

"I know," I said. "I just hope the kid doesn't find something that used to be his mom in there."

*****

346

Chapter Fifteen

"I don't know how much ammo we'll need when we get inside," I said. "We could kill all these, but it would take too much."

"Why aren't they at the doors anymore?" asked Albert.

It was the question I dreaded. I wondered if I should lie to him, then thought better of it. He was nineteen years old; old enough to be told the truth when he asked a question.

It's that awkward moment when you wish an awkward moment joke was appropriate, but you know it's not.

"They scatter because there's nothing drawing them," I said.

He stared at me, only his eyes visible through the eerie mask. "What do you mean?"

"Albert, I think Hemp would concur that without the draw of human flesh or the direction of the red-eyed females, they just wander. All directions. Like they're doing right now."

"Why aren't they going to the doors? What about the people inside there? They smelled them before, right? What's different?"

Serena removed her mask and reached up and slowly pulled Albert's off. She stroked his hair and said, "What he's telling you is the creatures never sensed anything inside. The strong females focused them there."

"But why would they, if there's nothing in there? My mom's in there!"

"She might be inside, Albert, but she's not *right* inside," said Serena. "Maybe further in."

Albert ran and put his ear to the thick doors, listening. He stared at us as he did so, and his mouth turned into a semi-smile. "I hear them moving! I hear it! They're in there!"

"You don't know what –" I began.

"Mom! Mom! It's Albert! Pound on the door if you hear me! Pound on the door! I'm alive, mom! We've come to get you out of there!"

I turned to Nelson and the others. "He's not going to stop until we prove it to him," I whispered. "We need to just open them."

"Hold on," said Rachel. She took her radio from her belt and pushed the button. "Russell? Maddie? Come in."

A squelch, and a voice. "Who's this?" It was Maddie.

"It's Rachel, Maddie. You and Russell be ready. The creatures up here are heading into the woods. Lots of them. I'd get the girls inside, and don't come out. You have the guns we left you?"

"We do, but why is this happening?" she asked. "Rachel! Russell's down at the creek with Crystal and Linda!"

"Does he have a gun?"

"No, he didn't take one," said Maddie, worry in her voice.

"Does he have a radio?"

Silence.

"Maddie?"

"It's on the table," she said, frustrated. "I'm looking at it right now. Damnit!"

"Take a gun and go get him," said Rachel. "And I'm only calling as a precaution, Maddie. They started moving into the woods about ten or fifteen minutes ago, so they won't be close to you yet. Still, hurry."

"Okay," she said. "How's Albert?"

"He's fine. You just go. Now."

"Okay," said Maddie. "Be careful."

"You, too," said Serena. "Out."

Rachel looked at us. "What do you say we get these doors open?"

*****

"Something's holding it from the inside," said Albert. He still carried his sharpened rebar rod in a long, obviously homemade sheath on his belt. He was using it to pry between the two heavy, wood doors, but they pulled out less than a half an inch before springing closed again.

"We need to find another way in," I said.

"Where?" asked Albert.

"You smell exhaust at night sometimes, right?" I asked. "Fumes? I thought I smelled them last night, too."

"Yeah, so?"

"It's got to be him," I said. "If he's still got fuel and a generator, it's venting somewhere. It can't be that long a run, and he didn't blast his whole place into solid rock."

"You think it's camouflaged?" asked Rachel.

"Maybe," I said.

"I know the best way to spot it," said Rachel. "Now that we know where this place is."

"The helicopter," said Lola. "What about fuel?"

349

"We need it first," said Rachel. "Albert, we may have to prepare today and get this all ready for tomorrow morning, early."

"What good is a vent going to do us?" asked Albert. "You can't get in through a vent."

"My Uncle Bug wouldn't make this place without another way out," I said. "He was ready for a massive disaster or government takeover – martial law. There's not a chance in hell he'd let himself become trapped. There is another way in. At least one."

"And I ask again, what the hell good will finding a vent hole help?" he asked.

"It's a starting point," I said.

"Yeah," said Nelson. "Dude, you have to trust us more. We've never done this junk before, but we are *really* lucky."

"Uh, yeah," said Lola, smiling and unbelievably calm after her ordeal. "You guys found me."

"Okay," said Albert. "But I hope you know we're wasting all this WAT-5 stuff of yours."

"Doesn't need to be completely wasted," I said. "We're going back down to our ammo stock, so let's kill as many of these rotters as we can. Maybe that'll help secure the future of the Railroad Park Homestead."

We got to work. Bullet after bullet, we ridded the world of just under 140 more walking corpses with frightening appetites.

Even with such a successful hunt, we were acutely aware that many of them had gotten away clean and were now crunching along atop the forest leaves, startling buck and doe alike.

*****

350

When we got down to the park, with six more rotters dying along the way, everyone was back in the trailers, and we did not find any strays at the camp. With their speed, it would be a while, and without the red-eyed bitches directing them, they would simply have to follow the scent.

We decided to have a quick meeting. The younger girls were told to stay inside their respective residences, and everyone else gathered inside Russell and Maddie's rail car cabin.

Albert had shared with his friends the news of his father. He told them he "took care of it," which was accurate, but much easier said by the young man than done, I knew. He told us he wanted to go and sit with the kids, and we all just nodded and told him to take care.

"I'm glad Albert's not here for this part," I said. "Kid's had it hard enough. Anyway, if I had to make a bet as to whether there were living people behind those two huge doors, my guess would be no."

"Dude, the zombies were there, though," said Nelson.

"For months, according to Albert," said Maddie.

"I told Albert about the red-eyed ones. Did he fill you guys in?"

"Yeah," said Russell. "You think the red-eyes ordered them to stay there? Why would they, if everyone inside there's turned?"

"I do," I said. "It's my guess that the lower garage section has nothing inside but bones and zombies, pretty much just like outside."

"Then why would the smart females want them to stay there?" asked Russell.

"Because," answered Serena. "They know there are people inside. Maybe not right there, but inside."

"Yes!" said Nelson, throwing his arms in the air. "And they know that's a way in. They don't necessarily have to smell it, because the red-eyed ones can hear."

I nodded. "From Hemp's later experiments after we left Concord, the eardrum tissue was not only regenerating, but according to him, they were already functional and changed in shape. Like they evolved into something better."

"So you think," said Maddie, "that they might have developed some type of super hearing and they can detect the sounds of living people inside that complex?"

"They can probably hear you down here, too," I said. "Girls will be girls, after all. They run, they laugh."

"Not these girls," said Russell. "Not very much, anyway. They have their moments, but they're smart. Always ready, and some are well-tested."

"I'm sure they are," I said. "Anyway, here's the plus side of what I'm talking about. I suspect the red-eyes knew there are people in there. Alive."

Nelson said, "So the smart ones didn't let the dumber ones leave because they know there are a lot of survivors in there, not just a few. If left to their own devices, the dumb ones would have just wandered off with nothing drawing them there."

"Exactly," I said. "It's the only thing that makes any sense. Albert's mother might be one of the survivors. I really hope she is, anyway."

Maddie's eyes glistened, and she played with her hair as she said, "I hope so, too, but until now, I didn't have any hope at all. Albert's been clinging to that all this time. As bad as it sounds, I was almost relieved when I heard about his father, because I thought it would allow Albert to finally let that go."

Serena slid in beside Maddie in the dinette bench and took her hand.

Maddie continued. "I just never had much faith that Morgan and Ellie were alive, but I never would've shared that with Albert."

"Don't give up on his mother yet," said Lola. "I had a definite feeling of defensiveness when those chicks got in my brain. They had very strong reasons for being there, and while I don't know exactly what they are, I can tell you they were trying to throw everything at me to get me to stop our push."

"They don't know about the wafers," said Nelson, smugly. "So they're not quite as smart as they think."

"We don't know who's inside yet," Serena said. "In the way of zombies." She turned to Lola. "Did that feeling of control stay with you after you killed the two? Like they were in your head?"

Lola shook her head. "No. After they went away, I was pretty much back to me. My thoughts."

"I wonder," I said, "If the red-eyes need to see you to know to issue commands."

"As opposed to sensing us?" asked Lola. "Maybe. Can you guys ask your scientist?"

"Do you have a portable shortwave radio?" I asked.

"Not so portable," said Russell, "but yeah, there's one in cabin 1. That's the old office. We power it with a car battery and have solar panels mounted on top of the cabin to keep it trickle charged."

"I'm gonna get to talk to Hemp!" said Nelson, obviously excited.

"Maybe," said Serena. "If we can get him."

"8:00 PM, eastern time," I said. "That's when he starts monitoring every night. "We'll be on."

"I want to hear little Flexy," said Serena. "I miss the hell out of that little guy."

*****

Russell and Maddie had a pair of gasoline-powered golf carts, both of which were equipped with small service trailers. Russell said they'd used them at the park beforehand to run supplies to events, like bonfires and picnics. Guns loaded and ready, Nelson, Russell and Albert loaded the small trailers up with empty, ten-gallon gas cans and volunteered to get enough fuel to fill the chopper. Rachel didn't think there was enough left in the tank to fly it to the gas station and its underground tanks, so it was the only choice.

I felt like I needed more sleep. Not sure why, because I slept pretty well the night before. Either way, there wouldn't be any naps today.

Instead, I used the time to investigate the Ham radio and get more familiar with it. Hemp had showed me the basics on the handhelds, but what I walked into inside that cabin looked like something from a steampunk novel. There was a row of six batteries wired in series, connected to a power inverter. The Ham was plugged into the inverter, and when I fired it up, at first nothing happened.

It took me a few seconds more than one might expect to realize this old radio had tubes and I was going to need a bit of patience.

Hemp was always scanning the short wave frequencies at 8:00 PM eastern time, so we'd be three hours earlier. We'd need to attempt contact at 5:00 PM.

I had understood that a certain range of frequencies was typical for daytime use, and the other range was used at night; I just didn't know whether any protocols had changed and I'd never thought to ask Hemp if he still scanned all the channels. Judging from the desperate people who might be trying to communicate on the short waves, it made sense to me that Hemp would not limit his search in any way.

I decided I'd better ask Russell if he'd even tried to use the radio. The antenna was still mounted and the batteries had a charge, so I assumed all was still functional, but it would be interesting to find out if he'd ever heard from anyone.

I immediately thought about what was happening in other parts of the world. How were survivors in Russia or Brazil, or even Saudi Arabia handling this catastrophe? Was there anyplace in the world where ... I interrupted my own train of thought, sending it off the rails.

The gas emanated from the earth. There was no sanctuary anywhere. Democratic, Islamist, Communist.

None of it mattered anymore. Governments and regimes were all now meaningless, all power reassigned to the plague that darkened all their citizens' lives and hopes; even in countries where a bleaker life did not seem possible before.

The radio had warmed up and now emitted sounds. When I heard the static and a few strange whistles, I figured I had it where it needed to be. I found a scan button and pressed it.

The channel changed, then stayed there for about twenty seconds before moving on to the next. Whenever it changed, I would press the button on the handset and say, "Dave Gammon, Dunsmuir, California."

Hell no, I don't know why I said that – I just couldn't think of anything else. I got nothing back, so turned it off and decided to preserve the battery. I'd try again at 4:55 PM our time. I supposed if we could scare him up within a couple of hours, that would still work. After that, we needed to get a good night's sleep and get started at first light.

*****

The fueling went very well. Everyone said there appeared to be a good amount of fuel left in the tanks.

According to the wood dipstick they'd found in the service bay area, there were roughly 6,000 gallons left.

That was worth setting up sentries to protect it.

After getting cleaned up, everyone ate inside. Windows were cracked to make sure we could hear if any cowbells sounded in the woods, but none did. No place but cabin 3 was large enough for everyone, so we crowded in there and had one of Flex and Gem's old favorites; canned chili.

Nelson looked at his watch. "Fifteen minutes, dude," he said. "I'm nervous."

"So am I," I said. "We need to prepare a list of things to talk to him about."

"I have it," said Serena. "Rachel and I worked on it. I thought it would be good to have someone in on it who didn't have all the background we did with urushiol and the wafers."

"Good," I said. "Fresh perspective."

"I chipped in, too," said Lolita Lane. "I need to know if I'm changed forever. I don't know that I want these things in my head."

"You controlled them, Lola," said Nelson. "You brought them in for the kill."

"Maybe," she said. "But I felt something else. Not directed at me. It felt like a … I don't know. Like a call. A broadcast. I'd never felt that before, and you know I've been around these things for as long as you guys have, even though I didn't know about the pregnant ones."

Rachel looked at us. For now, Maddie and Russell were silent. The girls were all present, many of them sitting on the floor or nodding off on the beds after their dinners.

"Okay," said Rachel. "From the chopper, we came to the conclusion they can call their walking dead brethren for about a mile radius, right?"

"Yeah," said Nelson. "Unless there are red-eyes in the mix, then farther."

"Exactly," said Rachel. "But what happens when the source of the broadcast is killed? Do the other red-eyes continue directing them to the original destination?"

"Serena, put that down on the Hemp list of questions," I said. "I hope he's run into this." I checked my watch. "Okay, if you want to come, it's time. I recommend everyone else be ready for anything. That means guns for those who can handle them, and rebar spears for everyone else."

Russell and Maddie nodded and ushered the girls out of the cabin.

Albert joined all of us. He had a stake in this, too.

A big one.

*****

"You don't need to scan," said Rachel. "If you were to do that and he answered you, you'd miss it."

"That's right," I said. "Hemp scans anyway, so he could hear me when he hits my frequency."

I turned it on and awaited the tremendously slow heating of the tubes. The batteries had a good charge, for the lights lit up and the needles on the meters bounced.

"Turn it to 12 meters and just stay there," Rachel said. "I'm not that familiar, but I understand it's an overall good frequency for distance."

A dull static came from the speakers, and I heard a voice say, "Austin survivors. South city. 122 souls."

I pushed the button on the transmitter. "Hello? Austin?"

An excited voice came back. "Yes, this is Austin. Who is this, please?"

"Dave Gammon in Dunsmuir, California."

"Wow," the voice said, then static filled the airwaves until, "California. Northern?"

I looked at everyone. "Yes. Near Mount Shasta."

"How many of you?"

"Roughly seventeen," I said. "We think there are more."

"Only seventeen," the voice said.

"I'm sorry," I said. "We're searching for someone in particular, so if you wouldn't mind keeping this channel clear. I'm not sure how this works, but if he can't hear us, we are going to have some trouble."

"Understood. I'm not a short wave man, either. You could be right. We're glad you're alive. Stay that way. Over and out."

"Did he say 122 people? Souls?" asked Lola.

I nodded.

"Cool," said Nelson. "Hey. Call Hemp."

"I'll try," I said. "Hemphill Chatsworth. Hemphill Chatsworth," I said.

We waited.

"Hemp Chatsworth," I said again. I kept repeating it, pausing for fifteen seconds, then repeating it twice more.

I checked my watch. It was 5:30 PM, and still nothing.

"California," said the familiar voice from Austin.

"Yes," I said.

"This Hemp Chatsworth you're calling. I hear him every night. He normally comes on about this time."

Nelson reached down and took the transmitter and pushed the button. "You've talked to him, dude?"

"I have," said the voice. "A few times. Thought we could convince them to come here. They're happy where they are. Said they'd rather avoid the roads."

Eric A. Shelman

I took the transmitter back from Nelson. "Great, Austin. Thanks for getting our hopes up. He's a good friend."

"Well, thanks to him, we have a good supply of urushiol, and we're ready to manufacture the WAT-5."

I felt a swelling of pride. Without all the work we'd done together – as a family – none of us would have made it out of Concord. It felt good to have assisted in spreading the word about our zombie solutions.

"Glad to hear it," I said. "WAT-5 is amazing. Prepare to have your mind blown."

"Dude, you're starting to sound like me," said Nelson, smiling. He pulled a rubber band out of his pocket and pulled his blonde hair back. His ends were about as split as they could be.

"Good luck. We'll surf some other frequencies. If we run into Hemp, we'll tell him where you are," he said.

"What's your name?" I asked.

"My nickname's Zed," the voice said. "I know. Appropriate. Good luck. Over and out."

We went back to our routine of saying Hemp's name. At 5:51 PM Pacific time, we hit pay dirt.

"David, is that you?"

"Dave Gammon! Yes, it's Dave! Hemp?"

"Oh, my word! It is you! Are you safe?"

"We are for now, Hemp. Is everyone there?"

"They're in the house. Hold just a moment while I get on the radio and tell them to get out here. As you know, I have a little shed where I do this."

Nelson, his fists clenched, jumped in the air, spinning around as he landed. It looked as though the kid had won the lottery, and we all smiled watching him, even Albert.

Rachel stood up, and to my surprise, went to him and opened her arms. Nelson looked extra happy and pulled her into his arms, picking her up and spinning her around.

"Okay, they'll be right in. Now I know you didn't call for nothing, so tell me how I can help."

"We've run into some phenomena," I said. "God, Hemp, it's so damned good to hear your voice I can't tell you. Nelson's jumping around like a puppy."

"Nelson's there?" he said.

"Yes, he's here. Didn't he tell you?" I asked, looking at Nelson. He stopped jumping and looked guilty.

"No, I'm afraid. Can he hear me?"

"He can," I said.

"Nelson," said Hemp. "You're very lucky you shared some of your secrets with me before leaving. I knew that you wanted to go to California with them, and I told the others as much when you went missing."

Nelson leaned over and took the transmitter from my hand. He pushed the button. "I'm sorry, Hemp. But I'm glad you convinced them I was okay."

"The first status on your well-being is right now," he said. "Unfortunately, Charlie and Gem weren't as easy to convince. They were sure you were dead, even when I told them you were practically a genius. I don't even want to tell you how much Trina and Taylor miss you. Easily as much as David and Serena."

I took the mic back. "We're safe, Hemp. Nelson, Serena, me, Rachel and Lola."

"Your group has grown!" said Hemp, and I could hear the smile in his voice, even over the vast miles. "How's your battery? Got enough? Some people want to say hello."

"Push the button and let them all talk!" I said. "Is little Flexy there?"

"So's big Flexy," said a deeper voice. It was Flex. "But the stud's asleep in his mama's arms right now. Good to hear your voice, Dave."

"I'm here, too," said Gem. "Nelson, I'm going to kick the living shit out of you."

Before I could give the transmitter mic back to Nelson, a pair of much smaller, female voices came on. "We're kicking your shit, too, Uncle Nelson, but we miss you!" said Trina, and Taylor followed with, "Yeah! We love you guys!"

I knew I was smiling, and when I looked around, I saw that all of us were. It was like being home again, and I didn't want to turn to serious conversation, but it had to be done. I didn't know how long the batteries would last, and I needed to get answers.

"How old is that one?" asked Lola.

"The one who said shit?" asked Serena. "She's seven, ready to turn eight."

Lola shook her head, smiling.

"We love all of you, too," I said. "Serena wants to say hello, then we have to get to the point."

I handed the handset to Serena.

"How are my ladies?" she said.

"I miss watching you ride a motorcycle in your leather cat suit," said Gem.

"It's a body suit, but that's okay. Dave likes to call it a cat suit, too."

"You being safe?" asked Gem.

"As much as possible," said Serena. "Now. Charlie, Gem, David is right. Being separated from you is like my sisters are gone, and Trina and Taylor, you're like my girls. I love you all so much, and can't wait until we're back home."

Charlie's voice came on. "Same here, Serena. And tell David, that I miss those dumb awkward moment jokes and that crazy hair of his, and Serena, I *am* your sister. Did I hear some more are coming back with you? What ... Rachel, and what was it, Lola?"

"Yes," said Lola, into the mic. "Lolita Lane, actually."

"That's a name," said Charlie. "Well, I'm Charlie Chatsworth, and to say what everyone's thinking, we sound like a couple of comic book characters."

"You might be right," said Lola, laughing.

"Can't wait to meet you guys," said Charlie. "Be safe and all of you, just get back here. I'm giving it back to Hemp."

Hearing Charlie's voice over that microphone was amazing. All of them were missed, but Charlie and I had a special bond since Shelburne, Vermont when we joined forces to rescue her husband.

"Okay, now that *that's* out of the way, how can I help?" asked Hemp.

"Hemp, we're pretty certain my Uncle Bug's in his complex, but we've run into a lot of the red-eyes, and they seem to have more abilities than we initially thought."

There was a prolonged silence. "David, sorry – I don't think I realized you were already in California. How did you get there so fast?" asked Hemp.

"Chopper," I said. "A med-evac. Rachel flies."

"Oh, my," said Hemp. "Pardon me for sounding selfish and a bit creepy, Rachel, but you have *got* to come back here."

Rachel did not ask for the mic, but she said, "Nobody with that accent sounds creepy. I'm pretty sure he could say some creepy things and he'd just sound sexy."

"It worked on me," came Charlie's voice. "He had me at *zombie*."

Rachel laughed. Nelson didn't. I thought I saw a tinge of jealousy in his expression.

"Okay, here's the deal," I said. I told him about the mountain complex of Bug's, the lower entry we feared was inundated with zombies, and our logistical struggle finding another way in.

I touched on red-eyed females and how the vapor inhaled by Lola had not only made her a receiver of messages, but gave her the ability to call them.

"Are you absolutely sure about that?" asked Hemp.

"99% sure," I said. "Lola stood still, and two of them walked through the crowd and went straight to her. They set their horde on us and focused on Lola. She killed them both."

"And you say she was consciously calling them?" asked Hemp.

I looked at Lola. She nodded. "Just confirmed. Yes, she was calling them."

"Okay," he said. "Hold on just a moment. I'm going to bounce some ideas off Flex, Gem and Charlie."

We waited. It felt really good to have Hemp and the others on the radio, all of us working as a team again.

After less than a minute, we heard Hemp say, "David, did you check the helicopter for night vision goggles?"

I looked at Rachel and shrugged. "I didn't," she said. "Would it be equipped with them?"

"No," I said into the transmitter. "We hadn't thought of it."

"You said this was a medical evacuation helicopter, is that correct?" asked Hemp.

We acknowledged that.

"Then yes, most likely. They would use it to spot heat signatures of crashed vehicles, airplanes and the like, after any flames have died down. I do not believe they're exactly standard equipment, but if equipped with some, they'll likely be in a case somewhere. Search the cockpit and cabin areas."

In the end, Hemp had a fantastic idea. He gave it to us in detail.

"And David," said Hemp.

"Yeah, Hemp?"

"Call me in the morning, before you go. It's three hours later here, and I intend to be on this frequency, probably before you even awaken."

"Why?" I asked.

"Because I want to toss this around tonight. I may have more input in the morning. If you think it can help you, I'll be here."

"Hemp, I know we've just been gone almost a week, but I speak for Nelson and Serena, too. We miss you guys."

After some back and forth that we all really needed in order to bring our sanity back, and some questions that were on the list that we hadn't covered, we said good bye to our beautiful friends across the country, and I know without even asking that we all wanted to get back there about a million times more than we had earlier in the day.

The helicopter was fueled. The sun had set.

It was time to search for the vent, and hopefully, the door.

*****

Chapter Sixteen

Found something," said Lola. "Says *Thermal Eye* on the case. It's got something plugged into it."

Rachel moved back. "This is it. Your Hemp is a genius!"

"Ha!" said Nelson, watching Rachel open the box. "That makes two of us."

I got the distinct impression that Nelson was still trying to impress Rachel, despite the fact that she'd already taken to him.

Lola opened the box with us looking on. Inside was what appeared to be binoculars, but with only one eyehole to look through. A cable snaked through the case and was plugged into the side.

"That keeps it charged as you fly," said Rachel. "Perfect." She powered it up, and held it up to the woods around the camp. "It works," she said, lowering it. "Dave, we're ready. I think this might work."

"If the gen's running now."

"We might see heat signatures anyway. From something else related to your uncle," said Rachel.

"Okay," I said. "Tonight, you stay here, Albert. We're not making any moves, we're just searching. Once we find the vent, Rachel will mark it on her electronics and we'll come back. Tomorrow morning we'll load up and hike there.

"Is there a reason I can't go?" he asked, obviously disappointed.

"There are a few, dude," said Nelson. "If *we* crash, *you* won't be dead. Then there's fuel consumption to think of. Excuse me, but you're a hefty kid."

Albert smiled. "You don't have many filters, do you, Nelson?"

"Nah," said Nelson, smiling. "Filters just make it take longer to say what you wanna say. Still, it's tough to stay mad at me, right?"

"I hate to agree with you, but yeah," said Albert.

Nelson looked at Rachel. "See? If people think you're a genius, they treat you like a know-it-all. If they believe you're just a stoner who gets lucky with a good idea now and then, they love you like a puppy."

"We've already had some long conversations, Nel," said Rachel. "You're far deeper than your façade."

"So you love me like a puppy yet?" he asked, smiling.

Rachel shook her head and did not answer.

Albert dropped his arms to his sides. "Fine, I'll stay here. But take one of those handheld radios. I'm going to be checking in on you."

"We won't be compromised, so feel free," I said.

"If you're not doing anything, why all the weapons?" asked Albert.

"Preparation," said Rachel. "Just like the scout motto. "Be Prepared.""

"Got it," said Albert. "This sucks."

"It's for your own good," said Serena.

"Whatever," said Albert. "Just be careful."

"We will," I said.

With that, we got in the chopper. Lola, Rachel, Nelson, Serena and yours truly.

*****

We all put on our headsets and Rachel got the Eurocopter in the air. I couldn't help but wonder about the red-eyes and their ability to hear, and what they would surmise with this big bird flying over, its blades beating against the air with low, rhythmic *thwumps*.

Did they have that much intelligence? Could their advanced brains still process that this was a machine flown by man, their primary food source? If so, could they possibly anticipate our mission? If that was possible, would they realize it was the same as theirs?

I know we both wanted inside. There could be no other reason to hang around.

"Can you tell where you are?" I asked.

Rachel nodded. "Marked it as best we could. Who's going to use the goggles?"

"I'll give it a go," said Nelson. "Just tell me when we're there."

"There could be other vents," said Rachel, angling the chopper sharply to the right. "Now's good."

We slid the door open and Nelson looked out. He turned back. "Somebody hold my belt. This is pretty freaky."

Lola sat on the edge of the seat closest to Nelson and loosened her safety belt, allowing her enough room to reach out and grab Nelson's belt. She gripped it as he held the device up to his eyes.

"Wow," he said in wonder. "I can see all the trees like daytime. These are cool."

"Look for bright points of light," said Rachel. "Hold on. I'm bringing it around to the left."

Nelson steadied himself, and Rachel brought the chopper lower, and banked smoothly to the left. I was impressed with her abilities and again thankful to have her with us. She was a ton of contribution tucked into a little, five-foot frame.

"Hold on," said Nelson. "Something looks like a green snake down there."

"A green snake?" I asked.

"Yeah, and it's even moving," he said. "Rachel, can you hover just off to my side another hundred yards or so?"

"Roger that," said Rachel.

"You know my name's Nelson, babe," he said, smiling.

I looked over to see Rachel shake her head. She said, "And you know that façade doesn't work with me anymore, *dude*."

"Touché," he said, which was a word I would not have credited him with knowing before I discovered his goofball persona was just a ruse.

"There!" he said. "Davey, take a look. Right down there. Bright green spot, then like a snake coming off it."

He moved and I took his place. I felt a hand curling under my belt, turned and saw Lola holding me steady now.

"Thanks," I said, peering through the night vision goggles.

"We have to get lower," I said. "I see what he's talking about, but I can't tell what the hell it is."

"I know, it's weird, right?" said Nelson.

Rachel said, "I don't like to get too low because of visibility. Never liked night flying."

"If that's the vent pipe," I said, "the part shining bright, then what's the snake part?"

"It's the exhaust," said Nelson. "I'm so freakin' stupid! It's the exhaust stream!"

"Which way is it going?" asked Rachel.

I looked, then pointed. That way. Toward where the front of the helicopter's facing."

"Then Nelson's right," she said. "The wind is blowing that way. We've found it."

"Can you mark it?"

"The GPS satellites appear to still be functional," said Rachel. "I mean, we're triangulating okay. Even if they're off, we're marking a particular spot, so it should be accurate enough. We can cross-reference it to a map when we get back to the park."

"What?" asked Lola.

"Never mind," said Rachel. "I'm thinking out loud, really. Yeah. We'll be able to get back here tomorrow."

Nelson had taken the goggles again and was looking outside, a smile on his face. "Wait!" he said. His smile turned to concern.

"What?" asked Rachel.

"What are … those?"

"What do you see?" I asked.

"Wow," said Nelson. "A bunch of dots. Like … I don't know, more than ten. Pinpoints, almost."

"Want me to get lower?" asked Rachel. "Where?"

"Just below us," said Nelson. "Almost right under us. Does this thing have a big spotlight or something?"

"Silly question," said Rachel. She hit a switch and started moving a joystick mounted to her left.

The area beneath them lit up like daylight.

I almost asked why we didn't use that to find the vent, but caught myself before I sounded like an idiot.

We needed the heat signature of the vent pipe.

"Holy shit," whispered Nelson, almost inaudible in the ambient noise from the helicopter.

"What?" asked Lola and Serena together.

"Look at them," said Rachel. "How many? Hundreds?"

369

Below us, bathed in the light from our multi-million candlepower spot, the forest revealed body after body, standing among the brush and limbs. Among these, every so often, red eyes stared upward. These were the points that Nelson had noticed.

The red eyes. They were here, and they had called their army.

"Circle them," I said. "The hill drops off behind them there."

Rachel banked left and straightened the bird out. We came around and she directed the spotlight farther down the mountainous hillside.

The bodies snaked up the hill, bunched up here and there, but wherever there was a clearing, there was a rotter standing, pushing into the next one, all wanting nothing more than to feed on human flesh and to be where their intelligent, female leaders called them.

"Sky," said Lola.

Nelson spun around and grabbed her hand, which had again been wrapped around his belt.

I knew why. If her caring hold turned into a vicious shove from a command issued from below, Nelson would be falling to the earth to join the red-eyed corpses.

"Nelson," she said. "I wouldn't hurt you."

"Dude, I know, but it freaked me out."

"Okay," said Rachel. "I think we know where the door is. It's the only reason they would cluster down there."

"Mark it, and let's get back down," I said. "We really need to think this through for tomorrow."

We returned to the Railroad Park in silence.

This was going to be a bigger job than we'd anticipated.

But Hemp's plan still might work – with some tweaks.

*****

Hemp's instructions for building a bomb were precise. The design was a bit crude, and it took a lot longer time to extract the gunpowder from a variety of bullets than we anticipated. Several of us spent hours on it. Hemp had us locate other household items to use in there, and in the end, we had followed Hemp's instructions exactly.

Even Rachel had no idea how to put it together, so we were essentially like amateur chefs working off a cookbook, albeit a damned good cookbook.

I was more concerned with the strength of the blast; whether it would have enough power to actually blow anything open rather than just scorch. We *were* dealing with Uncle Bug, after all. I wouldn't bet against him being prepared for a bunker buster bomb, delivered by the US military.

The bomb was somewhat cone-shaped, heavily weighted on the bottom. If we had to drop it from the chopper for some reason, it would hopefully remain upright, which was crucial because it was designed so that the force of the blast would concentrate downward.

By the time we were done, it was past eleven o'clock. Nelson, Rachel, Lola, and everyone else hit the sack, but Serena and I had other plans. Hemp insisted the bomb would be quite stable, so we put it in the helicopter and got ready to call it a night.

Russell had developed an instant water heater of sorts, used solely for bathing. It was actually quite ingenious.

They had an elevated tank that they used to collect snow and rainwater. They conserved it, but because of the creek below, they did not need it for drinking water, therefore it was used mainly for cooking and bathing.

The main hose ran from the bottom of the tank, along the ground. About ten feet from the massive fire pit, the hose coupled to a pipe and disappeared underground. Russell explained that they had created a four-foot diameter, multiple-layer, copper coil that rested just inches below the fire pit; as long as there were even embers glowing, the water would pass through and be nice and warm upon exiting.

Placed fifteen feet away from the fire pit was a single, ball and claw-footed bathtub, just like an antique from an old Victorian home. Maddie said it had come from the same shop that sold the cowbells.

Under the stars, after everyone else had gone to bed, Serena and I filled the porcelain tub with water that was amazingly warm. Retrieving the soap from our railroad car, Serena and I risked full nudity, sinking into the water together washing away the dirt and grime accumulated over the last couple of days. We kept our ears alert for the sound of distant cowbells and to our relief, none clanked their metallic warnings to us.

Her head on my shoulder, Serena whispered, "They're not here. That's good."

I agreed with a nod. Where all of the disbursed infecteds that had waited outside Bug's huge doors for so long had gone, we did not know, and as long as they weren't here now, for the moment we didn't care.

But Serena's vocalized thought did momentarily snap us out of the bliss created by the full, wet contact of her bare skin to mine; her, seated between my legs, her back resting against my front with my arms wrapped around her; lathering up her stomach and breasts, moving down to slide between her legs – all the while trying not to make her seating position too uncomfortable with my involuntary contributions beneath the water.

But that diversion did it. As I shrank and our thoughts again turned to zombies, I said, "I wonder if they're making their way to join the hillside horde," I said.

"Maybe," said Serena. "Sorry I ruined the mood. We should get dried off and pick things up back in the CCT Caboose."

"I got the only caboose I need right here," I said, squeezing her ass beneath the water. She arched her back and laughed quietly.

"Let's go," she said.

*****

By midnight, Serena and I had drained the tub, toweled off, and gone inside our railroad car. I lay there in the queen sized bed with this beautiful woman in my arms. It was a fairly cool evening in the lower sixties, and just a thin sheet covered our bodies.

"David," she said, stroking my chest with her hand.

"Yeah," I said.

"I ... wow. I don't even know how to say this."

"You're not breaking up with me, are you?" I asked.

Serena laughed. She rested her head on my shoulder, and I could not only hear each word she spoke, I felt the vibration of it through me. It gave me an intense emotion of closeness with her.

"You know I love you, right?" she asked.

"God, I hope so," I said.

"I want to have a baby," she said.

"If you mean right now, I'm game," I said, which was entirely inappropriate, but a cover for the overwhelming sense of joy that had just flooded over me.

She slapped my chest. "I planned to start now," she said. "If you agreed."

That was it. I couldn't take it anymore. I jumped out of bed, standing there in all my naked glory, and ripped the sheet from atop her. I jumped onto the bed and straddled her, kissing her mouth, her neck, ears, breasts, stomach, and I stopped right there so we could finish our conversation.

She was laughing so hard, I was sure we would both be heard by everyone in the park.

"Okay," I said, still straddling her. "You'll have to use your imagination for this one. Pretend we're playing Cranium."

"What?" she asked.

I pantomimed reaching into my pocket and pulling something out. I had no pants on, so she *really* had to use her imagination. I held it in my fingers, took her left hand, and slid the imaginary thing onto her ring finger.

"I love you, Serena."

"David!" she said. "Does that mean ...?" she trailed off.

"Hell yes, it means," I said, excited.

I hopped over her and sat on my knees on the mattress beside her, taking her by the hands. I could see her smiling face looking up at me in the candlelight and the pale moonlight shining through the small window of the rail car.

"David, you're like a jumping bean," she said through a laugh.

"Serena," I said, bouncing on the bed again, "I wasn't even sure I wanted a kid, and I can tell you that as much as I loved Leona, I don't think either of us felt we had the time to dedicate to raising a kid. But now, with you ... and seeing little Flexy and knowing Charlie's about to pop any day now, I realized that I've known for months that I wanted that with you."

"You could've told me," she said.

"I would have," I said. "I'm not too sure what I'm doing anymore. Seems I feel everything so powerfully these days that I start to wonder if I'm the only one."

"You're not," she said, pulling me down to her. Her back arched as I kissed her, and she spread her arms wide, followed naturally by her legs. My hands stroked her sides, over her ribcage, and down to her squirming hips.

I knew an invitation when I saw one. I hopped off the bed, retrieved the sheet from the floor and wrapped it around my neck like a cape. "Guess who I am," I said.

"Batman."

"Wrong."

"Superman," she tried.

"Wrong again," I said. "I'm Captain Cunnilingus."

"Save me," she said, smiling. "I'm in distress."

"How can I refused a damsel?" I said, discarding my cape and swooping in. She laughed, and it was music to my ears.

The candles flickered around us, their dancing flames throwing shadows throughout the inside of the rail car. There was a new electricity between us now, and it seemed everywhere my fingers contacted her glistening skin, sparks flew. She was gooseflesh over every inch, and when I pressed my mouth to her and drank her in, it was as though she floated above the mattress, my only task to pleasure her and to keep her from flying away.

We made love for an hour and fell onto the bed, exhausted.

*****

The morning came, and as promised, I went to the main cabin and powered up the Ham radio. Serena went to help Rachel and Lola prepare the gear we'd need. Nelson and Albert came with me.

Drumming my fingers on the table, I waited for the meters to light up and bounce. I made sure we were still on the agreed-upon frequency and grabbed the microphone, pushing the button.

"Hemp, are you there?" I said. "Hemp Chatsworth?"

"David, yes!" came his voice. "Thank you for checking in. I do have something for you."

While we had zeroed in on our plan, I would change everything based on Hemp's recommendation, I knew. Nelson sat beside me, which I thought was a good idea. He was Hemp-like in his ability to analyze a problem – something I would not have uttered a week ago.

"Go ahead, Hemp. Anything you have," I said.

"Okay, first off," said Hemp, "I'm very confused about the red-eyes' focus on the bunker."

"Why?" I asked.

"Exactly what I was thinking," said Nelson. "Give me the microphone."

I handed it to Nelson, and he said, "Hemp, dude! I know exactly what you're going to say. This bunker was built like a brick shithouse and there's no doubt it's airtight. Am I headed in the right direction?"

"You are," said Hemp. "Exactly. If this place is sealed up, which I assume it is – except perhaps for a ventilated air system that likely vents far from the entrance around which you said they're clustered, how would these females know that living humans were inside?"

"I hoped you could answer that," I said. "Any ideas?"

"None at all," said Hemp. "Nelson, have you any thoughts on it?"

Nelson shook his head. "Not really. Maybe through the exhaust vent for the generator? We smell that."

"They must have some way of circulating the air in there, right?" said Albert.

"Who was that?" asked Hemp.

"Albert. He was here in Dunsmuir when we arrived. He suggested some sort of recirculation system for the oxygen."

"It's a better possibility than the generator exhaust pipe. Albert's right – there must be a fresh air supply somewhere. I don't know if it's at that entrance, but that might explain it," he said. "They would definitely have to have circulation and a place for it to escape."

"We haven't flown over the whole complex yet, Hemp," I said. "Just where we found the vent and door. There might be another group of zombies waiting near the vent you're talking about."

"It depends on how far away it vents," said Hemp. "If he's planned this place as long as you say, he may have several built-in protections."

"Well," I said. "Based on how long he's been holing up in there and doing nothing for the survivors we found, a lot of good all his protections did him."

"If he's alive, they did exactly what he planned," said Hemp. "David, don't begin judging your uncle until you hear his story."

Hemp was right and I knew it. I told him so.

"So any approach with this new information?" Hemp asked.

A new voice joined the mix. It spoke one word: *"David?"*

I stopped talking. The voice was familiar.

"Who's there, please?" said Hemp.

"It … wasn't you?" I asked, knowing it wasn't.

"Dave Gammon? Davey?"

"Uncle Bug?" I said, incredulous.

"Yeah," he said, his voice clear, the signal strong.

"Have you been listening in the whole time?" I asked.

"I've been listening to this Hemp guy for quite a long time now," he said. "Dave, how are you? Are you okay, kid?"

"Is this the famous Brett Ulrich Gammon?" asked Hemp. "How come you've never responded before? You've heard me talking in the past on the short wave?"

"I have. But excuse me for just a sec. I ask again," he said, this time with a slight edge to his voice. "Dave, *are you okay*?"

"Yeah, Uncle Bug, I'm fine," I said. "The only reason I'm here is to find you."

"I figured that, buddy," he said. "People don't just drop by Dunsmuir. 'Specially these days."

"So can you let us inside?" I asked.

"I'm afraid not," he said. "Can't risk it."

"I hope you're joking," I said. "We traveled all the way from South Carolina to find your ass."

"Sorry, buddy. Too dangerous. Tons of them dead things outside of here."

"I know," I said. "We saw them last night."

"Okay, so you get it," said my uncle.

"Not so much," I said, really starting to get irritated at his nonchalant attitude about the entire purpose of our trip and all we had risked to get to his bunker. "Uncle Bug, what *have* you been doing in there all this time?"

"You want me to be honest?" he said.

"Hell yes," I said. I noted that Hemp was being quiet, letting this conversation unfold.

"I've been hiding."

"Hiding. You."

"Yep," he said. "Me."

"What about all your preparation? Why do all that just to hide in a hole?" I asked.

"It's a helluva hole."

"How many people are with you?" I asked.

"One."

"Bullshit," I said. "What happened to the others?" I was growing angry. I'd come all this way to get attitude and evasion from one of my formerly favorite people in the world. "Albert from the Railroad Park saw a bunch of people get into the lower doors before they closed," I added.

"They did, and most of 'em are dead now," Bug said.

"Most of them?" I said. "You said there's only one with you."

"*With* me. Exactly."

"Stop being vague!" I said.

"There are more," he said. "But they're not *with* me."

"Where are they?" I asked.

"In another section of the complex."

"Do they have supplies? Are they still alive?" I asked.

"Goddamnit, Davey, some of 'em are dead, some of 'em are alive, and a whole shitload of 'em are somewhere between the two! I thought you said you came here to see about me?"

I wasn't sure how to respond to his last statement, so I just answered the question. "That's the reason we're here, but it doesn't mean you're more important than any of the other survivors," I said.

"Shit, dude," said Nelson. "Your battery's running low, man."

I looked at the lights on the Ham radio meters, and they were dimming. I pushed the button on the transmitter.

"Uncle Bug, I'm coming in."

"You can't!" he said. "I've got cameras set up, and these things are clustered around my upper door."

"I know that," I said. "We've seen it. From a helicopter."

"When?" he asked.

"Last night," I said.

"I saw a few flashes in my cameras," said Bug. "Thought that's what it was."

"You can't hear it from inside?" asked Hemp. "You're that well insulated?"

"Yeah," he said. "Hemp, I even got your urushiol info written down, from when you were talkin' to Austin. I even have a mini beer brewery here that I converted to a still using your instructions, but no poison ivy to produce the shit. Out of boredom, I did everything else to it I need. Just need the main ingredient."

"Were you listening last night?" I asked.

"Yeah," said Bug. "Sorry for not saying anything, but I don't trust too many people. I'd been listening to this British dude for months, but I had no idea he knew you, Dave. I was sure it was a setup last night."

"A setup?"

"What are the odds that a stranger I've been listening to on the short wave radio knows my nephew?"

"So you thought it was some … what? A government plot to draw you out?" asked Hemp.

"Look, I didn't know," said Bug, sounding upset. "As for the others trapped in here, there's nothing I can do about it. If you think you can clear that door, I'll let you in, but don't use that fuckin' bomb Hemp had you make. I have control of the upper door."

"Excellent," said Hemp. "I'd rather you not use explosives anyway."

"And Dave, you'd better have some fuckin' plan to get yourselves back out or get all of us out, because if you don't, then forget it. I'll just stay where I am, and those folks can do the same – maybe until all this crap is over."

"You didn't build that complex to just hide inside it," I said.

"No, that's right," said Bug. "But I always thought the need for this place would be because of a government out of control – not these God-forsaken creatures that are somewhere between alive and dead tryin' to kill everyone."

"David," said Hemp, "how much urushiol do you have left? Of the canisters we sent you off with?"

"Only like an eighth of a canister," I said.

"Is there any poison ivy or oak in that area?"

"Russell said there was," said Nelson.

"Hell yes, there is," came Bug's voice. "I see it on my surveillance cameras. Lots of it around."

"David, then you have to –" Hemp began.

The voice cut off mid-sentence.

Nelson tapped me on the shoulder and pointed at the radio. "You're done, dude," he said. The dark meters now read a frequency of zero.

"Shit."

"If we make a push to get inside," said Nelson, "I think we need to have as much poison ivy with us as we can carry. I think that's where Hemp was going."

"And Bug can use his modified brewing equipment to extract it."

"Exactly, dude," said Nelson. He pulled a pipe from his shirt pocket, lit it with a Bic lighter and took a big hit. He held his breath and stared at me, smoke leaking from his nostrils.

"We need to try our regular radios," I said. "We won't get Hemp, but we might get Bug."

*****

The operation was not going to be simple, and now that we had confirmed – in the vaguest terms – that there were other survivors with Bug, we now needed to figure out how to rescue them as well.

I turned on one of the cheap handheld radios and started on channel 9. I went up the list and on 19, I got a response.

"Dave?" the voice came?

"Uncle Bug! Thank God," I said.

"We'll see what God has to do with it when this is all done. Davey, for now I need to know your end game."

I sat there in stunned silence, everyone ready to roll and all of it for this man on the other end of my walkie.

Finally, I was able to address his comment: "End game? The goddamned end game has always been to come and see if my uncle was alive. You. You *are* my end game."

"I figured that, Davey, and I appreciate it. I thought about you a long time over the last few months. Figured you probably knew I was immune to this urushiol shit from me showin' off with the poison ivy when you were a kid."

"You learned about it from Hemp's radio broadcasts?"

"Yep. Problem was, I never let you get into the shit, so I didn't know if you were immune or not."

"Well, apparently it's one of those good hereditary things," I said. "We need to come in. If we can clear the door, will you open it?"

"I can open that one. I'll do it for you."

"What do you mean, you can open *that* one?"

"You'll understand when you get inside."

"Me and some friends. We're going to need brainpower to figure out the rest of this."

"The rest of what?"

"I want you to come back to Whitmire with us."

"Where the hell is *Whitmire*?"

"South Carolina. Nice place," I said.

"Fuckin' South Carolina?"

"Yeah."

"What in God's name for?" he asked.

"If I told you, you'd probably tell me you're just fine here."

"So, there's no reason?"

"You're family. That's reason enough," I said. "See? You'd rather put all this planning you did to use than be with me – your damned family."

"Wait a fuckin' minute, Davey. I want to remind you that I love you, kid. You were my first nephew, and as it turns out, my only nephew. I love Lisa, but her dad and I ain't brothers."

"Lisa's dead," I said.

"Oh, shit. I'm sorry, Davey. Real sorry."

"Yeah," I said. "I'm a bit short on family these days, so if you don't mind a whole lot, can I at least see you and find out what our options are?"

"It ain't pretty, Davey. I can get you in, like I said. If you can clear away that bunch that's been camped out here for about eleven months now."

"Everybody's going to put their radios on channel 19," I said. "Please, keep yours on, and if you come up with anything that will help, just feel free to chime in."

Once we put the word out and everyone in the camp pitched in, we ended up with four large garbage bags filled with poison ivy leaves and stems. We rolled them very tightly, compacting them as much as possible. Everything we needed or thought we would need was thrown into the helicopter. We intended to fly it to the closest point to Bug's place and unload there.

We met again in the large cabin. Everyone was there, including all the girls. Most were half awake.

"Is anyone going with me?" asked Lola. "Not that I need company," she said. "I was on my own for quite a while, you know."

"We know you can take care of yourself, Lola," said Serena. "That said, you're carrying out a dangerous part of this. I think someone needs to be with you in case things go wrong."

"You mean in case they actually catch me?"

"Exactly, dudette," said Nelson. "I'll go with you, 'cause you're not going to be on WAT-5. You'll need some backup."

"Nelson, I need you with us," I said. "And we need Rachel available to fly the helicopter if necessary."

"I'll go," said Russell. "Maddie's taken care of the girls by herself plenty. I'll go with Lola. In fact, I know where you want us, so we can take a trail I know about up there and practically beat the helicopter. We'll take one of the golf carts. Fully fueled and ready to go."

"Will it maneuver the trail?" asked Lola.

"Absolutely. I've done it a hundred times, hunting. With the trailer, which we'll leave behind."

"Okay," said Maddie. "But only if he's on the WAT-5 stuff. Period, end of story."

I looked at Maddie, and while there was worry in her eyes, she nodded at me. Russell had been watching her, too.

"Thank you, Maddie," he said.

"Be careful," she said, unsmiling.

"I'll let Bug know when we're airborne," I said. "Make sure he's monitoring channel 19 and he's ready to open the door when we get it cleared."

*****

After dousing with WAT-5 – we used all but the powdered residue in the bottom of the baggie and even gave the last red-eye wafer to Lola just in case – we shook off the cobwebs from our mini-naps and got going. Lola and

Russell took off well ahead of us. I had warned Russell about Lola's connection with the red-eyes, and how if she began to say strange words, to keep his weapon ready and his eyes on her. I stressed that unless any irrational actions ensued, she was fine and could be fully trusted.

Lola would not take one of the AR-15s, but she agreed to take a Ruger .22 caliber revolver that carried ten rounds, plus her trusty blade. Naturally, she wore her running shoes, and as we lifted off in the chopper – me, Rachel at the controls, Serena, Nelson and Albert, we flew overhead and were all amused to see Lola running alongside the cart while Russell drove, almost already at their destination.

His head was turned as though he were saying something to her, so we figured he was trying to convince her to get in the damned cart and preserve her energy.

He didn't know how much energy that girl had.

Rachel set the Eurocopter down on the road near the trail to Bug's place just as Lola and Russell emerged from the trail and into the middle of Interstate 5 about a quarter of a mile south of us. We waved to them, and they waved back.

"Everybody grab a bag of poison ivy," I said. "If we each take one, it should be a breeze."

"You're a skinny dude," said Albert. "I'll carry yours, Nelson."

"Awesome, bro," said Nelson. "Be careful. It's more valuable than weed these days."

"That it may very well be," I said. I pressed the button on my radio, "Uncle Bug. You copy?"

"I read," he said almost instantly. "You in position yet?"

"No, no," I said, "Not yet. But we're ready to take the trail from I-5 to your place. Your cameras on?"

"They will be. I'll cycle them on in ten minutes for a quick scan. I'm conserving gen power a bit more these days. When you get there, the trail up here is to the left of the garage. Be careful. That place was swamped last I looked."

"We cleared it out yesterday. Verify it when you look and let us know if anything's changed."

"Got it," he said.

"Okay, when you get eyes on the exterior of the main door up there, let me know if our plan's working," I said.

"How will I know?"

"You'll know," I said.

"Okay. Over and out."

"Later," I said.

"We're almost there," said Lola, over the radio.

"Okay," said Rachel. "Lola, you can start any time. We're about to make our way up the trail, and we're going to push it."

"Got it," she said. "I'll start now."

"Good," said Rachel. "I think it'll be a good idea to give your radio to Russell so he can keep us updated."

"Wish me luck," said Lola.

"Check in and let us know when you know it's working," said Russell, a moment later.

Ten minutes later the radio clicked. "Davey, come in!" said my uncle.

I grabbed my radio. "What is it?"

"I don't know what the hell you're doing, but there are fewer freaks out there now."

"How many fewer?"

"Hard to tell, but they're all looking to the south, like they're waiting to go. I'd guess right now there's forty fewer than before."

"Holy shit," I said.

"Keep doin' what you're doin'," he said.

"Got it."

"Over and out," said Bug.

"Russell, come in," I said.

"I heard all that," said Russell. "And we can see them now. Lola's standing on this big rock, just staring up the trail. That whole line of them you said were heading up the hill?"

"Yeah," I said. "So she's calling the red-eyes?"

"She's not making any noise, but yeah – I assume that's what she's doing. They're coming. Looks like all of them. I'm freaking out a bit, to be honest. You sure this shit works?"

"On the regular rotters, yeah," I said. "Move when you have to. Keep them moving toward you, but don't get cornered. Watch behind you, too. I know I don't have to tell you because you live here, but I don't need you falling into a creek or a canyon."

"I'm thinking it's time to get in the golf cart and drive a bit farther. We'll let you know."

We reached the huge bay doors on Bug's lower level they were still clear. Just piles of bones and the fresher bodies of those creatures we had killed. Flies avoided the putrid, rotting corpses, making me wonder what was different within the meat itself.

"There's the trail," said Serena. "Bug said it'd be just to the left of the garage."

"Let's double time," said Nelson, breaking into a jog. Hauling our guns and bags of poison ivy, we all followed, keeping pace. Albert brought up the rear, and I could tell he was laboring.

The surrounding woods were eerily empty. No animals, no walking dead. The trail ahead was spooky in its emptiness, the trees creating a shadowy canopy over the narrow, leaf strewn trail. With a decent night's rest under our belts, we all had adequate energy to make good time.

"Stop for a sec," I called out, trying to project enough for everyone to hear me despite my lack of breath.

Rachel, who had passed Nelson even with her shorter legs, slowed to a stop, then leaned down to put her hands on both knees and catch her breath. She then withdrew a bottle of water, took a drink and passed it around to the others.

Albert drank long and hard.

I pushed the button on my radio. "Bug," I said. "We're at the fork in the trail. The first one. Is that where we cut right?"

"No, man" said Bug. "Second fork. The second one. It's a bigger trail. You take that fucker there, it leads right off a goddamned cliff."

I looked around at the others. They all nodded. I smiled.

However, it was that awkward moment when only I knew that I almost didn't make that call and just told everyone to cut right at the first fork. I didn't know how far the drop off was, or what was at the bottom of it, but we might have lost Rachel – not to mention Nelson, who was right on her tail.

For that brief moment, I questioned everything. The plan. My competence. My fucking intelligence.

"David, let's go," said Serena.

"Fine, but I lead," I said, jogging past Rachel and taking the first position on the trail. If anything was going wrong, it would be me who took the fall.

Literally, if necessary.

My AR-15 was ready and my Walther was loaded, too. I hoped not to need either.

We made it in another fifteen minutes. When we got to the top, not one abnormal – not one red-eye – waited at the entry hatch. I got to the top of the hill and saw the steel door embedded in the earth.

"David," said Serena, touching my shoulder and pointing. "Look."

We all looked. Just thirty yards down the hill, we saw twenty rotters moving away, over the rough terrain. They were being drawn by Lolita Lane, I knew. I prayed there were no red-eyes within view who might turn their rotting bodies, topped with their eerily perfect heads and crimson eyes, spotting us and forsaking Lola's call to instead come after us.

None did. We watched them until their heads slowly dropped out of sight, and only then did I grab my radio.

"Uncle Bug," I said. "We're here. Turn on your camera."

"Roger," he said. A moment later, I heard the hum of a tiny motor and saw a camera painted with camouflage mounted on a similarly painted rod sticking out of the earth. It panned us for a moment, then stopped when it was pointed at me. I waved.

"Holy shit, Davey! Is that you?"

"In the flesh. Why?"

"You'll see," he said. This was followed by the sound of metal sliding in a slot. We all took a step back and watched as the doors embedded into the rock slid open from the center in both directions, revealing a stairway leading down inside.

"Well, what you staring at, kid?" he said. "You guys get in so I can close it up. Now!"

I waved the others in and got on my radio. "Russell, you read?"

"Yeah," he said. "We're about a quarter mile farther back down the road, Dave. Tons of them. Red-eyes and the others, too. Never seen so many pregnant things at once."

"Just be happy they'll never be born, Russell. And stay clear of them. Tell Lola to keep calling them, but you be careful. The WAT-5 doesn't fool the red-eyes."

"Roger that."

"Okay," I said. "We're going inside now. You guys be careful."

"I didn't last this long being anything else," said Russell. "Keep in touch."

With that, I followed Albert, Nelson, Rachel and Serena into the hideaway home that had become my Uncle Bug's private prison.

*****

Chapter Seventeen

"Wow," said Serena, looking from Bug to me. "Crazy resemblance. You guys could be twins."

"Yeah, if I were twenty years younger or the other way around," Bug said.

I hugged my uncle, and it did register that our hair was about the same length, and we both had long beards and the same blue eyes. We were identical in height, and he wore a brown pullover tee-shirt and jeans. Being unable to see any wrinkles beneath all the facial hair, it was almost like looking in a mirror.

"So what you're saying is that my uncle's good looking, too," I said.

Serena smiled and moved in for a hug from Uncle Bug. Rachel held out her hand and Bug shook it briefly, then pulled her in for a hug, too.

Albert was not in the mood for hellos. Instead, he slowly walked the perimeter of the huge room, touching the many metal doors embedded into what appeared to be a solid rock wall.

Nelson got his hug and said, "Dude, I've never met a Bug before. But I hear you grow hydroponic pot."

"Not anymore," he said. "Grew enough to last me a lifetime before all this shit ever got started."

"Good to know," said Nelson.

"Uncle Bug, where are the other people?" I asked.

"Yeah," said Albert, walking back up the small flight of steps and standing directly in front of my uncle. "How many, and where are they?"

"I don't believe we've been introduced," said Bug. "But I recognize you, kid. I saw you on the cameras down below once in a while. You'd come out of the woods and just stare at all the crazies."

Albert nodded. "That was me. My dad was with those crazies."

"Sorry," said Bug. "Lots of good folks turned."

"None as good as my dad," said Albert.

"Maybe, maybe not," said Bug.

"Where are they?" asked Albert.

Uncle Bug turned to me and said, "This guy's a fuckin' buzz kill. I didn't open the door after over a year for this shit, and —"

"Uncle Bug," I interrupted. "Albert is hoping his mother's inside here somewhere."

"Oh," he said. "Kid, I'm sorry."

"What about?" asked Albert. "Sorry, buddy, but your mom's not here, or sorry for being a greedy hermit for a year and letting everybody fend for themselves?"

"I feel for your situation, buddy, but you have no fuckin' idea what you're talkin' about." He turned to me and clasped me on the shoulder. "We've got a lot to talk about, Davey. Man, it's good to see you. Good to see anyone."

"Uncle Bug, we don't have a lot of time. The only reason that horde isn't out there right now is because Lola and Russell drew them away."

Bug nodded. "So I have a decision to make. About leaving."

"Yeah, you do," I said. "And you don't have long to make it. You said you were here with one other person. Where?"

"In the nursery."

"The nursery?" I said.

"Yeah. It's my daughter. Isis."

"What?"

"Isis. After the Goddess of motherhood, magic and fertility. She's just over a year old," said Bug.

"Where's Angela?" I asked. "You said you –"

"Now it's my turn to interrupt," he said. "I didn't finish the story, and it's a long one that I've never told before. Don't know if I can, but you're my blood, Davey, so if there's a time, I guess it's now."

I nodded. I had some idea of what he would say from the sadness in his eyes.

"Anyway, I suppose we have a little time if we're going to use what you've brought in those bags. You guys need a shower? Some food?"

"We're good," said Serena. "The shower sounds great, but I think we can wait until after we set up the still to extract the urushiol."

We got the four bags of poison ivy unwrapped and opened. All of us sat down and began shredding the plant matter with our hands until the pieces were as small as we could make them. After that, we stuffed them into the tank and Bug got it closed up and powered on. At the end was a half-gallon sized, glass container. I hoped to see oil in there within a couple of hours.

When we were done, we rinsed the sticky residue off our hands and sat down.

"Alright," said Bug. "I suppose I'll tell you how things got to be the way they are right now."

393

"Got any of that pot?" asked Nelson. "I wouldn't mind a little toke before story time, and mine's in my backpack." He smiled, and Bug smiled back and glanced at me for approval.

"Helps him focus," I said.

Bug laughed. "Me too, once upon a time. Sure, Nelson. See that white desk over there? There's a tray and a pipe in the top drawer. Knock yourself out."

"Why would I do that?" asked Nelson. "I just want to get high."

My uncle just stared at him. Rachel shook her head.

Nelson shrugged and laughed. "Sorry man," he said. "My kook act dies hard." He was already halfway to the desk.

The dude was pretty funny.

*****

The room was almost a perfect circle. Around the perimeter were massive steel beams for support, and eight metal doors of some kind, which Bug explained led to various storage and living quarters. The main room had to be sixty feet in diameter, the floors bare concrete. Rubber mats were placed in work areas, like the kitchen, and he had spread out large, carpeted area rugs beneath the sitting areas.

Overall, it looked like a industrial-themed loft in New York, but without a view.

Bug had hung paintings, too. Mostly scenes of a snow-capped Mount Shasta and the town of Dunsmuir, and I even noticed one painting of the Railroad Park in which we had stayed. An old, framed photograph of me sat atop the white desk where Nelson got the pot. In the picture, I was about twenty years old, my hair still long, but my beard pretty much non-existent.

Albert said again, "Look. I know I'm not the reason Dave and these guys came here, but I can't do or think about anything else until you show me where these other people are," he said.

"The problem is getting them out," said Bug. "The garage level is the base. It's like a 5-car, so it's big. In the northeast corner, which is just to your left as you walk in from the outside, there's a set of four steps that lead to a steel door. Behind that is a 20' x 30' chamber where they're trapped. It's got one gravity flush toilet that still seems to be limping along and tons of food storage in recessed alcoves, and there's plenty of that. I hadn't gotten my water stocked up in that area yet, but they had enough for a couple of months. They've been staying alive by drinking runoff from the mountain streams and snow that I could never seem to completely seal up."

"Good thing," said Albert.

"It was, in retrospect. God's plan, maybe."

I thought it strange that my uncle, who didn't trust anyone, had any belief in God at all.

Bug continued. "I can't leave the lights on for them all the time, but I turn them on once in a while, and I talk to them."

"Do you know their names? Ever make a list?"

"Most of them. I didn't have anyone to give the list to," said Bug. "They're alive, and they're eating."

"What's beyond that room?" I asked.

"Where you are now," he said. "The whole configuration is shaped kind of like a Z," he said. "From the garage, you'd open the lower door and go up the steps on your immediate left. When you get inside the chamber where they're trapped, you'd turn right and walk to the end. There are storage alcoves at the end and on the right, but at the end on the left is the door into this chamber. Three steps up and you're in."

"So why the hell didn't you just let them in?" asked Albert, incredulous.

"Don't you think I would have?" asked Uncle Bug, looking directly at Albert. "Buddy, I know it's no fuckin' picnic in there after a year, but I can't open that door to let them in here without opening the lower door, and with all them zombies in there, that'll kill 'em."

"Why?" asked Albert, not breaking his gaze with Bug.

"Something happened to the electrical lines," said my uncle. Wires fused or something. The button for the lower door doesn't do shit. If I hit the button to open the door into this chamber, the lower door from the garage opens, too, only it starts opening first."

"So they could be inundated with infecteds before they could even start to move," said Serena.

"Yeah, and I'm pretty sure there's a nice number of your red-eyes down there and they're not exactly lackadaisical."

"You painted a picture that meshes with what we thought as far as the garage occupancy goes," I said. "You got any surveillance in there?"

"Yep," he said. Bug walked across the room to where a bank of LCD computer monitors were arranged on brackets that ran them three high and seven wide. It looked like a setup an ambitious day trader would put together. Twenty-one monitors in all. At the moment they were all dark.

"You can see why I keep them off," he said. "It's a lot of power draw."

He reached under the table below them and pushed a button. The monitor marked MAIN ENTRY came on, and showed the exterior entry hatch.

"This is where you came in." He pushed another button on the one marked GARAGE EXTERIOR.

"Shit," he said. "I haven't turned this one on. You guys did a number down there, too. What a mess."

"It was a lot of work," said Rachel. "Some close calls, too."

"The question was, what's on the lower level?' asked Albert.

Bug leaned forward and pressed the button on the monitor marked GARAGE INTERIOR.

A mass of something appeared on the 27" monitor, but it wasn't clear what it was.

"Too dark," I said. "No such thing as low light cameras?"

"Don't need 'em," said Uncle Bug. He slid a panel up on the table and pushed a button that said G.I. LIGHTS.

When the light chased away the darkness, I think we all physically drew away from the monitor. The room was packed with the stinking, walking dead, and as we looked, several faces featuring piercing, red eyes turned toward the light and the camera. In a massive push, they came toward it. The gnashing and chewing was visible in the HD monitor, and at their feet we could see what appeared to be chunks of bone, some pulverized to powder. Several skulls littered the floor, and among it all were torn pieces of clothing and shoes – so many pairs of shoes of all kinds.

"Oh, my God," whispered Serena.

"Are they all … infected?" asked Albert.

"In this room, yeah," said my uncle. "The ones that weren't died pretty nasty deaths a long time ago."

I cringed. "Can you show us the survivors?" I asked.

Bug thumbed a joystick by the button and the camera panned to the entirely opposite direction until another aluminum door appeared on the monitor.

"This is the door to their chamber," he said. Bug then tilted the view downward, and we saw a skeleton – or rather, half a skeleton – on the floor, part of it beneath the door, keeping it about an inch from closing completely.

"What happened?" asked Nelson, still holding the now extinguished glass pipe in his hand.

"When everyone came running up my trail to get away from the creatures in town, me and my wife, Angela, had just gotten inside. By then, I knew that whatever happened was worse than anything I'd ever expected. Like I told you, Davey, I thought I'd be fighting our fucked up government – not some extremely efficient human transformation shit where your neighbors turn into monsters and try to kill you."

"Hey," I said. "I'm sure all the people running were as surprised as you."

"Yeah, I know" said Bug. "Anyway, back to what happened. The only doors that aren't on electronic controls are the two big ones down there. I planned on it, but didn't have enough fuckin' time to finish the work before this came on. It all happened too fast. So I went down and got those doors opened manually. Before people from town got here, I got my ass back up here and monitored it with my cameras. I used my speakers to instruct them what to do, but before long, I saw too many infected motherfuckers were getting inside with the healthy ones."

"Wow," said Rachel. "We tried to open those doors," she said. "So if they're not electronic, what's holding them closed?"

"Belts, believe it or not," said Bug. "I yelled at 'em, told 'em too many sick fucks were getting inside. That's when the normal ones rushed the doors and started pulling them closed. It was crazy, man."

At the memory, Bug broke out in beads of sweat. He stared at the shuffling creatures in the monitor, obviously remembering. "You can see it's a big room. I figure there are two hundred or so biters in there right now, but there were over three hundred people at first. More were pouring in, but the people were freaked out and they were desperate. They started pushing new arrivals away and pulling the doors closed. I watched for what seemed like forever, because everyone rushing the doors started panicking when they saw those doors swinging shut. Fought like crazy. The people inside finally got 'em almost closed, and the guys with baseball bats – about four of them, just started pulverizing anyone who blocked them from closing the rest of the way."

"Even uninfecteds?" asked Serena. "Killing people?"

"I suppose they figured it was a *them or us* thing. They finally got the doors closed, but so many people got bit and scratched in the process that eventually it turned into what you see now. Just a bunch of those things. Everybody got infected."

Bug panned the camera over to the inside of the huge doors, and we saw what looked like twenty belts buckled between the two heavy, interior handles. It would be impossible to open them as we had tried to do.

"Like I said, I hadn't gotten everything in order yet – the electrical shit. Not dialed in. I intended to get as many healthy folks up here, to where we are, and with access to my storage area where I kept almost as much food as I have up here. I got thirty or so into the middle chamber, off the garage. That's the one between there and here."

"Do you have a camera in that room?" asked Albert.

"I do," said Bug.

"Which one?" he asked, poring over the bank of screens, his eyes darting along the many labels, no doubt trying to figure out which button he should push.

"I'm almost scared to turn it on, Albert," said Bug. "I'll be responsible for ending your hope."

"Putting it off won't change it, sir," he said, solemnly. "Please."

Bug nodded and pressed the button by the monitor called STORAGE CHAMBER.

It was as dark as the garage had been. "You ready?" asked Bug.

Albert nodded, his eyes locked on the screen.

"Okay," my uncle said, and pushed the button.

Light bathed the room and we heard everyone inside scream as they threw their hands over their eyes, clearly shielding them from the brightness.

We all began to cry at the sight of the prisoners. The many gaunt faces remained covered by thin hands, and one man was cupping his hands in a trickle of water that flowed down the interior of the stone wall, drinking.

"I don't see her," said Albert. "Shit, I don't see her!" He, too, was crying. No. Albert was sobbing.

"Hold on," said Bug. "Just hold on, kid. Take this, Albert. I lost control of the pan on this camera a long time ago. There are dead spots I can't see."

Bug passed Albert a microphone and adjusted a volume potentiometer very low, putting it at 2.

"Go ahead," said Albert. "Say her name. Tell her who you are."

Albert held the mic up, watching the room. "Mama," he said. "Ellie Brookins? It's me, Albert. Mama, are you there?"

We all held our collective breaths and stared at the monitor. A light, almost indistinguishable voice met our ears. "Bertie?"

Albert's eyes brightened and his sob caught in his throat. He raised the microphone. "Mama?" he whispered.

A head moved from the bottom to the top of the monitor. Black hair. A dark dress with white spots. The face turned. I didn't know what Albert's mother looked like, but this was a black woman.

She stared at the camera. "Bertie? Is that you?"

"Mama!" he shouted, and the crowd standing behind her cowered at the loudness of the sound.

"Albert," said Uncle Bug. "Softly, please. For the others."

"Mama, it's me," he said. "I'm okay. I'm alive. You're alive. Mama, I've come to get you."

The crowd behind her became more animated and the murmur behind her grew to a loud mumble, then a cacophony of voices. "Help! Help us! Get us out of here!" they shouted in a variety of pleas.

"Albert, please," said Bug, holding out his hand.

Albert looked at my uncle and raised the microphone again. "Mama, I love you," he said. "I'll be right here. I'm close to you. Just outside the door." He passed the microphone.

Bug pushed the button. "Everyone, I have some help here now. I haven't until now. We're going to figure out how to get you out of there, I think. I think we finally can."

*****

"When all this started, we were still living in town," said Bug. "I wanted this place empty while I was doing all the electrical and blasting out the main rooms. These rooms are all solid concrete walls with craploads of rebar running through them. It all took years to build, but I had the main door installed right away. Remote controlled. There was no reason to move here until we had to, because I knew if the government turned on the people, we could be here in twenty minutes."

He pointed at the entry door, then the door behind which the other survivors were trapped. "Those two doors are impenetrable. All the others lead to storage and living area, but those two are the ways in. I don't care what you throw at them, you're not getting them open. Try to blast

401

'em and you're just going to bend 'em up so they're jammed permanently. It seemed like a good idea until those folks got trapped in there."

"I guess it did," said Rachel, who being military, could appreciate the value of fortified bunkers.

"Until I heard updates from your friend Hemp, I didn't have any idea what was causing this crap or what anyone could do to protect against it," said my uncle, stroking his beard the way I did when I was deep in thought. "Locked in here, I didn't have the stuff I needed to make your urushiol mix, and because of the sheer numbers of the freaks outside, I couldn't go on any runs to pick poison ivy or anything else."

"You have a ton of weapons, right?" Albert asked. "I heard you did."

"I got the best, and tools of all kinds." Bug got up and went to the third aluminum panel to the right of the entry stairwell. He turned a lever and slid it aside. Behind it was every type and style of gun I could have imagined. Along the wall were rack after rack, and at the base of the compartment were what looked like hand grenades and other incendiary devices.

Albert stared, but said nothing. I suppose it just confirmed his suspicions. My Uncle Bug had all the weapons in Dunsmuir and Lake Shasta. The kid turned and went to sit on the couch.

"And I only picked up on Hemp's broadcasts about six months ago, so this was way before that."

Bug walked back to a plain, beige couch and sat down and we all walked over and stood beside him.

"I'd lost track of Angela for a while," he said. "I started seeing crazy stuff on the news, and before I knew it, the crazy shit was right outside my door. I had guns at the other house too, so I loaded up and took out my share, then set out to find Angela."

"Where was she?" asked Rachel, sitting beside him.

"She'd gone next door to check on our pregnant neighbor. Her husband was deployed with the Marines, so Angela got friendly with her – went to check on her, seeing as how they were both with child."

He picked up a bottle of water from the table and took a long drink. "I knocked, but nothing. Then I kicked the damned door in and saw my Angela standing there, this friend of hers completely turned into one of those things. It's crazy how fast they just don't look alive anymore. There was this red mist hanging in the air around Angela, but I had no idea what it was then."

"But I thought they evolved to have that vapor," I said. "I'm pretty sure Hemp believes the red vapor came over time."

"Maybe that was instantaneous," said Serena. "And the other things – the telepathy, the hearing – was part of the evolution."

"Maybe," I said.

"So what did you do, Bug?" asked Nelson, getting us back to the previous discussion. I could see he was fascinated.

"What the hell do you think I did? I grabbed my wife and pulled her away, and I shot at the thing. It dropped to the damned ground so fast I didn't see it coming, and I put a hole in the wall. Next thing I knew the bitch got her hands around my legs and was probably just about to flip me on my back when I put that double-barreled shotgun against her head and sent her brains across the room."

"Holy crap," I said. "Close call."

"Angela was freaked out and confused, like she was in a daze. I scooped her up, pregnant and all, and ran up here. And I mean jogged my ass the entire distance, killing the freaks one-handed along the way. I probably just barely beat the rest of the folks from town up here."

"You got lucky," said Rachel.

"Not so lucky as I'd have preferred," said Bug. "All that shit sent Angie into some kind of labor. By the time I got inside with the doors sealed up, she was cramping and bleeding bad. I had medical supplies – enough for almost anything, but I didn't have the expertise, and had no idea I'd need it. She wasn't due for a couple more weeks."

"Planning for stuff you never really thought would happen and still didn't think of everything?" asked Serena.

"That's the understatement of the century," said Bug. "Anyway, I got her on the bed. The bleeding stopped on its own, and I still felt the baby kicking, so I figured all was well. Angie was awake, and I'd feed her and keep her comfortable, but after those things started collecting at the top hatch, she started mumbling weird shit. She quit eating and just walked the perimeter of the room like she was going stir crazy. Her eyes had turned blood red, but the baby seemed content to stay put for the time being."

"So the labor pains just went away?" asked Rachel. We'd told Rachel about the control the red-eyes had over fertile women, so questions about *what* Angela was saying probably seemed unnecessary.

"Must have been a false labor or something. Just enough to freak the shit out of me. Anyway, every time I let her get out of bed, she'd go to the controls and try to open the doors. This went on for a week. No sleep. Watching her all the time, grabbing catnaps when I could. She wasn't one of *them*, but she was doing crazy stuff, and I had no idea why."

"What did you do?"

"Strapped her, finally. She begged me not to, but that was in her moments of clarity and those became more and more rare. Pretty soon all she said was *open* and *in* and *door* and shit like that. She didn't seem to know who I was or care who I was. Broke my heart. She went in and out, but she never stopped trying to get to the doors. Another two weeks passed, and then she was past her due date. I was exhausted as hell, and more worried than I'd ever been. Just when I thought I'd have to make some major decision about the baby, she went into full blown labor, and this time it was bad. She was bleeding like crazy, and I didn't have any goddamned blood supply or a way to get it in her. Like I said, I didn't plan for every contingency, even though I thought I had."

"You delivered the baby?"

"I did. Angie was gone, but she still pushed – I could see her doing it, and she worked that baby out of her body. Isis slid into my arms, and I sat there, thankful that little baby girl was alive, but worried as hell about Angela."

Rachel took Bug by the hand and squeezed it.

"You lost Angela then?" she said, quietly.

Bug nodded. "She did something strange before, though."

"What?" I asked, mesmerized. We all were. Even Albert. He stared at Bug as he continued, and Rachel couldn't keep her eyes off of my uncle.

"Her eyes opened real wide," said Bug. "And they were redder than I'd seen before. She sat bolt upright and said *baby*. Then she fell back and that was it. She was gone."

"Oh, my God," said Albert, finally affected by the story, and perhaps understanding that Bug wasn't the horrible person he'd made him out to be in his mind.

"I'm so sorry, Bug," said Serena. "Baby?" asked Serena. "That's all she said?"

"Yeah," said Bug, putting his hands on his knees and standing up. He took a deep breath. "Whew. I don't think I ever want to tell that story again."

I went to him and put my arms around him and pulled him in tight for a long time. He put his arms around me and his head against mine, and we just stayed that way. In my ear he said, "It's damned good to be with you again, Davey. I had no idea what it'd mean to see you again. Can't even tell you."

"Double that," I said. "Love you, Unk. Missed you more than I knew."

He pulled away and his eyes were watering. At least that's what he'd say if anyone called him on it.

"I'll go get Isis. She's probably bored by now."

"Is she having a nap?" asked Serena, a kind smile on her lips. "I can't wait to meet her."

I knew Serena's mind had drifted to Trina and Taylor, and the baby we'd talked about having together. I hoped she wasn't worried.

Bug looked at her for a moment before answering. "No, Serena. She's not having a nap."

"No?"

Bug shook his head. "Nope. Isis doesn't sleep. Ever."

We all stared at him. He left to bring out his daughter. The moment he left, I wondered to myself what my uncle had done with his dead wife's body.

And if she had become something that he really didn't want to talk about.

*****

The moment we saw Isis, we gasped.

Bug wasn't surprised. Isis had glowing red eyes.

"Uncle Bug," I whispered. "Is she … okay?"

"She is," he said. "She's perfect. Just doesn't sleep, like I said."

"She *has* to sleep," said Rachel. "Babies all sleep."

"Like I said. Not her."

She was cute as a button. Her hair was dark like Bug's and her face was round and cherub-like. Everything about her, save for her eyes, which you could tell were blue beneath the red, looked like any other baby. Pink skin, perfect fingers and toes.

She looked at us with some trepidation, it seemed. Her little, red eyes went from one of us to the other, and started over again.

Bug put her down, and she walked very well. She went immediately to Rachel – I wondered if it was because she was the closest to her height – and raised her arms. Rachel leaned down and lifted her up. Now Isis gave everyone a closed-mouth smile.

"She's a little beauty," said Rachel. "Nelson, look at her."

"Dude's pretty cool," he said. "Makes me miss little Flexy."

"That would be a dudette in your language, Nelson," said Rachel, bouncing her in her arms.

"There's something else," said Bug. "The moment she was born, the floodgates opened up top."

I looked at him. "What do you mean?"

"The zombies, man. They started coming. In hordes, if you'll excuse the use of a cliché."

"I wonder why," said Rachel. "You did have quite a concentration of the pregnant red-eyes up here."

I stared at the baby and wondered if Angela's last word came from her, or from outside. It was as though a revelation came to me. I squeezed Serena's shoulder. She'd been around more red-eyes than probably anyone besides me.

"What if Isis is the draw? What if she's the only reason they're coming here? Blocking you in?"

"What do you mean?" asked Bug.

"You said it yourself," I said. "The moment the baby was born, Angela said baby, and the horde got thick. Has it ever died down again?"

Bug shook his head. "Nope. Just keeps growing."

I decided to let that go for the moment. I wasn't sure I was right, and I wasn't sure he was ready to think about it. But I just kept thinking of Lola's power and how coincidence was often not that at all.

"Where's your ventilation come out?" I asked. "You said this place is sealed up tight, but you have to vent fresh air."

"That fresh air vent has multiple filtration systems," said Bug. "and it comes out a pipe that runs underground for about six hundred feet. Well away from here."

"Why did you do that?"

"Because I figured it might carry some heat with it, and I wanted to eliminate signatures. I can cut off the generator if I need to and let the pipes cool, but I can't stop breathing. I'd switch to oxygen tanks if things got dicey, but I still have to exhale."

"So there's absolutely no reason for these things to be gathering here. You're sure they can't smell you or the folks trapped in that middle chamber."

Bug shook his head again. "No way."

Hemp's gonna shit," said Nelson. "This is new knowledge. He loves that."

"What you're saying sounds more scary than helpful," said Bug. "The question is, can it help us?"

Jim Morrison's voice floated through my mind and I thought, *My brain is squirmin' like a toad ...*

*****

While the still did its job – and it was working very efficiently, having created around four ounces of the crucial oil already, we discussed our plan for freeing the people in the middle chamber, including Albert's mother.

Bug had given Albert permission to get back on the microphone, as he said he often did, to talk to the people trapped inside. Albert learned that two people had died since they were trapped in there, which was actually impressive.

There was still quite a lot of food left, but the water had run out after two months. Since that time, they had been living on the trickle seeping in from up on the mountain. The extra just trickled down into the garage area through the door that was held open about an inch by the bones of an unfortunate escapee.

Nelson asked him why they didn't just use water from the toilet for a drinking supply, but Bug told him he'd installed an incinerator toilet. He didn't want to plumb the water in and electric was already available, so it seemed to make sense. Unfortunately, with all those people down there, Bug had to turn the power on more than he liked, though he had plenty of fuel. They had even used it for an emergency heating source during the cold months, but Bug had extra blankets and towels stored in one of the closets there, so it was only for when temperatures dropped to their lowest.

Albert put the microphone away after telling everybody we were working on a solution – finally – and telling his mother again that he loved and missed her. I was happy for the kid. *Really* happy. I'm sure in his heart he had believed she was dead. When he came back over to where we were monitoring the urushiol progress and Bug was preparing to feed Isis, he actually looked to be at a sort of peace for the first time since we'd met him.

As he watched the oil slowly dripping into the container, he suddenly turned toward me.

"Davey, I got it."

"Holy molars!" shouted Nelson, and we all turned to look. "Dude, what are you using on her teeth? Fertilizer?"

"What do you mean?" asked Bug.

The baby hadn't opened its mouth for any purpose other than a shy smile at the girls, so I hadn't noticed what had caught Nelson's attention. Isis's teeth – she had a mouthful for a baby of her age.

"Wow," said Serena, putting the spoonful of food in her mouth. Isis immediately spit it out and if it was possible, looked disgusted.

"Not hungry, are you?" asked Serena.

"Oh, she's hungry alright," said my uncle. "Just not for creamed corn. Sorry, I should have told you."

"What does she prefer?" Serena asked.

"Meat. Any kind of meat."

Serena ran her finger up and down over the infant's lips and Isis opened her mouth and made sounds while Serena apparently counted. "Nineteen teeth at what, eleven months old?"

I looked at Serena, then back at Uncle Bug. "You think there's any tie-in to her red eyes?"

Bug looked at me. He wasn't smiling. "What are you gettin' at?"

"I'm not as smart as Hemp," said Nelson, "but you got a red-eyed baby here – cute as a button, though I've never really figured out what's so cute about a button – and all she likes to eat is meat? Have you looked outside lately? Seems to be an epidemic."

"Shit," said Bug. "I've thought about it, but she's never tried to use those choppers on me. Never had a baby before, so I didn't know if that was normal."

"I've seen babies with a lot of teeth before," said Rachel, "but these grew fast, and it's not just the size. They look a bit more pointed than normal, especially the molars.

And just so much bigger than those of an ordinary eleven-month old."

I was wondering if it was time for me to go back to what I'd begun to think about earlier. Isis and the connection to the red-eyed hordes and their minions. We'd kinda broken the ice and my uncle would know that none of it was Isis's fault.

I decided it was time.

"Uncle Bug," I said. "I'm going back to what came to my mind earlier. You said the rotters started to gather outside when Isis was born, right? You're sure?"

"Yeah, that's about the time the numbers got enormous. Before that they were just milling around, just downstairs."

"So they never showed up at the upper entrance until the birth?"

"No, just down by the garage."

"You only had cameras on the entrances, correct?" I asked. "So you wouldn't know if they were other places, right?"

"No, I got cameras all around the surrounding woods. I only saw them in any big numbers outside my place."

"And how long were you in here before Isis was born?"

"Just about three weeks," said Bug.

"And you're sure there were none by this entrance?" I asked, pointing at the steps leading up.

"No. Davey, just down at the garage. What are you gettin' at, man?"

I ran my hand over my mouth and down my beard and looked into his eyes. "I'm seriously wondering if there's something about Isis," I said, finally re-stating my suspicion. "Can your daughter be the draw?"

"How so?" Bug was confused, and I understood why. He'd been confined in this bunker for over a year. He'd

411

recently heard Hemp sharing information, but you had to be out in the real world, confronting them, being hunted by them and being surprised by them to really grasp the full potential of what powers the red-eyes truly possessed.

Serena looked at me. "David, are you saying that the red-eyes are drawn to Isis? Like they call one another?"

I nodded. "It first hit me when Uncle Bug said they started showing up right after she was born. I understand why they'd have gathered at the lower door, because at the time there were lots of uninfecteds running for this place. Even after the doors closed, there were lots of our kind in there that could have drawn them through scent. I don't know how long it took for them all to be changed or … well, you know. Eaten."

"So what brought them up top?" asked Bug. "You saying it could be proximity to Isis?"

I nodded again. "Maybe it's an involuntary thing. As long as she's awake – and you said she never sleeps – she's … I don't know … broadcasting or something."

"Or they sense her," said Rachel.

"That's what I was thinking," said Nelson. "I thought I was just spooking myself, so I didn't say anything, but if that's what you're thinking, too."

"A maternal pull?" asked Serena. "It's possible that there aren't many like Isis. Where the pregnant woman was exposed to the red-eye vapor but not infected, and the baby was born. I can't imagine that scenario would have played out very much. Isis may be one of a kind."

"Wow and shit and fuck," said Bug. "Like a fuckin' siren calls sailors from the sea onto the rocks."

"I'd take rocks over zombies any day," said Nelson.

While people often joked about dogs chasing cars and what they would do if they actually caught one, I thought the same thing about the red-eyes.

It was my guess they'd do more than stand there and stare at little Isis. I suspected that she would either become their Oracle or their delicacy.

*****

Chapter Eighteen

Isis was a trip. Bug was concerned about her lack of vegetables, so he told Serena that he often mixed in some creamed corn, spinach, and other veggies with her puréed meat. Beef was her favorite, but she also liked pork, and last on her list was chicken and lamb.

When Serena had put the first spoonful of the creamed corn and beef mix in her mouth, she closed her lips, worked her mouth around, and through her lips, she excreted only the corn. Isis busily chewed the rest and swallowed, then opened her mouth again for more.

Serena grabbed a towel, wiped Isis's chin and the bib off and looked at the cloth. Then she looked back at us. "There's not a shred of beef in this. It's just the corn."

"It's what she does," said Bug.

We all gawked at him. "She filters out the veggies?" asked Rachel, her mouth open.

"I keep hopin' she's getting some of the nutrition from the vegetables I put in there, but she'll only eat what she eats, and it's pretty much meat."

"As I've heard Flex say," said Nelson. "This gets curiouser and curiouser."

*****

As Bug had told us, he had dismantled his brewery and essentially converted the equipment into a still using other supplies, quite like we had done to the brewery in Concord. Based on Hemp's detailed instructions, he had added some heating elements and re-worked it, but could never get outside to get the main ingredient – the poison ivy.

Now, with what we had brought, the makeshift still had done its job. When it was all complete, our harvest of poison ivy had yielded six and a half ounces of pure urushiol oil. It was enough to destroy literally thousands of zombies. Not the red-eyes, but it would slow them down.

There was enough seating when we moved some chairs from the dining table over by the sofa and armchairs. Once we arranged all the chairs in a circle and sat, I checked my watch and said, "We need to check in with Lola and Russell. We've been in here four hours now."

I got on the handheld. "Russell, come in. You read?"

He came right back. "I was just about to call you," he said. "We keep retreating, but they keep moving on us. I had to shoot two of the red-eyes already – they started flying toward Lola, and I swear I'm not exaggerating when I say that. Those things can move. Took me five rounds to take them both out."

"They *can* move," I said. "Sorry, Russell, but we have to figure out how to get about thirty people trapped in a middle chamber out before we can leave. We need you to keep them occupied a bit longer."

"Well, Lola's like a damned Pied Piper over here, and we're gonna be out of radio range soon unless we circle them back around to the north. That brings them too close to the Railroad Park for my taste. Maddie and the girls are down there alone, and Lola looks like she's exhausted."

Four hours was a hell of a long time, and I had no idea what Lola was going through. "Okay, just hang in there a little longer," I said. "Bug said he has an idea to get them out safely using our urushiol. After that, we'll all get out, radio you and we'll make a run."

"Hurry," said Russell. "Seriously."

"Gotcha," I said. "Talk to you later."

"What's your plan?" I asked Bug.

"See that hatch in the ceiling there?" said Bug, pointing.

"Yeah," I said.

"My water supply tank is up there. The one that's fed by rainwater and runoff and supplies the shower and flush toilets up here. None of the lines lead into the middle chamber, but I have extra hose that we're going to need to plumb in. It's up there in the crawlspace, by the tank. Only it's more of a walkspace."

"I don't get it."

"We dump the urushiol in that water tank," said my uncle. "Then we run the hose from the drain valve on the tank and connect it to the electrical conduit leading to the middle chamber. I got shitloads of duct tape, so I can secure it pretty well. In the chamber, we'll need a couple of them to lift someone up high enough to reach the light fixture, take out the bulb and try to break the fixture out."

"Why?" I asked, not sure where he was going.

"Davey, I used a waterproof conduit – one of the things I did think of – so if we run the water through it, it'll be just like a hose."

"What good will it do to pump it into their room?"

"Because," said Bug. "That skeleton has been lodged under that door the entire time. That's a gap for the water to flow downhill. Down the steps it goes and floods the garage. What do you think?"

I smiled, and everyone's eyebrows went up. "That's a damned good idea," I said. "Really good!"

"You think it'll work?" asked Albert.

"If it touches them, it takes them out," said Nelson. "The junk will eat up their legs, dude. When they fall down it's all over. They're like freakin' mashed potatoes."

*****

Isis was closed in the nursery. She was a good little girl, and like any infant, she was still mesmerized by mobiles and angelic music, so Bug got her set up and closed away for the moment.

As for our plan, everything had gone like clockwork. Using a ladder, Nelson entered the hatch wearing one of our headlamps, and located the lower drain. He was able to stretch up high enough to access the lid of the tank – which held about 3,000 gallons and was partially embedded into the wall of the building.

Bug said it had to be inserted into the wall and held on the other end with 4" x 4" steel legs because when the tank was full, it held over 400 cubic feet of water, and at just over 62 pounds per cubic foot, it would weigh almost 25,000 pounds.

We didn't need to know this stuff, but Bug offered, and we knew he'd most likely be leaving his sanctuary soon. He might as well be able to brag a bit in the meantime.

Albert turned on the lights and got on the microphone. "I know you're all tired and weak," he said. "I can see that. But we need two or three of you – more if that's what it takes – to get someone up high enough to take out that light bulb and see if you can rip down that light fixture. We need to have that conduit disconnected."

Nobody asked why. Three of the men got slowly to their feet and looked up at the nine-foot, concrete ceiling. "We should be able to do that with a foot boost," said an older man. He had the remnants of a dress shirt on, both sleeves torn off, and he had wispy, grey hair. He was bone skinny, and had lived like a rat for the last year.

"Do it then, Larry," said Albert, who had talked to several of them and knew many by name. "Just get it done. It's the last step."

"Bug," said Albert. "Go ahead and cut the power to that chamber so they don't get shocked."

"Good call, kid," said Bug and went to the electrical panel.

In fifteen minutes – which encompassed several tries before the plastic electrical junction box broke free – Larry held it in his hand, up to the camera.

"Ready to try this?" Bug asked.

I shrugged. "Hell yes. Let's do this."

"Wait a minute," said Serena. "That oil's in the tank, but it's not mixed. How are you going to mix it? It's got to be blended somehow, or it might not disburse properly. The oil might come out last and just dribble onto the floor."

"Jesus, you're right."

"You got a compressor, dude?" asked Nelson.

"I do," said Bug. "Little portable jobbie. Why?"

"We'll aerate it," he said. "I'll jump back up there, hook the air to the bottom of the tank real quick, and just crank the compressor on. We force enough air up the bottom of that tank, it'll bubble to the top, churn it up real good, then we re-connect the hose and let 'er flow."

"Where did you get this guy?" asked Bug, looking at me.

Serena answered. "I don't know who he is," she said. "He's not the same Nelson Moore who rode up on his scooter a few days ago."

"Oh, he'll be back when he's needed," said Nelson, climbing the ladder. "I got my kook on standby."

Nelson yelled a signal and Bug cranked on the compressor. We could hear the churning from down below, so it seemed to be working. Nelson closed the bottom valve, dropped the compressor hose back down, connected the spare hose back to the tank's drain line, and taped the other end to the conduit. "Should I open it now?" he asked.

"Wait," said Rachel. "That gap. The garage is pretty big, right? That water needs to build up a while so it really cascades down those steps and gets all the way across that floor."

"Wait," I said. "That room is big. There won't be enough water to get any depth."

Everyone's faces drooped.

"Bullshit!" said Bug. "That entire floor angles toward the door. Never leveled it, 'cause I didn't need to. So it's got a good slope and it's all gonna flow that way anyway."

"Perfect!" said Rachel. She studied the room for a minute, swiping her short, brown hair behind her ear and biting her lower lip. "Okay. Tell them to pack something around that gap below the lower door first. They can wait until the water builds up a bit in that chamber, then let it go."

I didn't know if it was military training or what made Rachel such a great thinker, but she was right there with the new Nelson.

Though I kind of missed the old Nelson. Just a bit.

I shared the information with our refugees and soon, several of them grabbed towels and packed them under the base of the door, tucking them tightly around the skeleton as well. It was effectively sealed off.

Bug got on the microphone. "Okay, everyone. We're gonna need three or four guys down by that lower door. Keep your feet pressed on those towels. The chamber's

419

going to start to fill up with water, and in that water is something that's going to kill those bastards on the other side of the door. They are the reason you've been locked in there for so long, but it's almost over."

"When it gets around a foot deep in there, pull those shirts off and rush toward the upper door," said Rachel, taking the microphone from Bug. "Bug, can you turn on the cameras in the garage so we can see what's happening? Then you'll know when to open the door."

"There are going to be red-eyes in there, too," said Serena. "Right, David?"

"We saw them on the camera," I said. "A couple, anyway. Give me the microphone real quick."

Rachel did. I said, "When this upper door starts to open, so will the lower door. That's why I want all of you up by this door ready to get your asses through it fast. Leave room for me to slide by on your left, so hang right."

"I'm smaller," said Rachel. "Let me do it."

"She's right," said Serena.

I shrugged. "I can't argue with that, but Rachel, be careful."

Nelson did not look happy. "Rach, are you sure?'

"I am," she said. "I'll worm by them and take out any pursuing red-eyes that come through that door."

I handed her my AR-15. "Use this."

"Fuck that," said Bug, walking to his arsenal door. He withdrew a tactical-looking weapon of some kind and gave it to her. "Mossberg 500 Persuader. Not an expensive weapon, but it's reliable. It should blow the heads off two or three at once. It'll give you plenty of time to slide another shell in it."

Nelson scrambled back up the ladder. As he got in position, the radio clipped to my belt erupted.

"Dave! Dave! Come in!"

I snatched it and pushed the button. "Russell, what's going on, man?" I said.

"It's Lola," he said, breathing hard. "She was standing there, and I knew she was getting tired. She moved her foot and tripped. She fell backward, and rolled down the hill. I was far enough away from the things, so I scrambled down after her, but I'm not down there yet. I can see her from where I am. She's laying there. Knocked out, I think, Dave. I don't even know if she's alive."

"Jesus," I said. "You have to get down to her, Russell? Can you?"

"I can, but as soon as I was in the clear I had to call you. They're going back. Back up the trail."

"Who?"

"Who the hell do you think? The zombies, man. The minute she fell they turned back toward the trail and they're moving."

"Hurry up with that water, Nelson," I said. "Open the valve now!"

*****

Bug still had cameras in the center chamber, but no lights. For this reason, you could see some images, but nothing was very clear, and it was very grainy. The lights had been turned on in the garage, capturing the attention of the many rotters milling around in there, all in various stages of dress and decomposition.

We counted four red-eyes in the room. The moment the lights went on and the cameras panned, their ugly faces turned toward it and they moved forward with bone chilling speed. I shuddered. I suppose everyone else was doing what their own bodies commanded.

The water was flowing into the center chamber fast, raining down from the conduit pipe and splashing down onto the floor. We could barely see at all now, as it had created a fine mist that could only help the situation – the more airborne urushiol, the better.

We waited. Bug was by the door control button and Rachel stood to the side of the door with the Mossberg in her hands, clutching it tight. Nelson had come down the ladder. He would not need to shut the water off. If the red-eyes did make it past the shotgun, they would have to run directly beneath the urushiol-contaminated water, and that could not help their condition at all.

"We're almost at a foot!" one of the men shouted, dropping out of the camera's view for a moment. He stood again. "Can't seal it where the bones are jammed. Water's leaking out. This has to be good enough!"

"No time like now," said Bug. "I'm ready on the button."

"Pull it!" I yelled into the microphone. "Get it flowing and run back to the other door as fast as you can."

"Wait until all of it drains before you open the door, Bug," said Rachel. "Take out as many as we can first."

Our eyes were peeled on the monitor. They yanked their makeshift stopper out and as the water rushed past their feet and legs and the light filtered in from beneath the flowing water, we could see them slightly better. Not much, but it was clear that all of them were now crowded toward the upper part of the chamber.

"It's almost drained!" shouted another woman. "Please, open the door!" She pounded on it, and we all heard the desperate plea from inside.

Our eyes remained peeled on the garage monitors now, and as we watched, zombies went down, one after the other. The normal rotters stood for a brief moment as the water hit their feet and ankles, eating them away. When their legs dissolved, they collapsed among the shoes and bones of human and zombie alike.

Like dominos, down they went, and I heard a strange screaming coming from the room, combined with the familiar popping-hissing as the rotters dissolved and fell over one another, the red-eyes pushing off of them in an attempt to stay upright as the flood of deadly oil and water rushed farther and farther into the room.

This served to push the red-eyes back, and now the door area was clear for ten to twelve feet.

"Hit it, Uncle Bug! Open the door!"

Bug hit the button. The upper and lower doors began to rise.

When the interior door was two feet up, filthy bodies began pushing through, and Nelson and Serena pulled them inside, to safety. Rachel stood aside, staying clear for the initial rush. Five, then ten were through, and as Albert's mother fell into the room she was quickly scooped up by her son, her frail, thin body nothing in his arms.

"Mama!" he said, lifting her and carrying her to the sofa across the room.

Rachel pushed by them and into the room.

"Three coming!" I shouted, watching the monitor as the focused red-eyes flew up the steps toward the middle chamber, the door now all the way open. I watched as they deftly clamored over the skeleton and took two steps into the room.

Rachel fired her first shell, and I cringed at the sound of the explosion echoing through the chamber. The shotgun was as effective as Bug said it would be, though, and the bitch in the lead's head disintegrated, the blasted chunks destroying the head of the one behind her so effectively you literally couldn't distinguish one's body parts from the other. Both creatures flew backward with the shell's impact, slamming into the third red-eye that was now spattered with the gore from her formerly undead sisters.

She was down and out of the camera's view, but not for long. She had apparently escaped serious injury, for she moved into the camera seconds later, and I had a direct, head-on view. Not for long. Now fully illuminated by the light streaming in from the garage and Bug's chamber, I saw that she was another of the fully nude creatures.

Despite the gore running down the front of her body, She appeared well-preserved, her skin gray but not mottled and pustule-covered, the eyes bright, red points, and again – the disturbing phenomena of long, straight hair, in this case as white as cotton. With her clothing long stripped away, I was amazed to see her visible baby bump churning and roiling within her as though the undead infant forever trapped inside was as angry and bent on reaching either the survivors or little Isis as was her deceased mother.

Rachel slammed another shell into the Mossberg, pumped the weapon and raised the gun again, firing directly into the face of the reanimated mother that would never be, blowing her too-perfect, dead face into fleshy particles that painted the camera lens and the wall around it like a Kandinsky abstract.

All of our refugees had now made it into the upper chamber, so I grabbed Rachel by the shirt and yanked her backward. Once we were clear, Bug slapped the button again, starting the doors on what seemed to be an agonizingly slow downward crawl.

We were wrong about there being only four. Two more red-eyes had entered the middle chamber and were charging for the upper door. As the gap drew to two feet, they left their feet, diving toward the gap. Rachel eyed the monitor and saw what they had done and with the Mossberg already reloaded, she aimed downward. As the monsters slid beneath the door, both making it through to their knees, it slammed down on them both, trapping them there.

Rachel fired, destroying the head of the one on the left and sending chunks of flesh, gore and bone in all directions.

We all covered ourselves, but none of us escaped the flying meat that had, just a split second before, been the creature's physiology.

Rachel managed to ignore it and went to reload again, when I ran forward, wiping the stinking muck from my face and beard, and said, "No!"

Following my single word, there was relative silence, broken only by the low sobs of people who had been locked away and living in hell for a year. I turned around and saw what we had accomplished, and looked back at Rachel.

"We need to save that last one," I said. "She needs to see Isis."

"Jesus," said Bug. He walked quickly over to the bank of monitors and pressed a button.

The main exterior camera monitor lit up, and it was our turn to gasp in unison again.

They were back. The horde that had been drawn away by Lolita Lane was back and growing larger as we looked on.

The siren calls, I thought, then almost laughed out loud that I had even used such ridiculous, poetic phrasing, even if only in my head. And still, when I considered how overdramatic the words sounded even to me, I followed that with another thought: *Isis, the first goddess of the new world, beckons.*

*****

While Serena and Rachel got towels for everyone to wipe away the biological debris that had spattered them, Bug and I went to the nursery. He had a blue Steve Miller Band tee-shirt, complete with the Pegasus logo, that he let me put on to replace my nasty shirt, and he pulled a new one on, too. Led Zeppelin, Houses of the Holy.

I thought of Charlie then. I remembered putting her in the Hall & Oates tee in Shelburne and having her so pissed off it was hilarious.

These little memories kept me sane.

"If she gets scared, she's outta there," said Bug.

"Absolutely," I said. "We need to see if she's it. The draw."

"I'm telling you," said Bug. "This room is airtight. Especially when that door's closed, but ... hold on."

Bug walked out of the nursery and back to the monitors. I was on his heel. He pushed the button on the garage exterior cameras.

My heart sunk. The creatures were there, too. Now there were twenty or so. There had been zero when we approached the place.

"Your girl was really working a number on them," said Bug. "She must still be out of commission."

I took my radio off. "Russell, come in. Russell."

We waited. I tried again. "Russell! If you can hear me, answer, please!"

I heard something, but it was low, tentative. "Dave, I hear you, but I have to be quiet. The last of them are making their way up the trail."

"Where's Lola?" I asked.

"She's about five feet below me," said Russell. "I was about to work my way down to her, when I saw more of them coming. No red-eyes over here right now. This WAT-5 works."

"Yes, but we're down to the wire," I said. "You might have fifteen minutes left. I need you to get to Lola. Can you tell if she's alive?"

"Yeah, yeah. She is. I can see her breathing from where I am."

426

"We need her awake. It's the only way we'll get out of here. The only way out is packed with them again."

"I'll do my best, Dave, but I don't know if she's going to be in any condition to do what she did before. It was a good tumble she took."

"Do your best. We've got some ideas. Long shots, but we're working on it. Have you heard from Maddie?"

"They're fine," he said. "I got them on channel 16."

"Good. Do what you can. God, I hope she's alright."

"Going down now," said Russell. "Path is clear."

I clipped the radio back on my belt. "Let's go."

We got back into the nursery and Bug picked up Isis. She laughed and looked at him, smiling as he bounced her. "I love you, kiddo," he said.

"Dada!" she said, smiling, slapping his face with her tiny hand.

Bug had a smile on his face, too. It was hard to look at the baby and not smile, despite what lay ahead. We carried her toward where the last red-eye was trapped.

The first thing we noticed was her singular focus. From the second we walked into the chamber, the creature stopped all moaning, all bodily movement. Its head turned toward Isis and it stared intently at the child.

Had I walked into a Halloween haunted house, I would have believed it a rubber statue. Not one iota of motion.

Bug walked slowly toward it, then carried his daughter off to the side. Now the zombie turned her head to follow. Its mouth did not gnash, or chew at a blackened, rotted tongue. It was fixated.

"Mama," said Isis.

"No!" shouted Bug, and turned on his heel, charging back toward the nursery.

"Uncle Bug!" I shouted, and followed.

427

"Where did that come from?" he said, hyperventilating. "Why did she say that?"

"I don't know, man. I don't know," I said. "It's that thing, getting in her head."

"That thing is not her mama!" said Bug.

"I know! You know that! Let's figure this thing out, Uncle Bug! Don't freak out on me. That's why we took her out there, to see what would happen."

"I wanted to see what that thing would do," he said. "I don't like that bitch in my baby's head."

"Neither do I," I said. "But we still need her."

"For what?"

"This," I said, reaching into my shirt pocket and withdrawing the baggie that once held the WAT-5. I held it up.

In the bottom corner was about a quarter inch of powdered residue from the wafers. "We need to see if we can put Isis out with this."

*****

Everyone was settled onto the floor of the room, and Bug had plenty of pillows and blankets to make them comfortable. As it turns out, Angela had been one for comfort, and insisted that Bug have loads of plush bedding if she were going to be living inside a mountain for any amount of time.

He had complied. Serena, Nelson and Rachel had gotten them all clean water and had also brought out several containers of baby wipes, which was the first time most of the people in that room had removed any of the grime from their bodies in a year. It was unknown how many infections or other issues existed among them, but considering how long they had been locked away, the gaunt-looking group was in pretty good shape.

While our new charges rested, many of them falling into what may have been their first comfortable rest in a long time, Serena, Albert, Rachel and Nelson joined me and Uncle Bug.

"First off, we're about five minutes from being off WAT-5," I said. "So that protection is out the window. But if this stuff puts Isis out, we can take her in there and see if old red-eyes is still so interested."

Nelson stuck his head out the door. "She's still staring right here," he said. "All those tasty people there on the floor off to her right, and she's staring right where we are."

"Confirms my suspicion, but not like this will," I said.

"Give it to her," said Bug.

"We'll need to mix it in with the beef," said Serena. "Think she's hungry again?"

"Isis is always hungry," said Bug.

One WAT-5-laced bite later, little Isis took the first nap of her strange, young life.

*****

"I'll carry her," said Serena. "We don't want to throw things off. She might just be drawn to Bug because he was carrying her last time."

Nelson poked his head out again. "I don't even know if you have to," he said. "Look"

We all stepped into the room. The entire group on the floor – the ones who were awake, anyway – had turned away from the red-eye trapped beneath the door. It had turned its head toward them now, and was pushing out a light, crimson mist, though not nearly strong or dense enough to reach them or affect them in any way.

They did not want to look at her, and they did not want to watch her watching them. Who could blame them?

I'm sure any one of them would have jumped at the chance to be the one to kill her when the time came.

Serena walked closer to her, standing off to her right. Still, she focused on the larger group, and did not turn her head. "Should I wake her?" asked Serena.

"Stand back a couple more feet," said Bug. He grabbed his hair and pulled if up off his neck. "Sweatin' bullets, guys."

"It's nervous work," said Nelson. "Go for it, Serena."

Serena, now a good four feet away from the ensnared red-eye, began rubbing Isis's cheek gently. The baby did not awaken right away, apparently unwilling to forfeit the first nap of its life.

Serena then kissed Isis's cheek, and I had to smile. She was so tender with her that I found myself looking forward to the day she told me she was carrying our child.

Isis finally stirred, her mouth opening in a yawn, those major teeth looking a little strange as her eyes fluttered open.

We were all watching when the silken-haired, living dead bitch with the red eyes jerked her head sharply toward the baby and again became singularly focused.

"Okay, that's enough," said Bug. "I think we've figured this shit out." He walked forward, withdrew a small carry pistol from his side holster, and held it down toward her head.

"If you're jumpy, close your eyes and ears." He didn't wait. He fired, and the last enemy in the room finally passed beyond.

Now the body continued to move. She was clearly dead, but the head and shoulders slowly gyrated.

"What the hell?" asked Nelson. "Why's she still moving?"

"The baby," said Serena, turning to carry Isis back to the nursery. "It's still alive inside her." She disappeared through the door.

"Not for long," said Bug. He went back to his armory cabinet and withdrew what appeared to be a large caliber handgun of some kind. He grabbed a magazine for it, put it in the gun and chambered a round. Without looking anywhere but his destination, he knelt down, placed the gun barrel gently against the very crown of the dead zombie, and fired three quick rounds.

He stood and looked down. No movement. Then he looked at me. "Killed my first baby," he said. "Oh, what a feeling." He wasn't smiling.

We just looked at him and nodded.

"What's next?" he asked.

"Bug, is there any other way out of here?" I asked. "Any weak spot? Somewhere we can punch through, using some of this artillery of yours?"

"He's got a trash chute," said Albert.

"What?" asked Rachel."

"At first I couldn't figure it out," said Albert. "When I used to come up here, I just didn't go far enough to find the upper hatch. I did turn on that other trail, Dave. The one at the fork?"

"Yeah, I remember. Bug, you said it led to a dropoff."

"A hell of a dropoff, man. About four hundred feet down into a river canyon. Rocks and brush."

"I was there once, and something below me caught my eye," said Albert. "I held onto a tree and leaned over the canyon and there was water coming out of this pipe. And some paper and stuff, too."

"Dude, you're littering?" asked Nelson. "That was your plan?"

Bug almost laughed. "Nelson, I didn't think I'd be in here for a year," he said. "Had no clue my trash would have an environmental impact – and with the scenarios in my head at the time, not to mention this one – I don't think a little garbage in a canyon is gonna change the world for the worse."

"Where's the chute," asked Rachel. "Show me."

Bug walked into the kitchen area and opened a smaller, aluminum door in the wall. Behind it was a round chute.

Rachel peered inside. "What is that, around twenty inches?" she asked.

"Good eye," said Bug. It's exactly twenty, inside diameter."

"Where exactly does it come out?" I asked.

"Just where Albert said. Just below that path at the fork, in the canyon wall."

Rachel looked at us. "I have a crazy idea."

"Go on," said Serena. "I think we're all open to crazy, if we can get these people out of here."

"It involves a couple of us at first. Maybe three."

She told us her plan. It sounded insane and plausible at the same time. I wasn't too sure about the second part – we weren't likely the best judges of what made any sense anymore. Our brains were probably twisted beyond the ability to recognize what was or wasn't common sense.

In the end, we decided to give it a go. None of us were getting any younger, and Bug, while far from convinced, didn't have anything better to offer.

*****

Chapter Nineteen

"There," said Bug, tearing off the last piece and turning Rachel around to inspect.

It was a good thing Bug had as much duct tape as he did. When we were done, Rachel stood there with that infant taped nine ways from Sunday to her chest. We made sure it wasn't too tight, and that little Isis could easily breathe, but the tape was eight layers before Bug felt comfortable that she wouldn't be going anywhere without Rachel.

"Okay," she said. "You have cameras on that trail?"

"I have one," he said. "But it's where we need it," he said. "I put it there to monitor if anyone found my trash disposal. Never saw Albert because I pretty much forgot I'd installed that camera."

He went to the monitors and hit a button marked TCC. It was a wide shot, but the 20" diameter tube in the wall could easily be seen, and the ledge about a foot above it.

"How the hell are you going to get from the chute to the ledge?" asked Bug.

"Time to practice what Don taught me," she said. "I need a length of some stiff rope. I'll prep it before we leave. Bug, you'll need to tape it over my shoulder."

Rachel worked with a length of rope, probably twenty-five feet long. When she had it configured and threw a couple of practice tosses, she nodded, coiled it, and Bug taped it in place.

"Nelson, I need you," she said. "You're skinny enough to come with me, and I need another set of hands."

"I'm in, Rach," he said. "I told you that."

"Just making sure," Rachel said, smiling. "Let's go then." She planted a kiss on the back of Isis's head, whose eyes were on her father, her gleaming teeth exposed in a toothy smile that was still as cute as could be.

"You each got a little Ruger .380 auto," said Bug. "Should get you down the hill, but you only got seven rounds each, so use 'em sparingly if you need 'em."

"Break a leg," I said. Bug and I lifted Rachel and tucked her, head first on her back, into the trash chute. A rope was looped around her right ankle, and further up, was looped around Nelson's. Once we got her inside we lowered her down about ten feet and did the same with Nelson, sliding his thin body in the same way; head first and on his back.

"I coulda used a hit before this," he said.

"You'll have to run on residual THC," I said. ' This is too important, Nel."

"Gotcha. Pray for us, dudes," he said.

"Feed it slowly," called Rachel from the tube. "Isis is quiet ... she's fine," she added.

Bug shook his head. "I'm worried as shit," he said.

All faces were turned toward us. Their lives depended on our success, too and they all knew it.

Albert and Serena watched the monitor while Bug and I kept feeding in the hundreds of feet of fine, hemp rope.

At least Nelson could take comfort in that.

*****

"There they are!" shouted Serena, and several people got up and moved over to the monitors. My uncle and I were still holding the rope, and when we got word that Rachel, Isis and Nelson had reached the edge of the canyon, I saw that we only had about thirty feet of rope remaining.

"Close," I said. "So what now?"

"We watch," said Bug. "She told us what she could do. Let's watch her do it."

On the monitor, we saw Rachel's shoulders emerge from the pipe. Bug's fingers tightened on the rope, as did mine. With each inch she scooted out over the nothingness that could swallow up both the woman and the baby, our tension grew. Rachel reached up and pulled the coiled rope from her shoulder, then struggled to get both her arms over her head.

She had it. Looking up, she peeled the remaining duct tape from her makeshift lasso, and eyed the tree hanging over the canyon above her.

You could hear a pin drop in that room. Nobody breathed. We stared at the monitor.

Rachel held the rope in her right hand and rotated her entire arm several times. I could see that it was not as easy for her in a supine position while suspended over a canyon – the rope must have been weighted much differently than when standing upright.

She made her first attempt. In the camera, we clearly saw the rope fall short of the large branch above and drop back down, threading into the gaping mouth of the canyon.

435

She held to the end and began coiling it back up, using both hands.

She was patient and careful. I wanted to offer her some encouragement, but for now there was no way to communicate with her.

"She'll get it," said Serena, meeting my eyes with her own. She nodded. "She will."

Rachel prepared again. She wound her arm and threw, and I could see it was with all her strength. The rope caught around what looked to be a pretty substantial branch, and this time it drew closed and cinched.

"She got it!" shouted Bug, a huge smile on his face. "Damn it, she fucking got it!"

I watched the scene unfold and marveled at how every little thing that happened to us along the way turned out to be for the best. Situations that seemed like sacrifices at first turned out to be the best decisions we could have possibly made.

To bring Rachel. To bring Lola. These strangers who seemed to offer nothing but additional burden at first, ultimately saving our lives. Maybe there was a God, and maybe this was his way of saying, *See, Davey? I may throw a zombie apocalypse at you, but I don't pull every rug out from under you. I help those who help themselves – and others.*

Well, good on ya, God. Thanks.

We watched as Rachel secured the end of the rope around her waist. We couldn't tell what was happening next, but we imagined that she was getting Nelson to unhook her ankle tether. She had to be free to get out of the pipe and onto terra firma.

Next, she came out farther, and though we could not see her from our angle, Isis was still in place as Rachel looped her hand on the rope and pulled herself free of the pipe. Her legs automatically found the bottom of the now dangling lasso rope, and she shimmied upward. Five shimmies and she had her elbows on the earth.

Two knee pushes and she and Isis were safe.

We still had Nelson on our tether, and now we saw his head and shoulders emerge from the chute. Rachel got clear of the rope and lowered it to Nelson. We could see her issuing some instructions. Before we knew it, our rope went slack, and Nelson was dangling over four hundred feet of nothingness, his legs windmilling frantically as Rachel wrapped the other end around a tree and pulled him up. He wasn't doing much climbing.

Again, I thought of this woman's ingenuity, overcoming her lack of strength. Rachel Reed was an amazing woman.

Nelson was on the ground. With a quick wave, they disappeared from view, running down the path toward the fork.

*****

We checked five minutes later, and while what we saw was comforting in some ways, it was frightening in others. The zombies at the main entrance were drifting away, toward the fork in the trail where Rachel, Isis and Nelson had been.

They were following the siren. Little Isis.

All we could do was wait until we heard from them again.

"Dave, come in!" came a voice on my radio. It was Russell's voice.

"Russell," I said. "What's happening? Is Lola okay?"

"I got her to the road," he said. "Down to five rounds of ammo left."

"Is she awake?"

"Nope, but she's breathing steady," he said. "Got a pretty nasty head wound, but it's clotted. I got her on my back and hauled her from the riverbed up to I-5. If any come now, I'm fucked. Not enough energy for anything at this point."

"Can you see the chopper?" I asked.

"I can see it from here, but it's about a quarter mile down the road," he said. "It's locked, right?"

"Not for long, Russell. Are you near the golf cart?" I asked.

"No, it's the other way," said Russell. "I'll carry her. I'm still running on adrenaline. I'll get her to the chopper."

"Okay," I said. "Good. Rachel and Nelson are on their way there now. Hurry."

"I'll try," he said. "Talk to you later."

He was gone. I was thankful that Lola was alive, but who knew in what condition. Man. We all deserved to come out of this thing.

Twenty minutes passed before we heard Nelson's voice on the radio. "Dudes! We're in the chopper and we have Russell and Lola! We barely made it past the garage! There were two red-eyes there, and when we showed up with this baby, it was like a freakin' blue light special at K-Mart."

"Is Isis okay?"

"She's fine, I shot two of 'em, plus a whole bunch of the normal rotters. Glad I got used to this gun," he said. "Anyway, I don't know if there were any other red-eyes at the garage doors, but we didn't see any and they didn't come after us."

I could hear the noise of the rotor blades winding up as he spoke. "Is Lola awake?"

"Dude, she's not," said Nelson. "She's breathing steadily, though. Her eyes are fluttering, so there's something going on in there."

"Keep an eye on her," I said. "She hasn't met Isis, and those two might have some sort of kinship."

I wasn't sure exactly what I was worried about, but any unknown was bad unless proven otherwise.

"Did you find the rescue harness? Can it be modified?"

"Are you sure it's necessary to hang her outside?" asked Bug. "Goddamnit, can't you just have her in the helicopter and fly low?"

"The trees are too canopied there," said Rachel. "I can't get it low enough. We have one shot at this thing if we want to draw them over," she said. "Isis will be safe. I promise."

Nelson came back on. "We're adjusting the harness now," he said. "There's one for a kid, but it's still kind of big. We're using clips and rope to make it snug."

"Make damned sure it's more than snug," said Bug.

I immediately thought of a bug in a rug. That was just me, and I didn't say anything about it to anyone. I felt crazy enough and I didn't need anyone confirming it for me.

I stood there holding Serena's hand in mine, watching that monitor for all it was worth. When I heard the sound of the Eurocopter's rotor blades beating through the camera's paltry speaker, my heart quickened to match the *thwumps.*

*****

We couldn't see the skids of the chopper, but we saw little Isis, dangling in that modified rescue harness, directly in front of the trail that led to a sheer drop hundreds of feet into jagged rocks and a trickling creek below. As the copter hovered above her, the rope swung back and forth, and with every pendulum motion of his child, I watched Bug's body sway to match it, his eyes never leaving the image on the screen.

439

Far below her was where we hoped to soon create a massive zombie graveyard.

Bug held his breath and tears streamed down his cheeks. I wondered how Isis was handling it. Some things that we think will frighten infants just make them laugh, and I hoped that was the case now. Perhaps her little laugh would draw the hungry creatures with even more fervor.

Bug had initially forgotten to turn back on the garage monitor, but did so then. Now all three, the entrance camera, the garage camera and the canyon monitors were powered on and our eyes constantly shifted between them. The creatures left alive at the garage were now making their way up the trail, and as they left, I saw the dead bodies that Nelson and Rachel had left behind.

In the camera, beyond the dangling child, we finally saw them emerge. The trail filled with zombies.

We waited for the next step. It would have to be done soon. The hungry dead pushed in the narrow path, approaching the edge of the steep cliff. They were fifteen feet away now.

Throw it, Nelson! Throw it!

"Why isn't he fuckin' throwing it?" asked Bug, in a panic. "Jesus!"

Something flew toward the path, landed a foot from the ledge and began billowing smoke.

"Yes!" shouted Bug. The smoke in the monitor grew thicker and thicker, and completely obscured the trail. But it also served to obscure the danger from the rotters, who had a way of realizing when something could hurt them.

Seconds later, we watched as bodies began emerging from the thick haze, toppling over the sheer ledge and plummeting from the trail into the empty space beyond. The damned drone zombies, for the most part, dropped silently. The red-eyes, in sharp contrast, shrieked in haunted frustration, their shrill, harrowing cries diminishing as they dropped away from Isis, the helicopter and the microphone that allowed us to hear them, down into the deep canyon – perhaps all the way to hell.

There hovered our little siren, our goddess of the zombies, our little Isis. She beckoned them into nothingness, and they continued to pour forth from the path, staggering into the vacuum that sucked them downward to crash onto the toothed rocks below. Shattered bones, skulls and brains would put an end to even the most powerful red-eye, and we now knew the draw toward little Isis was not something they could fight.

Two by two, sometimes five at a time, pushing and clawing at one another for the opportunity to reach the dangling baby, just 10 feet off the cliff, but a chasm away from reaching her.

I began to notice something, but I was afraid to say it aloud. Isis had begun to swing more wildly, and closer to the cliff's edge.

Bug grabbed the monitor with both hands and yelled, "What the hell's happening? She's swingin' too close to the cliff, Dave! Give me that goddamned radio!"

I held it out and Uncle Bug snatched it from my hand.

"What the fuck is going on!" he screamed into it. "Get her the hell back! You're too close!"

"Stabilizer or something!" yelled back Nelson, sounding frantic. "She's having trouble holding it here!"

"Then pull the fuck back!" yelled Bug, sweat pouring from his face.

"She says she's got it!" shouted Nelson. "We're still safe!"

Then something happened. A red-eye emerged from the smoke and launched off of that cliff. I hadn't seen it coming. Nobody had.

As though catapulted, it flew toward the harnessed baby, now dangling only six feet or so off the edge of the precipice.

Its fingers caught the bottom strap of the leather and it clung there, one arm loose and swinging in the air, trying to gain purchase. Isis now hung at a frightening angle and Serena screamed and turned away, unable to watch any more.

"Jesus!" shouted Bug, pushing the button and screaming into the radio, "Get that bitch off her! I don't care what you have to do!"

Serena clutched my hand, her eyes squeezed closed. My heart tripled in speed. This was a scenario none of us had anticipated. The harness breaking, Isis plunging hundreds of feet to her death; of course that came to mind, but not this. The red-eye clawed her way up, and as the monster's other claw-like hand hooked around and clutched the leather harness, it pulled itself upward.

Something shiny flew through the image, and we all squinted at the monitor.

A change in the rotor beat, followed by a quick swing of the rope, left the creature again clutching at Isis' harness with just one hand, and moments later we saw something attach to the creature's head.

A Ninja star. As we jammed our faces closer still to the monitor, another one flew, and another one. All cleanly missing Isis and embedding into the head of the dangling creature less than two feet below the baby. Black blood began running down its face, then dripped in inky blobs from its body, and out of the camera's view.

Her fingers released. A harrowing shriek echoed through the canyon as one of the most powerful creatures of this apocalypse dropped to its death.

Bug's head drooped and he let out his breath. He looked at me. "Nelson, I presume?"

I nodded and squeezed his arm. "Yeah."

He pushed the button on the radio. "Thanks, man. Thanks for getting that thing away from my baby."

"It was nothing, dude," said Nelson. "You think you were freaking out. I was shitting my pants up here."

"Is that chopper stable?" asked Bug.

"She bypassed something," he said. "We're good now. She's okay, and they're still coming."

Bug turned to look at the monitor. Almost all of them had now fed onto the path at the fork. He looked at me.

"Shouldn't be too long now," he said. "Another five minutes or so and they should all be there."

And so it went until the parade of walking dead came to an end. At the conclusion, when the smoke cleared and the path was revealed, only three zombies remained on the trail, now milling about as though unsure why they were there. We watched as the cable swung away yet again, moving Isis out of the line of fire.

We heard several gunshots and the last three creatures dropped into the dirt, a black-red mist settling down atop their crumpled, destroyed bodies.

A cheer erupted from the group behind us, who had all been watching the scene unfold. We turned to see faces that likely had not smiled in months, showing us their teeth.

I took a deep breath and pulled Serena into my arms. Albert held his mother.

In the monitor we saw Isis swing back into view, then her harness began moving upward quickly, then past the chopper's skids.

"Got her!" said Nelson. "No worse for wear. She's laughing!"

"That's my girl," said Bug, crying. "Thank God."

"Nelson," I said.

"Let me get her secured," said Nelson.

After a few seconds, he came back on. "Yeah, Davey? What's up?"

"You got that bomb still?"

"The one Hemp had us make?"

I laughed out loud. "How many bombs do you have, man?" I asked.

"Okay," he said. "Good point. What about it?"

"Light the fuse and drop it into the canyon."

"Good idea," he said. "I don't like bombs anyway. Something else I need to do first, though."

A few moments later, something fell past the camera. It didn't look like the bomb we'd made.

"What was that, Nel?" I asked.

"Test drop," he answered. "I counted how many seconds until it hit."

I knew exactly what he was doing. Hemp had told us how many feet per second the fuse he had specified would burn, so Nelson was making sure the timing was right to actually do some damage if there were any surviving rotters at the bottom of the canyon. He intended to cut the fuse to the right length before dropping it. There was, after all, no reason to waste a good explosive.

A few seconds later we saw the large, dark, conical device drop past the camera. None of us saw what happened next, but about six seconds later, we heard an enormous explosion outside the bunker and through the speakers. We'd done pretty good, because we felt the vibration in the solid floor of Bug's bunker.

I looked at Bug and smiled as he wrapped his arms around me and my girl. We provided guns to all who were comfortable with weapons and prepared to leave my uncle's fortress and prison. The monitors showed the coast was now clear.

I knew without asking that my uncle would be coming back with us to South Carolina. At the same time, I wondered how my family there would feel about our dangerous little zombie goddess, Isis.

Perhaps Hemp could work something out to alleviate the frightening implications of her involuntary talent.

*****

Epilogue

The woods were clear as we walked back into the Railroad Park grounds. At our arrival, all of the young girls were mesmerized at the large group of survivors and Maddie and Russell found many of their friends among our refugees.

Bug's expertise in planning for things that were not supposed to ever happen had its benefits. He shared everything he could with the survivors and over the next week, made several runs back up to his place to gather weaponry and supplies.

The morning after the rescue, I got up early. As I got a fire going in the pit outside, I heard the flapping of wings and turned my eyes skyward.

An eagle flew overhead, soaring just twenty feet above me. I whispered, "Leona, there you are," and smiled.

It *was* her. I knew it in my heart.

As for the group, nobody had any desire to live inside of a mountain or in a concrete bunker. If these *were* the last days of their lives, these people had decided it was their distinct right to live it in the bright sunshine and warmth of outdoors.

Among Bug's supplies were several generators, which were rolled down on their carts and installed. Making several runs to town, Bug got them started on an effective fence to protect their masses from attack. They left the cowbell sticks, as they would alert them to the threat, which could then be taken out with a bullet through the fence.

Or a sharpened rebar spear tipped with urushiol oil ... whatever made the most sense.

As for our group, Lola rested for three days before she felt well enough to eat regularly and move around the park. Her head hurt and she'd had a hell of a goose egg over her right eye, but I believe much of her necessary recovery was due to almost five hours of calling the red-eyes – in direct competition with a natural like Isis.

In the end, both had saved us. Along with Rachel, Nelson and Russell. I shook my head when I thought of this.

None of them were supposed to have been with us at all. Kismet. Fate. The universe at work. God. Put the credit where you like – the only thing that mattered was the outcome. Though it would be nice to duplicate that kind of luck, if called upon to do so.

Nelson held classes for the girls, and for whomever wanted to participate. Subdudo classes. And yeah, I followed along. It was more complex than it initially seemed, but everyone got the hang of it after about five sessions. Since it was more pressure and touch points, the girls could use it on one another without inflicting any pain. I even showed Serena what I'd learned.

I thought it was funny. Her reaction was just a tad less jovial as I helped her up and tried to kiss her, reminding her that she was lucky I did it in the grass.

Despite how nicely the Railroad Park was coming together, what with the new arrivals organizing and helping to get railroad cars that were not being used back up to livable condition, Lolita Lane and Rachel Reed decided they were coming back to Whitmire with us.

I was glad of it. It meant we got to ride in the helicopter on the way home instead of driving our asses there. At that point, I just couldn't imagine a road trip.

So now we're on the way home. We got on the Ham radio again and told Hemp to let everyone know we'd be there in just a few days. He'd called them into the room again, and damned if I didn't hear a nice cheer erupt from my friends and family.

Screw that. They were *all* my family. It felt like everyone close to me was family now. And soon enough, I'd marry Serena and start a real family.

As I watched Serena cradling Isis in her arms, the baby's bright, blue-ish-red eyes taking it all in, I thought, *When she does get pregnant, that woman's not leaving my sight for nine months.*

The last night we were there, Nelson broke out his Elvis Costello guitar and began to play and sing. He did some Bad Company and he sounded pretty good. Then he did Clapton's acoustic version of Layla, and everyone smiled. The older of us sang along.

I realized I was proud of myself. Dave Gammon had set out to do something, and holy shit if he hadn't gotten it done. I'd lost my mom and my sister, but I had found my last blood relative. Small favors it would seem, in comparison to what had been lost, but not so small to *me*.

It's that awkward moment when you shrug off the imposter complex and realize that you might actually be some sort of a hero. I smiled. I *felt* like a hero.

Even if only in my own mind.

THE END

If you enjoyed this book, please do the author a BIG favor and visit Amazon.com to write a review!

Try retyping this damned link: (You *will* have to sign into Amazon.com to actually write a review!)

http://www.amazon.com/s/ref=nb_sb_noss_1?url=search-alias%3Ddigital-text&field-keywords=eric+shelman

MORE BOOKS BY
ERIC A. SHELMAN
AND DOLPHIN MOON PUBLISHING

Keep an eye out for the next book in the Dead Hunger series:

Dead Hunger VI: Homecoming

ABOUT THE AUTHOR

Eric A. Shelman lives in Southwest Florida with his wife, Linda, and their whippet, Beau. Eric was born in Fort Worth, Texas, and left there as a teenager in the early 1970s when his widowed mother remarried and his new stepfather moved the family to southern California.

Eric first took on zombies as a genre in 2011, but has been writing poetry and stories since he was in elementary school. In fact, when he was a young longhair living in Laguna Beach and Dana Point, California, in the late 70s and early 80s, he'd write ridiculous short stories with no plot and no end, all with his friends' names in them. In fact, you'll find the names of many people Eric knows today in his stories and books.

Eric has an author fan page on Facebook – and it's the best place to find out when his next release is coming – just search for Eric A Shelman Author, and you should find it just fine. You can find him on Goodreads, too. Last resort, you can also check out his website – www.ericshelman.com.